M000072830

Shattered VESSELS

A NOVEL BY **NANCEY FLOWERS**

Shattered Vessels

This is a work of fiction. The author has invented the characters.
Any resemblance to actual persons, living or dead, is purely coincidental.

Cover art by Lydell Jackson
Interior Design by Nancey Flowers
Edited by Chandra Sparks Taylor

Printed in China, by Kaleido Graphics Services Group, Inc.

For more information, or to contact the author, address correspondence to:

Flowers in Bloom Publishing
P.O. Box 473106
Brooklyn, New York 11247

Or visit: www.nanceyflowers.com

Library of Congress Control Number: 2002094328

ISBN: 0-9708191-1-0

First Flowers in Bloom edition printing, January 2003

10 9 8 7 6 5 4 3 2 1

ACKNOWLEDGEMENTS

The year 2001 proved to be filled with many trials and tribulations. The year 2002 has been extremely prosperous and a blessing. I've seen the eye of the storm and came out unhampered. I give God all of the glory for exorcising all of the demons that were in my life who no longer have a presence. God is good!

My mother, Rose, is and has always been my biggest cheerleader my entire life. Without her love and support, this journey wouldn't have been half as easy. I feel the need to elaborate. My mother's love is and always has been unconditional. If children worldwide were able to receive an ounce of the love that my mother dotes on me, they would truly be blessed.

To my cousin, Orane Haughton aka, O, who is more like my son, thank you for all of your love and support. Always remember that hard work, honesty, determination, and perseverance will bring your dreams to fruition in abundance. I also have to thank my beautiful niece Aisha Flowers for loving me enough to travel and be my sales representative.

I have a wonderful crew of family, friends and salespeople for my first novel *A Fool's Paradise*, and of course *Shattered Vessels*. Your assistance enabled me to move forward with this project. You all are stuck with me for better or worse. Maxine McIntosh, Majida Abdul Karim, Léone D'Mitrienne Williams, Tracy V. Green, Marvette Richardson, Gary Lovelace, Andrea Haye, Dawn Green, Aleshia Harmon, Uncle Bill, Diana Flowers, Judy Lockhart and the staff of Hair Studio, Sharon Davis, Andrea Flowers, Tanisha Lisle, Carla Tyler, Akwete Hinds, Frank James Thomas, Jr., Raymond Griffith, Dr. Charles Grannum, Kyra Solomon, Tina Lewis, Monique McNeil, Willette Hamilton, Kama Walcott, Marcia McIntosh, Melrose Hall and family, Trust Graham, Richlieu Dennis and my Nubian Heritage family.

New friends and people that I've met along the way, each of you have touched my life in different ways. Some of you held my hand in my time of need, helped me move residences, provided me with shelter, typed my manuscript, set up signings, gave me a ride, cooked and fed me, hung out with me, offered me advice, made me laugh, or simply called to say hello and check on my well-being. Your existence has been quintessential and I'd like to thank each of you. Michael Presley, Marlon Green, Joylynn M. Jossel, Sandra A. Ottey, Donna Hill, Jessica McLean-Ricketts, Tracy Grant, Anike Ajagunna, Timmothy B. McCann, Linda Dominique Grosvenor, Travis Hunter, Kenji Jasper, Lolita Files, Victoria Christopher Murray, Mondella Jones, William Fredrick Cooper, Jacquie Bamberg Moore, Jamellah Ellis, Bernice McFadden, Tonya Marie Evans, Carl Weber, Antoinette of Hair Plus, Tracy Price-Thompson, Carla Canty, Brian Egeston, Regina Lynn, Mary B. Morrison, Toni Staton-Harris, Michelle Washington, Ron Kavanaugh, Troy Johnson, Deborah Maisonet, Max Rodriguez, Johnny Holman, Jr., Nicole Bailey-Williams, Yvette Hayward, Zane, Regina Clark, Culture Plus, Afrikan World Books, Pageturner.net, Black Writers Alliance, Authorsontour.com, Ourstory, Sibanye, Monique Ford and Circle of Sistah's Book Club, The Nubian Chronicles, RAWsistaz, Melonie Payne, United Sisters Book Club, and a host of others that supported me.

A special shout-out to my sorors of Delta Sigma Theta and my Florida connection, Maleta McPherson of Heritage Bookstore and More Inc., Felicia Wintons of Books for Thought and Jackie Perkins of Montsho.

Thanks so much for your love, support and guidance.

Again, I'd like to thank my wonderful friend and editor Chandra Sparks Taylor for all of her insight and words of encouragement and patience. I revere your friendship, and I am glad to include you in my fold of people I consider friends. Thank for extending a listening ear to me whenever and wherever you are. You are the finest in the business. Please don't ever stop doing what you do best.

I can't thank all of the above people enough for being there for me in more ways than I could ever imagine. I also want to thank all of my readers, because without your letters, e-mails, and support there would be no reason to continue this mission. Thank you!

Please visit me at www.nanceyflowers.com I would love to hear from you. If you haven't read *A Fool's Paradise,* please purchase your copy today along with *Twilight Moods* and stay tuned for *The Other Woman.*

Peace, Blessings and Love

Nancey Flowers

In memory of Aunt Jeannie.
The first person to ever hold me lovingly in their arms.
I will always hold you with the same love in my heart.

Shattered Vessels

Shattered VESSELS

The body is a vessel
That vessel is contained
Your soul, spirit, emotions, moods, thoughts,
feelings, intellect, knowledge and wisdom are
embodied within that vessel
From the outside your vessel may appear whole,
unhampered, rejoiced, but when you see yourself in
the mirror, you know the truth
You know that the life you are living is merely a
façade
Your vessel may overrunneth
Your vessel may be chipped and cracked and
glued back together or painted to hide the ugly truth
You need not worry, your shattered vessel can
once again become whole
Realize your inner strength and love your vessel
This vessel, your vessel, is fragile and should
always be treated as such

—*Nancey Flowers*

1

Reason For Celebration

edford Jackson sat comfortably in his plush green leather chair, behind his mission-style desk made of strong-grained solid oak, and lightly tapped his pen on the desk. He had a one o'clock appointment with a prospective client. His account director, who had been pitching Truman and Haughton Associates, said that he really needed Bedford to help him close this deal. Since Bedford rarely got out in the field to pitch to clients anymore, he jumped at the opportunity. Yes, life was good. Not to mention that this year alone his firm had had to hire four new heads. Jackson and Jackson had recently relocated to a big office across the street from Madison Square Garden, One Penn Plaza. Yes, life was good.

Bedford's internal line buzzed. He glanced down at his new forty-five-hundred-dollar Cartier Pasha 38mm watch. The silver guilloche dial told him his potential clients were not due for at least another forty-five minutes.

"Yes, Shirley?" Bedford answered.

"Sir, Mrs. Jackson is here to see you."

What could Felice possibly want from me now? Bedford thought. He tried never to mix business with pleasure, especially during work hours. Felice always seemed to choose the wrong and most inopportune times to come by and chat.

"Send her in," he responded reluctantly.

Five years earlier, no one thought it possible for Bedford to accomplish all that he had. Sure he held his undergraduate degree from Morgan State University and his MBA from Columbia University. There was never a doubt in his mind that he could start his own financial consulting firm, but his former friends from his childhood home in the Lafayette Garden projects in Brooklyn did. It was that type of ghetto mentality that Bedford had decided to leave behind. Bedford felt it was time for blacks to stop blaming the white man for shit. Find their craft and build on it. That's exactly what Bedford did. As a result, his firm Jackson and Jackson Financial Consultants Inc., had been featured in *Essence, Ebony, Savoy, Upscale* and *Black Enterprise* magazines. As a matter of fact, Earl G. Graves, the owner of *Black Enterprise,* also an alumni of MSU, had recently inquired about retaining the services of Bedford's firm.

Bedford propped his feet up on the desk and held the Truman & Haughton portfolio in front of him. The door to his office opened, and Felice waltzed in, looking better than ever in a navy pinstriped suit, which flattered her figure-eight shape. The suit was undoubtedly a Dana Buchman and the three-inch heels were either Prada or Gucci. Bedford pretended to be consumed by the portfolio.

"Hi, B.J.," Felice said as she sat down opposite Bedford. "You can stop pretending to be busy. Don't you think that I know you by now? How long have we been—"

Bedford's impatience got the best of him, and he cut her off.

"Felice, for your information, I am busy, so what is it that you want?"

"For your information, I have good news for us. I stopped by to tell you about my latest acquisition."

Bedford immediately perked up after hearing the word *acquisition*. He loved that word. Acquisition meant more money, more money, more money! *Ka-ching.*

"Remember when you came into my office a few months back, and I told you that I was working on a project, but I wouldn't tell you what or who the client was?" Felice asked.

"Go on," Bedford replied anxiously.

"Well, my account team and I were toiling day and night on these sons of bitches. But all of our hard work just paid off, baby. About an hour ago, I received a call confirming that my new client would like to come onboard. B.J., I'm still in shock."

"That's great, Felice. But whom have we added to our prestigious roster of clients?"

"Oh yeah, I did leave that out, huh?"

"Yes, Felice. Now would you stop toying with me and spill it already."

"B.J., honey, are you ready for this? She stood placing her hands firmly on Bedford's desk, legs slightly spread apart. "We are now the choice consulting firm for Key Pieces!" Felice screamed with excitement.

"You mean the fashion designers for Geto Genius urban wear?" Bedford questioned, already knowing the answer.

"None other. I had a meeting with Mr. James Huntley, the president of Geto Genius, and we practically sealed the deal with a kiss, so to speak and like I said, he called about an hour ago," Felice bragged. "We have finally broken into the fashion world, baby. Geto Genius is one of the fastest growing urban clothing companies around today."

The look on Bedford's face corroborated his excitement. Felice's account team was responsible for clients in the entertainment industry; Bedford's team focused on finance companies. Jackson & Jackson was also slowly trying to branch out into the fashion world. This was the second largest account that the company had landed this year outside of the entertainment and finance arenas. Life was definitely good!

"Felice, you better not be lying to me, woman. Because if you're not, please tell me that I'm dreaming."

"B.J, honey, you are far from being in snooze land. Need I add that this is definitely reason for celebration? Where are you keeping the Dom Perignon, because I know that you've got some hiding up in here?"

Bedford opened his bottom desk drawer where he kept his Dom. He didn't want Felice to know where he kept his goods because she was known for pilfering and never replacing, but to hell with it. Jackson and Jackson was on a roll. When he and Felice decided to go into business together it was a match made in heaven.

Bedford and Felice met as undergrads at Morgan State. They were both business majors and immediately hit it off. Bedford was serious about his studies and was not trying to get involved in any serious relationships. That was, until Felice Monét Pryce stole his heart. Bedford had started a study group for business finance majors scheduled for every Tuesday and Thursday at the Soper library. Initially, the group had eight regular attendees; three were already on the dean's list. Once the group began its study sessions, three more made the dean's list. The following semester, word got out about how well the group was doing, and before the semester was out, seven more people joined, including Felice. Although the business department was relatively small, Bedford had never seen Felice prior to her joining. He didn't know how he could have missed her and couldn't recall them being in any classes together.

Felice was a fast-talking, tongue-in-cheek, gum-chewing, around-the-way girl from Brooklyn, like Bedford. Bedford was smitten the first time he laid eyes on her. He knew that he wanted her, no questions asked. She would become his next conquest. Felice was fierce, and she knew it. She was tall, slender, and had the complexion of maple syrup. Her skin was flawless, and she wore her naturally curly hair in a short-cropped cut. Felice also had the most luscious lips that Bedford had ever seen, and a strong chin. He could suck on those lips all day if she would let him. The features that caught Bedford's attention most were her large brown eyes, and it didn't hurt that she had a fat ass, either. Word in the business department was that she was a big tease. Bedford was up for the challenge.

Bedford later learned that Felice was after him too. She had had her eye on him for an entire semester, and when she heard about the study group, she couldn't think of a more opportune way to meet him. To Felice, Bedford was the definition of fine. No he wasn't fine, he was *foine!* The brotha was six-feet-three and had a body that wouldn't quit. She'd first spotted him playing racquetball at the Hill Field House. He had on a white Adidas tank, which clung to his sweaty pecks, while his matching shorts exposed his very defined muscular legs. Bedford's eyes were dark and brooding, which Felice found to be mysterious, and he had the deepest dimples she'd ever seen. She stood there watching him as he skillfully played, running around the court rarely missing a shot. Staring down at him from the upper level, the only words that would register to her brain were *ump, ump, ump* and *damn!*

Felice had gotten the 411 on Bedford, too, so she knew that he never kept a woman for longer than two months, three at max. It wouldn't take long for her to convince him that they belonged together. Three years later, she became Mrs. Felice Jackson.

Felice took two wineglasses from Bedford's credenza and moved around to his side of the desk. Bedford popped the top of the Dom and poured it.

"Here's to success and more success in the future," Bedford toasted.

"Here, here," Felice said, clinking her glass with Bedford's. "I noticed that you've gotten a couple of new toys in your office. When did you get this shiny new desk?" Felice asked, rubbing her hand across the smooth wood grain. "You haven't invited me up to christen the new furniture. B.J., are we growing apart? When were you going to invite Mama up?"

"Felice, not now, okay? Don't get any ideas. I'm expecting Truman and Haughton Associates to arrive in the next half hour."

"Then that gives us plenty of time," she said, grabbing his waistband, causing them to collide. "If I recall correctly, all we need is a good fifteen."

Bedford was tempted, but he just didn't feel like tasting Felice at the moment. Shirley, his secretary, was right outside his office and Greg, his account director, was probably waiting for him in the conference room. He eased away from Felice hoping that she would get the message.

"Felice, I have to meet Greg in the conference room. He probably needs my help."

"B.J., honey, Greg is a big boy. He can set up the presentation without you. Besides, Shirley will let you know when your clients arrive. Now stop being so stubborn and give Mama what she wants."

Before he could object, Felice was already taking him in her mouth. How in the hell did she manage to unbuckle his belt and undo his pants? Felice was always too quick for him. She'd make a good thief, Bedford thought, as he threw his head back to enjoy the ride.

Bedford watched as Felice kept her eyes open to admire his tawny brown and nicely sculpted thickness. She always commented on the fact that even after all of these years she never tired of looking at Bedford's dick. Her exact words were, "It's a lovely sight to behold and to receive." Felice continued to marvel at him as her mouth continued to engulf his flesh until it miraculously disappeared.

When Bedford could stand it no more, he used his hand to swipe all of the papers and office supplies from his desk to the floor. The metal items crashed noisily and scattered about. He gently pulled Felice off her knees and laid her across the desk. As he unbuttoned her blouse, he showered her bosom with long wet kisses. She was wearing a new Victoria's Secret lace bra in fire-engine red. Bedford loved it when she wore red undergarments. Especially lace.

Bedford felt the blood racing from his head to his head. *Why did Felice have to do this to me now?* Bedford thought. Damn, now he had to get his nut off. Bedford moved to Felice's favorite spot and began nibbling on her ear. Felice moaned.

"Touch me there," she whispered, cradling her breasts.

Bedford slowly moved his hand up her thighs. To his surprise, Felice was not wearing any underwear. He felt the slickness between her legs and got even more excited. He continued to rub the area until he felt her sail begin to swell and he knew she was ready. Felice pulled him down on top of her and guided him to her milky way.

"B.J., baby, why do you hold out on Mama like that?" She purred.

"I promise, I won't do it again. Okay, baby?" Bedford said as he continued to please her.

Felice was on a mission. She moved from beneath Bedford who was in no condition to argue, and he surrendered himself to her. Felice removed the bra and her 34D's spilled out. This always drove Bedford wild as she rode him to ecstasy. Their bodies were intertwined as they rocked and moved together as one. Felice moved like a professional jockey riding a horse, swift and skillful. They both indulged in the pleasures that each had to offer as they kissed, sucked and basked in glory.

"B.J, honey, I'll always love you," Felice said as she felt her body reach its peak. "I need you, baby I need you," she exclaimed as her body convulsed.

"This shit is sooo good," Bedford replied. "I love this shit, you hear me. This is the shit." Bedford pulled away from Felice as he released. He held on to the edge of the desk to steady himself. "Whoo! Damn that was so good," Bedford said again, out of breath.

"Isn't it always? I don't know why you deprive yourself. Especially since you know it's good."

"Felice, I'm not even going to dignify that with an answer. As a matter of fact, you know the answer. I'm going to go clean myself up before my soon-to-be clients arrive. Now if you'll excuse me." Bedford headed into the private bathroom in his office and shut the door. When he came back out, Felice had everything back in place, including herself. She was once again seated in the chair across from his desk.

The intercom went off again.

"Yes, Shirley? Are they here yet?"

"No sir, but you have a call on line one."

"Who is it?" Bedford asked as he looked adoringly at Felice.

"It's your wife, sir."

2

Hiding Under Makeup

ndia McCall had an assortment of every type of makeup imagin-
able. She was on the mailing list to receive everything from Mac
and Black Opal to Fashion Fair and Iman. After all, she was beauty
director for *Shades* magazine's Beauty section. It was something to do
in her spare time, since it wasn't like she needed the money. Her husband, Grayson, made plenty. The magazine wasn't the real reason that
she received the makeup. As she was applying Iman Corrective Concealer to cover up the bruise that Grayson had left below her cheek
from the previous night's little tiff, she realized the Clay 2 Color blended
right in with her complexion. India was glad that someone had finally
created makeup concealer that matched her skin tone perfectly. It also
helped that she wasn't as pale as her mother. India's fair complexion
always allowed her to hide bruises. She stared at her reflection in the
mirror and batted her long baby doll eyelashes and thought, *Damn you
look good, girl. Look at those bedroom eyes, perfectly arched eyebrows that any woman would die for and those gorgeous high cheekbones. India, girl, you are what dreams are made of.*

After perfecting her makeup, India decided that she wanted something to snack on, so she pressed the intercom for Lenora, the maid, to
whip her up a strawberry tart. It would soon be dinnertime, and the tart
was a good fat-free light dessert. What could be better? It was never
good to overindulge and eat fatty foods. What man would dare want a
woman who was as big as a house? There was a reason that Grayson
still found her desirable and didn't stray. India made sure to hire a

personal trainer after she had Sierra to help her lose that god-awful weight. She would never put her body through that torture again. She gained twenty-seven pounds from the pregnancy. The mere thought of it disgusted her.

"Lenora, are you there?" India asked. She could hear the clanking of the pots, but there was no answer. India knew darn well that Lenora was down there and was deliberately ignoring her. It was so hard to find good help nowadays. Lenora was the third maid that they had hired over the past two years. The last two servants left complaining to Grayson that India was demanding and irreverent. The nerve of them. Who did they think they were? They worked for her. It wasn't her fault that they were too lazy to serve. They had known what the job entailed when they were hired. She made sure that they were compensated well and got to go home every evening to their families. Most of her neighbors had maids who lived with them. India thought that she was being thoughtful, but she learned that you couldn't please everyone all the time.

"Lenora, if you are there, please answer." *She better not make me have to come down there,* India thought.

"India, is that you?" Lenora asked. India could hear the woman's smile through the intercom. India once heard Lenora refer to her as Ms. Parvenu to someone over the phone, implying that if she weren't married to Grayson, she wouldn't be as well off, but she didn't care. India's only concern was that Lenora did her job and did it well.

"What are we having for dinner tonight?" India asked.

"Well, ma'am, I've prepared a spinach salad for the first course, sliced roast lamb, ginger baby carrots and roasted red potatoes garnished with hollandaise sauce for the second. Is that to your liking?"

"Yes, whatever. Have you made dessert yet? I have a taste for a strawberry tart."

"Well, we still have the lemon meringue pie from the other night—"

"That's not what I asked you," India barked, cutting Lenora off. "I said I have a taste for strawberry tart. Does that sound like lemon meringue pie? Just make the strawberry tart. Thank you!"

India could hear the attitude in Lenora's voice, but she didn't give a damn. All she knew was that after dinner she expected the dessert of her choice. A small knock at the door distracted India from her thoughts.

She knew that it was Sierra, her daughter, awake from her nap. Sierra was getting so big now. She was four years old and too smart for her own good.

"Mommy, are you awake?" Sierra asked from the other side of the door.

"Yes, sweetie. Come on in."

Sierra entered the room, rubbing her eyes with the back of one hand and clutching her stuffed elephant with the other. Her long hair was in two plaits and decorated with yellow barrettes to match her Baby Dior outfit. She walked over to her mother and handed her the stuffed elephant while she attempted to climb atop the bed. India placed the elephant to the side and assisted Sierra onto her lap. Sierra then planted a big, wet kiss on India's face.

"So how is my little sunshine today? Did you sleep well?" India asked as she patted a few loose strands of Sierra's hair back in place.

"Yes, Mommy. But I'm hungry. What are we having for dinner?"

"Ms. Lenora is cooking our favorite. Baby carrots and red potatoes, yummy."

"Mommy, can I have some ice cream for dessert? I promise that I've been a really, really good girl," Sierra said, batting her lashes, showing off her puppy-dog eyes. She was definitely a miniature India. From the eyes, the well-defined cheeks, beautiful hair and pouty lips, Sierra was certainly going to cause many hearts to flutter.

"We'll see about that. Are you excited about going to Melody's birthday party tomorrow?"

"Yes, and I didn't tell her what I got her, either."

"That's good, because you want it to be a surprise, don't you?"

"Mmm-hmm."

"What did I tell you about saying that? What's the proper response to my question?"

"Yes, Mommy."

"That's right, so stop nodding your head and answering 'mmm-hmm' when you know your reply should be either yes or no. Okay?"

"Yes," Sierra said.

India could hear the doorbell ringing, but she wasn't expecting company. Who could it be at this God-forsaken hour, she wondered. It was almost dinnertime, and her friends knew better than to stop by when the family was about to eat. Maybe it was a special delivery from Grayson. He always knew how to apologize after an argument.

About two months ago, India had said some things that she knew would make Grayson fly off the handle. They had a little tiff, and later that evening he came home with a four-carat diamond bracelet. It was a beautiful bracelet and well-thought-out gift. India had been eyeing it at DeBeers for months. Grayson always knew how to charm and win her over. If only she could learn to shut her mouth and stop provoking Grayson, things would be much better between them.

Everything Grayson did was for the benefit of his family. He was a good provider. He worked hard and devoted much of his time to the Professional African American Men Association. The PAAMA, which Grayson chaired, focused on uplifting the status and creating awareness for the black man in his community and society. The group mentored inner-city youth and created opportunities through networking. Many of the men in the organization held prestigious positions. Some were political figures, big-time lawyers like Grayson, doctors, engineers and architects.

Grayson was a go-getter. When he first heard about the organization and learned that there were no chapters in Prince Georges County, Maryland, he set out to start one up. Grayson couldn't understand how the richest African American community in the country could be devoid of such a prized organization. After a year and a half of lobbying, brick laying, sweat and more hard work, his dream had come true. They had one of the best chapters in the country. The year before at the PAAMA's annual gala, his chapter had won the award for outstanding achievement and best campaign for the war against drugs. This year Grayson had his eye on winning at least three of those awards and was putting forth one hundred and fifty percent of himself into making that dream a reality. That was exactly why he and India had gotten into an argument the previous night. She shouldn't have mentioned Grayson's absence from home. It was only for a short time, and sacrifices had to be made.

"India," Lenora called on the intercom, disturbing her thoughts.

"Yes, Lenora. Who is it?" India answered, sounding annoyed.

"It's your sister, Patience."

Damn, India thought. The last person she needed to see was Patience. She needed to finish getting herself together.

"Sierra, go prepare yourself for dinner, okay? And if dinner isn't ready when you're done, ask Miss Lenora to turn on the television so you can watch Nickelodeon in the family room. Now, scoot," India said, after putting Sierra down on the floor and tapping her bottom as she walked toward the door.

"Yes, Mommy," Sierra answered.

"Close the door behind you, sweetie," India said as Sierra exited the room. "Lenora, please tell my sister that I'll be down in five minutes."

"Patience is already on her way up, she insisted that she knew the way," Lenora said.

Before India could reply, her sister swung the door open and barreled her way in. Damn, damn damn! India thought. It was as if her sister had some kind of radar and always chose to visit when she was at her worse.

India and her sister looked exactly alike, except Patience was about thirty pounds heavier and had her mane cut into a natural like a little boy. It was a good thing that they had naturally wavy hair. India never understood why Patience had cut all her hair off in the first place. When they were younger, people constantly mistook them for twins. However, today Patience was a prime example of India's earlier sentiments regarding weight. Patience had never bothered to lose the excess after she'd had her children. Not even an ill attempt. Here she was five years later and the fat had made itself a home on what was once a beautiful figure. It amazed India that Patience's husband hadn't strayed yet. Or maybe he had and she just wasn't aware of it. Oh well, what did it matter to her?

"What's happening, sister-girl? If I don't bring my big ass out here to see you, we'd never see each other," Patience gushed. "That huge luxury jeep sitting out front must be for show."

"Big ass is an understatement, okay! And we moved out here for a little privacy, peace and quiet. So I'd appreciate it if you would call before you came all the way out here for a visit. Suppose I wasn't home?"

"What in hell crawled up your stank anorexic ass and died? Besides, you *are* home, and I'm your sister. Therefore, I don't have to call, I can just show up whenever I like. Now, if you have a problem with that, tough. Can I have my hug?" Patience asked, ignoring India's attitude as she walked across the four-hundred-square-foot bedroom to embrace India.

India prayed to God that Patience wouldn't notice the bruises on her face. She was in no mood for a lecture. Patience didn't understand the pressures of being a model wife.

When they were through embracing, Patience took a few steps back to look at India who was dressed to the nines as usual in designer sportswear. India hadn't even left the house, but she was high maintenance and made it a point to always look good—hair freshly permed, French manicure and pedicure, lips lined and glossed and eyebrows plucked to perfection.

"Something about you has changed. I can't pinpoint it, but I'm sure you've done something to yourself."

"Patience," India said, relieved that her sister hadn't noticed the bruises. "You are tripping. Nothing has changed since we saw each other last month."

"You can't fool me. Anyway, I came by to thank you for the restaurant review that *Shades* did for us last month. Girl, *Pájo Soul* gets so busy now we have to take the phone off the hook. Literally. Jonathan and I really appreciate the hook-up. You saved our lives!"

"What's new?" India replied unenthused. "If *Pájo Soul* weren't so tucked away in the first place, you wouldn't have had that problem."

"India, for once, can't you be happy for me? Damn, well anyway, it worked out for us. Jonathan and I couldn't be happier, and we have you to thank. Besides, not everyone can afford to have a restaurant at the Harbor Place. Real estate is unbelievable down there right now. Plus, we have double the space for half of the cost on Charles Street, which is only five minutes away from the harbor."

India realized that she was being short with Patience for no particular reason and decided to let up a little. Otherwise Patience would only continue to study her attitude and take notice of her appearance. "You're welcome. I'm glad it worked out to your advantage."

"Girl, did it ever. Little John is downstairs playing with Sierra. He wanted to be with his momma today, but Veronica wanted no part of me. She begged to stay with her daddy. I tell you, for them to be twins, they are nothing alike. Night and day, those two."

"Patience, what did you expect? One is a girl and the other a boy. The similarities ended with their looks."

"I know, but sometimes, not all the time, I wish that Veronica could be a little more relaxed like her brother. She's all over the place. If I had to sit home and watch her all day, I'd be dog tired by day's end. I get so many complaints about her misbehavior in school. She's always talking and disrupting the class, or not paying attention. Little John, on the other hand, is like a saint. It's a good thing that they're in the same class. If they weren't, the teacher probably would have thought that Veronica didn't have any home training. However, since they are, she can see how well-mannered and behaved Little John is."

"I hope you don't compare them to each other aloud, because that would not be good," India said.

"Of course not. I know better than that. It's just a little observation that I'm sharing with you is all. Anyway, you know that Daddy's birthday is coming up soon, right?"

"And you're telling me this because you think that I care?"

"India, you should stop being that way. Regardless of what happened, he is still our father. Put the past to rest."

"Yeah, the way we put our mother to rest. Patience, if you've decided to have a change of heart, then I say more power to you, but please don't impose your crap on me."

"Fine, but, again, he is our father, and we only have one parent left."

"And why do we only have one parent left? I'll answer that for you, because of *him!* He's a poor excuse for a man. He couldn't take care of business when we were younger, and he's still not able to handle things now. Grayson, on the other hand, would never fall prey to such nonsense, and he's a real man. Grayson's got it together both professionally and financially. He is a real committed family man."

"You know what, I didn't come to argue about Daddy or to discuss Grayson's career track or portfolio. I stopped by to give you a little something for helping me out."

"What?" India asked, only half interested.

"A strawberry shortcake and a strawberry tart. What else? I damn sure won't experiment with anything else on you. You're so particular."

"Correction. Not particular, I just know what I like and Cool and Minty party cake is not my idea of what tastes good. Who in the world told you to add mint to a cake for flavoring? Mint was made to keep your breath fresh. So, when I see or hear mint flavor, I expect it to be hard candy, chewing gum or toothpaste. Even tea, but I damn sure won't eat any cake that has mint. Cake should taste like cake."

"Whatever. It sells extremely well at the restaurant, so forget you with a capital F. So what's for dinner tonight? I can smell Lenora cooking up a storm."

"Are you staying for dinner?" India asked, hoping she wouldn't.

"Did I say that? All I asked was what's for dinner. But you know what? It's time for me to leave. Your attitude stinks. No wonder you don't have any friends. No one can stand to be around you for more than ten minutes."

"Patience, good-bye."

"I love you too." Patience walked out into the hall and yelled down the stairway, "Little John, put on your jacket and let's get ready to go."

"So, where are you headed to next?" India asked, standing in the bedroom doorway.

"I have a sorority meeting tonight."

"Again? Speaking of friends, those are your only ones," India said, facetiously replying to her sister's earlier comment about her lack of friends.

"Correction, those are the friends who you are aware of because they live out here in your neck of the woods. My best friends, who are not Deltas, live in Baltimore County near me. So don't try to bring me into your lonely little circle. Your only friends are the people you work with, and even they don't like you, but they have to make nice since you're the head of your department."

"Whatever," India answered.

"Shallow," Patience mumbled under her breath.

"What did you say?" India asked.

"See you next month. Same bat channel, same bat place," Patience strolled out of the room, leaving India alone.

"Thank you for the tart," India yelled. "Bitch," she said as she headed toward the master bathroom.

Patience reappeared in the doorway. "I heard you, and don't think that I didn't figure out what was different about you. You can hide all you want under that makeup, Miss Beauty Director, but I know that Grayson beat that ass again. I may be a bitch, but you're a stupid bitch. Give that some thought." Then she left as quickly as she had appeared.

3

Business as Usual

oney, I'm ovulating. Are you in the mood?" Wanita Freeman asked, trying to wake her husband. She was wearing her latest lingerie purchase, a silk chemise with a deep keyhole that was derriere-skimming. William always did like the feel of silk against her body, so she figured tonight was no exception and that once he took a look at her, he'd be ready to jump her bones.

It was three in the morning, and William had arrived home from his business trip a little after midnight. He was the vice president of Acquisitions for Radio One headquartered in Lanham, Maryland, but they lived in Atlanta, Georgia. Radio One had recently closed on twenty additional radio stations across the country, making it the largest African American–owned company in the United States.

William rolled over and stared at his wife who was slowly becoming a nag. It was always "Honey, when are we going to have children?" and "When are you going to spend more time with me?" Hell, somebody had to bring home the bacon. *This luxurious house ain't made of gingerbread,* William thought.

"I just got home from an exhausting trip where I covered six cities in five days. I sat through excruciating meetings negotiating contract after contract, puckered up more times than I cared to in order to meet our seller's needs. I missed my flight and sat in the airport for three hours. Then I sat on the plane for another five hours and pulled together a full report about the entire acquisition for Ms. Hughes that's due.

So, Wanita, what do you think?"

Wanita didn't know what to do anymore as far as winning her husband over. She was thirty-three about to turn thirty-four in August, which was nine months away. She definitely wanted to have a baby before she turned thirty-five, but at the rate that she was going with William, it could take her another two years to either convince him to have kids or strap him down and make him.

Wanita was thrilled that her husband was doing so well at his job. They both had made many sacrifices to get him to where he was, but their relationship felt so incomplete. And Wanita knew exactly what they were missing: children. Three years ago, when she told him that she wanted three children, William had laughed at her and said, "What are you trying to do, kill me?" *Just for argument's sake,* she thought, *would it really kill him to spend a little quality time with me? Take me to a movie every now and then? Perhaps even go to the Four Seasons like we used to.* Now, the only time they did anything together was when he needed a shoulder piece for one of his banquets or other big bash events. She was left alone to do her volunteer work down at the children's hospital and to shop with her friends. At first, Wanita had thought that this was the life that she wanted to lead, but the novelty quickly wore off.

"William, when are *we* going to start a family?"

"Wanita, can we not go into this right now? I just told you how tired I was, and you want to start a full-scale discussion at—" William paused to glance at the stereo CD clock radio. The Indiglo night-light brightly displayed the time—"three-seventeen in the morning?"

"Fine," Wanita huffed, and turned over to switch off the lamp on her side of the bed.

"Good," William answered, ignoring her attitude.

Wanita was a happy-go-lucky person, so when she woke up that morning, she decided to make breakfast for William and herself. It had been a while since they'd sat down at the breakfast table together. She diced the green peppers and onions so that they would be caramelized in the scrambled eggs. Then she fried the turkey bacon on their rarely used stainless-steel Viking range, and put the kettle on for tea.

William loved turkey bacon. Wanita prayed for the day that she could convince him to eventually cut meat out of his diet altogether. She was a semi-vegetarian. Her indulgences were fish and dairy products.

When breakfast was complete, she went outside to get the newspaper that arrived like clockwork at their gate daily. Just as Wanita re-entered the foyer, William was walking down the spiral staircase nicely dressed in casual wear and freshly shaven.

"Good morning, beautiful," William said as Wanita stood at the bottom of the stairwell waiting for his arrival. She handed him the newspaper while he planted a kiss on her anticipating lips. William was always a very good kisser, even though they rarely did that anymore, either.

"Good morning. Did you sleep well?"

"I always sleep well when I'm sleeping next to you."

"You're such a charmer," Wanita replied as they walked into the breakfast nook in the kitchen. "So it sounds like your trip was rather successful."

"It was very successful. I might add that this deal will give us a very nice commission. I know you have your eye on that new Benz sports model, and in a couple of weeks, we can go down to the showroom and get it, cash and carry," William said with an enormous grin on his face.

"Come here, baby, let me give you a little more than some sugar in your tea," Wanita said, strolling over to William's side of the table. A new car, she felt like wiping all the food off the table and celebrating.

"We'll have plenty of time for that later," he said, rubbing her round mound. What did you make us for breakfast? It smells so good, and I haven't had a home-cooked meal in a while."

"I made all of your favorites: eggs with peppers, cheese, onions and tomatoes; turkey bacon; challah French toast with raisins and cranberry tea."

"That's why I love you so much. You do it up the right way, baby. So, tell me what you did while I was away."

"The usual," Wanita said as she put the food on serving plates to place them on the center of the table. Then she returned to the stove.

"What's the usual? Do you need any help over there?" William asked.

"No, I'm fine. Layla, Maxine and I did a little shopping. I worked down at the children's hospital. We're preparing for the annual fund-raising benefit. This year we have costume character appearances from Nickelodeon. One of their popular programs, *Rugrats,* or something like that. Anyway, this year we were able to partner with the local cable company and they're paying for that portion of it. I've sold more than sixty tickets already. By far, this will be one of the most successful fund-raisers ever."

"That's great. Well, you can give me a couple of tickets to sell for you. I have a meeting this afternoon that I have to attend."

"What meeting?" Wanita asked, trying not to show her frustration.

"The Professional African American Men Association. You know that we meet third Saturday of every month, and today is third Saturday."

"Oh, I just thought that since I haven't seen you all week that we could go out. I got tickets for *Tapping from the Soul,* and tomorrow is the play's last day at the Fox Theater. I would hate for the tickets to go to waste. It seems like such a great show."

"Don't miss it on account of me. Take Maxine or Layla with you. Surely one of them will be available to accompany you either today or tomorrow. Can you please pour me some more tea, honey?" William asked, extending his mug.

"Why can't you go with me tomorrow? What other plans do you have for the weekend?" Wanita asked, fighting the urge to pour the hot water down his crotch instead of in his mug.

"You know that I have season tickets to the basketball game, and there's a game tomorrow."

"Well you don't have to attend every game. It's only two months into the season and there are lots more games. Why can't we go to the play tomorrow together?"

"First of all, I don't go to every game. I missed all of the games this week and last week. Now it's important that I attend this particular game because the Knicks are playing the Hawks. I can't miss my

Knickerbockers. I can't afford for them to lose either. They need me."

"What the hell do you mean they need you? I need you," Wanita quipped.

"Honey, you know what I mean. I paid top dollar for these tickets, and me and the guys already planned to spend the afternoon letting loose. Now, I promise that I'll spend some time with you. I have two weeks vacation coming up, so plan a nice trip for us. Anywhere you want to go. Keep me in the loop about the date and place, because you know that I have to renew my passport if you want to leave the country. That way I'll be all yours for the entire trip."

"Listen, I'll plan the trip, but that doesn't get you off the hook as far as tomorrow is concerned. Your game doesn't start until the evening, anyhow."

"Sunday games begin between noon and two o'clock. So, just take one of your friends with you, and I promise that I'll go with you the next time there's a play in town, but you have to let me know in advance."

"In advance!" Wanita flung her head back in disbelief. She couldn't believe what she was hearing. "What the hell do you mean by that? You're my husband and I shouldn't have to make appointments with you. It's business as usual for you, isn't it? You're unbelievable. Should I check with your secretary for openings and availabilities?"

"Wanita, don't be ridiculous. Comments like that are not very becoming and make you sound stupid. Now, all I'm saying is, if you want to ensure that I'll be able to attend, it would be in your best interest to give me advance notice," William said, wiping his mouth with a napkin and pushing his chair back.

"Well, the same way you would like to be given consideration and advance notice is the same way I have to give my friends notice. They have husbands, too, and that's their quality time. You can't expect me to intrude upon that."

William stood and began adjusting his pants and tucking his shirt in. Now was definitely a good time to leave.

"Listen, I don't really care who the hell you get to go with you, but I can't do it. It's as simple as that. Like I said, the next time something like this comes up, I'll happily go with you. Tomorrow is just a very bad time. Unfortunately, I have to get going, because PAAMA is planning our annual gala. It's in Atlanta this year, so we definitely have to come correct. We could probably use some of your expertise on our catering and decoration committee. This way we can spend more time together. How does that sound?"

"Whatever, William."

"You haven't touched your food. Aren't you hungry?" William asked.

"I just lost my appetite," Wanita said, standing to throw her food in the waste bin. She didn't see the sense in bringing up their conversation from earlier. He would be just as nonchalant anyway.

They had been married for eight years and were together four years before that. Yet they still hadn't started a family. Every year there was a different excuse. First, it was his career, then money, travel, then a career switch, then his mother took ill and passed away. Of course, he had no control over the unfortunate passing of his mother, but what was next? What was waiting for her behind door number six? Wanita gave up her career when William's mother took ill. He was too busy to tend to his mother's ailing condition and, since Wanita was a nurse, it made sense for her to stay home with her. Besides that, Wanita had had some issues with her job, so it hadn't been a hard decision. Wanita spent eleven months taking care of his mother. What a shame that she didn't live to see her only son's children. His mother was probably turning over in her grave because one of her dying wishes was for William to carry on the Freeman family name. He was certainly doing an injustice to her.

"You need anything while I'm out this afternoon?" William asked, trying to redeem himself.

"No, have fun," Wanita said as she cleared the table. All the while, she thought, *Yeah, bring me back my old husband—or a new one.*

It was just like William to leave her alone with her thoughts. One of these days she was going to plot some serious stuff against him and he'd be sorry he ever messed with her. Did he even realize what he was doing to their relationship? He didn't even know who she was anymore. The last time they spent quality time together was more than a month ago. He could have asked her if she wanted to go with him to the game. She enjoyed basketball just as much as he did. Hell she used to play on the girl's varsity team in college. Her basketball scholarship had paid her way through college. At five-foot-ten, she was one of the best shooting guards on the team. In case William had forgotten, that's how they met. He was so impressed with her skill that he just had to talk to her after one of her games.

William was visiting some friends at the University of Connecticut and ended up going to one of her games. After the game, he approached her with some weak-ass rap, but she found him very attractive and decided to give him a little play. He was much taller than she was, which was a big plus. Most of the guys she had dated in the past were either her height or an inch taller. By the time she put on her three-inch heels, she would tower over them. William was brown like the wood grain in her car; he had a unibrow like Al B. Sure and nice teeth. Wanita always had a thing for men with beautiful teeth. It was a sign of good hygiene. That night William ended up ditching his friends and they went to a little burger joint and talked until two in the morning.

They were both in their senior year of college and had a lot in common. William's visits became more and more frequent, and he didn't miss any of her home games. She found him charming and enjoyed learning new things about him. They partied together, went to plays, movies, the works. One thing led to another, and she decided to attend nursing school in New York. He had already been accepted into the law program at his alma mater, St. John's University, and they would graduate a year apart. The nursing program at Downstate Medical was only two years long. Wanita obtained a job after graduation, and they decided to live together. Two years later, they were married. Shortly after that, he was offered a job with Radio One. They relocated to Atlanta and never looked back.

Wanita was slowly beginning to realize that William had no intentions of starting a family, at least no time soon. It was too much of an inconvenience for him. Wanita decided to call her friend to help her cool down.

"Hey, Layla. What's up and popping with you today?" Wanita asked.

"The book club is meeting. I thought you were coming over here to help me out."

"Girl, why are you lying? You know damn well I told you that

William was coming home and we were going to spend time together today."

"Oh yeah, that's right. Well, listen, I'm trying to prepare the food
for all these greedy-ass women coming over to my house for the
meeting, so I can't chat long. You know how they don't eat, expecting to be fed when they come. I swear most of them come for the
food first and the book discussion second."

"I know that's right. What book did you all choose for this month?"

"*A Fool's Paradise* by Nancey Flowers."

"I read that. It was hot. Okay, count me in. I'm on my way over.
Do you need anything before I get all the way over there and you send
me out to the store?" Wanita asked.

"I thought you said that you were spending time with Big Willie
today?"

"Long story. I'll tell you when I get over there," Wanita said.

"Fine. Since you offered, you can pick up two bottles of Chardonnay,
two bottles of Martinelli's sparkling apple cider and paper plates."

"Now suppose I wasn't coming. What would you have done then?"

"Just pick up the stuff and bring your butt on over here. Let me ask
you real quick, is it business as usual with William?"

"You know it is. Same ole shit, different day," Wanita said with a
deep sigh.

"Woo-woo. We'll chat when you get here, so hurry."

"Alright, see you in about an hour."

4

The Silent Treatment

B edford tried to regain his composure before picking up the phone to speak to Sandy. She always had a way of detecting when he was lying, and the last thing that he needed to do was give her reason to doubt him, especially over the phone. Bedford was already on her shit list. Less than a month ago, Bedford received a telephone call from a woman he had met at a business function six months earlier. He didn't recall giving Keyanna his home phone number. As a matter of fact, he never gave female acquaintances his home number. He wasn't that simple. Yet, she found it, called and took the liberty of introducing herself to Sandy. She even gave Sandy a play-by-play of their sexual escapades. Women were trifling and vindictive. Keyanna knew from the get-go that he was married. He never withheld that information from her, and still she tried to get possessive. If only women came with warning labels like "possessive," "unstable," "crazy," "will puncture condom when not looking," "drama queen," "diseased," or "looking to get laid, no strings attached," life would be so much easier, but they didn't, so he had to take his chances.

Felice sat across from him looking smug, and for good reason. He really didn't want Felice in the room when he spoke to Sandy, but he knew that she wasn't about to leave. Plus, he didn't want to burn any unnecessary bridges with her. After all, she was still a good lay. Sometimes he didn't know why they'd broken up in the first place. Yeah, he knew. She caught him in bed with Davonna. He couldn't exactly talk himself out of that one, now could he? Though he did try. That's the last time he risked taking a woman to his house to fuck. What made it even worse was that Davonna was Felice's personal assistant at the time. It went without saying that Davonna was on the unemployment line bright and early the next day.

Bedford cleared his throat as he picked up the phone.

"Hey, Sandy. How's your mini vacation going?" Bedford asked.

"Everything is going well, but I can't wait to come home. What took you so long to answer the phone?"

"Oh, um, I was preparing for a meeting. You know the one that I've been preparing for with Truman and Haughton Associates? Well, the meeting is in less than fifteen minutes and I wanted to make sure that I had everything in order before I picked up the phone. You deserve my undivided attention."

"Oh, because Shirley said that you had someone in your office and that you were busy," Sandy said.

Think quick, think quick, Bedford thought.

"I was going over some figures with Greg, but when Shirley said that it was you on the line, he left. He's in the conference room now setting up."

"Oh, for a minute I thought that it was Felice," Sandy said, sounding concerned.

"Why would you think that it was Felice? Even if it was, sweetie, you've got to understand that there is nothing going on between us. Felice is my business partner. We work together and are bound to run into each other from time to time, but she means nothing to me. From the moment that I met you, the fire I once felt for Felice was extinguished. There's not even a flicker of interest now. Okay?"

"Bedford, I want to believe you. You understand that, right? It's just that…well, you know, the Keyanna incident."

"Baby, I can't tell you enough how sorry I am. When we go back to see Dr. Barton, we'll discuss all these unresolved issues. I want to regain your trust," Bedford said.

"Okay. By the way, the flowers that you sent are beautiful. If only I could bring them home with me."

"There are plenty more flowers where those came from, and since you like them so much, when you get home, you'll think that you were in a florist shop."

"Bedford, you are so silly."

"Which ones did you like best?"

"The stargazers are so aromatic, but the yellow roses with the reddish tint were beautiful."

"I knew you'd like them."

"You know I did."

"Then I'm happy. Tell your mom hi for me, okay? Listen, honey, I've got to go. Truman and Haughton Associates may already be here, and it's not good business to keep potential clients waiting."

"I know," Sandy said with disappointment. "I'll see you tomorrow then, okay?"

"I love you," Bedford whispered.

"I love you too."

The intercom sounded as soon as he hung up from Sandy.

Good timing, Bedford thought.

"Sir, they just arrived," Shirley announced.

"Thank you, Shirley. I'll be right out."

Felice no longer had that look of contentment on her face; she appeared downright pissed.

Bedford ignored her while he gathered his portfolio and the presentation that Greg had put together for the meeting. Whatever it was that was bothering her would have to be dealt with later. Right now, he had important people waiting for him.

"Are you going to wish me luck?" Bedford asked Felice as he walked from around the desk to leave.

Felice only huffed and shook her head.

"Is that a no?" Bedford asked.

No answer.

"Are you going to answer me at all?"

No response. Felice gave him a gaze that was sharper than a paper cut.

"Oh, so now you're giving me the silent treatment." Bedford quickly looked at his watch to see how he was doing with time.

Felice pushed out her chair, cut her eyes at Bedford and strolled past him without uttering a word. Her perfume lingered as she passed by.

"Fine, suit yourself," Bedford replied. The one thing that he was grateful for was that Sandy wasn't nearly as temperamental as Felice, who was like a time bomb. You never knew what would set her off. It was so much work trying to figure out what was wrong when she was upset. She always figured him to be some kind of psychic. Then, when he'd take a stab at guessing what the problem was, she would rile herself up even more if his presumption was incorrect. Aside from the good sex, what Bedford could remember best about Felice was tick, tick, tick, *kaboom!*

Felice blocked his entrance before he could open his office door.

"You are such a fucking bastard," Felice said.

Oh, now she was in the mood for a discussion. Great.

"I'd appreciate it if you lowered your voice," Bedford said, concerned that Shirley would hear on the other side of the door.

"Don't tell me to lower my voice. I'll scream my lungs out if I choose."

"Okay, Felice, so what's bothering you now?"

"You know what! That shit you told Sandy just now."

"What shit, Felice? Speak up, because time is money."

"That shit about I mean nothing to you, and the moment you met her the fire you felt for me was extinguished. What the hell was that all about?"

Bedford knew that he should have made her leave the office. Though he didn't see why she was tripping. She of all people knew his situation best. Why did he keep putting himself into these spots?

"Felice, I couldn't very well tell Sandy that you were in my office. That's number one. Number two: What do you expect me to tell her? That every time that I see you I want to fuck you? Now, our relationship has been plain and simple for the past couple of years. Why are you trying to complicate matters?"

"I'm not upset at what you said, but it's how you said it. You made it sound like I wasn't worth crap. How do you think that made me feel? I'm sitting right in front of you and you blatantly insult me. I would never do that to you."

"Oh, but it's okay for you to flaunt your boy, Aaron, in my face, right? Listen, let's not create a double standard here. Sandy's my wife. If she needs reassurance that I'm not sleeping with you, then that's what I'm going to give her. I'm sorry if I hurt your feelings, and I hope that you accept my apology."

"You're still a bastard," Felice said as she opened the door and stormed down the hall.

"Thanks for stopping by," Bedford said innocently as he stood in front of Shirley's desk.

"What's wrong with her?" Shirley inquired, peering over the frame of her glasses.

Shirley had been Bedford's assistant for more than ten years now. Before he began working for himself back in 1995 she was his secretary at Becker and Coles Financial Group. Due to a personal family crisis, Shirley had to take a six-month leave of absence. Instead of holding her job, the company decided to replace her. At the time, she also assisted two other team members who complained that Shirley was going to be gone too long and that they needed someone reliable and stable. What they really meant was someone young and white.

Bedford was very fond of Shirley and thought of her as a surrogate mother. He knew that it would be hard for her to find a new job in such a competitive marketplace. She was what he considered top notch, but it was getting harder and harder for people over forty, much less fifty, to find gainful employment. So, when he decided to venture out on his own, he gave Shirley a call. He explained to her at the very beginning that he wouldn't be able to pay her much, but as his business grew so would her salary. Bedford kept his word. Shirley was the highest paid secretary in the company, and with bonuses she almost made what he paid his account managers. He wanted to make sure that she was happy, especially since she'd stood by him when he couldn't quite afford to pay her full salary.

"You know how difficult she can be," Bedford said, trying to cut their conversation short. "By the way, thank you for sending those flowers to Sandy."

"You're welcome, sugar," Shirley said, grinning.

Looking at Shirley one would never figure that she was fifty-nine. If a stranger were to guess he would figure forty-five at best, and a good-looking forty-five too. Bedford noticed that immediately. He used to daydream about her at his former job. That was until he learned how old she was, and then she became less desirable. There was nothing sagging or drooping, because she never missed her jazzercise class. How could someone that old look that good? But that syrupy southern drawl and the fact that she was always showing pictures of her grandkids gave away her age.

"Why didn't you warn me that you were sending them? It's a good thing that I know you so well and went with the flow when Sandy mentioned that she liked the flowers."

"Sugar, I help out when I can. I want people to feel good whenever possible."

"Well, thanks, Shirley. I don't know what I'd do without you."

"Wallow in your filth," Shirley said, laughing.

"You're probably right," Bedford said as he headed down the hall for his meeting.

5

If That Diamond Ring Don't Shine

t was Friday night and *Pájo Soul* was jumping. Patience and Jonathan were celebrating their restaurant's one-year anniversary. *Pájo Soul* was closed to the public for the evening for a private bash. What a difference a month could make. One little blurb in a magazine and, boom! As much as Patience hated to admit it, India did them a huge favor by getting them a review and in the process, saved their lives. Patience and Jonathan were *thisclose* to calling it quits and getting regular-paying jobs, the same regular-paying jobs that they both gave up to follow their dreams. They left the familiar (corporate America) to begin their own enterprise. It was a scary notion, but as the old saying goes, "nothing ventured, nothing gained."

Patience wanted to do more than bake India a cake and a tart, but she couldn't think of anything of which her sister was in need—other than a new husband, but that was another story. It would have been a lot easier if her sister weren't so particular, but she was. During their exchange of gifts last Kwanzaa, Patience bought India a beautiful cashmere scarf. It was the best money could buy, or the most money that Patience could afford. The fact of the matter was that it wasn't cheap. Patience knew better than to buy India anything that could be classified as cheap. India valued herself according to her material wealth. In that respect, they were night and day. Patience was day. She was bright, not a cloud in the sky, perky, full of life and to her, the glass was always half full. India was night. Her entire disposition was best defined as petulant. She was dark by nature and neither their parents nor Patience ever figured out where she inherited that poor quality.

Patience loved India unconditionally and prayed for her safety daily. She also hoped that India would see Grayson for who he was, come to her senses and leave him. As far back as she could remember, India had always been a gold digger. Even as a teenager, she lived above her means. India always had to be a fly girl, and it was hard to be fly when your parents were blue-collar workers. She wasn't happy unless she could outshine everyone else. She prized herself on stomping out any and all competition when it came to her peers. India was always pretty enough, so that was never an issue. She only dated money. It didn't matter where or how these guys earned their money, just as long as they could support her habit, which was shopping.

The problem was that there were three children who needed to be clothed and fed living off their parents' measly income. Their father started out working for an automobile manufacturer and had worked his way up to floor supervisor before retiring; and their mother was an assistant librarian at a public school. They lived in a modest-sized home in East Baltimore and never wanted for much. Their parents always told them to climb to the farthest heights because the world had much more to offer them than it had in their day. Patience knew, it was natural for parents to want you to do better than they did, but at what cost? Nothing could be worth sacrificing your well-being.

Though Patience was supposed to be celebrating, she wasn't really in a celebratory mood. How could she be? Yesterday her sister had had so much foundation on it would require a chisel to remove it all. She didn't know what to do anymore. If India wouldn't go to the police and report the abuse, what could she do? She had tried talking to her on more than one occasion: The first time it happened, the second and third, and this was the fourth. It wasn't like Grayson beat India every day, but then again who knew. She really didn't see her sister but once a month. They talked on the phone all the time, but you can't see bruises over the phone. It probably occurred more frequently than she cared to think about.

Patience thought back to the first time a guy had put his hand on her. She was dating this older guy name Cedrick when she was in high school. At the time she was sixteen and Cedrick was twenty. He had already graduated from high school, had a full-time job making dollars as a construction worker and was rolling in a brand spanking new 1985 Volkswagen Golf. Cedrick was the shit—light skinned, curly hair, gold cap on his front tooth and a body built like steel.

Patience was sitting on her porch on Thirty-third Street on a warm summer day in July. She was gossiping with her friends when Cedrick strolled down the street looking real good in his Air Jordans, Guess jeans and red-and-white Coca-Cola polo shirt. He was about five-nine, and they noticed each other right away. Shortly after, they started dating regularly. Cedrick took Patience to the movies and dinner. They didn't frequent McDonald's like the rest of her friends' dates. Instead, they went to Red Lobster and Sizzler. Every paycheck Cedrick bought something special for Patience—clothes, a name ring with diamonds and matching necklace, you name it, Patience got it. Patience was his boo. They were tighter than a pair of jeans on a hoochie momma. You wouldn't see one without the other the entire time they were dating. That was, until Tameka entered the picture. Actually, Tameka was always in the picture, but Patience didn't know that at the beginning.

Patience had a ten o'clock curfew on school nights and midnight on the weekends. So after Cedrick safely dropped Patience home, he would go to Tameka's house three city blocks away from Patience. One of Patience's good friends told her that Cedrick had been seen with Tameka on several occasions. Patience refused to believe such lies. Lots of people were jealous of her relationship with Cedrick and would say anything to break them up.

The rumor kept spreading and spreading until one day Patience decided to ask Cedrick about it. He denied it and wanted to know who and where her sources were. Patience told him she didn't believe the rumors anyway, so it wasn't important. Over the next couple of weeks, Cedrick was extra attentive and Patience believed that everyone was lying.

April rolled around bringing spring with it. It just so happened that their parents had to drive to North Carolina for a family emergency, and Patience convinced them to allow her and her older brother, Cleveland, to watch the house. Since she was sixteen her wish was granted, and she was entrusted with the care of India. Her cousin Yvette who lived in the adjoining row house, was also told to keep an eye on things. This was a joke, especially since Yvette and Patience were extremely close. That night, after they watched their parents drive off into the night, Patience convinced Yvette to drive her to Cedrick's. They weren't going to stay long, but Patience wanted to surprise him. Cedrick had dropped her off at ten o'clock like he normally did and said he was going straight home to rest for work the next morning.

After convincing Yvette to take her, they packed Yvette's siblings and India in the backseat. They pulled up in front of Cedrick's building and parked across the street. Patience saw Cedrick sitting on his steps and got out of the car. She slowly approached him, not really taking notice that he was not alone on the steps. She was so caught up in the moment she failed to realize that he was seriously preoccupied.

"Hey, Cedrick. How ya doin'?" Patience said, chewing gum and smacking her lips while giving him her biggest smile.

"Patience? What you doing here? Why you ain't at home?" Cedrick asked, alarmed.

Patience still hadn't noticed that he was engrossed to say the least—until she did a double-take and saw Cedrick's two-finger ring on Tameka's chain. Strike that. The ring was on his rope chain, which was around Tameka's long neck.

"Cedrick, who is this and why is she wearing your chain?" Patience asked as calmly possible. She was livid, but her mother had always taught her to be a lady.

"Baby, listen. Come inside my hallway with me for a minute. Let me talk to you."

"Talk to me about what? Tell me why this girl has on your chain," Patience demanded.

Tameka couldn't have weighed but a buck five and was as plain looking as they came. She and Patience were both about five-five, and Patience wanted to kick her ass. What the hell did Cedrick really see in this girl? She couldn't hold a candle to Patience. Tameka was rail thin, bald headed with peas laced around the edges and looked cheap.

Tameka obviously knew about Patience and gave Cedrick a look like "the jig is up, so what you gonna do now?"

Yvette heard the ruckus and pulled into Cedrick's driveway, then hopped out of the car, advising her siblings and cousin to remain inside.

"What's going on, cuz?" Yvette asked, staring into Patience's tear-filled eyes.

"This bastard... he-he," Patience stuttered, but the words wouldn't come out.

"Come here," Yvette said, pulling Patience away so she wouldn't break down in front of Cedrick and Tameka. "Listen, Patience. Pull yourself together. Don't let that bastard or that tramp see you cry, okay. I know this is messed up, but take a deep breath and try to relax."

"I-I-I can't believe... believe this punk is playing me like this. What did I do to him, Yvette? If he ain't wanna be with me, he shoulda just quit me."

"I know, girl. I know, but some negros ain't worth shit. He's real fucked up, but just keep taking deep breaths and relax. We gonna go back over there, because I have some choice words for that bastard and that ho."

"I'm okay," Patience said, wiping her face on her brand-new white Gap T-shirt. "Don't say nothing, though. I'll handle this, okay?"

"Whatever," Yvette answered, taking off her jewelry and plaiting her ponytail in case they needed to throw down.

Cedrick and Tameka were having a little argument of their own when Patience and Yvette returned. But it ceased once they noticed that they were no longer alone.

"Cedrick, who is this and why is she wearing your chain?" Patience asked.

"Patience, just come inside with me for a minute and I'll explain."

"No, you can tell me right here in front of whoever this is," Patience said, nodding in Tameka's direction.

"You said you was gonna tell her, so tell her now," Tameka interjected.

"I'm listening, and don't give me no bullshit about this being your cousin 'cause I don't wanna hear it," Patience said, scowling.

"Please come inside with me, Patience. Just let me talk to you privately."

"Go ahead and see what that liar has to say," Yvette said.

"Please," Cedrick pleaded. He paused long enough to give Yvette a threatening stare to mind her business, but she wasn't fazed one bit.

Patience looked at Yvette and she nudged her to go ahead.

"I'll have a talk with her while you're in there listening to him lie," Yvette said.

Cedrick opened the front door and allowed Patience to walk in first. He flicked on the hall light and rested himself against the radiator while Patience positioned herself directly in front of him with her arms crossed. She put all her weight on her right leg and leaned back and had an "I wanna kick your ass" look on her face.

"Well," Patience said.

"I'm sorry, baby. I didn't mean for this to happen this way."

"You didn't mean for what to happen this way?"

"For you to find out about me and Tameka like this. I never wanted to hurt you."

Patience was mad as hell and was two minutes from crying, but she kept hearing Yvette telling her not to let Cedrick see her cry.

"You bastard. Why didn't you just 'fess up about her when I asked you two months ago? Why the heck did you have to lie? How long were you going to string me along?" The questions could have gone on and on, but Patience didn't want to lose her self-control.

"Well, me and Tameka been kicking it for like… four years now."

"What? Oh, hell no. What you mean you been kicking it for four years? Then why in the hell did you start seeing me?"

"Me and Tameka had just broke up when I met you. I had been wanting to kick it with you for a while, but I was always with Tameka. Then, when we split up and I saw you, I had to take my chance. It was real good between us, but see Tameka is my age and we got history together. Then a couple of months ago, she said she wanted to get back together. I told her no and that I was seeing you. She was like, whatever. Then stuff started getting in the way, like your curfew. You know, sometimes when I'd ask you to spend the night and you'd tell me no, it's like I gotta suffer because you're young and can't hang."

"I can't believe this. You ain't shit," Patience screamed.

"Let me finish. Please," he said, trying to unfold her arms in an attempt to pull her closer. Patience was stiff as a board. "See, when me and Tameka was together she used to come over and cook and clean my place for me and she don't gotta worry about no curfew. You can only hang on the weekends and even then you have to be home by midnight. I need more than that. I need a woman."

"My pussy was woman enough for your ass earlier today. You bastard, punk ass, lying motherfucker."

"All right, stop cursing. That shit ain't ladylike. I ain't say nothing before, because I knew you was upset, but stop," Cedrick warned.

"Fuck you, negro. Who you giving orders to?"

"I'm not gonna tell you again. Don't let me hear you cursing again."

"You know what, Cedrick, you can go to hell. You and your bitch out front. You belong together," Patience stated boldly.

Whap! The sound was accompanied by a stinging sensation to her cheek. The entire scene had taken place so quickly Patience wasn't sure what had happened.

Whap! Again and then again. Cedrick laced Patience with a procession of smacks. He didn't even give her cheek a moment of relief, slapping Patience three times in the face-twice on one side and once on the other.

"I told you to watch your damn mouth. Who you think you talking to like that?" Cedrick asked.

Patience couldn't even react. She was too shocked. All she could do was massage her cheeks and exercise her jaws. Patience didn't know where the hits came from, but she knew that she didn't want another backhand slap.

"You all right?" Cedrick asked.

Patience just wanted to get out of the hallway and back outside. The cherries on the wallpaper only served to remind her of how red and bruised her face probably was. The incense that he had burning in his apartment only nauseated her.

"Mmm-hmm. Yeah, I'm okay," Patience responded.

"You sure?"

"Yes, I'm fine."

"I'm sorry that things had to end like this between us because I really liked you. If you were older, we could have kept on kicking it. You know what I'm saying."

"It's okay. Really, I understand," Patience said, grabbing the door-knob.

"I got it," Cedrick said, putting his hand over hers to open the door. "I'm still a gentleman."

When they walked back outside, Yvette and Tameka were talking. Not talking like friends. More like Yvette was bullying Tameka. Yvette was slightly taller than Tameka and used her height to hover over her. Patience walked straight to the car and didn't look at either one as she passed them.

Yvette immediately followed. India had taken a front-row seat outside and was leaning on the car, but Yvette's siblings were fast asleep. It was almost twelve-thirty in the morning.

"Girl," Yvette said, pumped up from her session with Tameka, "did you know that Tameka lives two floors above Cedrick's? She said that they had been kicking it for two months, but were doing it on and off while you two were dating."

Patience was only half listening. She was trying to plot a way to kick Cedrick's ass. She couldn't do it. Not even with Yvette's assistance. Cedrick may have been small, but he was quick and a good fighter. Patience had witnessed him kick a couple of guys behinds on the street for staring at her before, but at the time never thought anything of it. Yvette noticed that Patience wasn't really paying attention.

"Patience, you okay?" Yvette asked, concerned about her cousin's silence. "What did he say to you?"

Silence.

"Talk to me, girl," Yvette said, not taking her eyes off the road.

That's when Patience broke into tears and sobbed uncontrollably. Not only did she catch her man cheating on her, but her cousin was also there to see it. And it wasn't like Tameka was cute or fly. Then, if that wasn't bad enough, Cedrick beat her like she was his child and had the nerve to ask if she was okay. Hell, in all of her born days her parents had never even slapped her.

Yvette pulled up to the curb in front of their homes and took a good look at Patience, but it was dark, and the streetlights didn't provide that much illumination. She turned on the light inside the car.

"What the heck happened in there?" Yvette did a double-take after she saw Patience's face. "What did that punk ass do to your face?" Yvette asked, holding Patience's face toward the light. "Oh, hell no! He hit you? We are going right back over there."

"We can't go over there alone," Patience countered.

"I had no intentions of doing that," Yvette said, getting out of the car and waking up her siblings. "Get up. We're home. Go inside and go to bed. India, stay in the house and watch them. We'll be right back. Patience, I'ma go see if Tony, Terence, Big Tye and Cleve are inside the house, okay?"

"All right," Patience answered. How could she forget about her brother and cousins? They would kick Cedrick's ass for her. That's right. Bring it on. Cedrick didn't know what he had gotten himself into. Her older brother, Cleveland, and cousins were not to be played with.

Sure enough, they were home. They came barging outside and rolled up to the car.

"Yo, we'll meet over there," Tony said, and the four of them put their helmets on and hopped on their motorcycles.

They all pulled up in front of Cedrick's building at the same time. Cedrick didn't see it coming. He had his arm placed firmly around Tameka's neck, and they looked like new lovers. By the time Cedrick realized what was happening, it was too late. Tameka jumped out of the way, and Yvette, who wanted to kick her ass, anyway, hauled after her.

Cedrick got his ass kicked, badly. Patience had to beg her cousins to stop pounding his face into the ground. They said that they wanted his face to ache the way hers had. Patience also broke up the fight between Yvette and Tameka, but not before getting a few punches and slaps in herself.

From that day forward, Patience swore that she would never, ever let a man abuse her in any way. Cedrick hadn't shown any abusive signs in the beginning, but then he'd just flipped. Patience realized that there probably were warnings all along, but she was so caught up in the rapture that she hadn't allowed herself to see them.

Patience later found out that, prior to their relationship, Cedrick used to beat Tameka all the time. None of that seemed to matter, because they still got married and had three children together. Now, it seemed that her sister was in a similar situation, if not worse. Grayson was a big-time attorney and knew all the right people who could get him out of such a situation; but they also had a child, and the last thing that Sierra needed to see or be around was an abusive relationship of any kind, especially between her parents. It wouldn't do well for her in school or when she got older. She would probably end up socially dys-functional, if there was such a thing.

In hindsight, Patience realized how naïve she had allowed herself to be back then. She also knew better than to *ever* date Cedrick again. No sense in walking into the fire twice when she'd already been burned once. That was plain common sense.

"Honey," Jonathan called as he danced over to Patience with drinks in hand. "Here's a frozen margarita. I made it special for you," he said, handing her the glass."

"Thank you," Patience said, taking a sip.

"You wanna dance?" Jonathan asked as he did his famous two-step.

"No, I'm really not in the mood."

"My baby girl don't wanna boogie with Big Poppa?" Jonathan asked, still doing his little jig and bumping a reluctant Patience.

"Jonathan, sweetie, I'm just not in the mood, okay?"

"What's wrong? Yesterday you were so excited about today, now you're moping around. Tonight is our one-year anniversary and we should be celebrating. Instead you've been solemn all night. Talk to Poppa."

The music was blaring and even though Jonathan was right within earshot he was still talking at the top of his lungs. Patience downed her margarita and wiped her mouth with the back of her hand while trying to maintain her balance. She was already starting to feel a bit inebri-ated, which could have come from too much alcohol or too little food. The margarita was definitely going to be her last alcoholic beverage for the evening.

A waiter was passing by with a tray of hors d'oeuvres containing glazed sesame chicken on a stick. Patience lightly tapped the waiter on his arm. When he noticed that it was the boss lady he put on a huge grin and handed her a couple of napkins. Patience returned the smile, took three of the shish kebabs and thanked him by name. This display of acknowledgement stunned the young man causing him to bare all thirty-two teeth as he nodded to say "you're welcome" and walked off.

It was not unusual for Patience to know the names of her workers. As a matter of fact, she made it her business to know all the names and a little bit of history about her employees, temp help included. She didn't want anyone to feel like a number in their establishment. Corporate America already had that covered. For years, both she and Jonathan had felt like talking heads or robots at their places of employment. Clocking in, clocking out, logging onto the computer terminal and logging out, swiping a badge in and swiping out. Then there was the monotony of repeating the same thing over the phone almost verbatim every day: "Sir or madam, I'm sorry to inform you that our audit reveals that you are in arrears of X amount of dollars. Now, we can make arrangements to resolve this over the next couple of weeks or months." Then came the interruption, followed by an objection from the client. Nine times out of ten the client was in the wrong and ended up having to live by her firm's provisions.

It took Patience and Jonathan ten years to leave their cushy, but boring jobs and follow their dreams. Patience was an accountant by trade, but worked as a senior account analyst at a major advertising firm. Jonathan started out as a chef at a restaurant, but had worked his way up into management. However, he found management to be very political, stressful and cutthroat. At the time, it was a good move for him because, if not for that fundamental experience, they would have had to hire outside consultants to help them run *Pájo Soul*. That would have equated to more out-of-pocket expenses, which they couldn't afford. The sacrifice was well worth it, and whoever coined the phrase "God bless the child who has his own" was speaking the truth!

Patience finally gave in and began dancing with Jonathan, since she saw that he wasn't going to give up. She wanted to tell her husband what was bothering her, but she didn't feel like screaming above the music and this was neither the time nor place. When Jonathan saw that she really wasn't into it, he gently pulled her in closer by the waist and kissed her forehead. Slowly they waltzed to the soulful sound of Al Green's "Let's Stay Together." Jonathan sang the words in Patience's ear. Patience loved it when he sang to her. The sweet sound of his voice always managed to lift her spirits. When Al and Jonathan got to the verse that told her to come running , she could bare it no more. The tears began to stream a little river down her face and Jonathan instinctively held her even tighter.

"Do you want to go in the back and talk about it?" he whispered.

"Yes," she replied, nodding.

Patience was sensitive by nature. In the confines of her room she cried to movies and television programs like *Roots, Little House On the Prairie, Beaches, Terms of Endearment, The Color Purple, Malcolm X, Amistad* and the latest tearjerker was the movie *The Hurricane.*

When they got to their office located in the rear of the restaurant, Jonathan handed her a tissue, which she gratefully accepted. Gently, he guided her to a seat and pulled up the extra swivel chair to sit beside her.

"Talk to me. Something has been bothering you, and you won't tell me what's wrong. I can't help if you don't share with me. Now, is it something that I've done or have one of the employees upset you again?"

"No, it's not you or the staff," Patience said, sniffling. "It's India."

"What? She didn't like our token of appreciation? I told you that we should have gotten her a tennis bracelet or a designer purse. I knew she was going to give you another headache."

"Jonathan, it's not that. It's happened again."

"What's happened again?"

"Grayson. He put his hands on India again."

"Really? Are you sure? Did she tell you this?"

"Yes, I'm sure and no she didn't tell me anything. I just know."

"If she didn't tell you how can you just assume."

"I'm not assuming anything," Patience said, straightening herself up in her seat. The tears began to coast down her cheeks again. "Her face was bruised, and she had a welt on her upper right arm."

"And you're sure that Grayson did that?"

"Jonathan, quit being so naïve. India didn't fall down any steps, she didn't walk into a wall and she wasn't roughhousing with Sierra. Grayson hit her," Patience said irritably.

"Why? What would make him do such a thing?" Jonathan questioned innocently.

"What do you mean, what would make him do such a thing? I don't care what she did. That man has no right to lay his hands on my sister. She is not his child, and even if she were, that would still be considered abuse. My question is why does she continue to stay with him? It's not like she has to."

"It's lifestyle, plain and simple. Your sister is accustomed to a certain standard of living and Grayson provides that for her. She's comfortable."

"There's not that much comfort in the world. She can more than provide for herself."

"Sure she can, but she wouldn't have the big house, the fancy car, clothes and jewelry."

"My sister makes close to six figures on her own. She could still have her car, clothes and a nice condo or town house."

"India in a town house or condo? Patience, get real. Your sister is dependent; Grayson is her security blanket, and she will take all the warmth that he can provide. You know that tune, if that diamond ring don't shine…"

"She can buy her own damn diamond ring. There's no possible excuse as to why India should remain in this situation. The environment is too negative for Sierra and her. It's not like we were raised in an abusive household. I just don't understand why she puts up with it. Money is not the end all and be all of life."

"Grayson seems like such a nice guy. We don't hang out, but when we have family functions and we shoot the breeze, Grayson is always fun to be around. Good conversation, smart, cool, relaxed. I don't understand."

"It's not for us to understand, but we do need to help India come to her senses before this gets any worse. Who knows how often this is happening? This is the fourth time that I've been aware of this, but I'm almost positive that the abuse is ongoing and I don't…I-I can't let this happen to my sister."

"Patience, it's going to be okay, honey. Don't cry." Jonathan wiped her face with the back of his hand and held her chin up. He held her tightly as her body shuddered from the tears. "I promise, honey, it will be okay. I'll help see to that."

6

Keeping It Real

"Did you cut the cheese?" Layla asked.

"What?" Wanita asked, knowing Layla was trying to be funny.

"The cheese. Did you cut it?"

"Was I supposed to? Forget the cheese. What should I do about William?" Wanita questioned.

"Do you want my honest opinion?"

"Of course I do."

"You know that I don't like to meddle with affairs of the heart."

"That's a lie right there!" Wanita said, laughing.

"Okay, here goes. William is a nice guy, hard worker, smart, charismatic, kind and handsome. Those are the positive qualities, but he is also selfish, stubborn, inconsiderate, neglectful and difficult at times. I guess you have to take the good with the bad, but you say that you want children and it's quite obvious that he doesn't. His career comes first, friends and hobbies second and you last. Now, I know that I've told you this time and time again, but you need to go back to work and get your life back in order. Stop being so dependent on him. Money isn't everything and you know it. Charles and I are fine on our measly incomes; we can still afford to do things together, and we have a wonderful family. Now, I'm not saying that we don't have our ups and downs, because that comes with the territory, but we're happy, and money has absolutely nothing to do with that. I've already said a mouthful and more than I intended, but take all that I've said with a grain of salt. Only you know if you're happy, and, personally, I don't think that you are. I can't advise you to leave him, because that would be wrong, and you know that I believe that marriage is sacred, but something has got to change or you won't have much of a marriage."

Both Layla and Wanita were silent as they continued to chop, cut and dice the hors d'oeuvres. Wanita was a little hurt, but she couldn't let on that most of what Layla had said bothered her. Yeah, some of it was true, but not all. Truthfully, Layla hit the nail on the head. Wanita didn't think that her life was that transparent. Or maybe it was because Layla had known her since they were both in pigtails, and they had attended grade school, high school and two years of college together. Basically, they knew each other like the back of their hands. Before her third year of college, Layla became pregnant, got married, dropped out and moved to Atlanta with her new husband, Charles, in that order.

"I can't stand you. Do you know that?" Wanita blurted out.

"Don't hate the player, girl. Hate the game. I only speak the truth and you know it. You also know that I'm not trying to be mean, but wasn't it just yesterday that you were telling me about all of these great plans that you had for today, which included spending quality time with William?"

"I know, but he's...."

"Soror, what did we learn about excuses when we pledged. I haven't forgotten, and, since you're the active one, I know damn well that you haven't. So, work on improving your relationship instead of defending William's sorry butt. Put your foot down and tell him that you want to go back to work. Stop allowing him to make you feel like you're incapable of doing things. You are one of the best nurses that I've ever come across. It was your occupation that enabled him to make those giant leaps in his career. You had the steady income and held things together when stuff was slow on his end. Girl, you better act like you know and let him know while you're at it."

"I don't know...I mean he has so much going on, and I know that he means well."

"Means well? Wanita, we never did discuss what happened or why you left your job, but I know the reason that you haven't gone back is because of William. I've been around the both of you on several occasions when you mention something in the health field or you try to give someone a recommendation. I've heard his smart remarks. So you made one mistake."

"Layla, it wasn't one mistake. My patient lost his life because of me and my incompetence."

"Listen to yourself. Why are you so quick to deem yourself incompetent?"

"I am listening to myself. You weren't there. You don't understand how traumatizing my life has been since that day. If I had paid closer attention, that man would be alive and well today, probably home with his family. He was young…you know in his early sixties. Earlier that day when I attended to him, he was watching *The Golden Girls* and laughing at their silly antics. I remember everything as if it were yesterday. I went to take his blood pressure, and while I was doing the procedure, he made a comment about how much he liked Rue McClanahan, who played Blanche, and her sexual appetite. His pressure was high, but nothing that I hadn't seen before. I told him to keep laughing and enjoy his program because a little rest and relaxation would help him improve his hypertension."

"If you don't want to talk about it you, don't have to," Layla said, coming to her friend's aid by massaging her shoulders.

"No, it's okay. I think that it's time that I talk about it openly so that I can put it to rest."

Wanita walked over to Layla's four-piece glass dinette set and took a seat. Layla finished setting out the last of the snacks, and, before joining Wanita, she poured them both a glass of water. She placed the water on the table and sat across from Wanita.

The stern look that Wanita had worn earlier while talking to her friend began to soften.

"It was my first month on the Surgical Intensive Care Unit. You remember that I was on the Medical Surgical floor before?"

"I think so, but go on," Layla urged.

"Well, after taking my patient's vitals, I went to the station to write my observations. The attending physician came by and read my patient's file and noticed that his blood pressure was two hundred and fifty over one hundred and ten. The physician asked if this was a recent escalation in his pressure levels, and I told him no. Then he continued to look at his chart."

"So you didn't prescribe him any medication at that point, right?"

"No, the doctor is the only one who can prescribe the medicine. I only administer it. Anyway, the doctor wrote the medication down that I was to give the patient. The drug is called Brevibloc, which is also known as Esmolol Hydrochloride. I know this means squat to you, but it helps decrease blood pressure."

"Thanks for clarifying that for me, but I get the gist of what you mean. Continue," Layla said.

"Okay, so when I went back into the room the patient...let me just say his name, Mr. Bowen, was eating his dinner. His wife was visiting in the room with him, and they were talking and laughing about something or other. Mr. Bowen had a wonderful spirit and always had a smile on his face. I told him what I was about to do as I began to prep him for the procedure. He was already used to us poking and prodding him, so he sat up to make himself comfortable."

"So his wife stayed in the room while you gave him the medication?"

"Yeah, there was no reason for her to leave. It was supposed to be a simple procedure."

"Had you ever administered that drug before? The Brevibloc, or whatever it's called?" Layla asked as she took a sip of her water.

"Well, yes and no."

"Wanita, you either have or you haven't."

"The drug comes in both tablet and liquid form. When I was on the Medical Surgical floor, I gave hundreds of patients the capsule, but never the liquid, so the adverse effects aren't as conspicuous."

"Just out of curiosity, what are the effects?" Layla asked.

"The usual stuff like dizziness, fatigue, headache and sometimes vomiting."

"Oh," Layla responded, and nodded sympathetically.

Wanita sat silently as she gathered her thoughts. It had been three years since the event had occurred, but she could still see Mr. Bowen's face as if it were yesterday. The only people that she had shared the details of the tragic incident with were her mother, William and Sandy.

Her mother was extremely supportive, and Sandy was there for her when she made her final decision to leave her job instead of going to trial and risk losing all credibility. That's when things started to fall apart between her and William. The tone that he began taking with her was filled with disdain. He no longer asked her for medical advice, and when she volunteered, his response was, "That's okay, I'll consult a professional." At first, she really didn't pay attention to the change, but in time she noticed that he no longer held her in the same regard as he had before. That's when the light that used to illuminate her soul started to diminish. Wanita no longer believed in herself or her abilities, and William did nothing to encourage her. If anything, he made her feel even worse.

"Like I said, I prepped him and Mr. Bowen said, 'ouch' when I stuck him with the needle. Then he laughed to reassure me that he was kidding. I began the loading dose by inserting ten milliliters of the Brevibloc." Tears began to fill Wanita's eyes as she continued. "Seconds later, Mr. Bowen started gagging, and then his eyes…they…they started to roll to the back of his head. I started to panic, so I immediately called code seven-seven from the bedside phone. His wife was sitting there witnessing the entire ordeal. Not even a minute later, he lost all color and became ashen. Two minutes later, several doctors filled the room. There were two respiratory therapists, the attending physician, and two anesthesiologists. Mrs. Bowen watched as the respiratory therapists did CPR. Then the anesthesiologists did an endotrachial intubation, and she became hysterical. I should have asked her to leave earlier, but I was so frightened that I forgot. She put up a fight when I tried to guide her out of the room, and a physician assistant helped. We had to practically lift her up, and she pounded the PA in the chest the entire time. It all happened so fast."

"Wanita, if you don't want to go any further, you don't have to," Layla said as she rubbed Wanita's back to console her. "Here, drink some water."

Wanita took the glass and drank all of the liquid leaving the ice cubes.

"I'm okay. It's just that I don't remember when I lost control of my life. It is at a complete standstill. I'm about to turn thirty-four, and I feel like my world is crumbling. I feel like a shattered vessel."

"Listen, that may be the case right now, but you can pick up the pieces and make yourself whole again. Stop allowing others to control your future. You are more than capable of doing things on your own, and you simply need to prove that to yourself. I've never lost faith in you. We all make mistakes."

"I don't know if I can call taking Mr. Bowen's life a mistake. It's more than that. I really messed up, and I can't bring this man back. This isn't something that can be repaired. His wife is left without a husband, and his children and grandchildren have lost a loved one, all on account of me. How could I have been so careless?"

"What went wrong?" Layla asked softly, trying not to pressure her friend any more than necessary.

"When I administered the drug, it was supposed to be diluted first. I could have given him ten milligrams without it being diluted, but not an entire ten cc's. It was the large dosage amount that killed him, but I didn't know. I didn't know that I was supposed to dilute it first. I was only following the doctor's instructions. I didn't realize that I had to do something special. When the Brevibloc is in pill form, it's hard to over-dose. The whole scene was horrible. Mr. Bowen's heart rate disap-peared almost instantaneously and in no time we lost his pulse. After working on him for twenty minutes, his heart was asytoli," Wanita paused. "I'm acting like you know what asytoli means. His heart stopped. We couldn't bring him back, and he was pronounced dead. He died be-cause of my ignorance. William is right when he calls me stupid. If I were smart, I would have known better."

"You can't be serious? You are not stupid. Didn't you graduate at the top of your class in nursing school? Didn't you take the registered nurses examination and pass on the first go-round? Didn't you set up shop for William and get his damn career off the ground? Who was the provider in the beginning of your relationship? Wanita, I think that you need to really sit down and take a second look at things and stop feeling sorry for yourself."

"It's just that William said…"

"Girl, like I said earlier, I really don't like getting into people's busi-ness like this, much less marriage, but you need to put your man in check. He's the one who's incompetent. If he can't see the beautiful and smart person that you are, then he's the one who's a shattered vessel. Not you."

The sound of the doorbell took both women by surprise. Layla got up to get the door, but before walking off, she stopped to give a few last words of encouragement. "Girl, keep your head up. It looks like our reading group is beginning to arrive."

"Yeah, I guess so," Wanita said, picking up the glasses to put them in the dishwasher.

"Go clean yourself up before everyone gets here. We're about to have some fun, discuss some girl stuff and chat about *A Fool's Paradise.* Now, I know you have some interesting things to say about the book, so I fully expect you to put your two cents in."

"I will," Wanita said, trying to mask her morbid mood with merriment.

"Wanita, cheer up and remember life is for the living. What happened to Mr. Bowen is sad, but you have to pull yourself together and move on with your life."

7

Wake Up and Smell the Coffee

andy sat on the wrap-around porch of the huge blue-and-white Victorian house with her mother. Gently, she placed the large glass of lemonade on the table and beads of condensation bathed the sides leaving moisture at the base. Sandy gazed at nothing in particular, but never tired of staring at the strawberry fields. Her mother, Mama Mavis, still grew fresh fruit on her couple of acres of land and provided strawberries and melon for the farmers market.

Sandy held her head back as the evening breeze softly brushed across her bronze skin. The weather was unseasonably warm for this time of year. In exactly one month, winter would claim the east coast skies. Yet, here she was soaking up the North Carolina sun during her short visit. She sorely missed the peace and tranquility that accompanied southern living. Though she was now accustomed to the fast city life that New York had to offer, she still craved the simple life. Lately, she had been craving it even more, especially after her recent dilemma with Bedford. She couldn't understand what was wrong with him. Why did he feel the need to go outside of their marriage to seek sexual gratification? Didn't they have a normal sex life? When did he find the time? They made love at least four times a week, which was better than normal to hear her friends and coworkers speak. She'd heard talk of women only having sex with their spouses once or twice a week at best. Bedford's sexual appetite was insatiable, but Sandy was up to the challenge. At least she thought that she was, until she received the disturbing call from her husband's lover, Keyanna.

The new position as vice principal at the Daniel Hale Williams elementary school was beginning to take a toll on Sandy and the marriage as well. Administration wasn't all that it was cracked up to be. To make matters worse, they were short two teachers and since she had been a science teacher prior to accepting the vice principal position, Sandy volunteered until they could find an adequate replacement. She was not only taking papers home to grade, but also budgets, proposals, quarterly teacher curriculums for approval and anything else that was required of her. This was harder than obtaining her master's degree, Sandy thought, taking a sip of her drink. She uncrossed her legs and pushed herself forward in her seat as thoughts of Keyanna continued to cross her mind.

After Keyanna's very explicit phone conversation, Sandy decided that she had to meet this woman in person to see for herself if she was for real. Sandy figured that a face-to-face meeting would enable her to determine if Keyanna was telling the truth. Sandy was usually very on point nine times out of ten when it came to judging a person's character. She had never confronted anyone like that before and was nervous even when suggesting it to Keyanna over the phone, but when Keyanna agreed, she felt like she had made the right choice.

The evening that Keyanna called, Bedford didn't deny knowing her. He said that he did in fact meet her at the benefit dinner that she mentioned over the phone. However, he claimed that everything else that Keyanna said on the phone was a bold-faced lie. According to Bedford, the evening that they met, Keyanna was coming on to him rather strong. He knew better than to be rude to her, because she held a particularly high position at a pharmaceutical company. Bedford said that he found that much intriguing about her, since this was an area that he wanted his firm to eventually delve into. Nevertheless, he made it clear that he was a married man and wanted nothing to do with Keyanna. Sandy would have left well enough alone and believed his story, but he said several things that didn't corroborate with his earlier account regarding the events of that evening.

On the evening in question, Sandy was unable to attend the event with Bedford because it was the evening of the parent-teacher meeting.

Bedford arrived at home a little after three A.M. This wasn't unusual, since Sandy knew that Bedford liked to get out and have a good time. But when he got home, he quickly showered and threw his suit in the hamper instead of letting it air out, which was his normal practice before taking it to the dry cleaners. When Sandy inquired, he said he was so tired he didn't even realize what he was doing. If he was so tired, why hadn't he come straight to bed? Upon further inspection, Sandy found smeared lipstick, a color she did not own or dare wear with her toast-brown complexion, along the neckline of his shirt. Bedford's quick answer was it could have been any number of women he came in contact with, since many of the event's attendees were either clients or associates. Sandy left it alone, but in the back of her mind the wheels were spinning a mile a minute, and the lame excuse never left her thoughts for a moment.

Second, he claimed that he did indeed give Keyanna his office number, since she could potentially become a client, but that still didn't explain how she had gotten their home phone number when it was unlisted. Sandy knew good and well that Shirley would never give a client their home number, whether it be male or female, but Bedford insisted that was the only way Keyanna could have gotten it. He stooped so low that he blamed poor Shirley for his indiscretions. How low can you go? Sandy knew that Bedford must have called Keyanna from their home phone and, in his haste, forgot to block their number, thus giving Keyanna access to it. Keyanna obviously had Caller ID, got lucky and then decided to save the number for a rainy day and it poured on the day she decided to call!

"Girl, why don't you go on home to your husband and stop being so damn simple," Mama Mavis said, jolting Sandy back to reality. "I ain't never heard nothing like this in all my natural-born days. Bedford is a good man. So what if he cheated? Turn a blind eye to it and move on. That man ain't done nothing that every other man out there ain't done. Only he got caught, so shut your damn eyes to it and move on with your marriage."

Sandy listened to her mother speak, and knew that she was probably right. After all, her mother and father would have been happily married for another fifty years if he were still alive. They were married thirty-six years before he passed away from kidney failure.

"You see, Sandy, sometimes men think with the wrong head, but as long as he's taking care of business at home, you don't never mind about it. Shoot, look at you in them designer clothes he done bought for you and that fine house y'all living in up there in New York. Humph, I wish your father, God rest his soul, and I had those kinds of luxuries. I can tell you one thing, I bet he's smiling down on you right now proud as a peacock. Another thing you need to take into consideration is that Bedford is trying his best to better himself. Look, he's going to a shrink for your behind. What more do you want? Go home to that man and don't give him the opportunity to be out there chasing some skirt. You've been down here for a whole week now. What you think he up there doing in the meantime? Ain't nothing down here in Charlotte for you. Everything you need is up there in New York."

Mama Mavis sat on her freshly painted porch rocking back and forth in her chair while the crickets chirped and the night grew brisk. She reached over to the glass table that sat beside her and grasped the tangy but sweet ice-cold lemonade that she had made earlier that day. After finishing off the last drop, she put the glass back in its place, smacked her lips for emphasis and breathed "aahh."

"What you over there thinking about now?" Mama Mavis asked. "You ain't said a word since."

"Mama, I don't want to appear out of place or nothing, but how did you feel when Daddy cheated on you? Did it bother you any?"

Mama Mavis chose her words wisely before answering her daughter's question. "Your father was very discreet with his business. He didn't go off gallivanting for the world to know, and if he didn't slip up that one time and have your brother, Robby, I'da never known or been the wiser. My point is this: Things could be worse. Now the problem with you young folks today is that you all are too damn quick for your own good. Always ready to get a divorce at the drop of a hat. That's why we got more baby daddies than we do successful marriages. When you say I do, that is serious business. You can't just up and leave because you feel like it. You got to hang in there like a champ. Your father and I managed to work things out and, as a result, you and Robby are as tight as ever."

"I know, but you know the reason that Bedford and Felice got divorced is because he cheated on her and she caught him in the act."

"Listen, you hang on to your man. Cheating is what men do. Now Bedford wasn't the first, and he won't be the last, you understand? That's Felice's loss and your gain."

Sandy sighed from exhausting thoughts of what to do next. She wanted to take her mother's advice, but it was hard for her to be as forgiving and understanding. Times had changed, and women weren't putting up with the same nonsense they used to in her mother's day.

"Sandy, I'm not telling you anything that I wouldn't do myself. You not too long ago spoke to the man and told him you'd be home tomorrow, so stop acting so silly."

Sandy got up from her seat, smoothed out her linen two-piece outfit that still looked perfectly ironed, and headed down the porch steps.

"And where might I ask are you going now, missy?" Mama Mavis asked, peering over her glasses and watching Sandy as her shadow slowly began to disappear into the night.

"I just want to cleanse myself by taking a long walk along the countryside by my lonesome before I return home."

"Alright, sweetie, but don't stroll too far or too long by yourself. Ya hear? I'll leave the porch light on for your return," Mavis said as she grabbed the arms of the chair for support and pulled herself out of the chair.

"Don't worry, Mama. I won't be long," Sandy replied as the sound of her voice echoed into the smooth wind of the night.

Sandy needed reassurance from her longtime good friend and brother, Robby. Yes, she loved Bedford and wanted things to work out between them, but she needed to get the male perspective. Her brother would be truthful. Sandy knew her mother had good intentions, and Mama Mavis had never steered her wrong before, but this wasn't Sandy's typical, everyday problem. How long could she be expected to turn a blind eye? Would counseling really help solve their problems? Or was Bedford merely doing it just to keep her satisfied? Sandy was getting dizzy thinking about it.

After a thirty-minute walk, Sandy arrived at her brother's house. He and his wife, Nettie, were both outside. Nettie was tending to her rose garden, while Robby looked after their baby. Sandy never thought she'd see the day when Robby would settle down, but Nettie was good for him. Robby was a good man, but he had a little wild streak. It wasn't women that made him stray. His weakness was gambling. No matter what the game or stakes, if there was money involved, you could bet Robby already had his foot in it. He was finally able to learn his lesson after his gambling caused him to lose the love of his life, Ella, and his job. Ella was his 1964 Ford Mustang. Robby was able to clean up his act after attending Gamblers Anonymous meetings, and that's where he met Nettie. She was the counselor of his group, and Robby was smitten at first sight. Nettie helped him get through his rough period and even managed to set him up with a better job. A few months later, they started dating, and the rest was history.

Robby saw his older sister approaching and got up to greet her as she entered their property.

"Nettie, look who the wind done blew in," Robby said, grinning from ear to ear, pleased to see his sister.

Nettie turned her attention to see what was getting Robby so excited. When she saw that it was Sandy, she got up and brushed herself off to greet her. Robby allowed Nettie to hug and greet Sandy first.

Robby was only a couple inches taller than Sandy. He was broad and muscular, and had the same build as their late father. He grabbed Sandy and gave her a big bear hug, lifting her completely off the ground, leaving her legs dangling. Sandy giggled until she could no longer breathe from the exhaustion of trying to release herself from her brother's grip and laughing so much.

"Are you going to hug me to death?" Sandy asked.

"Maybe. It's not often that I get to rub shoulders with city folk like yourself." Robby chuckled. "I didn't think that I was going to get the chance to see you before you left, but I'm glad you're here."

"I had to stop by to see my favorite person. Let me hold Jillian," Sandy said, laughing and pushing Robby aside to get to her niece. "I can't believe she's getting so big. She's not even six months yet, right?"

"Actually, she'll be seven months next week," Robby answered proudly.

"Oh my goodness. Have I really been away that long? It seems like it was only yesterday that she was born. The time has just been flying right past me."

"We know what you mean," Nettie said, packing up her gardening tools and heading over to the shed. "I'm gonna clean myself up and then I'll come back out for Jillian Pearl's feeding, okay?"

"No rush, honey," Robby called out. "She's no trouble. Sandy and I have it all under control out here. Sandy cuddled Jillian for a couple more minutes before cooing her to a light sleep and resting her inside of the bassinet.

"She's such a good baby, Robby. She looks like both of you. It still amazes me that you are actually somebody's father. My little brother," Sandy said poking her finger into his deep dimple. "I remember when I used to beat you up. You remember that?"

"Woman, you trippin'. You mean when I used to let you beat me up. I didn't wanna hit you back because you were a girl."

"Robby, whatever," Sandy said, faking a blow to his jaw.

"So, what brings you down here to see us country bumpkins? You left your high-society life to come hang with us down here?"

"Boy, don't make me pop you. I came to spend a quiet Thanksgiving with Mama Mavis, and I needed a change of scenery. I get tired of looking at all that concrete up there. It's nice, but sometimes the hustle and bustle can wear you down. Plus, I'm still trying to deal with Bedford and his antics."

"Yeah, you were telling me about that. What ever happened?" Robby asked, kicking back and putting his feet up on the porch railing. For the first time, Sandy noticed that her brother had stripped the porch of its green paint and gotten it back to its original wood state. It was nicely shellacked all the way around. Her brother was always the handyman. He was certainly doing wonders to the house that had looked ramshackle a few years ago. No one thought that it could be restored, but Robby took it and refurbished the place room by room.

"You really want to know?"

"I asked, didn't I?"

Sandy shrugged and put her head in her hands and went into deep thought. She had wanted to talk to someone long before this in great detail, but she didn't have anyone at home to discuss her personal business with. She didn't trust anyone enough to tell them the hell that she'd been going through. She shared the story with their marriage counselor, but it wasn't the same. Sandy wanted to break down and share her inner thoughts with someone. The nightmares that she had been having lately were a result of her restlessness. The past two months had been pure hell and torture for her. She hated Keyanna for sleeping with her husband and she hated her husband for succumbing to his weakness. Even more, she hated herself for not knowing what to do.

Sandy took a deep breath.

"You know we're in counseling now, right?"

"Yeah, I believe you told me that the last time we spoke. How's it going?"

"Well. I guess."

"Sis, it either is or it isn't. Which one is it?" Robby asked, angling his head so that he could keep an eye on Jillian.

"As far as I can see, things are getting better, but I'm still a little leery," Sandy replied, slowly massaging her temples.

"Why is that?" Robby asked, in a concerned tone, emulating the posture and manner of a psychiatrist. The only thing missing was the lavish office that she was becoming all too familiar with lately.

"A few weeks back, I met with the woman who called our home."

"Are you crazy?" Robby asked in amazement, losing the calm demeanor he'd held only seconds ago. "Why would you put yourself in danger like that?"

"Robby, hear me out. I met her at a very busy restaurant, and I had enough information on her to know that she wasn't a loony bin."

The morning of their meeting, Sandy had awakened extra early to make sure that she looked her best. Their meeting was on a weekday, so Sandy had to take the morning off. Bedford was already aware of the disturbing phone call, and he denied everything. However, he was unaware of the length to which Sandy was going. Sandy pretended that everything was honky dory, so to speak, and followed her usual morning routine. Bedford never suspected a thing. She had gone to the beauty salon the day before and gotten a manicure, pedicure and her hair styled. She was careful to sleep on her stomach the entire night, head propped up on her arms to avoid messing up her do. She dressed in her newly purchased Earl Bannister tobacco-colored suit, matching plaid shell, and trendy shoes with matching handbag to boot. The shoes gave her an extra three inches, making her five-nine. She didn't want to appear short, since she had no idea how or what Keyanna looked like. Her makeup was flawless. She drew on her eyebrows so they looked warm and inviting and put on a taupe-colored eyeshadow that had glimmers of silver and complementary lipstick.

Sandy arrived at the Stardust Diner on the corner of Broadway and Fiftieth at nine sharp, though her meeting with Keyanna wasn't for another forty-five minutes. She still couldn't believe that she had the gumption to set up a meeting with her husband's alleged lover. Nevertheless, she was there, nervous and waiting. Sandy pondered what she would say once Keyanna arrived. How would she steer the conversation, since she was in the driver's seat? Sandy ordered decaffeinated coffee from the waitress. The last thing she needed was to be wired on caffeine. She didn't know what she was capable of doing to this woman, especially if she was lying.

Sandy had the hostess seat her at a small booth facing the door. Her back was opposite the video screen and she watched as the indoor choo-choo circled the mezzanine above her. Sandy was keeping a close watch on the door and saw when the woman in the soft yellow double-breasted pantsuit entered the diner at 9:20. The woman took a quick glance around the restaurant, and upon spotting her target, she began her descent. The woman walking in her direction strode with confidence, and if Sandy was correct in her analysis, arrogance as well. Sandy's heart began to flutter at an unbelievable pace. Her mouth was drier than a desert on a scorching day, and she felt like she was losing all of her wits. Was she doing the right thing by meeting this woman? *What would meeting her really accomplish now?* She wondered. Why couldn't she have found a man who could keep his dick to himself? Oh yeah, she had back at home, but he was too countrified for her. Jim was his name. He double-majored in agriculture and horticulture in college and wanted them to live on a farm. Looking back, Jim probably wasn't such a bad choice after all. He probably wouldn't have put her through this crap. It was funny how we always let the good ones slip away, Sandy reflected.

The woman stood staunchly in front of Sandy. Out of courtesy Sandy stood to greet and shake her hand and she reciprocated. Girl-friend was decked out and dressed to impress. The double-breasted pantsuit had a very stylish oversized collar and a brown silk shirt beneath it. Her briefcase, satchel handbag and shoes all matched perfectly. Sandy immediately recognized the designer shoes and bag since she, too, had been admiring the ensemble for a little over a month. After seeing it on Keyanna, she no longer felt the desire to purchase them. Bedford seemed to have a knack for selecting women who shared the same tastes and looks—all of them seemed to be the same height, color, and all sported the same short-cropped hairdo.

"Hi, I'm Keyanna Harrington, and you must be Sandy Beulah-Mae Jackson," she said, extending her hand to meet Sandy's and looking her up and down with a slight smirk.

"Yes, I am. I appreciate you coming to meet me today," Sandy replied, trying not to sound nervous. "Please have a seat." Sandy's bout of anxiety was quickly passing as she noticed the way Keyanna gave her a once-over. Who in the heck did this woman think she was looking at like that? She should have been dispensing the disparaging look. The nerve!

"No problem. I had an appointment for this morning, but I resched-uled it for later on in the afternoon. You know, as top executive at my job I have to stay—"

"Listen, Keyanna," Sandy brusquely interrupted. "I'm really sorry if I've caused you any inconvenience coming down here today, and, again, I really appreciate you being so cooperative, but let's do away with the niceties and cut to the chase since this is not a social call."

"Fine," Keyanna snapped. She situated herself in the seat, tugging at the waist of her blazer. Her patience waned after Sandy failed to speak immediately once they'd sat down. She picked up the menu and, after making her decision, she placed the menu back on the table.

Sandy didn't want to mince words any longer than necessary. It was obvious from the scornful look on Keyanna's face and her tone that she thought very little of Sandy. What was really the reason behind her saying her own middle name? It's funny how Keyanna nicely omitted her middle name during the introductions.

"What were the circumstances under which you met my husband and how long have you been sleeping with him?" Sandy asked.

"Well, I see that this country girl does have some spunk after all," Keyanna retorted. "Touché. You are not at all what I expected. From what Bedford told me…anyway that's really not important. Bedford and I met back in January at the African-American United Scholarship Fund Benefit. We hit it off immediately, seeing that we both had gone to predominantly black universities. I understand that you went to some women's college in Virginia."

The waitress reappeared to take their orders.

"I'll have black coffee and a lightly toasted bagel with lox and a side of non-fat cream cheese. Thank you," Keyanna said abrasively, not once looking at the waitress as she handed her the menu. Sandy ordered freshly squeezed orange juice, home fries, scrambled eggs with onions, green peppers, cheese and politely gave the waitress eye contact while returning her menu.

"Shall we resume?" Keyanna said, not waiting for an answer. "If you continue eating like that, you won't have a husband for long."

"Look, Keyanna, I didn't come here for you to bash me. The college that I did or did not attend is none of your business nor is my food selection, but my husband is my concern. Now, that is the purpose for us both being here today, so please let's stop with the showering of the pleasantries and get down to the matter at hand, shall we?"

"Whatever. What do you want to know?" Keyanna responded in an acidic tone. She arched her thin, but nicely plucked eyebrows and clasped her hands under her chin for emphasis, and leaned forward.

"How long were you seeing my husband?"

"It was sometime after the gala. We stayed in touch for business purposes…one thing led to another and you know," she said with an insincere smile, then waved her hand in the air.

Sandy was beginning to feel tense as the words rolled out of Keyanna's mouth, and the momentary distraction was almost as welcoming as rain on a humid day. She listened and felt her heart sink with every word that tumbled out of Keyanna's mouth. She spared no details ranting about places that they had been including a weekend visit to their summer home in Martha's Vineyard, Chelsea Piers for golf lessons so she could improve her handicap. There was even a purchase of a very expensive sapphire necklace. It was given as a small token of forgiveness when he had to break a date with her because his wife was threatening divorce. The icing on the cake was when Keyanna announced that Bedford said that the reason he had remained with Sandy was because of the kids. Whose kids, Sandy wondered? Jerry's? On that note, Sandy had to shake her head in disbelief. She uttered a dry laugh drawn from the bowels of incredulity, but was really meant to be derisive. Sandy may have been a country girl, but for a city girl, Keyanna was the embodiment of "complete idiot." She had to be, why else would she fall for such stupid lies? Didn't she notice that Bedford didn't have any pictures of children on his desk at work? She claimed that she had been to his office on several occasions for their spontaneous trysts.

The waitress returned with a large round tray and gingerly sat their respective orders in front of each of them. Noticing that the table was devoid of salt and pepper shakers, the waitress quickly grabbed a set from the empty booth behind them. Before leaving, she asked if there was anything else that they would like and both responded in the negative.

Keyanna spread the cream cheese on her bagel and put the thinly sliced lox on both sides. Neatly, she held the bagel in place and cut it into fours. Sandy had seen some strange habits before, but, to her recollection, most people cut their sandwiches in two. After nibbling a small piece of the bagel, Keyanna picked up where she had left off before the waitress had appeared with the food. Sandy simply listened and continued to watch as Keyanna nibbled like a gerbil.

Sandy was slowly beginning to lose her appetite, only tasting a forkful of her eggs. She couldn't believe that Keyanna was sitting in front of her flaunting the affair she'd had with Bedford. Forget the fact that his wife was sitting directly across the table from her. She gave details like two girlfriends venturing to the mall on a Saturday afternoon. Revealing the night-after talk. It was obvious that Keyanna was a conniving and ruthless little tramp. Keyanna expressed no sense of regret or remorse for her shameless act and obviously had no respect for Sandy's feelings. This probably wasn't the first nor would it be the last time that Keyanna had an affair with a married man. Most likely it was a hobby of sorts for her, Sandy thought. What could her expectations be of a married man? That he would leave his wife for her? And, even if he did, then what would make Keyanna so different from the woman that he left? Women failed to believe, once a cheat always a cheat and, if a man he left his wife for another then he'd probably leave the other woman too!

"Are you still seeing my husband?" Sandy asked, unable to hide the emotions that seemed to be twisting inside of her like a tornado.

Before answering Keyanna took a long swig of her coffee. "Listen, I don't know what problems you and Bedford have had in the past, but he needed a shoulder to lean on... and—"

"Keyanna, again, I'm not at liberty to discuss my marriage with you. All I asked you was a yes-or-no question Are you are still seeing Bedford?"

"As of last month, no," Keyanna reluctantly responded. It was the first time that Sandy had noticed a look of defeat on Keyanna's face. Sandy internally breathed a huge sigh of relief.

"My last question is who broke it off? You or Bedford?"

"It was sort of consensual. After he told me that he wasn't leaving you, I decided that I didn't want to prolong the relationship."

"Are you always that gullible? I mean, men always tell the other woman that the reason they are cheating is because of problems that exist in the marriage and, nine times out of ten, it's just bull. Well, Keyanna," Sandy said, removing her wallet from her handbag and placing a twenty-dollar bill on the table. "I truly feel sorry for you." She then stood, gathered her belongings and left her food untouched. She had long finished her juice while Keyanna was giving her rendition of her affair with Bedford. She then walked past Keyanna, refusing to glance back as she walked out of the Stardust Diner.

"Wow," was all Robby could say after Sandy finished her story. He stroked his goatee and shook his head for several moments. "Umph, sounds like brother man done fucked up, huh? Well, I'm not going to tell you what to do, but I will tell you what not to do. Just a few words of caution: remember that a tiger never loses its stripes. Now, don't listen to your Mama or me. Follow your heart. It will help lead you in the right direction."

"Robby, you're right. Bedford is trying to turn himself around, and my heart is telling me to return home and plaster the small holes that have been made in our home. Everything is almost perfect and there's no problem too big that love can't solve, right?"

"Now don't 'low them fast-talking, no-men-having, too-educated-for-they-own-good city friends of yours to talk you into leaving your man 'cuz half of them wouldn't know a good man if he bit them in the butt, ya hear! Now go on home and behave like a good wife and re-member Mama loves you, baby."

"Thank you, Mama. I love you too!" Sandy exclaimed as she tightly hugged her mother, taking in the strong scent of Mama Mavis' Eau de Toilette perfume. It was a smell that reminded Sandy of her mom's strength, years of security, love and stability throughout her child-hood and calmed her even as they released and Mama Mavis disap-peared in the distance and she headed through security to get to her terminal.

Those were the last words Sandy's mother said to her before she got on the plane for her assigned mission. Deep down, she hoped that going home was the right thing and, even more, that Mama Mavis' sentiments rang true.

8

He Didn't Mean Them Any Harm

ndia was under a great deal of stress. Her beauty department was falling apart at the seams. India's associate editor, Linda Grimes, had resigned a month ago. India then promoted her editorial assistant to fill the spot. However, the new assistant didn't stay for long because she took a job at a new magazine with India's former associate editor, Linda.

The deadline for the June issue of *Shades* was less than a week away, and India was short-staffed. To make matters worse, she couldn't locate her two feature stories, which had been written and completed by Linda, and India's boss wanted to have them both delivered to her by Friday. India would have rewritten them herself, but they were celebrity interviews and she couldn't falsify information. If she at least had the notes, she could embellish a little, but India didn't even have those at her disposal. India was in a quandary and there was no way that she could go to her boss and tell her that she had no clue as to where the stories were. These were things that India was supposed to be on top of. The June issue was scheduled to come out in mid-May. The issue was one of the largest; it focused on beauty tips for the summer, and the entire section was India's responsibility. It fell under her reign and department. One of the interviews was with Sanaa Lathan on her fresh new look and the other was with India Arie on her au natural appeal and her recent success as a songstress.

India knew she should call Linda and ask about the stories but the day Linda quit, things didn't go over so well. Instead of India questioning why Linda wanted to leave and possibly making a counteroffer she behaved irrationally. India ordered Linda to gather her belongings and to leave that very day. When five o'clock came around and Linda was about to leave, India had security check her bags to ensure that she wasn't taking company property. Linda was also forced to leave her Rolodex with her media contacts behind. The relationship was severed from that point on. Needless to say, India couldn't call, e-mail or even drop Linda a line.

The relationship that India had with Linda prior to that day wasn't volatile. It was actually very amicable. However, India took Linda's departure personally and looked at it as an act of betrayal. The sad thing was that Linda was one of the few people that she could call or consider a friend. India wanted to call and apologize to Linda the next day, but the damage had already been done. Even so, her pride wouldn't let her.

India was always a mess after she and Grayson got into an encounter. It threw her off in every way. She always had to take a few personal days off, because she was branded with bruises. Then she had to make excuses to Sierra and, this last time, Sierra happened to be home during their carousing. At first, Sierra was fast asleep, but the noise woke her. She knocked and banged on her parents' door until she began to cry. It was a good thing that India had decided to lock the door that night. After Grayson was done with her, he opened the door for Sierra and took her back to her room. Thank God for the little things.

India never wanted Sierra to witness her father beating her. She knew that it could possibly impact Sierra in her adult life. India knew that it wasn't healthy for the relationship to go on the way it was, and she would eventually confront Grayson about it. Grayson was level-headed and rational, and, if she spoke to him from the heart, then he would try to curb his behavior. She knew Grayson had a hard life as a child and was working to overcome his shortcomings as an adult. India wanted to be there in his corner to support him wholeheartedly. She understood that he loved his family and didn't mean them any harm. The good thing was that he never lifted a hand to Sierra.

The internal line buzzed. India didn't want to answer it, but whoever it was could just as well come to her office for a visit.

"Yes?" India answered.

"India, it's Nala. How are we coming with those stories?"

Nala was the person with whom she least wanted to speak. India decided to try to stall her boss one more day. If she couldn't locate the stories by the next day then she would just confess.

"Nala, I'm on it. Is it possible that we can get together in the morning?"

There was silence. India heard the sound of paper being shuffled.

"Hold on while I look at my schedule…okay, that's fine. I have an availability at ten-fifteen sharp."

"I'll see you then," India said, relieved.

Now if she could only conjure up two lead stories featuring Sanaa Lathan and India Arie, her work life could continue unhampered.

9

It's Our Anniversary

andy was on a high and had no intentions of coming down. It had been four months since her North Carolina visit, and she had decided to remain with Bedford. Although they still had a few hurdles to cross, their counseling sessions proved to help tremendously. Sandy never doubted Bedford's love, but she was starting to lose faith in his commitment to her. She figured, he'd probably still be married to Felice if Felice hadn't caught him cheating. There were times that she wanted to pry the sordid details out of Felice, but it really had no bearing on Sandy's marriage to Bedford. She was inclined to think about a line from her favorite movie *Love Jones*: Not to ask a question she didn't want to know the answer to.

What a difference a few months made. Marriage was a sacred bond that required a tune-up every now and again. If Sandy's mother was able to forgive Sandy's father, Larry, may his soul rest in peace, then she could definitely forgive Bedford's one indiscretion. No one was perfect. It wasn't like he left a trail, just a pathetic woman who seemed incapable of attaining her own man. Sandy tried, but would never understand why women did such underhanded things to one another.

Sandy was in the process of getting ready for a night out on the town with Bedford. They were celebrating their three-year wedding anniversary, which also coincided with the anniversary of their monthly counseling. Their doctor felt that they could decrease their weekly visits to bimonthly. Although they didn't have children, he wanted to start a family badly. Bedford had never expressed this to Sandy, but his reasons for not pressuring her were not selfish; on the contrary, he knew how much her career meant to her and didn't want to hinder her rapid progression. If she had gotten pregnant a year earlier, the school board might have overlooked Sandy for the vice principal position. It wouldn't have been fair if the board had, but the fact of the matter was that it was a strong possibility. It was definitely a man's world, and any fault the board could find to not promote a woman would be to its advantage. The last thing Bedford wanted was to be a setback in her climb to success. Sandy had to admit she was grateful for Bedford's thoughtfulness.

Bedford was also having a hard time coping with the senseless killing of Shiloh, his only nephew. Shiloh had just graduated from Bedford's alma mater, Morgan State University and majored in finance just like his uncle. He was a bright and ambitious kid with big dreams that were cut short due to ignorance. Bedford played a large part in Shiloh's rearing. His sister's husband died of a heart attack at the age of thirty-one. Shiloh was a kid at the time and needed guidance, so Bedford stepped in to help his sister, Isis. The bond that Shiloh and Bedford shared was infallible, the two loved each other without limits, and it was as if Bedford was Shiloh's father. Bedford made sure that his nephew received only the best. He made sure that Shiloh set high goals for himself and taught him responsibility, but Shiloh was a good kid even before Bedford came to his aid. By the time Shiloh was eight, he had won a poetry contest sponsored by a newspaper, was MVP for his Little League team and on his way to becoming a star player on the community basketball team.

Bedford cried during this particular session. Sandy had never seen him so emotional. She wanted to help her husband through his pain. This awareness made her even more determined to give her all to their marriage; Bedford deserved that. She needed him, and he needed her. That day she held Bedford to her chest and rocked him as he sobbed. Sandy's blouse clung to her skin from the tears and perspiration. Her heart weighed heavy as she thought about how selfish she was being for remaining upset about Bedford sleeping with Keyanna. It was simply a moment of weakness after Shiloh's death.

Sandy applied the finishing touches of makeup to her face. She enjoyed using the lip brush over the actual stick. It required precision and time, but it made all the difference to her. Now all she needed was her toasty glittery eye shadow to enhance her perfectly plucked eyebrows. She emptied her makeup case on the vanity table. Lip liners, lipstick, mascara and several casings of eye shadow darted and rolled around, but none of them were the one for which she was looking. Sandy heard something hit the wood floor behind the vanity, so she got on her knees to retrieve it. Before she could return to her seat, she felt a pair of hands covering her behind. She turned her head to greet her naughty husband with a mischievous smile.

"I don't know if I want you going out looking like this tonight," he said, still holding Sandy's butt. Sandy was unable to analyze the look on his face. She couldn't tell if he was serious or joking. Sandy was cautious and took a gentle approach. She didn't want to upset him or sway his mood.

"Sweetie, if you want me to, I'll change into the peach-colored dress you purchased for me last week."

She really had no desire to change, but to appease him she would. Tonight was a special evening, and the last thing she wanted was see it destroyed over attire. Tonight, compromise was the name of the game. She lowered her position from beneath the table and pulled back to avoid bumping her head. As she eased back, she felt Bedford's groin pressed against her butt. It was then that she realized why he had made that remark. When she was bent on her fours, her entire pubic region was exposed, and it didn't help that she had on thong panties. They were supposed to be a surprise for later—so much for surprises. Well, he still didn't know that they were edible. However, he was about to find out since his face was nuzzled between her fur-trimmed center. Sandy wriggled as Bedford darted his tongue in and around, using it as a navigational tool.

"Bedford, you're going to make us late," Sandy whispered.

"We have time, baby," Bedford said, turning Sandy around and throwing her legs over his shoulders to devour her. She wanted to stop Bedford so they wouldn't mess up whatever he had in store for her, but it just felt too good. Sandy moaned.

"Not yet," Bedford said, lifting his head. "I want to taste some more of this sweetness."

Sandy swung her legs from off his shoulders and stood. Bedford was still crouched on the floor, so Sandy hovered above his face allowing him to continue his exercise.

Sandy unfastened the button on her gold sequined dress and slowly and carefully pulled it over her head to avoid getting the sequins hitched on her diamond hoop earrings. When she looked down she could see Bedford's erection straining, making the zipper of his pants bulge.

"You like it, baby?" Bedford asked between courses.

"Oh yeah," Sandy said, trying to suppress the raging below. Bedford knew how to further arouse her, so he unbuckled his belt and unzipped his pants to release Duro.

The edible panties were now completely gone. Sandy licked her full lips as she hungered to swathe them on his throbbing penis.

Bedford wrapped his large hand on the lower part of his shaft leaving only a small portion and the head exposed. Sandy's knees buckled as she allowed herself to succumb to the feeling she held back earlier. Bedford glided his tongue faster, and Sandy wailed a tune he was all too familiar with. He held her legs firmly to the ground. Her legs went weak and her body slumped forward from exhaustion. When she was able to steady herself she let out a gasp, inhaling deeply through her mouth and exhaling through her nose.

Sandy leaned forward and her exposed puckered nipples, brushing them against the side of Bedford's moist lips. Bedford couldn't resist sucking her pacifier-size nipples, but Sandy desired more and made her way to Duro. Her warm mouth sucked and licked him in circles. When she was done, she got up and walked over to the bed. She propped two king-size pillows beneath her and laid on her stomach. She motioned for Bedford, and he popped up off the floor. He knew how to take directions. Bedford knew how to satisfy her wants. He entered slowly into her slick, savory walls. He lunged deeper until he lost himself. Sandy hung on to the pillow for dear life, and Bedford dunked into her depth. She moaned and Bedford complied. Shudders of pleasure passed through their bodies. He leaned closer to Sandy's warm body and wrapped his arms tight about her waist and buried his head in the crook of her neck. He stroked both fast and slow, rocking back and forth. They moved together in unison. Without warning, Bedford went over the edge.

Bedford remained on top of Sandy, not applying his full weight. Eventually, he found enough strength to roll over and on to his back. Sandy joined him and lay on his chest of smoothly sculpted muscle. Bedford ran his fingers through Sandy's hair.

"Bedford."

"Yes, love?" he responded.

"Don't mess up the do, okay?" Sandy said in a playful tone.

"Woman, you weren't worried about that do a few minutes ago, hell an hour ago."

"That was then, this is now, and, like I said, don't mess up my do," she said, waving her fist in the air.

Bedford wrestled her onto her side and pinned her hands down.

"Oh, so you wanna play now, huh?"

"Bedford, stop," Sandy squealed. "You're hurting my wrists."

"Oh, I'm sorry," he said, kissing the spot she complained about.

In one swift move, Sandy maneuvered herself from his strong hold and flung her body on top of him.

"What has gotten into you, woman?" Bedford asked, tickled at Sandy's playful behavior. Sandy wasn't a prude, but she wasn't exactly playful, either. She was taking a new lesson on life and love. Bedford's renewed interest in their marriage had reformed her, and she wasn't going to take it for granted.

"You know what's gotten into me, and I wouldn't mind a replay if we weren't already so late," Sandy said as she got up hastily and rushed into the adjoining bathroom. "I have to pee."

"You always have to use the bathroom after sex," Bedford said, laughing and putting his shirt and pants back on.

"Where are we going tonight?" Sandy yelled over the running water from the faucet. "You still haven't told me." Sandy returned to the bedroom and put on the gold sequined dress and her strappy open-toe sandals. She was finally able to locate the toasty shadow that further enhanced her outfit.

"And I'm still not telling," Bedford answered as he headed downstairs.

Bedford went into his private study while Sandy freshened up her hair and makeup. This room was his solitude and was off-limits to everyone, including Sandy. He needed to pull himself together for this evening. He had a full night of activities planned and wanted everything to go smoothly. It was his workspace where he received innovation and inspiration for new accounts. His study was also where he went to get his thoughts straight. Ten minutes passed before Sandy knocked on the door to inform him that she was ready, and they headed out.

It was a beautiful March evening when they stepped out of their three-family Brooklyn brownstone. Global warming seemed to be in full effect because, under normal conditions, the weather would have been between fifty-five and sixty degrees. Instead, it was in the high seventies.

A black Mercedes Benz limo was waiting out front. The driver who had been waiting close to an hour, quickly jumped out of the front seat to open the door for the Jacksons. As they approached the car, they were full of giggles and swinging hands like newlyweds. Instead of allowing Bedford room to pass, the driver stood peering at Sandy's butt. It wasn't until Bedford cleared his throat that the driver snapped out of his trance.

"You got a problem, man?" Bedford asked. The look that he shot the driver was frightening, and the response that he received let him know that he'd put the guy in check.

"Pardon me, sir. I apologize for my rudeness," he said as he backed away to let Bedford in.

Bedford didn't bother to reply, because, for the first time the word *sir* made him feel old, and at thirty-eight he was far from being old. The word *sir* knocked him off balance and made him uncomfortable.

He merely stepped into the car and possessively embraced Sandy and gave her a warm kiss. Sandy was oblivious to what had just taken place and simply obliged by returning the kiss with ferver.

The car was stocked with the best bottles of wine, champagne, beer and snacks possible. The first song that played upon entry of the limo was Tony! Toni! Toné's rendition of "Anniversary". Then, the smooth sultry sounds of Luther Vandross filled the air. The Bose speaker system made it feel as if they had front-row seats at a concert as Luther belted out the lyrics to "A House Is Not a Home."

Bedford poured them both a glass of champagne and made a toast to unconditional love.

"Sandy."

"Yes, Bedford?" Sandy replied.

"Baby, I know that I haven't exactly been the best husband, and I want to express how bad this has made me feel. I'm far from perfect, and I can't make excuses for my behavior, so I won't. I want you to know that you mean everything to me. I love you and appreciate your patience and tolerance of my shortcomings. Love knows not its depth till the hour of separation. I have never been as afraid as the day you packed your bags and went to North Carolina. I had no idea if you were coming back, and I lost it. I was flat out lost, and I never want to feel that way again. If it weren't for Shirley, I don't know how I could have gotten through Thanksgiving much less that week."

Sandy held her head down as Bedford revealed his heart. His confession soothed her soul, and she was now prepared to put the past to rest. She caressed his hand as he continued his speech and gently brushed her lips on his cheek.

"I live to love you. From the first time I saw you, I knew that you were the one who would bring a smile to my face. The one to stand by me. Your beauty goes beyond the exterior, and anyone who knows you is blessed, but to be married to you is an honor and good fortune bestowed upon me. I love and revere you, Sandy." Bedford reached into a small side compartment and withdrew a palm-sized aquamarine box with a white bow. Sandy gasped, because she immediately recognized the Tiffany box. As Bedford handed it to her, a tear escaped and rolled down the side of her face. Taking the box from Bedford's extended hand, Sandy excitedly hugged him and whispered words of love into his ear.

"I open my heart to you. There is room for only one, and I choose you. You, Bedford, are the man that I live to love and enjoy loving." Her voice trembled, and more tears accompanied the love tear that had departed before the rest. As she opened the box, she was surprised to see a necklace with a flawless solitaire princess-cut diamond. Sandy knew it had to be at least two carats. Her mind was void of all thought as her mouth gaped open.

Marvin Gaye and Tami Terrell's "You're All I Need" played in the background. Bedford took the chain from the box while Sandy removed the pearl necklace that she had donned for the evening.

Bedford tapped the partition for the driver. Once the partition went down Bedford reached over and retrieved a long white box and, with a smile, he handed the gift to Sandy. She was completely overwhelmed. She opened the box and found a dozen of the most perfect red and white long-stemmed roses she had ever seen. Her earlier gift to him of a golf club membership at the prestigious club in Connecticut paled in comparison.

Once the partition was closed again, Sandy didn't waste any time. She undid Bedford's shirt, loosened his tie and began to sensuously spread kisses over his chest. Her kisses traced down to his mid-section and Duro broke free. She lowered her head and before long they were repeating scenes from their earlier play.

10
The Speech

E veryone waited for the guests of honor to make their appearance. Patience, Jonathan and India had pulled everything together, including the guest list, menu, floral arrangements, hotel and transportation, in less than three weeks.

Soft music played in the background, and people who had not seen one another in ages mixed and mingled. Patience and India were surprised at the huge turnout, considering everything had been tossed together last minute. This particular Saturday evening was already booked for another party, but then she had received a mysterious call from a relative and had to alter the schedule a bit. The client who was scheduled for that evening was livid about the change, but Jonathan offered a percentage off the catering, and he quickly shed any animosity.

Three and a half hours later, the stretch limo pulled up in front of *Pájo Soul*. The streetlights were in full effect as pedestrians strolled the avenues. Sandy was fast asleep when they arrived. She was worn out from Bedford as well as the very long ride. After two hours of begging Bedford to give her an idea as to where they were going she finally decided to just take a nap. Sandy and Bedford were connoisseurs when it came to restaurants. So when Sandy saw the rave review of *Pájo Soul* written in *Shades* magazine and showed it to Bedford, he had Shirley make the initial call for the arrangements, and he followed up with the details.

Bedford gently nudged Sandy to make her aware of their arrival. Sandy's eyes fluttered open as she raised her head off Bedford's lap. She moistened her lips and cleared her throat while peering out the car window to check out her surroundings. She still didn't have a clue as to where they were or even what state. The last thing she remembered seeing were signs for the Delaware Memorial Bridge. She had fallen asleep and, since it was dark, it could have been any time of the night. Sandy heard the limo driver's door open, so she quickly dug into her handbag for a breath mint. Before closing the bag, she offered one to Bedford who declined. When the back door opened, Sandy returned Bedford's blazer. The young driver gave Sandy the biggest grin as he assisted her out of the vehicle, and it didn't escape Bedford's attention. Bedford decided it best to let it rest; after all, Sandy was his wife and was with him. She was extremely attractive, and eyes were meant for looking. At the same time, he wasn't a sucker and would have a word with the driver at the night's end. It was apparent this young kid didn't know any better or simply didn't give a fuck.

Bedford took Sandy's hand and walked the few feet to the restaurant. When Sandy finally looked up at the awning and read the name of the restaurant, she made a high-pitched squeal, squeezed Bedford's hand and tiptoed to give him a generous kiss on the lips. When they got to the door a sign read "Private Party." The look of excitement immediately extinguished from her face.

"Bedford, I can't believe we drove all this way and *Pájo Soul* is closed for a private party," Sandy said, sulking.

"These are your people, baby. I'm sure they won't turn you away."

"I know, but it's the principle. I haven't spoken to Patience and India in so long. I can't impose. Look how long ago that review came out, and I was supposed to call and congratulate Patience and her husband on their success. At least if I had called I wouldn't feel so much like an intruder."

"Baby, San, come on. We came all this way, what do we have to lose?" Bedford said as he tapped on the door several times.

"Okay, but I really feel bad about popping up unannounced. I'm still uncomfortable."

"Stop worrying," Bedford said, just as someone opened the wooden engraved double doors.

"Hi, may I help you?" a young woman exclaimed.

Bedford immediately took notice of her beautiful skin and hour-glass figure. He quickly cleared his throat and peeked inside the restaurant before answering.

"Yes, my wife, Sandy, and I drove all the way from New York to visit your restaurant, but we see that you have an exclusive engagement happening this evening. Is there anyway that we can dine here tonight?" Bedford asked. There was definitely a hint of seduction in his voice. Sandy remained behind him, embarrassed that they would come all this way without reservations; the evening was going to turn out to be a bust after all.

"It is a private function, but let me get the manager for you; maybe he'll make a concession this one time, okay?" the young woman said and walked away.

Bedford nodded and his eyes remained glued to her behind as it swayed in the Saran Wrap–fitting dress. The fact that her back was exposed only further served to arouse him. She wasn't much to look at in the face, but Bedford could work it anyway.

Sandy thumped Bedford in the shoulder.

"Ouch!" Bedford said, stunned for a moment. He'd almost forgotten Sandy was present.

"What is wrong with you? Now she's going to go and get Patience or Jonathan. This is just what I wanted to avoid."

Bedford sighed a sound of relief. He thought that Sandy caught him staring at the hostess.

"Sandy, would you relax already? Please, just let me handle this."

Just then the young woman reappeared.

"Follow me," she said enthusiastically.

"Thank you, young lady," Bedford said sarcastically as he turned to Sandy. "Are you happy now?" he asked. The young woman led them down a narrow corridor. The peach-colored walls were lined with pictures of celebrities that had visited the restaurant. Dimly lit track lights softly illuminated the walkway. They passed a room that had a wooden placard that read coat check and diagonally across were doors leading to the men's and women's rest rooms. Within seconds they were in the main room of the restaurant.

"What's your name?" Bedford asked the young woman.

"Oh, I'm sorry. I thought I said it when I greeted you at the door. It's Je'Nae." Sandy trailed a few feet behind, and Bedford held his hand out to lead Sandy into the room. Sandy was still a little peeved with Bedford and, even though she had an attitude, she reluctantly took his hand.

Suddenly, the dim lights became bright, and were accompanied by a group of people yelling "Surprise!"

Patience and India came to the front to greet their cousin Sandy. Sandy looked at Bedford and Je'Nae and almost broke into tears. Everyone clapped as Sandy gasped for air and covered her mouth with both hands. She really felt like crap. There she was getting upset at Bedford for being so unorganized, when he really had an entire evening planned. He had gone through a lot of trouble to pull this together. As Sandy looked around, she spotted people that she hadn't seen in years: Patience, India, Tony, Big Tye, Terence, her old roommate from college and a few others. Sandy's heart raced. She was overwhelmed and knew that Bedford had gone through hoops and pulled tons of strings to make this evening happen. How could she ever doubt his love again?

Sandy counted at least twenty-five people who had traveled near and far. She couldn't believe her eyes.

"Girl, welcome to *Pájo Soul*," Patience said as she hugged Sandy tightly.

"Welcome to Baltimore stranger," India chimed. Instead of hugging Sandy, she blew air kisses on each cheek.

"Oh my goodness, I can't believe this and you all. You knew about this? How? When? I'm still shocked," Sandy exclaimed. "Let me grab a seat. I'm feeling a little light-headed."

Patience directed Sandy to a table and, just as Sandy was about to sit down, Mama Mavis, Robby and his wife, Nettie, appeared. Again, Sandy couldn't believe her eyes. She looked across the room for Bedford and spotted him standing next to Jonathan returning her gaze.

"You're unbelievable," she mouthed.

He smiled and responded, "I know."

She waved at Jonathan and, instead of sitting, she remained standing to embrace her family.

"Baby," Mama Mavis drawled, "we were beginning to wonder if y'all got lost. But I'm glad you got here safely. Happy anniversary!" Mama Mavis said, holding on tightly to her daughter. "I told you that Bedford was a good man. Stick with him."

"Thanks, Mama, and I know," Sandy said obligingly.

Robby and Nettie stood patiently waiting for their turn to talk. When Mama Mavis let go, she gave Sandy's hand a little squeeze and headed over to Bedford.

"I can't believe you all drove all this way from North Carolina. How long did it take you?" Sandy inquired as she stepped into Robby's massive arms.

"We didn't drive, girl. Your husband flew me, Nettie and Mama Mavis in and we left Jillian with Nettie's parents."

"What? He really went out of his way to make this night grand."

"He sure did," Nettie added. Then she joined her husband and hugged Sandy.

"It seems like things are back to normal with you and Bedford," Robbie said, but it sounded more like a question.

"Yeah. We've been to counseling, and we're working through all of our problems, but things are better than ever, especially tonight."

"That's great, Sandy," Nettie said. "All relationships have their ups and downs. You just have to work through them. Keep in mind, marriage was never meant to be easy or else everybody would be doing it."

"Amen," India linked in on the conversation. "You just rained a river with that last statement."

"Whatever," Patience said. "That all depends on the situation. Sometimes you need to keep your wits about you and leave while the going is good," Patience continued and shot her sister a spiteful look that made India cut her eyes.

"Would anyone like something to drink?" India asked as she began backing away.

"A glass of chardonnay," Sandy said.

"I'll take a Heineken and Lynchburg lemonade for my Nettie. Thanks India," Robby said.

"Coming right up," India replied.

Sandy, Patience, Nettie and Robby sat together at a table for ten. Sandy cased the restaurant from her seat. She noticed it had all of the original crown molding and wooden arches around the doorways, and the ceilings were high. The furniture was an eclectic mix of round, octagon and square tables. The chairs were a dark cherry finish and high backs. The chair cushions matched the floor runners on the beautifully polished wood floors. Beautiful and vibrant artwork masked each wall. Each piece appeared to be done by a different artist, but they were all framed in similar gold-colored frames. Candles in gold artsy wired holders were lit in the center of each table with matching napkin holders. The overall ambiance of the restaurant was magnificent. Sandy was impressed and couldn't wait to sample the eats. The smooth sound of Musiq mellowed the mood, and Sandy couldn't have been happier.

India returned with the drinks and her husband in tow. Grayson was looking better than ever, always dapper, as if he'd just emerged off of the pages of *GQ* or *Esquire*. Both he and India were looking sharp and made a stunning couple.

After they set the cocktails down, Patience abruptly excused herself. Sandy could feel the tension in the air, but she refused to get caught up with family business on this particular night. As far back as she cold remember, Patience and India had always had their issues. When they were younger and their parents would send them down south to stay with her family for the summer they would get into it something awful and over the most trivial of things. Sandy always served as their mediator. Time passed, and they were adults now, but their bickering and differences remained the same.

Sandy mixed and mingled and saw friends that she hadn't seen in two years or better. Prior to living in New York she had lived in Atlanta, and her friend Wanita and her husband, William, were present. Wanita looked stunning as usual. Sandy always thought that Wanita should have been a model. She was tall and regal. She had cheekbones that would make an African jealous, and plain features, but her personality made her radiate. At five-ten with a figure that would make someone's daddy crash his brand-new Cadillac if he wasn't paying attention, Wanita could have easily given Tyra Banks and Naomi Campbell fever.

Bedford didn't pay Wanita's airfare, but he had extended her an invitation. William happened to be having a meeting at Radio One's corporate headquarters, which was a little less than an hour away from *Pájo Soul*.

The melodic sound of metal striking glass calmed the chatter and the music was lowered. Bedford took center stage and held up his glass to propose a toast.

"Does everyone have a full glass?" Bedford asked, turning to see and hear the responses. A few guests replied "no" and Bedford directed the waiters that already had champagne on their trays. A two-minute period passed and Bedford resumed and beckoned Sandy to stand by his side. He wrapped his arm around Sandy's waist affectionately and looked adoringly into her eyes.

"First, I'd like to thank all of you for coming out this evening from near and far to share this auspicious occasion with me and my beautiful wife, Sandy. You all witnessed the look on her face when she walked into this room."

A few people agreed and said "umm-hmm" and "yeah" and others laughed as they recalled the look of astonishment on Sandy's face. Bedford laughed and pulled Sandy into his hold a little tighter, and she bumped him with her hip.

"Seriously, I'd like to also thank our cousins—Patience, for allowing me to invade at the last minute and use this beautiful and well-talked-about restaurant, and India, for helping out with the arrangements and for being so thorough. You are both angels. Jonathan, man, I'm not leaving you out. Thanks for the use of this place, and the good food that we're about to eat. If the food is anything like these appetizers you are going to have to get a couple of wheelbarrows to roll folks out of here tonight."

"No problem, man," Jonathan replied, cracking up at Bedford's good humor. "It's all love, my brother. It's all love."

"Much appreciated. Four years ago I went to Chicago to a convention for work and the United Federation of Teachers happened to be having their convention as well. I had had enough of the daylong seminars and decided to take a walk, and to my good fortune, I literally bumped into this beautiful woman that you see standing beside me now."

Sandy tucked her head into her neck and smiled bashfully while clinging on to Bedford's bicep.

"I wasn't paying attention while trying to escape and walked out of the hotel ballroom and into Sandy. She was a good sport, because I did some damage to those toes. I offered to buy her a drink, but she declined. I couldn't get that sweet face and innocent smile off my mind. Then, I saw her again later that evening, and I almost tripped trying to run across the room and, once again, I managed to step on her foot, however, I did it on purpose this time, just to get her attention, and, since she was already at the bar, she couldn't deny me the second time around. It was then that I lured her in hook, line and sinker. She didn't even know what was happening to her. One year later, I tricked her again into becoming my wife, and I'm here today to share this with you. It's been three wonderful years, and I'm looking forward to multiplying that number by forty or better. Baby," Bedford said, and held Sandy's chin in his palm, "you are my reason for being. I plan on loving you today, tomorrow and always."

Sandy's eyes misted as Bedford finished and planted a full kiss on her lips. The guests applauded as Sandy and Bedford continued to kiss like it was their wedding day.

Jonathan and his team of cooks really put their all into the presentation and preparation of the meal. The menu was mainly soul food with macaroni and cheese, potato salad, collard greens, black-eyed peas, sweet potato soufflé, snap peas, salad, fried chicken and catfish. But they also added a few Caribbean dishes to the mix. They had jerk chicken, mango baked chicken with plantains and rice and peas.

Sandy sat at the largest table with Bedford, Mama Mavis, Robby, Nettie, India, Grayson, Wanita and William. Patience and Jonathan didn't eat with everyone else. Patience was busy supervising the staff, ensuring that everything went smoothly on the front end of the restaurant, and Jonathan did the same with the back end. This night was equally important to both of them. Sandy was family and this was her anniversary celebration, so everything had to be just right. Bedford could have chosen any other restaurant, and in New York where they lived no less, but he specifically chose *Pájo Soul*. Patience was extremely flattered. On top of that, Patience and Jonathan offered to cut him a break on the rental and catering, but he refused saying, "Skimping and trimming edges isn't my style." He asked them to treat him the way they would any other paying customer. Then, he sent them a check for the entire amount when all they required was a deposit to get the gas burning. Patience and Jonathan didn't argue, because they weren't stupid, but they planned to lay everything out nicely and even decided to get them a really nice gift.

After dinner and dessert, the staff cleared the tables and pushed them aside to create a dance floor. Jonathan hired his friend who was a disc jockey as a side gig. Old-school R&B songs filtered through the air. Sandy and Bedford danced most of the evening away with each other and, on occasion, a friend would cut in. The other half of the evening, Sandy and Wanita caught up on the happenings since Sandy's last visit to Atlanta, which was only a few months shy of a year. Wanita shared how things had changed between her and William, but she said he didn't seem to think anything was wrong with the relationship and refused to seek counseling. Wanita said that William's exact words were, "If you have some personal issues that you want to resolve, then by all means seek help. If you need a counselor, psychiatrist or whatever, I'm here to support you. Just handle your business." Then he stated that he was to be left out of attending any sessions because he wasn't the one with the problems.

Sandy thought that William was cruel for behaving that way and didn't know what to say other than "Hang in there. Maybe he'll come around soon." The thing that saddened Sandy most about their conversation was the urgency in Wanita's voice. Wanita desperately wanted to start a family, and William felt that at this point in his life it would only be a burden. Sandy felt that she needed to reevaluate her own priorities after hearing her friend make that remark. Surely that wasn't the way she came across when Bedford mentioned the prospect of starting a family. She was definitely going to stop taking the pill soon. She'd discuss it with Bedford as soon as the summer break was in session. Sandy didn't bother to discuss her past problems with anyone because they were just that, past problems. Everyone seemed to have one problem or another, and some were worse than others. The fact of the matter was that no relationship was flawless. Bedford really and truly had made a turnaround and redeemed himself back to one hundred percent as far as Sandy was concerned.

Sandy watched the antics between India and Patience. She didn't bother to inquire, but figured their bantering had something to do with Grayson. The stares and looks that Patience gave him whenever he came near them were appalling. At one point, Patience whispered to India, but loud enough for Sandy to hear, "Please go fetch your drunken-ass husband."

India retorted, "Why do you always have to exaggerate and make a mountain out of a molehill?"

"India, listen, just get him away from the bar. He is harassing my bartenders because they won't serve him any more drinks, so take him out for some fresh air or something."

India spotted him at the bar, and she did as she was told and rushed to Grayson's side.

The evening began to wind down and the crowd began to thin. Everyone vowed to remain in touch. This was usually the way most engagements ended, anyway. People had tons of fun, got caught up in good conversation and then made empty promises to visit, write, call or whatever. Some would actually keep them, while the majority would not. Either way, Sandy was happy to have been among her friends and family.

Sandy sat at the table twirling a stirrer in her cocktail and watched as Robby gracefully glided across the floor with Nettie. She listened to the serenade of The Commodores' "Three Times a Lady." Nettie swayed her hips and head to the music.

Sandy looked around the room, taking the last sip of her drink as she tried to locate Bedford. She wanted one last dance to complete her fantasy evening. Bedford was nowhere in sight, and Mama Mavis came and stood directly in front of her, blocking her view.

"Sandy, baby, I'm tired. I'm going to call it a night."

"Okay, Mama. Did you have a good time?" Sandy asked.

"I sure did," Mama Mavis said, smiling from ear to ear. "More importantly, did you?"

Sandy noticed for the first time that her mother had some brand-new dentures. During Sandy's last visit, she had begged her mother to replace her old ones and even gave her the money, but Sandy figured that her mother had spent it elsewhere. Truthfully, she probably did, but when she got the invitation for her anniversary party, she probably just broke down and withdrew the money from her bank account. Sandy's mother hated to spend her own money, much less take some out of the bank. She much preferred to call Sandy, or even Robby, to complain about her money problems knowing that they would cave in and come to her rescue. Sandy was constantly reminding her mother that she couldn't take the money with her to the grave, and she wasn't getting any younger, so she might as well spend some of it. Sandy encouraged Mama Mavis to consider traveling or refurnishing her house or investing in a reliable car, but Mama Mavis did none of those things. Sandy knew that her mother was holding for dear life to the insurance money that she'd received from Sandy's father's policy. The only investment Mama Mavis has made to date was to pay off the balance of her mortgage. Now she owned her home free and clear.

"Mama, nothing could ever top this evening. You were so right about Bedford. He must have gone through so much to pull this together, and he must have talked your ear off in order to get you to fly. You've never flown anywhere before."

"Well, it didn't take much convincing once he explained what he was doing. Besides, I've never been against flying, just flying alone, and I didn't have to do that, either, since Robby and Nettie came. Bedford is such a kind and generous man. His business must be doing pretty well for him to splurge like that."

"As a matter of fact, Jackson and Jackson is doing nicely. He just signed and added a few new clients to his roster," Sandy replied.

"And the counseling?"

"Wonderful. We've made a lot of headway, and as you can see things couldn't be better," Sandy exclaimed. Sandy's hands danced in the air with each word that seeped through her mouth. "So Mama, where are you staying?"

"Child, I'm staying at the Hyatt down at the Harbor Place. I have a view that will remain etched in my memory along with that smile of yours. Bedford has made my weekend too! I haven't had this much fun since that T.D. Jakes revival last summer. Now that was something. Anyway, let me go see if those two dirty dancers are ready to go. Don't make sense we take two taxis over there when we can share one."

Mama Mavis got up and put her gold knit shawl over her shoulders and waltzed toward the make shift dance floor to the rhythm of the music.

Patience immediately filled the void when Mama Mavis stepped away.

"Girl, you look good!" Patience said, taking a seat to join Sandy.

"You don't look too bad yourself," Sandy exclaimed. "You and Jonathan seem to be doing pretty well. You all are getting write-ups in magazines and newspapers. Shoot, not bad at all."

"Please, you know that's all due to India pulling strings for us. If it weren't for her, I don't think we would have lasted this long. I've got to thank God for her, even though she gets on my last nerve from time to time."

"You two still go at it, huh? Well, what good is family if they don't inflict a little pain on you every now and again?"

"Humph, if you only knew half of it. Anyway, you can only imagine my surprise when I received the call from your enchanting husband. At first, I was like, 'Bedford who?' Then he said 'your cousin.' I still couldn't identify him. I thought someone was playing games, and I was in the middle of a little crisis and in no mood for jokes. Then, he mentioned you, and my ears perked up. He told me his plans, and we went from there. He went all out, girl. You have definitely snagged yourself a winner."

"Speak to me, because don't I know it! Jonathan looks like a winner too," Sandy exclaimed.

"He's that and then some. If only we could package and shelve them for display so these other trifling men could see a real man. Sort of like action figures: Jackpot Jonathan and Bona Fide Bedford. I'm so sick of these people masquerading around pretending to be real men."

"Patience, you are still crazy," Sandy said, laughing uncontrollably.

"But can you hear me, though, 'cause you know I'm speaking the truth." Patience held her hand up for a high five and between laughs,

Sandy swiped hands with her.

"Speaking of husbands, have you seen mine? He seems to be MIA."

"He's probably out walking Grayson's drunk ass. He is always ruining shit," Patience said, footprints of disgust on every word.

"Oh yeah, that's right. Does he always get so blasted?"

"Grayson is a true piece of work. I don't know what India sees in him. Anyway, it's your night, so let's end it on a positive note."

"Jonathan," Patience yelled across the room and waved him over. "Honey, can you please go into the office and get that box for me?"

"Oh yeah, sure; give me a minute to finish cleaning up the bar, and I'll go get it."

"Thank you, baby," Patience blew him a kiss, which he caught then pretended it fell, retrieving it before allowing it to hit the floor.

"He's such a kidder," Sandy said, enjoying Jonathan's act.

"Tell me about it," Patience said, laughing.

Jonathan headed into the office located in the back of the restaurant. He'd had a good night, but it was definitely the hardest that he and Patience had worked. He knew how important it was for her to have the opportunity to entertain her family. Family meant everything to Patience. Since Jonathan and Patience came from humble beginnings, as a couple they had learned to work well together. Their relationship displayed all the finest qualities: love, honesty, respect, compromise, compassion, passion and, the most important of all, communication accompanied by understanding.

Jonathan strolled down the dimly lit walkway. His feet and body ached from preparation and long hours of labor. He was going to retrieve the gift and go back to the office for a quick nap. He was hoping that they hadn't left the door unlocked because, although they treated all of their employees like family, the favor wasn't always returned. Less than a month earlier, one of their beloved family members had stolen money from them.

When Jonathan got to the door, he heard voices, and his pulse increased like a locomotive on an express track. He listened outside to hear if the voices sounded familiar. Then he heard a smacking sound and a man yelling what sounded like, "Is this what you want?" Then, if he wasn't mistaken, he heard a female making an agonizing sound.

Damn, Patience had warned him about India and Grayson, but he didn't think that he'd witness the massacre first hand. He pulled himself together, since he didn't know what could jump off when stepping into a domestic violence dispute. He'd seen enough episodes of *Cops* to know that getting involved in such a situation when a man's adrenaline is so high could be dangerous, but he could take Grayson without any problem. He just didn't want to have to hurt him too badly. The sounds grew more violent as he began to turn the doorknob. The door was locked. He quickly found the key in his trouser pocket and unlocked it. Jonathan cracked open the door and peeked inside, prepared to take Grayson head on. He was totally unprepared for what was actually occurring before his eyes. Je'Nae looked like a deer caught in headlights, and the astonishment on her face concurred with Jonathan's startled look. Je'Nae's black skirt parachuted like an umbrella. It opened and closed as Bedford rammed her from behind. Unaware of Jonathan's presence, Bedford's hands smoothly glided across Je'Nae's exposed behind. Je'Nae tried to jerk away from Bedford's grasp, but she was unsuccessful. On her second attempt, she managed to heave away, but by then Jonathan had merely closed the door and headed back to the main dining room.

11

Rewind

The flock of birds decorated the sky and the sun cast over the
harbor, putting everything it touched in iridescence. The song
of the seagulls pierced the air along with the swooshing sound of
Patience's workout suit. She felt like she was walking on cotton clouds
in her new cross-trainer sneakers. Patience took deep breaths to wind
down as she approached her town home. There were few people up at
the break of dawn. Patience loved living near the harbor and, at least
three times a week, she'd get up for her hour-long, three-mile brisk
walks. The unity of the sun and the light, balmy breeze was soothing.
Patience lived for days like this and was in no immediate rush to head
back home, but the twins would be up soon, and she had to get them
ready for school.

Patience entered through the screen door of her kitchen. Jonathan
was already awake and whipping up breakfast. Bacon, eggs and French
toast filled the air.

"You're in a rise-and-shine kind of mood this morning, aren't you?"
Patience said before she kissed Jonathan full on the lips and headed for
the fridge for some orange juice. "I thought you'd be exhausted from
partying 'til two this morning."

"Me? What about you? I'm surprised you're fully functional without receiving your usual eight to nine hours worth of sleep. By the way,
there was fresh-squeezed juice on the table."

"I can't believe you let me pour the glass and then decided to tell me," Patience said, and walked up on him to tickle his stomach.

"Woman, when will you learn that your man is not ticklish, and don't blame me because you're blind. You walked right past the table and stole a piece of bacon. Yeah, you're not slick. I saw, everything then you headed to the refrigerator. You were so busy stealing you failed to see the juice."

"Whatever," Patience said, laughing, and Jonathan joined her. "By the way, you really outdid yourself last night. The food was excellent. We need to give the staff a nice round of applause for being so on point and gracious."

"Yeah, with the exception of Je'Nae," Jonathan interjected. "She was extremely helpful."

"She's a great hostess and you know it. Good help like Je'Nae is hard to find."

"She was a little too helpful and gracious if you ask me," Jonathan sniped.

"Jonathan, what do you mean by that?" Patience inquired, curiosity piqued.

"I caught the wonderful Ms. Je'Nae in a very compromising position last night."

"Oh my goodness, please tell me it ain't so. Damnit, she was doing such a great job. Who else do we have to fire besides her? Not West, I hope. He seemed to be clocking her."

"No, not West. He knows better."

"Hunt?"

"No?"

"Elijah? Reggie? Thomas?" Patience queried.

"No, no and no."

"Well, I've run out of male staff members. Was it one of the women? Is she a lesbian? Oh my goodness," Patience said excitedly, believing that she had some good gossip.

"It wasn't anyone on our staff."

"It was one of my perverted relatives, wasn't it?"

"Yes, it was."

"It must have been Big Tye. You know he just got out of jail, right?"

"No."

"Terrence?"

"No."

"Tony?"

"No."

"Not my cousin Robby? He's much too much of a gentleman to do such a thing."

"No, not your country-ass cousin either," Jonathan said and laughed.

"I thought you said it was someone related to me?"

"It is," Jonathan said.

"Oh, hell no!" Patience said, infused with anger. "Not that lowlife alcoholic bastard, Grayson. That son of a bitch and poor excuse for a man."

"Patience, Grayson may be all those things, but I don't think that he's a cheat."

"But that's everybody, and you said it was one of my family members."

"Well, you left out one," Jonathan replied, filling his lungs with air and sighing. "It was Bedford," Jonathan finally admitted.

Jonathan continued washing the dishes he used earlier and restoring them to their proper place. His back was to Patience, but he knew without even turning around the look of shock, disgust and anger that was plastered on her face. Who could blame her? She was just made aware that the man everyone was fawning over the night before was a fraud. Bedford was a swindler, trickster, an out-and-out charlatan.

"Back up. Rewind! You're telling me that you caught Je'Nae and Bedford screwing? The same man who made the speech to my cousin Sandy? The man who went through all of the trouble of pulling together the event of a lifetime for his wife?"

"Yes."

"Are you sure?" Patience asked, one octave away from yelling.

"Patience, I may be senile on occasion, but brother ain't blind."

"How? When?"

"The how you already know. When doesn't really matter, but, if you must know that detail, it was when I went to get the gift. Remember, I came back empty-handed, and I told you I'd left the keys to the office in the kitchen by mistake."

"Where's the cordless?" Patience asked, walking in circles.

"In its cradle on the wall," Jonathan said, pointing. "But it's only 6:45 in the morning. You can't call people this early in the day."

"Oh yes the hell I can," Patience said as she grabbed the phone.

12

One Too Many Drinks

ndia's office resembled a cosmetics boutique. Samples of makeup and perfume fragrances were strewn across her desk, shelves and floor, atop the file cabinet, and there were unopened packages that required her immediate attention. Her office never gave the appearance of being unhampered. It was quite the contrary. Everything was stored neatly, either alphabetically or by the date received.

India had been out of the office for three days. Sierra had come down with the flu, so she stayed home to nurse her daughter back to health. Apparently, little John and Veronica had both had the flu, so when Lenora baby-sat the three of them on the evening of Sandy's anniversary party, Sierra caught their cold. India didn't understand why Patience would bring her sickly children around her healthy angel. When India called Patience on her mistake, her sister's response was "Sierra is not fragile and she's not made of glass. In case no one told you, children get sick from time to time, so deal with it." India was so shocked at her sister's insensitivity that she merely placed the receiver back on the base and hadn't called her since.

There were larger issues at hand. As a matter of fact, India was going to need both hands to help her grasp her situation and get it under control. India began noticing that Grayson was drinking a lot more than usual. The fiasco at Sandy's anniversary was only one of many over recent months. A month earlier, they had attended two functions for his job, and at both he got extremely wasted. *Shades* magazine had had its annual awards banquet two months earlier, and he was two minutes away from embarrassing her there. And now this mess at Sandy and Bedford's anniversary party. Grayson got blitzed beyond reason in front of her friends and family. India didn't know what she would have done if Jonathan and Bedford hadn't taken him for a walk to help sober him up. Her intentions were to address the situation that night, but what good would that have been? Grayson wasn't in any condition for her to reason with him. Then Sierra got sick with a fever of 101 and India, being the overprotective mother that she was rushed her to the hospital. First, she put in a call to her pediatrician, but it was after hours and when she didn't get a response after waiting a little more than a half an hour, she felt it best to play it safe. Sierra rarely got sick, and although she'd had colds as a baby, she wasn't prone to getting them. On occasion, she got the sniffles, but it was never accompanied by a fever.

India eased her shoes off by the heel and flung them under her desk and stretched her arms.

The foyer and the rooms that led up to the main dining area were fragranced by the scented candles. Lenora had done an excellent job of preparing the food and making sure the presentation looked superb as India stood over her micromanaging her every move. Her behavior toward Lenora was downright despicable. At one point, Lenora turned to her and said, "Maybe I should go on home and allow you to finish this up properly." India got the message and left Lenora in peace. Perhaps not in peace, but she didn't pester Lenora quite as much.

Grayson called to report that he would be home later than he expected, which bought India some additional time. She was a little sweaty from running errands, doing light housework and being in her kitchen, which felt more like a sauna. She was able to take a quick shower, using her favorite Satsuma body wash, and pull together a more tantalizing outfit. Grayson would be pleased.

It was a few minutes to eight, and Lenora had set the table before she left and placed the food on silver serving platters. Sierra was fast asleep and everything was on schedule when Grayson arrived home.

"Welcome home, honey," India said, greeting Grayson with a big kiss as he entered the door. Grayson appeared to be in a cheerful mood as he returned India's peck with a sensuous open-mouthed kiss. India was surprised, but did not refuse him. However, she smelled and tasted alcohol. She started to address the situation right then and there, but she didn't want to spoil the mood. That discussion would have to wait until later.

Grayson feasted on his meal while listening to an update of his daughter's prognosis and the details of India's day. India was so electrified about sharing the night with her husband without any interruptions, she almost forgot the purpose of the evening.

"Grayson," India said, placing her dessert spoon beside her plate, "I wanted to talk to you about the other night."

"The other night, huh?" Grayson said, licking the last of his crème brulee off his fork. "It was good to see your people come together, wasn't it? Sandy and Bedford sure make a nice couple."

"Yes, it was nice seeing everyone—Sandy, Bedford, Aunt Mavis, my cousins, the whole lot of them."

"So, what's up?" Grayson asked.

"I feel that you need to slow down on your alcohol intake." Her tone reflected a bit of fear.

"My alcohol intake? What the hell is that?" Grayson asked with annoyance laced in his voice.

"You had one too many drinks—"

"First of all, the drinks weren't that strong, and secondly, it was a celebration among family and friends. One too many drinks? You must be kidding me!"

India was going to hold her ground because Grayson needed to be aware of the spectacle that he had made of himself at the party.

"Grayson, you were a complete embarrassment."

"Stop exaggerating. You didn't say nothin' about your cousin Big Tye. He was a real embarrassment."

"Grayson, Big Tye is not my responsibility, but you are. Did you realize that Bedford and Jonathan had to take you out for a walk, that you could barely stand without their assistance? I was so humiliated," India said, raising her voice with each word.

"Let's rewind, okay? You are my wife, not my mother or my guardian, so the only person responsible for me is me. We are responsible for Sierra, this house and the bills. Therefore, I could not have humiliated you. If you did feel that way and you were humiliated, that's on you." Grayson pushed out his chair and it scraped loudly against the beautifully shellacked wood floor. "Now, are you through?"

India couldn't digest the food she had just consumed, much less the heap of bullshit that Grayson had just force-fed her. She was appalled at his selfish attitude and his total lack of regard for her feelings. Her mouth was dry, and her heartbeat felt irregular. She took quick, deep breaths to relax herself, and closed her eyes for a moment to envision happy thoughts, because she knew he had to be deranged talking such nonsense.

"Grayson, as long as we are married, *we* being the operative word, we are responsible for each other. I don't know what has gotten into you. Maybe one or two too many drinks again before you got home tonight. Is that what took you so long getting here? Didn't you think that I'd smell the alcohol on you when you got home?"

Grayson hopped out of his chair and was in front of India within a second. India could feel his hot breath as he stooped directly in front of her. She could see the look of contempt shadowing his eyes. India felt vulnerable and was unable to move as he cupped her chin, forcing her lips to protrude like a fish.

Dear Lord, please spare me, India prayed silently. *I won't say another word on the subject if You let him take it easy on me. Please, I ask You, Lord.*

"If you had let me get a word in edgewise earlier, you would have known that my firm just landed a big case today and that I may be assigned as legal counsel. The staff ordered everyone margaritas with chips and dip to celebrate. I indulged along with everyone else and had two drinks. I didn't get drunk because I had to be responsible for me and drive home. I come home for a night of R&R, but instead I get the third degree. India, I want you to understand one thing, you hear me?"

"Yes," a petrified India answered, trying not to flinch and provoke him further. If he were to apply any more pressure on her jaw, she knew he could easily break it. It was already bad enough that she was bound to have bruises where his hand clamped her face.

"If I want to be chastised, I'll pay my mother a visit. When I want advice I'll see a shrink. When I want to know the latest breaking news in the entertainment world, or I want information about our daughter or this house, I'll see you. Now, I'm going to get ready for bed. Are you coming?" he asked as he let go of India's face and stood erect, his tone back to normal.

"In a while; I have to clear this stuff up. I sent Lenora home early."

"Okay. I'm going to take a shower, so I'll see you upstairs."

"Alright," India replied, trying to sound cheery. Once Grayson disappeared, India didn't budge; her body went limp and a sole tear channeled down her face.

13
Ruby

he warm sun softly grazed Wanita's face as she strolled down
Peachtree Road. Passing the Fox Theater, she glanced up to see
who or what was performing or playing, but, to her disappointment, the
black letters merely said "Coming Soon," which simply meant they were
scouting out an act or nothing was scheduled. She was more than sure
she'd end up purchasing tickets for whatever would be playing there
next; it was routine for her. She loved theater, dance, singing and the
arts in general. To date, the only three shows that she hadn't seen when
they came to town were *Mama, Poppa Done Ate Up All the Chicken,*
Mama Shot Poppa and *Mama Ain't Got No Man.* Wanita couldn't
understand how anyone could take those plays seriously. In her opinion, they were simplistic and degrading.

Wanita's thoughts were distracted when she came upon a new pet
store. There was the cutest little black terrier sporting a pink bow
yelping in the window. Wanita stood in front of the casement spell-
bound at the sight of the puppy. She watched the puppy extend its paw
and scratch at the window. Wanita fell in love almost immediately.
When she was a kid, her father bought her a golden retriever for her
tenth birthday. For years she had begged and pleaded for her parents
to get her a puppy. They weren't opposed to the idea, but were against
having a dog locked up in the apartment. She could still hear her father
bellowing, "An apartment is no place for a dog!" When she was nine,
they moved from their tenement in Sunset Park, into a nice Victorian-

style home located in the Clinton Hills section of Brooklyn. It was one of the few remaining homes of its kind in that area that was livable. Many of them were dilapidated and torn down by the city and later replaced with high-rise condominiums. Wanita's birthday was shortly after they settled into their new home, and her parents kept their promise by getting her the dog that she had longed years for.

The memories of her parents, her old house and her golden retriever filled Wanita with cheer. She loved that dog, her parents and her old house in Brooklyn. Moments later, Wanita found herself at the register talking to the clerk about the puppy. Shortly thereafter, she was filling out the necessary paperwork for pet adoption. After completing the forms, Wanita was told to come back later in the evening to pick up the dog. She even selected a name for her new canine friend. She couldn't wait to carry Ruby home.

Wanita headed back to her car, which was parked off of West Paces Ferry Road. It was almost noon, and she was due to have lunch with Maxine and Layla at the Fish Market restaurant. She knew that Layla would get there on time because she worked in Buckhead, but Maxine was a housewife like Wanita and would stroll in fashionably late as usual. They had these lunch dates biweekly, but sometimes schedules conflicted and it only ended up being once a month. It used to be Wanita, Maxine, Layla and Sandy. Wanita missed Sandy dearly. Sandy was the level-headed one of their foursome. She brought sanity and class whenever they were out together, but Wanita was happy for her. Happy that Sandy had found a man who loved and cherished her. Wanita knew Sandy longed to be married, and it now seemed that her wait was not in vain. Sandy was thirty-one quickly about to turn thirty-two with no prospects in sight before Bedford came along. Sandy always complained that the men in Atlanta were either already taken or gay and that she was only one step away from visiting Morehouse College to find herself a man ten years her junior, but she was willing to provide on-the-job training. They would laugh at her sarcasm, but the girls felt her pain. After all, she was the only one not married out of the group. The scary thing was that she passed the remark about visiting Morehouse so many times that Wanita was beginning to take her seriously.

Wanita was surprised at the lengths that Bedford went to for their anniversary party. All night, Wanita watched as Bedford doused Sandy with attention. While at the same time, she took notice at how William barely gave her the time of day. He did manage to insult her shoes and, if that wasn't bad enough, he was extremely unsociable. He exchanged a few words with Grayson about the Professional African American Men Association, to which they both belonged, but other than that, his behavior was ornery. Every ten minutes, he gave her a look that read "Can we get the hell out of here now?" Wanita had had to pull teeth to even get him there that night. She mustered up the power to ignore him and with that decided to have a good time and not leave early on his account. They were one of the last couples to depart that evening and, even though he bitched and moaned about Wanita being inconsiderate, she still managed to soar in the air freely like a dove.

It was a quarter after twelve when Wanita arrived, and the parking lot at The Fish Market was crowded. Wanita didn't want to be late, so she decided to valet park her car instead of circling the lot for a spot. The doorway to the restaurant was partially blocked by waiting patrons and Wanita must have said, "excuse me" and "pardon me" at least ten times before making it to the hostess stand. Fortunately she was smart enough to make reservations and was seated right away. To her surprise, both Layla and Maxine were already waiting at the table. Hugs and kisses were exchanged immediately.

Wanita took her time getting acclimated while her friends continued with their tawdry conversation. Wanita hated when they talked about their children. It was amazing how two strangers could stand at a train depot together waiting on the next arrival with absolutely nothing in common. However, if they stood there long enough and the subject of children was to be brought up, pictures would be taken out and exchanged. Then, depending on the age of the child, they might discuss day care, the school that their child attended, or if they had infants they would discuss potty training, teething or the terrible twos. It was the one subject on which she had no expertise, and she often felt left out. That was one of the reasons that she volunteered at the

children's hospital, to help fill that void. She also had enough godchil-
dren to last her a lifetime, but she didn't have a chick nor child to call
her own.

"So, what's new, ladies?" Wanita asked, bursting with enthusiasm.

"You tell us," Layla replied.

"Yeah, how is our girl Sandy doing? How was her anniversary
party?" Maxine inquired.

Maxine was the clown of the group. She had a colorful personality
and a warm disposition, but she had a habit of poking and touching
people when she talked, and today was no different.

"All I can say is that we should be so lucky as to have a Bedford in
our lives. I mean that man is hotter than a bed of burning coals."

"Say it ain't so," Layla said, leaning forward on her elbows.

"Well, first off, he flew her family from North Carolina to Maryland, rented out this beautiful restaurant, even though I found out the
restaurant is owned by her cousin. Girl, he even got a limo that drove
them from New York down to Baltimore. Then he professed his love
to her in front of the group. I was floored when that man spoke, tears
came to my eyes," Wanita said, wiping away pretend tears.

Both Layla and Maxine laughed at Wanita and her antics.

"Damn! Sandy found herself a good-ass man. Smart, sexy romantic, kind and considerate. Shit, I'm about to leave Chris' ass. Does
Bedford have a brother?" Maxine asked, laughing.

Before Wanita could answer, the waitress came by to take their
drink orders. They all ordered Chateau Nu Blous and picked up where
they'd left off.

"Whose turn was it to pick the restaurant?" Layla asked, looking
at both Wanita and Maxine.

"Who else do you think?" Maxine countered. "You know when
there's seafood involved, Wanita has to be behind the selection."

"Don't you ever get tired of fish?" Layla asked.

"Not really, since I'm a vegetarian," Wanita replied.

"You need to get off that kick, because true vegetarians don't eat
fish, either."

"Layla, please! No need to get technical, okay," Wanita lashed
back.

After carefully scanning the menu, Wanita finally settled on the swordfish, asparagus and couscous. The menu had more than twenty fish items, and several chicken, pork and beef dishes as well. The menu was extensive and often overwhelming to look at, but Wanita liked The Fish Market because, it gave her options, and she wasn't limited to the two or three fish dishes that most other restaurants offered.

"So what are you talking about leaving Chris for now?" Wanita asked.

"Girl, please. You know I am not leaving that man. He may be a workaholic, but he is a good man and wonderful father."

"Maxine, I hear that," Layla responded.

"I think things would be better between William and me if we had children, but I can't even get him home long enough to try and produce," Wanita said. "But, I bought a puppy for us today. She's a little terrier that I'm going to pick up after I run my errands. I've already named her Ruby. She's so cute."

"Umph, I am happy for you, but what is William going to say?" Maxine asked, smirking and looking at Layla.

"William won't say anything. He never said anything about not wanting a dog."

"He never said anything about wanting one either, right?" Layla interjected.

"Y'all are tripping," Wanita said, draining her glass in one swig.

"If you say so," Maxine said, and Layla nodded to concur.

On her way home, Wanita picked up everything Ruby would need to feel the comforts of home and more. Wanita was looking forward to a new addition to the family. If she couldn't have a baby, the least she could have was a puppy. It wasn't quite the same, but both required love and attention. Wanita was beginning to feel lonely, and this new responsibility would help take her mind off William's weekly business trips. Even when he was home, he was too busy to spend time with her. Between his work obligations, PAAMA involvement and season tickets to the Hawks and the Falcons, he was always preoccupied.

Wanita was on all fours grooming Ruby when she heard the front door open and slam shut. She heard William clear his throat as he dropped his keys on the side table. His wing tips scraped against the parquet floors in the foyer as he headed toward the rear of the house and into the kitchen. Wanita changed positions and sat crosslegged. She was stroking Ruby when William entered. He laid his briefcase on the table and walked toward Wanita.

"Hey, honey," Wanita said. "How was your day?"

"Too long. I swear, Radio One is out to buy every station that has a for sale sign on it, and even those that don't," William replied.

"Are they working my honey to death?"

"Nothing I can't handle. What's for dinner?" William asked. "I'm starving," he said as he walked toward the fridge.

"Oh, I didn't get a chance to make anything today, I got caught up with the girls and Ruby," Wanita said, smiling.

"Who's Ruby?" William asked, his head still buried in the refrigerator.

"Ruby is the puppy in my lap that you've been ignoring. Boy, you really are out of it. Would you like me to order you something to eat?"

"That would be nice. You really should have ordered something earlier. You knew that I was coming home and I'd be hungry."

"I'm sorry. It was an oversight on my part."

"An oversight? What the hell is that? You know, Wanita, I don't ask for much, and yet you still manage to fuck that up!"

William slammed the door shut after grabbing a beer then he headed back to where Wanita sat.

"Just to let you know, I hope you bought that damn dog for one of those kids that you take care of at the children's hospital."

Wanita sat quietly stroking Ruby and listened to William as he continued to reprimand her.

"You know how I feel about pets. If it's not in a bowl or a cage, I want no part of it. They are just like children, and you know how I feel about that."

"William, you're being irrational. Ruby is a puppy. She won't get much bigger than she is right now, and we have space."

"Wanita, space is not the issue. Listen, get rid of the damn dog, or I will. I'm going upstairs to relax. Call me when the food arrives." Wanita felt a surge of anxiety and anger wash over her. William was being cruel for no particular reason. Everything had to be done his way. Wanita slowly felt like she was losing herself, and fighting with William was no longer a winning battle.

Sandy was right when she'd said that in order for William to begin respecting her again she needed to get back to work. Things weren't like this when she had her career. It wasn't until she became completely dependent on him financially that he began to mistreat her like she was unwanted shit on the bottom of his shoe. Wanita was tired of being treated like a second-class citizen in her own home. She needed and wanted to be heard.

"William," Wanita called, her voice wavering slightly.

"What?" he snapped, not looking back as he approached the stairwell.

"Would you like some Cambodian cuisine?" Wanita asked, caving in to what she'd really intended to say.

"Whatever," William answered as he climbed up the steps. "Just make it quick."

14

"You're a Very Lucky Woman"

andy felt her face getting hot, and she used that as her seventh
sense. Her intuition was telling her that something was dreadfully wrong, but she couldn't pinpoint it. Things were going better than ever between her and Bedford, and she had just spoken to Mama Mavis and her brother less than twenty-four hours earlier. She sat at her desk and tried to figure out who was in trouble and why.

Sandy leaned her head back and reclined in her newly purchased executive-style leather chair. Crossing her legs, she swung her foot back and forth, admiring her Mary Jane shoes. She really needed to focus on the citywide testing program that her children were due to take in less than three weeks. The exams were administered annually to assess student performance in language arts and mathematics. Since this was Sandy's first year as vice principal, she had to prove her worth. The year before her school had made some improvement in both areas of study. However, many of the students were minorities, and the report showed that the majority of them were failing to learn. Both city- and state-administered tests showed that about sixty percent of elementary and middle school students weren't reading at an acceptable level, and seventy percent weren't at a proficient level in math. Elementary school numbers were particularly distressing, and Daniel Hale Williams, the school Sandy co-chaired fell right into the mix. There were 677 public elementary schools in New York City. Less than twenty-nine percent had at least thirty percent of their students reading at an acceptable level; less than fifty percent had at least forty percent at that level; less than ten percent had more than seventy percent of their students reading at that level. In New York, there were currently 105 schools on the state's list of chronically failing schools and, although Sandy's school showed improvement, it was still a statistic. It was her daily duty to check in with each class for at least fifteen minutes to make sure that the kids were taking their lessons seriously and that the teachers weren't slacking.

Sandy looked at the large round silver clock that hung on the wall. It was still pretty early, and school wouldn't begin for another half hour, so she reached over for the telephone and dialed the first number that came to mind. The phone rang twice before a low, groggy voice answered.

"Hello."

"Hey, girl, did I catch you at a bad time?" Sandy asked.

"No, I'm up. William just left for work. I was just sitting here in the bed thinking."

"Are you okay?" Sandy asked. She could tell from the sound of Wanita's voice that something was definitely wrong. Even though Wanita didn't work and wasn't obligated to get up early, she was still a morning person. She was always full of cheer and extremely perky—without coffee.

"Is everything all right? You don't sound like your old self."

"I'll be fine. It's just that…damn, girl, I'm just a little stressed out. Things are a little haywire around here. William and I have been going at it, and I'm at my wit's end."

Sandy got up from her chair and closed her office door for some privacy. Just like she figured, something was wrong and, as usual, she'd hit the jackpot. On the evening of her anniversary party she could sense that things had gone awry with Wanita and William. William was usually very outgoing, but on that particular evening he hadn't been very sociable and didn't work the party. He'd barely spoken to anyone. Sandy was aware of the fact that he worked himself like a horse, so she brushed it off, thinking that maybe it was late and he was probably tired. After all, he did mention that the trip to Baltimore coincided with his business. Then, Sandy noticed that, although Wanita was happy to see her and was sincere, her smile was faint and weak. It was as if

Wanita had put on a happy face just for her, but Sandy knew her friend much better than that. She didn't pressure Wanita to talk because it wasn't the place or time. Wanita did volunteer that she and William were spending less and less time together, and that she was feeling alone in their marriage. Sandy wanted to pry, but held back. She'd made a promise to herself to follow up with Wanita, but she had gotten so busy with the preparations for the citywide exams that it had escaped her. Especially after she'd gotten the results back from the practice exam, which was still well below average.

"You know that you can talk to me. I may not live in Atlanta anymore, but I'm always here for you," Sandy said.

"I know. I know. Girl, I do miss you. Even though Layla and Maxine are here, it's just not the same. I've been meaning to call you and give you the low down, but I didn't feel like burdening you with my problems."

"Wanita, you know better than that. I'm your friend through thick and thin. When I was manless, who was there to console me? You. When I sat at home lonely eating an entire Domino's pizza, who would come over to get my ass up to run around the track? You. When my father died, who flew to North Carolina with me to help out with the funeral arrangements? You. So, Wanita, please stop trippin'."

"Sometimes I feel like I'm just being silly, you know? That my concerns are trivial, and that if I voice them out loud, it'll sound petty and of no major significance."

"Wanita, if it's bothering you like that, then it's definitely significant. Besides you are not the only one with problems. I have issues too!"

"Yeah, right! Not the woman that I saw a few weeks back. I'm not going to lie, I was feeling a little envious watching you and Bedford and all of the attention that he was giving you. And to think, you used to cry because you thought that you'd never find the right man. Well, Prince Charming came riding on his big black stallion and swooped you away, and now you're living happily ever after."

"Wanita, there is no such thing as happily ever after, but you can come pretty close to it. So, enough about me, what's stressing my adopted sista out?"

"Where do I begin? Wanita paused. "I think that I need to go back to work. I feel like I'm too dependent on William, and I don't have a life anymore. Yes, I volunteer at the children's hospital, and I was recently asked to be the basketball coach at the local high school for the girl's team, but it just doesn't feel as fulfilling. There's something missing."

"Well, you wanted to have a baby, right?"

"Yeah, but William isn't ready to start a family yet. You know how hard he works, and I don't want to throw any extras into his already heavy load."

Sandy listened to the hurt in her friend's voice. She knew how much Wanita wanted to start a family. She didn't know what the holdup was and, although she and Wanita were close, she didn't think it appropriate to ask if perhaps she was having fertility problems. It was a very sensitive issue, and Sandy figured it best to allow Wanita the opportunity to tell her if that was indeed the case.

Again, Sandy looked up at the clock to make sure that she would have enough time to give her undivided attention before the morning fire drills began. Without fail, her teachers streamed into her office each morning with emergencies that most of them could very well handle on their own. Sandy didn't mind playing the Good Samaritan, because the vice principal before her never gave anyone the time of day.

"I understand that William works a lot, but you'll be the one having the baby, so what difference does it make if he's busy? Most of the time it's the woman who does all of the work, anyway."

"Sandy, that's true, but William is standing firm with his decision right now about the kid thing. Put it like this, last week I brought the cutest little puppy home. I was drawn to Ruby the moment I laid eyes on her in the shop window. Girl, I went all out and bought her a little bed, toys, and even had a little tag made with the name engraved in it. When William came home that evening, he basically said, 'pets are just like having children, a huge responsibility, and that's something that I don't want to be a part of right now.' I thought that I would be able to slowly talk him into allowing me to keep Ruby, and, in time, that he would develop a liking for her, too, but three days later, he returned her to the store himself.

Wow, Sandy thought. She never realized that William was so selfish. Why would he steal Wanita's joy that way? There really was no other way to put it other than William was really fucked up! How do you tell your friend that her husband is acting selfish without stepping on her toes? It was always easier to give advice when you were on the outside looking in, but she knew that if the shoe were on the other foot, she would want someone to tell her if her husband were messing up. She had to be tactful in her approach.

"Wanita, how did that make you feel?" Sandy didn't mean to come off as a psychiatrist, but maybe if she allowed Wanita the opportunity to think about the situation and come up with her own conclusion, she wouldn't have to say a thing.

"Honestly, I was really pissed off. I don't think that I ask for much, and it wasn't like I was asking him to take care of Ruby, you know. I would have kept her out of his way, but then he said that he would still be able to smell the dog, and he didn't want to come home to a house that smelled like dog, I could respect that, so I left it alone."

Sandy's idea wasn't working as planned. She didn't understand why Wanita chose to shelve her dreams of starting a family and still allowed her husband to rule her life.

"So, how does William feel about the idea of you going back to work?"

"We haven't discussed it yet. William is never home long enough for me to discuss much of anything. That damn job of his is going to be the death of me, and, since we are spending so little time together, I thought that maybe if I focused on my career again, it would enable me to take my mind off having children."

"So, you're willing to put your dreams of starting a family on hold? You're not getting any younger, you know. As a matter of fact, I've been thinking about having a little bambino," Sandy said, nestling the phone under her chin. A huge smile came to her face upon mentioning the prospect of a baby. This was the first time that she had said such a thing out loud. Her heart was spilling with joy. She never thought the idea of being pregnant would bring her such excitement. She always thought pregnancy to be an inconvenience. It looked like such a struggle to waddle around with a huge basketball as your navigational guide. You were no longer capable of tying your shoes, or seeing your shoes, for that matter. Morning sickness became your sun-up companion, along with possible gestational diabetes, hypertension—or both. What could be so exciting about those things? Then Bedford came to mind, and she knew he'd be a wonderful father. Before his nephew, Shiloh's murder, she saw the interaction that they had, and it was phenomenal. Anyone would have thought that Shiloh was his son, and Bedford never told anyone differently. He simply nodded to comply.

"Sandy, I'm so excited for you. Is that what Bedford wants?"

"He's mentioned it in our counseling session, but…"

"Counseling? Sandy, is everything alright with you two down there?"

This was just what Sandy didn't want. She didn't mean to turn the spotlight from Wanita on to her. Besides, it was in the past, so she wanted to put that mess in a trunk and lock away the key.

"Yeah, but that's done and over with. We went for a few sessions to help improve our already superb marriage. You know that Bedford's nephew was killed last summer, and he was having a hard time coping with it, so we decided to go to counseling. Why don't you and William try it? It sounds like you need to air some things out. Don't sit there harboring your feelings until you feel like you're about to explode because that is not healthy."

"Girl, as a nurse who minored in psychology during undergrad, I know this. But sometimes it's easier said than done."

Sandy heard someone knocking on her door. Once again, she glanced at the clock. On a normal day, she would still have had a few minutes to spare, but being a vice principal didn't allow for normal days anymore.

"Just a minute," Sandy exclaimed. "Wanita, girl, I want to continue this conversation later on. It seems that someone requires my assistance. I must admit, as much as I love my new position, it is truly time consuming, and I often crave the simple life of just being a regular teacher again."

"I hear you. We can definitely catch up later on today. I have to start getting ready, anyway. I have an appointment with the director down at the high school. They are being really persistent and deep down I'm really excited about becoming a coach. I can still see if I have skills on the court."

"You go, girl! Well, good luck, and we'll chat later. Tell Layla and Maxine that I said hi, if you see or speak to them soon."

"I will."

Sandy straightened herself up and went to answer the door. When she opened it, she couldn't believe her eyes. To her surprise, it was Bedford standing in her entry with a handful of stargazers that immediately occupied her office with their aromatic fragrance. Bedford was definitely on the road to one-hundred-and-ten-percent recovery. Just when she thought things couldn't get any better, he continued to outdo himself.

"Well, to what do I owe this unexpected, but pleasurable, visit?" Sandy asked, pulling him into the office by his tie and shutting the door behind him.

"I was just in the area, and I thought I'd stop in."

"Yeah, right. I work in Harlem. We live in Brooklyn, and you work in midtown Manhattan. How did you wind up in this area?"

"Sandy, baby, I have business up here. I have clients in the area," Bedford said. He buried his head in the nape of her neck and started kissing her passionately. Then he turned his attention to her ear, a spot that he knew would ignite her fire.

Sandy murmured sounds of pleasure, but she quickly realized where she was and pulled away from Bedford.

"As much as I would like to, I can't right now. The day is about to begin here, and the last thing I want or need is for my secretary or one of my teachers to come barging in here."

"I'm sure the teachers will knock, and as for your secretary, I sent her on a little errand to get us some coffee."

"Bedford, why did you do that? Now I don't have anyone to answer my phones or cover the front office. You are so crazy." Sandy returned to her desk, and Bedford took a seat across from her and leaned back comfortably in the orange-cushioned chair.

"Now what business do you have up here?" Sandy asked, returning to their earlier subject.

"My business up here is you, woman. You ran out of the house this morning like a bat out of hell without so much as giving me a good-bye kiss, so I had to come up here and get it. Then I thought, while I'm at it, maybe I can get something else too." Bedford had a Cheshire-cat smile on his face.

"Unfortunately, we can't all lie around in bed until we feel like getting up. I have to be at work by a certain time because people depend on me, and I don't have the luxury of working for myself."

Sandy picked up the stargazers and held them to her nose. She closed her eyes, allowing herself to get lost in the scent. She imagined herself wearing a soft white cotton dress, running through a field of flowers filled with tulips, stargazers, roses with baby's breath and dahlias. She sorely missed the living in the South. Nothing could replace the quality of life offered there. The air was fresh and clean, the houses were pretty nice in size, and there were friendly neighbors, southern cooking and the comfort of simply kicking back, just to mention a few things. But Bedford made it all worthwhile, along with her career.

"Do I detect a hint of jealousy, Ms. Jackson?"

Sandy removed herself from her seat, sauntered past Bedford and bumped her hip into his shoulder while placing the flowers in a vase.

"Where should I put them?" Sandy voiced.

"Are you ignoring me, beautiful?"

Sandy put the vase on top of her cherry-wood bookshelf and, before sitting back down, she stopped to plant a soft kiss on Bedford's lips.

"I could never ignore such a handsome man as yourself who stops by my office to get a good-bye kiss and bring me flowers. That would be unheard of," Sandy said, laughing.

"Oh, so it doesn't matter that this man is your husband? You would give your attention to any good-looking man with flowers, huh?" Bedford inquired, arching his brows.

"Give me some time to think that one over."

"Woman, don't play with me. I'll come over there and put you over my knee."

Sandy smiled at the thought. Now that was a new idea. Before Sandy could respond, she heard a knocking.

"Who is it?"

"It's Ms. Richards. Do you have a moment? I have a question for you."

"Yes, Ms. Richards, please come in."

Bedford stood to get ready to leave. When Ms. Richards came in,

Sandy introduced her to Bedford, and he kissed her on the lips and departed.

"Your husband seems nice. You're a very lucky woman!"

"Ms. Richards, if you only knew," Sandy replied and repeated the sentiment to herself again. *You're a very lucky woman.*

15

A Familiar Voice Over the Airwaves

atience was exhausted. She'd spent the last four days at home with her very chicken pox infected twins. They ran her ragged when they were up, but she didn't mind doing for them. She wanted to nurse them back to health as quickly as possible, and her deceased mother's old recipes seemed to be working wonders. Patience gave the children hot baths using tea prepared with some of the recommended herbs like clover, red ginger, goldenseal, Pau d'arco and Yarrow. She sponged the affected area with the tea. She used a wet compress to help control the itching, and before bed each night, they drank catnip tea sweetened with molasses. Patience figured that by the next day, they would almost be back to their little fire-starter ways, especially Veronica.

Jonathan had been running *Pájo Soul* without her, and he called every other hour for one thing or another. He wanted to know where she put the invoice book, if she had ordered the fruit and vegetables for their upcoming catering gig, where the employee schedule was located, and the inquiries went on. She knew that he was more than capable of handling things alone, because he had managed restaurants much larger than theirs in the past. However, she knew the reason he called her so often was because he missed her. He missed having her company, and when he got home late at night, Patience was either too exhausted to be attentive or fast asleep.

Over the past four days, Patience was able to catch up with her soap operas. She no longer had the luxury of watching her programs, and she'd stopped taping them well over two years ago. She fell back into the old familiarity of her favorite characters, Adam Chandler, Palmer Cortlandt, Erica Kane, Opal and Dixie. *All My Children* still held its appeal and charm for Patience, and it was good to be able to flip back and recognize the cast. There were a couple of new faces, but, for the most part everyone was still there.

It was almost five o'clock. Veronica and Little John had gone to sleep at a quarter to one. Restless nights made them have odd sleeping habits. Patience was just about done preparing the ground turkey for her famous lasagna. She finely diced the bell peppers, onions and scallions to add to her homemade tomato sauce. The noodles were soaking in the large pot. She added a touch of oil to prevent them from sticking together. Both Veronica and Little John requested that she make lasagna for dinner, and she was happy to oblige, since it was Big John's favorite as well. Jonathan was supposed to be the chef, but his lasagna still couldn't touch Patience's with a ten-foot pole, and she teased him about it all the time. She hoped that he would make it home in time to break bread with the family, but there was a good chance that he wouldn't be able to, since the executive chef had a family emergency, and John had to cover.

When Patience was done combining all of the ingredients, she put the lasagna in the oven at 350 degrees. It would be ready just in time for the kids when they woke up. Patience went back into the family room to watch the news. She needed to know what was going on in this crazy world. She couldn't understand why people were being so vicious to one another—terrorist threats every other day, brutal killings and bombings. It didn't begin to make sense to her. She and Jonathan had spent many nights discussing politics and world views, and they both shared the same sentiments. The world was slowly feeling the wraths of hell. It was no longer a safe place for anyone. Everyone was affected by what was going on. People were being laid off by the thousands, the stock market kept taking a nosedive and the poor were getting poorer. She and Jonathan were just grateful for being able to be together, to provide for their families and for their health. Anything negative that might have happened to them in the last year or so was minor compared to those who had lost loved ones, their jobs, or even the will to live.

Both Patience India had lost contact with their father long ago. After September 11, Patience had decided to let bygones be bygones and called her father. He was a trifling man, but Patience came to realize that, no matter what, he was still their father. India didn't seem to concur, but that was just one more thing for both sisters to disagree on.

Drugs were a serious problem in the city of Baltimore. Most families believed drug use could never happen to them, and when it did they were unprepared. Families often got comfortable in their routine and settled in their environment, never thinking that life would throw them an unfair pass. Well, their mother, Patience and India were one of those families, and they were definitely not ready for what their father had had in store for them.

It was Patience's sophomore year in college and India's senior year in high school. Patience was on the dean's list and India was being India. She did well in school, but gave her parents hell when it came to honoring her curfew. She was always out with one boy or another. Their mother was promoted to head librarian at the public school, and their father still worked at the auto manafacturer company. They had a nice savings set aside for their children's educations and were both scheduled to retire within a year or two. Their parents had plans to sail the seven seas and spend lots of time visiting Africa. Things were going great until they received word that Cleveland, their only son, had been killed in The Gulf War. Shortly after, their mother took ill and had a minor stroke, from which she never fully recovered. Then, their father began taking muscle relaxers for his chronic fatigue and depression. It started with quaaludes and slowly progressed to heavier over-the-counter drugs. His behavior began to change, but their mother was in no condition to address the change. Patience was away at school, and India was just too into herself to notice that things were simply falling apart. Patience entered her senior year in college and India started her sophomore year, and that's when things went awry. The check that their mother sent from their college fund bounced, and both of them had to apply for student loans. Their father often disappeared for days at a

time. Drug dealers would show up at their doorstep like traveling sales-
men, asking for their dad. The family was in dire need of repair. Their
father still opted to take early retirement to try to make amends and
catch up on the bills with the lump-sum of money that he was going to
receive. However, they had to use that to maintain the mortgage, which
was behind. They managed to keep the house, but their parents' dream
of traveling together became a dream deferred. Patience graduated
from college and ended up getting a job at the ad agency that she had
interned for, while India still attended college. Their mother's health
deteriorated, and the fact that the family seemed to be drifting even
farther apart made matters worse. Within a year, their mother passed
away. India graduated two months after her mother's death, and she
blamed her father for the demise of their family.

The television watched Patience as she lay on the couch, curled in
a fetal position. The timer woke her up. She raised her head just enough
to allow herself to see the time. It was now a quarter to six, and she
knew that Veronica and Little John would be up soon. She quickly sliced
the French bread in half to add butter, garlic and parsley leaves and
wrapped it in aluminum foil. Fifteen minutes later, the bread was done
and the kids were up. Patience made them sleep in mittens so that they
wouldn't scratch themselves and leave unsightly marks. They both
wandered into the kitchen, Veronica wearing pink mittens and Little
John wearing navy blue.

Patience untied the drawstrings that kept them from pulling the
mittens off their hands and ordered them to clean themselves up so
they could eat dinner. In their absence, she set out the tableware. She
went back into the family room to catch whatever she could on CNN
before the kids returned. There didn't seem to be anything interesting
on, so she flipped to WJZ to see her favorite news anchor, Kai Jackson.
Patience found him to be very sexy and attractive. He had visited *Pájo
Soul* in the past, and they even had a picture of him at the restaurant.
There still didn't seem to be anything interesting happening. There was
a female rapper who had made the headlines because she allegedly
beat her female lover, causing a miscarriage. Patience sucked her teeth
and was about to leave the room, until she heard a familiar voice over
the airwaves. She turned around, giving the television her full attention.

Patience watched as the young female rapper tried to make her way through the crowd, and the reporters assailed her with a tongue-lashing. Some of them were even as bold as to try to pull her aside for a personal interview. Then she saw him.

"At this time, my client is pleading not guilty."

It was Grayson, representing the female rapper. Patience couldn't believe her eyes and immediately picked up the phone to call her sister, India.

"Good afternoon, *Shades* magazine. India McCall's office, this is Nashelle, how may I help you?" India's temporary assistant said. As far as Patience knew, this was the fourth temp that India had hired over the past couple of weeks. There was Crystal, Fawn, Racy and now Nashelle. She didn't know what was wrong with her sister and her attitude. The sad thing was that India didn't see a pattern or think that she had an attitude problem. She had a hard time keeping assistants and an even harder time maintaining a housekeeper. Lenora was still employed in the McCall household, which was amazing.

Patience could tell that Lenora didn't play games with India, nor did she put up with her nonsense. She did her job, handled her business and went home, which was what separated Lenora from India's past help. Everyone else tried to suck up to India and into her ego, and she would use that to her advantage. People were drawn to her because she was beautiful and smart though, once introduced to her personality, the love affair quickly fizzled. India liked to prey on the weak—and she considered anyone who tried to befriend her weak. She also treated anyone who wasn't on her level like a subordinate. She used her position at the magazine and Grayson's community ties and status as a top attorney to make herself appear larger than she really was.

"Yes, good afternoon, Nashelle. Is India available?"

"May I ask who is calling?"

"This is Patience, India's sister."

"Oh, one moment, please."

While Patience was kept on hold, the smooth sound of Angie Stone entertained her. She was so fixated with the song, she didn't realize the amount of time that had passed.

"Hi, Patience, I'm sorry for keeping you on hold for so long."

"No problem. I was just enjoying the music. Is India busy?"

"No, I think that she left for the day. I was trying to locate her, and no one has seen her in more than an hour. She didn't say that she was leaving, but her handbag is gone, so I guess she must've left."

"Well, it is getting kind of late, but if you should see her let her know that I called."

"I will," Nashelle replied.

"Thanks, and don't hang out there too long. I hope that you're going home soon. Bye."

"I'm not. Bye."

Patience hung up the phone and immediately went to check on the lasagna. She could smell the wonderful aroma of the meat, sauce and cheeses blending together. Upon opening the oven door, the warmth enveloped her like a blanket during a cold winter night. She pulled the top rack out with the potholder. The ingredients had melted and were blending together slowly, but it wasn't quite ready. The lasagna needed to simmer for at least another ten to fifteen minutes.

Veronica and Little John ran into the kitchen hitting, screaming and tattling on each other. Patience had to pry them apart. She told them to keep quiet and have a seat at the table.

Patience still had a little time to kill, so she looked at her to-do list on the refrigerator door. The list consisted of things that she needed to do for herself, the children, the business, the house and things for Jonathan. She had accomplished most of the items. She had gone grocery shopping, picked up and dropped off the dry cleaning, paid the mortgage and utility bills along with the children's tuition, taken her car for a tune-up Jonathan's for an oil change and had made most of her phone calls. Still, there was one phone call to which she needed to bring closure.

Patience had already left more than four to five messages in the past month. Each one was brief and inconspicuous. She would simply say, "Hi, Sandy and Bedford. I hope all is well with you guys. It was great seeing you, Sandy. I didn't realize how much I missed you. Let me know when you're coming out this way again." However, she was more than sure that Bedford was aware that she knew about his little quest and wasn't passing the messages on to Sandy. It really didn't matter, because she had something that would throw a wrench into his little well-oiled machinery, but, in the meantime, it wouldn't hurt to try making one more call.

The phone rang four times before Patience removed the phone from her ear. She knew that the fifth ring would activate their voice mail service and that had already proved useless. Just as she was about to hang up, she heard someone pick up the receiver on the other end.

"Hello," Patience said, hopeful that she was finally getting through to Sandy.

"Hello, who is this?"

"Oh, hi, Bedford...it's Patience. How are you?" Patience asked, her enthusiasm now dust in the wind.

"I'm doing well. Thanks for asking. Hey, I never properly thanked you and Jonathan for going all out for me and my wonderful wife. You all really made our anniversary special. I'll never be able to top that again."

"I'm sure you won't," Patience exclaimed, wanting to end the niceties. "Is Sandy in?"

"No, I'm sorry she's not right now. I believe she has a parent-teacher meeting this evening and won't be in until late."

"Well, then I'll try her again another time."

"Would you like to leave a message?" Bedford inquired.

"No, I'll try my luck again next time. Take care," Patience said and hung up.

16
Lay It On Me

ndia left the office early after receiving a disturbing call from Sierra's school about a gas leak in the facilities. Everyone had to evacuate the premises immediately, meaning India had to get moving. This couldn't be happening at a worse time. She was in the middle of completing yet another project and couldn't spare the time. Right away, she called home to see if Lenora could pick up Sierra. Unable to reach Lenora, India began to panic. This was the last thing that she needed on her already full plate. What purpose was Lenora serving if she wasn't available when she needed her? She dialed Grayson's office number and didn't get an answer, which was peculiar, especially since he had a personal assistant. She then called his cell phone, but it forwarded directly to voice mail. At this point, India was fuming. Where the hell was everybody? It was times like this that she wished that Patience lived closer to her. As bad as things were between them, she could always depend on her sister. Desperation led India to make one last attempt at calling the receptionist at Grayson's firm.

"Good afternoon, Lever and Bard law firm. Lavelle speaking. How may I direct your call?" the overly cheery voice asked.

India was in no mood for cheer and barked her request at the receptionist.

"I'm looking for Grayson McCall. This is Mrs. McCall."

"One moment please."

India bit on the pen cap as she waited for Little Miss Sunshine to return to the phone. India looked at the LCD on her handset and noticed that she was on hold for well over a minute. Time was wasting, and India's patience was waning.

"Hello, ma'am? I apologize for the wait, but Mr. McCall is not at his desk right now."

"Well, page him then," India snapped.

"Is this call of an urgent nature?"

"It must be if I'm asking you to page him, right?"

India was again placed on hold without a response. This time she held on even longer than the first time around. India hung up and pressed speed dial. Her call was again answered by Miss Sunshine.

"Good afternoon, Lever and …"

"Yeah, yeah. Save the pleasantries. I was holding for Grayson. In case you didn't hear me the first time, I'm his wife, India. And FYI, I don't appreciate being put on hold for long periods. Now is Grayson in?"

"Mrs. McCall, I'm sorry. I can't seem to locate Mr. McCall. Would you like his voice mail?"

"That's fine."

Seconds later, India was listening to her husband's smooth baritone.

"Hello, Grayson, it's me. I was trying to find you so that you could go to Sierra's school and pick her up, but I don't know where you've scampered off to. Anyway, apparently there's a gas leak at Sierra's school, and we need to pick up our daughter. I can't find Lenora, either, so I guess it's up to me again to pick up where everyone else is slacking. I'll see you at home later."

India placed the receiver back into its cradle. Damn, if it wasn't one thing it was another. India slid her shoes on, grabbed her blazer and handbag and headed out of her office. Her assistant wasn't at her desk, and she didn't have time to wait around considering she was already late, so she just left.

When India arrived at the school, there were only a few children left outside with teachers. When Sierra spotted her mother's vehicle, she pulled away from her teacher's grip and ran toward it. India parked a few feet away from them and got out of the car to greet her daughter. Sierra ran and jumped into her mother's arms.

"How is my sweet Sierra doing?" India asked, embracing her.

"I'm fine, Mommy. Are we going home?"

"Yes, we are, sweetie pie."

"Mommy can we please go to Auntie Patience's house? I want to see Veronica and John."

India thought about the idea. She really didn't feel like taking the forty-five-minute drive out to Baltimore, but Sierra needed something to do, and she couldn't take her to work with her the next day. As a precaution they were closing the school until the next week. They had to wait for the inspectors to come out before re-opening the school, but were sure that it would be taken care of by Monday.

"Let me call Aunt Patience. I have to make sure that it's fine with her first, okay?"

"Okay."

When they arrived home, India went to Sierra's room and packed an overnight bag. She went into the kitchen, and Lenora was preoccupied with preparing dinner. The house was sparkling, and India could smell the scented candles that she'd bought a few weeks ago burning. It smelled like Lenora was preparing a feast fit for a king. India couldn't help looking into the pot with butternut squash soup. There was also chicken kiev in the oven, along with a casserole dish, which had brown rice and mixed vegetables. Seeing all of that food made India's mouth water. It was already a few minutes to five, so it wasn't too early to eat. She decided to make a plate for both herself and Sierra before they headed out, but Lenora told her that it would be another ten minutes before the chicken would be done. They sat down at the bar in the kitchen and watched the thirteen-inch television.

"Mommy, are we going to eat in here?"

"Yes, we are going to keep Ms. Lenora company." India looked at Lenora as if to ask her permission. Lenora simply nodded.

Lenora turned up the volume on the television for her guests and walked over to the oven to turn the temperature down. She went to the cabinet to get the plates and silverware. She then set out placemats and went to the stove to prepare their plates.

India simply wanted to relax. Her day was hectic enough, and, when she was with her daughter she tried to eliminate the outside pressures of work.

For the first time in years, India thought about her mother and how much she missed her. Being in the kitchen with Lenora reminded her of the times that she had helped her mother out when she was cooking. When her mother prepared meals, it was always a feast. She made that southern food like no one else could. And she made her baked goods from scratch. If her mother were alive today, she'd probably be helping Patience and Jonathan out at *Pájo Soul*. Her mother, Lillian, would burn that food like no one else could. Their father used to comment on their mother's culinary skills all the time. He never, ever missed a meal, and their mother lived to serve that man and her family. She catered all of the church and community events. She made sure that the family ate its meals together just about every night, although, when the kids got older, it became harder to bring everyone together. Nevertheless, they still had their holiday dinners together as a family. Family would drive up from down south for Thanksgiving, Easter, Christmas, New Year's and Independence Day. It didn't matter the occasion. Heck, there were times that they would show up uninvited, just assuming that Lillian was going to be behind the stove.

India wasn't a bad cook herself, and neither was Patience. She figured what attracted Patience to Jonathan most was the fact that he could cook his ass off. Patience loved to eat, and the fact that Jonathan was able to provide her with the three F's—feeding, fucking and financing—made him all the more valuable. He didn't make nearly as much money for India's satisfaction, but he was a good provider, and it didn't seem that Patience was in need of anything. Then again, Patience was very easy to please and had simple taste. India was often amazed at how much she and her sister differed when it came to likes and dislikes. The only thing that they both shared was their taste in men. When they were younger, they liked their boyfriends tall, dark and hung. India, of course, had to add paid to that list. It didn't make sense to date someone who couldn't afford to take her out. What was the benefit of dating a broke man? Realistically, what did he have to offer? India figured she had a lot to offer and needed some equal form of reciprocity.

At a very young age, India knew what she wanted and didn't want in a relationship. She did want a man with cash. India needed a brother who could supply her with some notes. Someone who was willing and able to spend some of what he had on her. India had an image to maintain. She didn't want a man who didn't have a car. Otherwise, he was wasting his time and hers. In all of her life, she never had to take public transportation, and she wasn't about to start. Although her parents weren't rich, they both owned their own car and, whenever she needed to go somewhere, they took her.

Her first real boyfriend was a very nice guy. They attended the same high school. He was on the junior varsity basketball team, and India was the co-captain of the cheerleading squad. He came from a very nice family, he was smart, very attractive like India and dressed nicely, which is what made her notice him in the first place. He failed to reach the bar for India's requirements. His parents weren't well-to-do, so he didn't have a car, and although he held a part-time job and was able to treat her to nice things every once in a while, they never went anyplace. The movie theater was a decent distance away, and India refused to take the bus or train anywhere. He wasn't able to borrow his parents' car. Both parents worked different shifts, and they only had one vehicle. So, that relationship ended as quickly as it started.

India then began dating older men, which her parents disliked. She dated all sorts of men and race wasn't an issue. At least not until she went to college and discovered that black was truly beautiful. India had never denied being black, but she was so fair that many just assumed that she was of Spanish descent. That couldn't be farther from the truth. Both of her parents were of African American descent. Her father was from Louisiana, and he had some of that Creole blood, but he was as dark as dirt, and her mother was simply light. It would have been easier to say that she had Indian in her family, especially since folks used to ask her that dumb question all of the time. Is your name India because you've got Indian in your family? There were times that India would just look at them to let them know how stupid they really were. Black people always wanted to be linked to something other than being black.

India played tic-tac-toe with Sierra and watched Lenora stir around the kitchen. She observed her movements and noticed that Lenora and her mother shared a lot of similarities. Her mother wouldn't be caught without her apron when she cooked, and she never saw Lenora without hers either. Lenora had long hair, but she only wore it in a twisted bun. Her mother was the same way, and they both loved to watch soap operas and the news. Her mother and Lenora probably had much more in common, but India never paid Lenora enough attention to even notice. The one thing that she really did like about Lenora was the fact that she knew how to mind her own business, and she didn't want anything from her. Her last few maids wanted to know what positions were available at *Shades* and if she could get them a job. That was one of the reasons she didn't like hiring younger women. They were always begging for one thing or the other and trying to advance their careers on her time. It would start out innocently enough, but then they tried to use her for free stuff from the magazine like perfumes and cosmetics or invitations to parties and award ceremonies. One of them even went as far as to take stuff out of her room, as if she wouldn't notice that her bottles of Vera Wang or BCBG perfume were missing. India only took home things that she liked, and, if it all of a sudden grew legs and took off, then that was definitely a problem that required immediate treatment. For instance, "You are fired. Please take your shit and go!"

India knew that both her husband and Patience thought that it was she who was intolerable, and at times she could be a handful. She never fired anyone for tardiness, absenteeism, or for not cleaning to her liking, though all of those things were more than valid arguments. There were always other underlying reasons for her giving someone the boot.

India didn't like when people used her for their own personal gain. That was one of the reasons that she had such a limited number of friends. She never knew who her real friends were. Over the past few years, it seemed like everyone she encountered wanted something—a favor, a job, goodies, anything. It was difficult to separate the fakers from the real thing. That was why India put so much stock into her home life with Sierra and Grayson and work. There were times when she wished that she had a life outside of the one that she presently had, but it wasn't a necessity because, for the most part, she had all that she needed within the walls of her home.

Sierra was telling Lenora about the events at school and how the fire alarm went off informing them that this was not a drill. Just like a child, she exaggerated the story so much that Lenora and India found themselves laughing hysterically as Sierra acted out the events.

Lenora placed India and Sierra's food in front of them and went to take a seat at the breakfast table by herself. To Lenora's surprise, India invited her to fix a plate and join them, to which she obliged. The three of them sat enjoying their food in silence while the soft hum of the television played in the background. India scolded Sierra for chewing her food and sticking out her tongue, a little something that she'd learned in school earlier that week. India told her that it wasn't nice for little girls to behave that way and that it wasn't proper etiquette. India was in the middle of telling Sierra about right and wrong, when Sierra interrupted her.

"Mommy, Mommy," Sierra said, excitedly, ignoring her mother.

India had taught Sierra better and was getting frustrated at her daughter's indignation. Sierra even went as far as to tug the hem of her mother's skirt. India grabbed her hand and was about to tap it lightly, when Lenora captured her attention.

"Good Lord, let me turn up this television. What in the world is Grayson doing on TV?" Lenora located the remote control and increased the volume.

"Mommy, I was trying to show you Daddy. Look, look," Sierra said.

India felt bad for not paying mind to her daughter when she'd tried to get her attention in the first place. She quickly apologized and turned her attention to the monitor.

"In the news today, female rapper X-Tasy, also known as Vontelle Jacobs, has been accused of allegedly battering her female lover, resulting in a miscarriage along with other major injuries."

The camera crews zoomed in on X-Tasy as she walked out of the courtroom escorted by none other than her attorney, Grayson. X-Tasy was accompanied by several other people, who must have composed her entourage. They pushed her through the frenzy and she refused to answer any of the media's questions.

India watched in disbelief. She couldn't believe that Grayson was on television, much less representing this hooligan masquerading around as a woman. Why was it that she wasn't made aware of his recent case? India was livid. The fact that she had to learn of her husband's whereabouts or business second-hand was upsetting. Over the past few weeks, Grayson was consumed with work, but so was India. She was putting out more fires than she could handle. India was also consumed with her daughter's extracurricular activities. She had to rush to Gaithersburg three nights a week after work to pick Sierra up from dance rehearsal. Then, on her available nights, she tried to visit the gym, though she couldn't remember the last time she was able to meet her personal trainer.

Grayson tagged along beside the young twenty-something female rapper and stopped to speak briefly to the reporters. The microphones and the newscasters swarmed in on him like bees to a hive. They made a mini circle around him as he made his statement, which was quick and to the point, while X-Tasy stood staunchly beside him.

X-Tasy was dressed in business attire, which someone had obviously picked out for her. She looked extremely uncomfortable as she pulled at the collar of her blouse. Her blond cornrows were trimmed with beads, and her makeup was overdone. For a female, X-Tasy was donning more jewelry than Mr. T. She smacked on her chewing gum as Grayson spoke. X-Tasy looked like a typical no-class, ghetto-fabulous little black girl who would have ended up in McDonald's or Wendy's flipping burgers if she hadn't made it in the rap game. Then, apparently, she'd made it and still managed to screw up! That was neither here nor there, but the young woman looked pathetic in India's eyes.

India continued to watch the telecast, but she tuned the sound out. For the last couple of months, their relationship had seemed extremely tumultuous. How could Grayson do this to her? There was a time when he would have told her what was going on in his life. He would have told her what was going on with his career. India knew that he was hoping to attain a position as an associate partner, but she didn't know where that stood. Asking anything of him nowadays was like begging a dog for his last bone. There were times when India felt as if she was walking alongside the third rail of a train track—one wrong move, and she could be electrocuted. Communication was almost non-existent, and the sex was quickly following. She attributed the changes to her overexertion with work; but as soon as she pulled together a new staff, that would be resolved. She didn't wait on Grayson hand and foot, but she was usually very attentive to his needs and, as a wife, she knew that she needed to clean up her act.

When she'd first met Grayson, things were different. Very different! She knew that he was a hard worker and would make it big one day. With that in mind, she planned to work her magic. If she'd had the ability to put roots on him, she would have done it. At the time, India was working at the *Baltimore Sun*. She was covering a local story on youth and inner-city crime. This was her opportunity to shine at the *Sun* and her ticket to stardom. Grayson was a well-respected assistant district attorney, getting paid little for his work, but, nonetheless, he was already establishing himself as someone with whom to be reckoned. He was working on one of the biggest drug cases of the year. Grayson was making headlines and receiving local news coverage every day for his staging in the courtroom and breaking information. India not only saw her chance for glory, but an opportunity to gain a husband. From the moment she laid eyes on him, she knew he was the one. He was the perfect height, dark and decent to look at. She immediately liked the way Grayson carried himself and that he was well spoken. He also didn't appear intimidated by her looks or her position at the paper, like most of the men that she came across. The truth was that he barely gave her the time of day, so India had to make the first move.

India was trying to get some dirt on the young man who was on trial. He was accused of gun racketeering, as well as being one of the biggest drug lords in Baltimore City. Grayson was the prosecuting attorney and was on a roll with the amount of trials that he'd won. The fact that he was successful in thirty-one trials out of thirty-three in his short career made him even more revered, especially in India's eyes.

India could smell a winner, and Grayson was going to be her prize. From what she could tell, he had every quality that she was looking for in a mate. He was confident, intelligent, driven, ambitious, possessed character, a career with endless prospects, no children, and he was financially secure. He was also single. There was no need in chasing a man who was unattainable.

India took note of the fact that he was a home owner and had several other investment properties that were doing very well. This was extremely important because it showed the type of provisions that he would be able to make available for his family. Grayson was driving the latest model Mercedes Benz and was the best-dressed attorney that India had ever seen. His suave look made him look like he'd just walked off the pages of *Savoy* magazine.

Grayson wined and dined India for six months, and they were married within a year. After they were married, India found one minor imperfection about Grayson's past. It was trivial in the scheme of things. India believed that it was probably that one speck that made Grayson so determined to succeed in the first place. He was stronger because of the events that had taken place when he was a child. Second, if Grayson didn't harp on being raised in foster care for twelve years and a halfway house for another two, then it really shouldn't bother India. Grayson's not having a steady place to call home during his youth only made him focus more on how he would subsist moving forward. His vision for the future included a family. He dreamed of having a stable family he could love and adore and be able to provide anything for which they could ever wish. These were the sentiments that Grayson shared with India while they courted. All of the above, stacked with his personal résumé, made him India's ideal man.

India didn't understand from where Grayson's actions were coming or where they were going. He had taken to binge drinking, and he seemed to be excluding her from the important things taking place in his life.

Lenora cleared her throat and continued smacking on her chicken kiev, twirling the cheese to her mouth like it was the last supper.

"Well, this looks like it will be an interesting case," Lenora stated.

"It looks like a joke, and I hope that it'll be over soon," India said.

"Mommy, is Daddy famous?" Sierra questioned.

"No sweetie. Daddy is covering a big case involving a famous artist, but he isn't famous."

"But he's on television, so that makes him famous."

India was getting frustrated and wasn't in the mood for Twenty Questions, but she didn't want to take her irritation out on her daughter.

"Sierra, I want you to understand that being on television does not make a person famous. Your father is not well known, eminent, illustrious or someone who everyone recognizes when he walks the street. Oprah Winfrey, Michael Jackson, Bow Wow, Jay-Z, Denzel Washington and the rapper X-Tasy your father is representing are famous. Do you understand?"

"Yes, a little bit."

India didn't want to ask, but she had to know what a little bit meant.

"Sweetie pie, what is it that you don't understand?"

"I recognize Daddy. You recognize daddy and Ms. Lenora recognizes Daddy, so that should make him famous. I know that my friends in school will recognize him too!"

Lenora burst out laughing, and India looked at her to see what she found so amusing.

"I'm sorry, but she just made a good point," Lenora said, giving an apologetic look.

"Go clean yourself up and go to your room and find a toy that you would like to take with you to Aunt Patience and Uncle Jonathan's house. Try to fit it into the small pulley that I packed with your clothes and make sure that you take your toothbrush and lotion."

Sierra jumped off the stool and ran through the kitchen and into the living area. She was about to run up the staircase, but India scolded her before her foot could touch the first step.

India and Sierra got into the car, and India immediately located her cell phone and dialed Grayson's office. He still wasn't there, but she left a message with his assistant. Then she dialed her sister. Patience picked up on the third ring. India was actually surprised that she was home, considering that it was still early in the evening. She was expecting to leave a message informing her sister that she would be stopping by in an hour.

"Hello," Patience answered.

"Hey, sis! What's going on?"

"Nothing much. To what do I owe the pleasure of this call?" Patience asked sarcastically.

"You can be so silly sometimes."

"Okay, now I know that you want a favor, because you're being too nice," Patience said and laughed.

"Please, why do you always think that I want something? Can't I just call to speak to my sister?"

"Well, for one, you really don't call me, and two, you only call when your sorry butt needs something; so what gives?"

"Girl, I'm on my way over. I've got drama in my life," India said.

"Is everything alright?" Patience asked, her tone increasing with an octave of concern.

"Yeah, everything is fine. I'm just tired. I'm bringing Sierra by for a few days. Is that okay with you?"

"That's fine, but please be warned. My two darlings have the chicken pox. I don't believe that it's in the active stage anymore because they've been home for four days now and, of course, they contracted it almost a week ago. They stopped itching, so that's a good sign."

India had to think long and hard as to whether she still wanted to bring Sierra to her sister's place. She had backed out of her driveway, but she was still parked in front of her house.

"Are you still there?" Patience inquired.

"Yeah, I'm here."

"India, I had to tell you. I know how you are when it comes to Sierra, and I don't want you blaming me if she gets chicken pox."

"Ahh, decisions, decisions. To hell with it! I'm on my way over. I'll see you in about an hour. I hope the traffic isn't bad."

"Keep dreaming. It's now the height of rush hour."

"Whatever happened to think happy thoughts?"

"I had two children. That's what happened to happy thoughts," Patience responded.

One hour, twenty minutes and a snoring Sierra later, India pulled up into her sister's driveway. When she turned off the ignition, Sierra woke up. Once she was familiar with her surroundings, Sierra hastily unbuckled her seat belt and attempted to open the door, but the child safety lock was on.

Little John and Veronica came bursting out of the front door and ran up to the car door. Little John began pounding on the side door, and India immediately lowered the window to tell him to stop. Patience came out of the house in her tennis shoes and sorority sweats. Her hair seemed to be growing out of the short natural do that she normally had.

"Little John, stop that. What is wrong with you? You know better than that!" Patience scowled.

Patience walked around to the driver's side and greeted India with a big hug. Then she hugged Sierra.

"How is my little cutie?" Patience asked.

"I'm fine, Auntie. Guess what?"

"What?"

"There was a gas leak in my school today, and I don't have school for the rest of the week."

"Is that right? Is everyone in your school okay?"

"Yes, I think so, but the school is kind of stinky," Sierra said, fanning her hand in front of her nose

"Is that so? Well I'm glad that you're here with us now. Are you hungry?"

"No, we ate before we came."

"Okay," Patience said, turning her attention back to India. "So, I saw my famous brother-in-law on the news this afternoon."

Why did she have to go and say that? India thought. *Damn.*

"See, Mommy! I told you that Daddy is famous."

India was tired of this argument and decided to leave it alone.

"You all go into the house and find something constructive to do," India advised.

India grabbed Sierra's travel pulley and followed Patience into the house.

Patience instructed the kids to go into the family room to read, play with the building blocks or watch an educational tape. Either way, they were told not to disturb the adults unless it was a dire emergency. Ten minutes later, Veronica had an emergency. She had to have something to drink because her mouth was dry from yelling at her brother to stop hitting them. Less than twenty minutes later, Sierra had an emergency. Little John didn't want to watch anything that they wanted to watch and then they all had to go to the bathroom.

When the kids finally settled down, Patience brewed some specialty French vanilla coffee and added a little creamer. She and India sipped on the coffee for a good five minutes without exchanging a word. The coffee was so good it deserved a moment of silence.

"So, tell me about the drama going on in your life," Patience said.

"Where do I start?"

"The beginning is usually a good place," Patience said, trying to break the tension that filled the room.

"You are such a wise-ass. Anyway, I had some things going on at work, which almost caused me to have a panic attack. That's almost resolved, but pretty much I had to hire a new team. Linda decided to leave and, in the process, took my editorial assistant as well. Girl, I've been having headache after headache. That crisis lasted too long and my ass was almost hung out to dry over that because when Linda left she purposely hid the lead stories from me. The damn editor-in-chief had to call her on my behalf."

"Why didn't you call her yourself? I thought that Linda was your girl."

"Yeah, she was up until she left. Then she flipped out on me. The other thing is that Grayson and I have been having problems. He's been drinking, and I told him about it and well…"

"What happened? He didn't hit you again, did he?"

"No. Why do you always think that he's hitting me? It's not that bad and, to be honest with you, it really doesn't happen that often."

"It doesn't happen that often? What will it take for you to wake up? It shouldn't happen at all. Jonathan has never, ever raised a hand to me and, if he did, he'd either be dead or he'd have two less limbs. I'm here to tell you I love him more than the sun shines, but I love myself even more."

"You're making a big thing out of nothing. He's raised his hands to me a few times and that's it. No harm, no foul."

Patience's expression screamed, "God, please help this child."

"So let me ask you, do you feel that you deserved to be hit?"

"No, it's not that I feel like I deserved to be hit, but at the same time, I understand that sometimes he's going through some things.

He apologizes, and I know that he loves me."

"Right, so that makes it all better, huh? You really need to listen to yourself and realize that you are not a child. Our own parents stopped hitting us when we were ten or eleven. I don't even hit my bad-ass children unless they really get out of hand, so what makes it okay for this grown-ass man to be hitting on his wife? You don't even have to answer that right now. You can just think on it!"

"Patience, there's nothing to think about."

"If you say so, but one day you're going to wake up and realize that there's a better way to live."

"I'll just take your word for it," India said, blowing her sister off. "Then, I get a call from Sierra's school, and I have to haul ass to go pick her up in the middle of my already hectic workday and when I get home, what do I see? Grayson on television and he didn't even tell me about the case."

"What? How can he not tell you something as big as that? Damn, everybody knows that slutty little rapper with her vile lyrics. I try my best to censor what Little John and Veronica listen to, but when they're not around me, it's out of my control. I heard them singing some of the lyrics to one of her songs the other day. I had to ask them whose song it was and where they heard it. I just don't know anymore, but this world is going to hell in a hand basket."

"I swear to you I better not ever hear Sierra repeating those lewd lyrics. I will spank that bottom until it turns raw. I do not play that crap."

"I don't understand why Grayson wouldn't tell you that he was representing X-Tasy. What's going on with that?"

"Well, when I get home, I have to deal with that. On my way over here, I left him a message on his cell phone and a message with his assistant at work. I told his ass that I was appalled that he would leave me in the dark. Can you imagine, there I was sitting in the kitchen eating my dinner with Sierra and Lenora when, all of a sudden, my daughter begins pulling my clothes to get my attention because she sees her daddy on television.

"I've got to tell you that that is some real messed-up shit. I called your job earlier to tell you the same thing, but you had already left. You must have been on your way to pick up Sierra."

"Probably."

"Well, when you get home, try your best to be civil. Maybe he has a good reason for not telling you, or maybe he's been so busy, like you said, lately that it slipped his mind."

"I don't know, and I refuse to assume anything," India said, shrugging.

"I hear you. Oh, guess what the hell happened at Sandy and Bedford's party." Patience rubbed her hands briskly together like two wooden sticks about to start a fire.

"You mean besides Grayson getting disgustingly inebriated?"

"That was nothing compared to what I'm about to tell you. If that were it, then I'd have nothing to tell you."

"Well, don't hold back, girl, share."

"Okay, so Mr. Bedford goes out of his way to pull the party of the century together for our cousin and his wife, right? He contacts us out of the blue about how he wants to make Sandy happy by bringing her family in and celebrating their anniversary at *Pájo Soul*. Now that's fine and dandy, right? So he flies in Mama Mavis, Robby and his wife. He pays full price, even though we give him a nice discount since he's family and all. He gives the best speech I've ever heard a man recite to a woman in public. The damn man almost had me crying, and come to find out he ain't shit!"

"Stop it, Patience. What the heck happened?"

"You are not ready for this."

"Lay it on me. You already set me up."

"This black man had sex with my hostess Je'Nae."

India gave Patience a little shove throwing Patience off balance in her chair.

Patience held up her right hand in the air.

"You know that I would not lie to you. Especially about something like this."

"I know you're telling me the truth, but I can't believe it. Not the same man who was fawning all over Sandy like she was the next best thing to sliced bread. Damn, that is hard to believe. I need a little drink. Gracious me, if you can't trust a man like that, who can you trust?"

"Listen, don't get me started. I know Jonathan would never do something as sleazy as that. I know that he would never cheat on me, for that matter."

"Damn," India said, getting up and walking over to the wine rack to select a bottle.

"Would you like some?" India asked, bringing the bottle over to the table.

"No, I'm fine. You know that alcohol makes me sleepy, and I'm going to need my energy to stay up with those kids tonight."

"I know that's right. So, how did you find out? I know that Je'Nae didn't tell you."

"Of course not. Jonathan walked in on them in our office. Now that is some bold stuff right there. They had the audacity to get busy in our office. I had to sanitize that place before going back into that room. I was so disgusted."

"Girl, I know you and Jonathan have had some play in that room, so don't even trip."

"That may be so, but it's our office and not the staff's. That office is and always has been off limits to all of our employees."

"You mean was," India said, laughing.

"I'm glad that you find this funny," Patience said, refusing to crack a smile. "This is really serious."

"I know. So what are you going to do?"

"I've tried calling Sandy on numerous occasions. I've left messages on their answering machine and with Bedford, but I'm sure he's not going to let Sandy know that I called."

"Why not? Do you think that he knows? Does he know that Jonathan caught him?"

"Jonathan said that he left as soon as he saw what was happening, but that Je'Nae caught a glimpse of him. Either way, he knows that I know."

"Why don't you call her at the job? Don't you have that number?"

"If I did, I sure as heck can't seem to find it now. When you want something you can't find it and when you no longer need the mess, it's right up in your face."

"Preach the truth, sister. Anyway, I know that you have a plan B, right?"

"I have a little something up my sleeve. Just wait and be patient."

"You have to bring me in on this one, because I don't want to miss out on all of the fun."

"Don't worry. I'll save you a seat front row and center."

"Damn, I know this is going to be good!"

17
One-Night Stand

edford was getting tired of the close calls. He was constantly looking over his shoulder because he knew that Patience was after him, and he didn't know how much longer he would be able to stall her. He knew that it was only a matter of time. Bedford didn't know how he was going to explain himself, and his previous act with Keyanna only made matters worse. If that incident had never taken place, then he could deny anything that Jonathan or Patience reported. Bedford could have easily said it was simply a case of mistaken identity. After all, it was late and it was plausible that Jonathan had had one drink too many, but his credibility at this point was shot to hell.

Bedford and Sandy's counseling sessions were now down to once a month. During their last visit, the therapist had mentioned that she felt Sandy and Bedford had accomplished a lot over the past couple of months. She also said that soon they would no longer need to return. Bedford was putting up a good front at the doctor's office, for his benefit as well as Sandy's. He didn't want to lose her. Bedford had never felt a love as deep as he did for Sandy. She was different from any other woman that he'd ever been with. Even though his business was flourishing when they first met, she had offered him the insight to help him go farther. Sandy was full of drive, ambition, brains, and constantly doted on him with attention, love and affection. Most importantly, she allowed him to be the man in the relationship. This was something that Felice had refused to do when they were married. Felice had to be the one in control and liked being the boss of all things. Sandy's big country heart and soft-spoken manner placed her summits above Felice. Sandy had all of that to offer, and the fact that she was beautiful only magnified his desire for her. Bedford realized that all of their problems were not solved, but they had made a lot of headway. It was the first time that he had openly expressed his feelings about his nephew Shiloh's murder. He didn't realize how much his actions and behavior affected Sandy. After Shiloh's death, he spent a lot of time in his study alone, a place that he never allowed anyone to enter, not even Sandy. He was also spending more time at work, and when he came home, he went directly to bed. Their weekend excursions became almost non-existent, and the affection with which he had once showered his wife slowly dwindled. None of this was done intentionally. That was why he had gone out of his way to make their anniversary so special. Shiloh was like the son that Bedford never had.

When Shiloh's father passed away, Bedford stepped in and assumed the role. He made sure that Shiloh had everything that he needed to become a man. Bedford reinforced the importance of education and taught him work ethics. Shiloh had just graduated from college and was enjoying his last summer of freedom. He was due to begin working at Jackson and Jackson two weeks before his demise. Shiloh was going to be his new junior account executive. Bedford had dreams of Shiloh eventually becoming a partner, and when he retired, Shiloh would be his successor; but this would never be. Bedford lost a part of himself when Shiloh died. Shiloh had helped to bring out the kid in him, and when his nephew departed the earth, that kid did too. Not having Shiloh in his life increased his need to have a child of his own, but he knew that Sandy had big plans for her career. The last thing he wanted to do was appear selfish and unsupportive. This was why, prior to therapy, he had never broached the subject.

He was still sleeping with Felice and, at times, he still ached to be with Keyanna. She was a good lay, and she had a body that could make him forget the day of the week. She practically lived in the gym, so her body was firm, but soft in all the right places. Keyanna had a sweet ass that felt like a pillow cushion and breasts that resembled ripe tangerines. They were the ripest breasts he had ever encountered, and when they were together, he nursed on them as if he were a newborn. She was a professional at everything she did sexually, including blowjobs. Keyanna was the first woman to make him cum in less than ten minutes by giving head. Keyanna was sexy, single and knew how to satisfy, and they had a good thing. But she got too greedy.

The evening he met Keyanna, he told her that he was married. From the very beginning, he never misled her as far as his relationship with Sandy was concerned. Sure, he blew smoke up her ass on occasion to make her feel special, but that was to be expected. Overall, Bedford thought that Keyanna could handle him on a sexual basis only, but he was wrong, and her actions had almost cost him his marriage. So, once again, he was on the prowl. He figured that once Sandy was pregnant, he would settle down and really become a family man. It was only a matter of time before he stopped his unfaithful ways. Sandy was beginning to be pretty open to different things sexually, so variety would no longer be an issue.

Another thing that bothered Bedford was his relationship with his sister, Isis. After his nephew died, their relationship became strained. It was partially his fault and half Sandy's. Sandy confided in his sister about his infidelity. Isis came to him to discuss his behavior, and he brushed her off. He told Isis that he was more than capable of handling his business, and he didn't want her meddling in his personal affairs. Isis knew that it was the same kind of conduct that had caused his first marriage to fail. Yet, here he was repeating the same mistakes again. His sister never really forgave their father for being unfaithful to their mother, so even though she loved her brother, he still disgusted her. The last remark she made to Bedford was that she was wiping her hands clean of him until he decided to turn his life around. Bedford and his sister had always been very close, and he was having a difficult time adjusting.

Bedford was lost in his thoughts when the front door slammed shut. The door to his office was slightly ajar, and the warm breeze swept across his face. It was so muggy outdoors that the air conditioner was set at sixty-five degrees. It was the first week in May, and the weather was in the high eighties, but the humidity was at a hundred percent. The light from Bedford's office shone through the crack of the door, so when Sandy entered the house, she greeted him and headed straight upstairs. Bedford ran out into the foyer area and called her to join him, but before she could turn around, the telephone rang. Sandy headed to the bedroom to get the handset and Bedford jolted back to his office in an attempt to intercept the call. He knew that Patience wasn't going to give up that easily and was probably trying to call his bluff about Sandy attending a meeting. Why did he keep getting himself into these situations? he thought, running for the phone. The other question he asked was why he continued to be so careless? He had common sense and, still, he found himself staring down the barrel of the gun. He was a simple man, all he really wanted was a little something on the side, no strings attached, but, at the moment, he had more twine than a five-string orchestra. Bedford knew that Sandy didn't deserve his constant infidelity, but he couldn't seem to help himself. He also knew that if she became knowledgeable about his one-night stand with the hostess at *Pájo Soul,* she would lose it, and he would more than likely lose her.

Bedford grabbed the receiver at the same time Sandy picked up. Instead of talking, he covered the phone with his hand and remained silent. It was a female voice and Bedford's heart felt like it was about to burst through his shirt. He felt beads of sweat forming on his forehead as well as under his arms. His Secret for women deodorant didn't seem to be doing the job, and it appeared that his secret was about to be told. After a few seconds, he heard the woman ask for Mrs. Jackson. When Bedford realized that it wasn't Patience, he quietly hung up the phone and heaved a sigh of relief.

18

"This Is Mrs. Jackson. How May I Help You?"

Sandy had had a long and hard day at work. The standardized test results came in and, to her surprise, the reading percentiles were up by seventeen percent, but they were still below average. She didn't really expect a miracle, and seventeen percent was more than she could have asked for. In comparison to the other city public schools, Daniel Hale Williams had fared quite well. Sandy was proud of her accomplishment, but still she expected more from her students. An increase of seventeen percent meant that fifty-two percent of the student population had above-level reading averages. However, she knew that if she could instill pride and a passion for learning in her children, they could reach even greater heights. Her dream was always to achieve the impossible. Sandy knew that when she took the position of vice principal, no one believed that she would soar the way she had. Sure, she was qualified for the position and since the city already had so many discrimination suits, the Board of Education felt obligated to give her the job. She was no fool and wasn't about to think that she had been given the position out of pity. Sandy knew that she was there on merit and merit alone.

Three years earlier, when Sandy first arrived at Daniel Hale Williams public school, the coursework offered to the children was in dire straits. The school lacked organization, and the teachers appeared to be disinterested in the students. It pained Sandy to witness other teachers treating the pupils with such disregard. It was unheard of to behave that way in the South. Sandy was under the impression that the majority of the teachers were only there to collect a paycheck. She took the initiative of pulling together several projects revolving around literacy and mathematics. She also started an after-school program, which catered to students who needed tutoring, or simply kept them off the streets. Sandy's dedication was infallible, and she gave up a lot of personal time to ensure that the program was successful. As a result, her efforts and valor did not go unrecognized and several other schools in her district were following suit.

Sandy had held several meetings with her staff. She met with each teacher individually to share the success and to congratulate him for a job well-done. Sandy was big on positive reinforcement and felt that if she acknowledged her people for their accomplishments, they would continue to keep up the good work. Some would even go the extra mile. She had a minor disagreement with one of her teachers. Sandy was accused of showing favoritism to certain teachers. Sandy laughed at the allegation, simply out of surprise. The teacher took great offense and carried the issue to the principal. Sandy didn't know whether to laugh or to cry, because she gave every teacher the opportunity to be creative. Every teacher was required to submit a syllabus along with his objectives for the term. Sandy reviewed each one thoroughly to ensure effectiveness and need. Some of the teachers had to go back and revise their curriculum, but that was to be expected. After all, not everyone was capable of turning in good work. It was just like giving a class of pupils a science project. The hard-working students would dissect an animal, build robots and solar systems, while the lazier individuals would make volcanoes. And everyone knew that the volcano was the easiest thing to make.

Unfortunately, this was what this particular teacher handed in, half-assed work. Sandy rejected it, and he was infuriated. The principal reprimanded Sandy for her behavior and apologized to the teacher, which had made Sandy feel like crap. Her principal's action only served to undermine Sandy's authority, which could jeopardize the relationship and level of respect that she had worked so hard to build with her staff. It was a well-known fact that Sandy and the principal did not get along, but this exploit only validated that sentiment.

Sandy was livid, but took her beating like a champ. She hated when people disliked her for no particular reason and from the moment she accepted the job as vice principal, her relationship with the principal had turned volatile. Her principal was an older white woman who was intimidated by Sandy. The school had been doing poorly for years, and along came Sandy on her big black horse trotting to save the day. Sandy's drive and determination never went unnoticed, especially by the principal, and it was fine to incorporate these things when Sandy was just a teacher, but once she applied for the vice principal position, the principal had felt threatened. It was only a matter of time before Sandy came after her job.

Lately, Sandy was feeling a little fatigued. She didn't know if it was due to the amount of work that she was putting in or what. There were a lot of things on her mind. Her mother's health was failing, and she couldn't be there to support her the way that she wanted to be. Robby and Nettie told her not to worry about anything, because they were there to help out. But it just wasn't the same. Sandy didn't know what she'd do if something happened to her mother. Mama Mavis was her rock, and she gave Sandy the strength and courage whenever she felt like giving up. Diabetes was nothing to play around with, and, apparently, her mother had been neglecting her health for some time, because now she was on a strict diet and had to go in twice a week for dialysis.

The other thing on her mind was Bedford. Although she felt that she could trust him again, something just didn't feel right. Things seemed to be a little strained between them. She was taking the advice of their therapist and trying to be more attentive to Bedford, but it had been hard to maintain that over the last two to three weeks. Sandy apologized to Bedford, and he said he understood—and it may have just been her imagination—but he seemed to be keeping to himself lately. She noticed that he spent more time than usual in his study, and she simply let him be. Sandy was in no condition to debate. She was too worn out from her day to even think about a long, drawn-out discussion. The most important thing to her was that he was home, so she had no reason to distrust him.

Sandy had plans for getting away for a while once the summer break came into session. She wanted to spend two weeks with her mother and a week in Atlanta with Wanita. She felt like she was abandoning her best friend in her time of need. She had forgotten to call her back the other day, and when Sandy got home, there were messages from Wanita and Patience on the machine. Sandy called Patience first, but the machine came on and she hung up. Then she called Wanita and they spoke for a little more than half an hour, but Sandy was so exhausted from that she really wasn't into the conversation. Wanita told her about something that William had done that was downright appalling. Apparently, Wanita's mother called and expressed that she wanted to pay them a visit, and he'd discouraged her by saying that Wanita was too busy helping out with the PAAMA's annual gala, and once that was done, they had plans to go on vacation. When Wanita's mother finally got in touch with her, she cried to her daughter and said, "Now that you have money and you're comfortable, you can't find time to spend with your mother." Wanita had never thought or even made that remark, and the fact that William took it upon himself to speak on her behalf enraged her. William was taking over every detail in her life, and Wanita didn't know what to do. When Sandy lived in Atlanta, William had been as sweet as pie, but the man that Wanita described over the phone was a nightmare.

Sandy answered the phone, a bit distracted.

"May I ask who's calling?"

"Yes, this is nurse Diana from the doctor's office."

"Oh, yes. I'm sorry for sounding so annoyed. I thought that you were a salesperson," Sandy said apologetically. "This is Mrs. Jackson. How may I help you?"

"Well, we've left a couple of messages and had been trying to get in touch with you for the past couple of days. Anyway, we have the results of your last visit. What day and time is good for you to come in?"

"Can you hold on a moment?" Sandy asked as she hung her purse on the doorknob. She kicked off her shoes and neatly placed them in the closet and then retrieved the day timer from her bedside table. "Today is Tuesday the eighteenth right?

"Yes, that's correct. We have several openings available next week.

I can tell you the times and you can let me know if any of them work for you."

"That's fine. Go ahead."

"Okay. We have availability at nine A.M. on May the twenty-fourth. Then we have another at four P.M. on the same day. The next opening in on the twenty-fifth at twelve o'clock, and last we have something on Thursday the twenty-seventh at two-thirty. Are you able to squeeze any of these into your schedule?"

"Yeah, I can make the Thursday appointment."

"Great. I'll pencil you in. Oh, by the way, your regular physician will not be in that day. Do you mind?"

"That's fine. I'm only coming in for results."

"Okay, then. You're scheduled to see Dr. Espinosa next week."

"Thank you, nurse Diana."

"You're welcome, and we'll see you next week."

Sandy hung up the phone and flopped onto the bed. She was too tired to remove her clothing. She was even too weary to go back downstairs to make her tea. Her body felt drained, and all she could do was curl up. Moments later, she felt a set of strong hands kneading her back. She stretched her body out and lay on her stomach. Bedford massaged all of the tension in her upper and lower back. He proceeded to remove her skirt and slowly slipped her stockings over her plump bottom. He rubbed her body in a gentle and sensual manner, and throughout the entire time, they didn't utter a word. She was grateful that he respected her need for quiet time.

Sandy knew where this was leading and wanted to tell Bedford not to get his expectations up because she was too exhausted to reciprocate any kind of loving. Bedford's hands continued to work their magic. He worked his way down to her feet and then returned to her midsection. He took extra care and time as he rubbed her thighs. Sandy was slightly aroused and hoped that Bedford wouldn't continue his little exploration.

Bedford had large, soft and firm hands. Slowly, he traced the curves of her silhouette. Sandy's body began to tingle and she responded with a shiver. Bedford immediately noticed the change and took advantage by rolling Sandy onto her back. He placed tasty kisses along her neckline. Sandy was turned on, but she felt lifeless and didn't want to do any work.

"Baby, I need you right now," Bedford said.

"Bedford, I'm really tired and…"

"Shh, shh, shh…don't say a word."

Bedford continued to work his magic just the way Sandy liked. She tried hard to appear uninterested with the hopes that he would discontinue his actions, to no avail. Without realizing it, she was making soft purring sounds of satisfaction. No wonder he wouldn't stop.

Bedford eased up from the bed and began taking off his clothes. Sandy didn't want to see his beautiful body. She wanted to sleep. Her day was beyond miserable and all she asked for was a little rest and relaxation. This wasn't such a terrible request, was it? Well, maybe this was exactly what she needed to bring her out of that funk that she was in earlier. The sight of Bedford's smooth, bare chest caused Sandy's heart to pulsate faster; her dark mood receded. Sandy loved to feast on Bedford's chest. Loved the sight of his coffee colored nipples and the thin strands of hair that circled them. She also loved the pleasure that it brought to Bedford when she tended to his areas of pleasure.

The mere thought of sucking Bedford aroused her even more. Her nipples began to ripen under Bedford's brilliant gaze. She was sure that Bedford knew what he was doing as he continued to strip. When his pants dropped, his manhood stood at full salute.

Without saying a word, Bedford pulled her legs to the edge of the bed, placed a pillow under her midsection and dipped his tongue into the pool and tested the waters. Once he became acclimated, his tongue did a few laps around the entire perimeter. Sandy writhed in pleasure. Exactly ten minutes later, Sandy began to inch away, trying to avoid the inevitable climax that was determined to press on with or without her permission. Bedford stayed with her for the long haul and, when she came, she clamped him tightly in a headlock with her thighs. The pent-up sadness and stress that she endured that day were no longer present. Instead they were replaced with satisfaction and joy.

When she finally released Bedford from her killerlike kung-fu grip, he wasted no time in filling her with Duro. He took his time as he stroked her gently, but he knew that she would quickly bore from this.

Sandy liked it faster and a little harder, which he had no problem fulfilling. Bedford began to increase his tempo and Sandy responded by interlocking her legs with his. She buried her head in his chest and nibbled on his nipple, kissing, sucking and licking. The dampness of her tongue on his chest made him thrust harder. He continued this way for another twenty minutes, changing positions as necessary. The sweat from his brow dripped into Sandy's hair and onto her forehead. As the sun began to retreat into the lavender sky, Sandy caught a shadowy glimpse of the chair that accompanied her vanity. She drew his attention to the chair and, within seconds, he was seated, allowing her to take full control of the situation. Sandy positioned her body, straddled Duro like a professional jockey, clipped her heels into his shins and rode him the way he liked it. She jumped a few hurdles knowing that this would be a short race. Less than five minutes later, Bedford was bellowing out an all-too-familiar tune, bringing a smile to Sandy's face.

19

"AIN'T-NOBODY-HELPING-YOU! THE-LORD, NOBODY!"

ndia and Patience sat and talked until Jonathan came home from work. It wasn't until Jonathan arrived that India realized that it was in the wee hours, and she had to go home to prepare for work the next morning.

The ride back took less than forty-five minutes and was uneventful as the roads were clear. India pulled into her driveway and saw that most of the lights were still on in the house. Grayson was known to pull long hours, but he never worked past midnight because he always said that he couldn't be at his best if he didn't get at least seven good hours of rest. India was drained from the long day at work and then having to rush to Sierra's school and driving to Baltimore and back. She was going to have a fitful sleep. She wanted to confront Grayson about his new high-profile case, but that would have to simply wait until the next day.

India opened the door and, for a quick second, she was thrown off balance. She could taste blood inside her mouth. Her vision was temporarily blurred. The hit caught her below her eye and her nose, making her nose, sting and her eyes water. She steadied herself and began to panic. She must have walked in while someone was burglarizing her house. The first thing she thought about was it was a good thing that Sierra wasn't with her. Then she thought, what if this person tried to kill her? Was Grayson okay? Her child couldn't grow up to be an orphan.

India fell to her knees and dropped her purse on the ground beside her. She closed her eyes and was about to beg for mercy. Then she heard Grayson's voice, and she quickly opened her eyes. Grayson grabbed India caveman style by the hair and yanked her into the living room. India stumbled behind him more concerned about losing a patch of hair than the beating she was about to receive. He moved so fast that India lost one of her mule sandals and had to hobble to maintain his speed. Her neck snapped back and a shooting pain ran from the base of her collar to her temples. India couldn't believe this was happening to her. This was unreal.

"Grayson, what are you doing?" India bawled. She was breathing heavily and trying to figure out what she had done this time to make him behave this way.

Grayson released her hair and shoved her, and India collapsed on the couch. He began to take off his belt, and India realized what he was about to do. In that split second, she attempted to run, but Grayson was one step ahead of her and extended his foot. India stumbled, but didn't fall. She regained her balance and sprinted toward the steps. India ran and, through peripheral vision, she spied Grayson on her tail. She never fully turned around because it would only slow her down. When she got to the landing, she jumped the steps two and three at a time.

India had never seen Grayson this crazed before. Her brain went from zero to sixty miles per hour in less than five seconds. She was still trying to guess what was causing him to react this way.

A few months back, he knocked her around a bit because she tried to manipulate him into cutting back on some of his extracurricular activities. She accused him of abandoning the family for the PAAMA. India knew this wasn't true, but she wanted him to spend more time with both her and Sierra. The only time he spent with Sierra was when he came home and put her to bed. By then he barely had time for her because he was worn out from his day at work. In hindsight, India knew that she should have approached him in a civil manner and expressed her feelings better. The fact was that Grayson valued his family too much and would never abandon them. India knew that he loved them unconditionally, and she could see the hurt in his eyes when she made those false accusations against him.

India could see freedom as she climbed the last of the two stairs that would lead her to the clearing and then into their bedroom. This, time around she wasn't quite as lucky. Grayson grabbed one of her ankles, and she fell, causing her breasts to be crushed flat against one of the steps. She managed to grab the handrail in time so that her face didn't hit the step, which might have caused her to chip or possibly lose a tooth.

Grayson was angry, and India could see it all over his face. She could see the veins straining in his neck. He was breathing heavily from chasing her, as well as from being upset. He didn't have on his dress shirt, but he wore his wife-beater undershirt and his slacks. Her running away from him only heightened the situation. If only she had stayed put.

Grayson rolled the thick brown leather belt around his hand so he could better grasp it, and he raised the belted hand to strike her.

India shrieked loudly and begged him not to. She wanted to know what she had done wrong and vowed she wouldn't do it again. India promised and pleaded as he grabbed her legs to drag her back down the steps.

When they arrived at the bottom of the landing India curled into a fetal position, her arms raised to protect her head. Her lithe body heaved with every breath she took, her sobs loud and uncontrollable.

Grayson pierced India with a look of disgust and disdain. He raised his belted right hand, and with every blow that connected with India's pale flesh, he spoke. "DON'T-YOU-EVER-CALL-MY-JOB-AND-LEAVE-ME-BULLSHIT-MESSAGES-LIKE-THAT-AGAIN. ARE-YOU-OUT-OF-YOUR-FUCKING-MIND? HUH, ANSWER ME. ANSWER ME, I SAID."

India writhed from both pain and fear. She wanted to answer, but she knew that wouldn't stop Grayson's diatribe. She knew that if she uttered even the slightest word that it would provoke him even further. It didn't make sense to say anything in her defense. She was damned if she did and damned if she didn't. In all of the years that they had been together, this had to be the worse attack yet. The last time they had gotten into a dispute, he slapped her around a bit and, when she attempted to cover her face, he punched her in the eye. Grayson didn't hit her hard, but she bruised so easily that she had to stay at home a few days to recuperate. No one had to know about the small altercation, and she was fine until Patience decided to pay her a surprise visit. Now, without even having to view herself in the mirror, India knew that she was definitely going to have to take the remainder of the week off. Her hands were sore from the grain and sharp edge of the belt lashing against her skin. Her back was bruised and welted from where the belt tore through her silk blouse and onto her bare flesh, and her legs stung with blood blisters.

"Lord, please help me," India sobbed. "Please make him stop."

"AIN'T-NOBODY-HELPING-YOU! THE-LORD, NOBODY!"

"Grayson, please stop. I'm sorry. I'm *sooo* sorry," India said, choking on the tears.

Grayson continued, and India decided to simply take the beating quietly, because the more she begged the worse he dealt the blows.

If India knew that this was going to happen, she would never have made that call. It wasn't as if the message that she left with his assistant earlier was bad. She merely voiced how disconcerted it made her feel to find out about her husband's new case via the media. Her exact words were, "Please tell my husband, Grayson, that I didn't appreciate finding out about his new trial with that gangsta rapper X-Tasy on television. When he returns, let him know that I have a few choice words for him later on this evening."

India was only being facetious when she mentioned the part about "a few choice words," and thought that Grayson would have been able to pick up on that, but evidently he hadn't. He felt that India was trying to make him look like a weakling in front of his office help. Grayson had an image to uphold, and he didn't like being made to look like a mockery. India knew that there were lines that she was never to cross. Grayson was the man of the house. There was to be no lip from her or Sierra. Grayson made the major household decisions, but he always consulted with India before moving forward. In short, Grayson was the boss, and he ran the show. He was a very important man and highly respected in their community. India's true job was to help Grayson maintain his image, take care of the family and be the perfect wife and mother. India took delight in doing all those things, because she wanted a take-charge kind of man. Grayson was that and more to her. He held the family down financially. If India decided the next day that she was tired of the rubbish at the magazine, she could quit with confidence. She knew that Grayson would always take care of their family, unlike her father. Grayson wasn't a weakling and would never fall prey to drugs. He had too much to lose to ever be that foolish.

"BITCH-DON'T-YOU-EVER-EMBARRASS-ME-AGAIN. DO-YOU-HEAR-ME? I-WILL-FUCKING-HURT-YOU!"

India heard the words and saw the belt as it flailed into the air and back down onto her, but she could no longer feel anything because her body was beginning to numb.

The beating seemed to be slowing down. India stole a quick look, and Grayson appeared tired, but she wasn't going to get her hopes up. His brow was crowned with sweat as he used the back of his free hand to wipe it away.

Grayson took a break and hovered above India. He knelt down beside her and spoke into the open crevice between her arm and her face. She could feel his hot breath burn into the welted areas of her skin.

"India, why do you make me do this shit to you? What the fuck is wrong with you? Huh? I just don't understand why you choose to cause me so much distress. Don't I do everything in this house?" Grayson asked.

India peeked through the space of her arm and nodded. "Yes," she responded in case he didn't see her head move.

"Don't I provide you with the finest of everything?"

"Yes."

"You know that I love you, right?"

"Yes."

"You know that you and Sierra are my world, and I will always do everything in my power to make things right for us, right?"

"Yes," India replied. She desperately wanted to unfold from her fetal position. Her body ached. From what she could see, her arms were badly discolored. Her light complexion made it possible to see the veins protruding alongside her bruises. She favored a cracked porcelain baby doll, but felt more like a shattered vessel.

"Then, why do you always bring me down to this? This is the type of shit that I'm talking about; you like to show out for no reason. I mean, you know that I would have told you about the case. You can't call my job and leave crazy messages like that. You know how they are at my firm. You know that I'm trying to make senior partner. So, why?"

India wanted to tell him that she hadn't meant anything by her message. Yes, she was upset, but she would have gotten over it. In another week, his trial would already be old news. What India really thought was that Grayson had withheld the information because he probably thought that she wanted the inside scoop for a story in *Shades*. Though she would have liked being privy to the case, she understood that it was information that couldn't be released because it could jeopardize X-Tasy. At the same time, Grayson could have mentioned it to her and at least allowed the magazine to contact X-Tasy for an exclusive interview. *Shades* had a good reputation when it came to interviewing celebrities about their problems. X-Tasy's case was high profile, and the editors wouldn't make her self-incriminate herself because, in the long run, it would reflect poorly on the magazine. If similar situations arose, and *Shades* wanted the opportunity to interview other celebrities in similar predicaments, the magazine's character would be questionable, thus making people hesitant to interface with the magazine. Lifestyle publications were becoming a dime a dozen, and everyone on the staff knew that *Shades* was in the game for the long haul.

"Grayson, I'm sorry," India said. She remained in the fetal position with her arms covering her face for fear that he wasn't quite done.

"Are you really sorry? Because seeing you like this really hurts me. Do you understand that?"

"Yes."

"Come here, let me wipe the tears from your face," Grayson said, extending his arms out to India.

Grayson gently pulled India into his arms, wiped her face and cradled her.

India sidled deeper into his arms. This is how it was supposed to be, India thought. Grayson stroked her hair and caressed her face. For once, it was left untouched, and for that India was grateful.

"Now, let me help you up. I want you to go clean yourself up."

India's body ached from head to toe when she woke up the next morning. The sheets beside her were crumpled and there was a hand-written note on Grayson's pillow. India reached over to retrieve it and saw that all of her wounds and bruises were cleaned with iodine and dressed. She had gauze in some areas and Band-Aids in others. She didn't even remember Grayson doing this for her.

India's movements were as slow as a snail. When her arm finally reached its destination, she didn't even bother to grab the note. She was too tired.

India was due in to work at 9:30 and it was already a quarter to ten. She propped her body so she could call her office. There was no way she was making an appearance at work for the remainder of the week. Her face may have been unaffected, but the rest of her body was a mess. It was too warm outside for her to wear long sleeves and it would look too conspicuous.

India was glad that Sierra was staying at her sister's house until the next day, which would give her time to recover. The bruises wouldn't look as gruesome the second day. At least that was what India hoped.

India had the number to her job programmed on speed dial and her line was answered on the second ring.

"Good morning, *Shades* magazine. India McCall's office. This is Nashelle, how may I help you?"

India liked this new woman, Nashelle. She was just what the doctor ordered after having gone through three nightmare assistants over the past couple of months. India admired her professionalism over the phone, her ability to multitask and think quick on her feet. The job didn't require a brain surgeon, just someone with basic office skills and common sense. India didn't think that it was a lot to ask for, but apparently it was. Nashelle had come on board three weeks ago and it had made such a difference in India's world. Prior to her arrival, things were, to say the least, chaotic, but Nashelle helped India out tremendously. She had great organizational skills and was making an excellent apprentice. India was thinking about offering her the job, but she'd wait out the ninety-day probation before jumping the gun. Ninety days would help give her time to see if Nashelle was the real thing or a fraud.

"Good morning, Nashelle. This is India."

"Oh, hi India. Are you running a little late?"

India cleared her throat and tried to make her voice sound groggy.

"Actually, no; I'm not feeling well this morning. I have a sore throat, and I woke up with a major headache. I won't be coming in this morning."

"Yeah, you don't sound too good. Are you coming down with a cold?"

"It could be either that or the flu. You know how this weather keeps changing. It goes from hot to cold and back again. I don't think that I was dressed appropriately yesterday. It was warm, but I had my chest exposed, and it got really chilly last night, and I was hanging out with my sister pretty late."

"I'm sorry to hear that. Well, then your sister was able to get to you, because she called here yesterday, and you were already gone for the day."

"Right. There was an emergency at my daughter's school, and I had to run and pick her up. Anyway, please pass the message on that I won't be in today. If anyone needs me, they can either call or e-mail me. If Veronica Webb's publicist calls, please give her my home telephone number. I really need to speak to her about the cover story for the fall issue. You have my home number, right?"

"Yes, I do. It's right here in the Rolodex, but let me make sure that it's current," Nashelle said, and recited the number to India.

"Good, it looks like you have everything under control. My fax is also available, so if you would please send me the papers in the red Pendaflex folder on my desk. I was editing a story, and I want to complete it while I'm home."

"Okay, consider it done, and I hope you feel better."

"Thanks, and I'll call you if I need anything."

"Alright."

India struggled to get to her feet, but she was experiencing some fierce hunger pangs. She really didn't have much of an appetite, but she wanted to, at the very least, drink some tea to settle her stomach.

India's legs hurt with every step that she took. The heels of one of her feet hurt, because the belt had struck her there, and she could feel a sore on the back of her head.

As she passed the mirror in the hallway she was able to examine herself. Just as she suspected, her face didn't have any noticeable bruises, but her lip was split and a little swollen from the first blow that she'd received when she entered the house. Her hair was matted to one side of her face, and it looked like she had large dreadlocks. Her eyes were swollen from crying, and she had a lot of red marks and welts on her arms and back. India wanted to cry. She honestly didn't know how much longer she could put up with Grayson's abusive behavior. She loved and worshipped the ground that he walked on, but enough was enough. It had affected everything around them. India had five remaining sick days and, one week of vacation left for the year. Her job would be jeopardized if this continued, Sierra would be scarred if she were to ever witness one of Grayson's beating, and it didn't do much for India's self-esteem.

India had seen the Tina Turner movie, *What's Love Got to do With It?* but she would never dream of retaliating against Grayson. She didn't feel that her situation was as drastic as what had occurred between Ike and Tina. Grayson never beat her in front of friends or family. These attacks didn't transpire every day or every month. They were actually isolated incidents happening two or three times a year. Ike only used Tina because she was his bread and butter. Grayson didn't use India for the purposes of advancing himself. Ike was a womanizer; Grayson wasn't. As far as she knew, he had never cheated on her because that wasn't one of his traits. Grayson loved her and Sierra and that was what mattered.

India put a mug of water into the microwave and set it on "beverage." One minute and thirty seconds later, India had a mug of steaming hot water. She looked at her selection of teas and decided to go with the Celestial Seasonings Tension Tamer. She needed something that would make her relax and eventually put her to sleep. She put the tea bag into the hot water to let it steep. The phone rang, and India slowly walked over to the other side of the kitchen to answer it before the machine came on.

"Hello," India said. She went back to trying to sound sick just in case it was someone from her office.

"Hey, girl," Patience said excitedly. "What's up with you?"

India was relieved that it wasn't her boss or Nashelle needing something already.

"Nothing much. I'm just feeling a little under the weather so I decided to take the day off from work."

"Oh, I was wondering what happened. I called your office and they told me that you called in sick, but I know you ain't sick. You just probably got home late last night and your lazy behind was too tired to get up for work today."

"Yeah, something like that, but I am feeling a little under the weather. I'm just glad that Sierra is there with you. How's my baby doing?"

"That's just who I called you about, and don't worry. She's fine. The reason I'm calling is because Jonathan and I had planned to take the kids to Busch Gardens over the weekend, and I wanted to make sure that it was okay for us to take Sierra."

"Of course you can," India said, relieved that her daughter wouldn't have to come home and see her looking a mess.

Sierra had a tendency of climbing all over her mother, and India couldn't deal with that. The last thing she wanted was for Sierra to be playful and for her not to be able to enjoy her daughter's company.

"Girl, you are truly a blessing," India continued. "I have a lot of work that I need to cover, and this will give me time to do just that while you all are away. When are you planning on going?"

"The kids seem to be all better so we're leaving tomorrow afternoon. Our plan is to make a nice weekend of it with the kids and, of course, Little John and Veronica ran around talking about it to Sierra, and we want her to come, but I didn't know if you already had plans."

"None! You can have her," India joked.

"Well, then we need to stop by and pick up some casual clothes for her. I don't know what you were thinking, packing two dresses and penny loafer shoes for her. She needs sneakers, jeans and a few tops."

"No," India said, alarmed. She didn't need Patience seeing her. It was bad enough that Patience already had an idea that something wrong was going on. "Why don't you just let her wear something of Veronica's?"

"Are you sure, because I know how funny you are about her wearing other people's clothing. The last time she came home with a pair of Veronica's panties on, you had a fit."

"Patience, those were panties. Clothes are different."

"India, bullshit! It's not like I gave her a pair of my panties to put on. Veronica and Sierra are children, and there is no harm there. Anyway, I just wanted to make sure."

India thought about it, and she really didn't like Sierra wearing other people's clothes, but this was different. Veronica was her little cousin and she knew that Patience was clean.

"It's fine. She can borrow something from Veronica."

"Okay. Oh, but there's still one problem."

"What?" India asked.

"Veronica's foot is larger than your little petite princess. We may still need to come over there for a pair of tennis shoes for her."

India was worried that Patience would show up unexpectedly. She needed to think quickly in order to avoid a fiasco. There was no way she could deny any accusations this time when she looked the way that she did. India had to give her sister more credit and refused to insult her intelligence by telling her that she had fallen down the steps, or she was robbed on her way home. If she were really robbed, she would have called Patience.

"Why don't you just buy her a pair for me, and I'll reimburse you. Sierra is due for a new pair of sneakers anyway. The ones she has now look awful. I'm embarrassed that I haven't even thrown them away yet."

Patience was silent for a moment, which concerned India. She was trying her best not to sound panicked. However, Patience was simply trying to get the kids in check. India could hear her talking to them in a hushed voice.

"I'll see what I can do, because we have a lot to cover before we head out. But if I get to the mall, you won't have to worry."

"It would be greatly appreciated. Besides, since I took the day off, I want to try to go out and run some errands."

"I hear you. Well, okay. On our way back, we'll give you a call. It won't make sense to travel all the way to Baltimore when we have to pass through your neck of the woods from Virginia."

"That's fine. I'll speak to you on Sunday then," India said.

"On Sunday."

India hung up and took a deep breath. She took a seat at the breakfast table to regain her strength and thought, *There is a God.*

20
"Grow the 'F' Up!"

ays were turning into weeks and weeks were quickly changing into months and time was flying by. A couple of weeks passed since William had told Wanita that she could go ahead and make vacation plans. Wanita visited all of the local travel agencies and even searched the Web to find the right spot for her and William to relax and revitalize their marriage.

William reassured her and even asked Wanita where they were going. She tried to get him to volunteer some places that he found of interest, but he told her that it didn't matter. He never chose their destination. He always left that up to Wanita, but she felt that it would be nice to have his input every now and then. He was surely quick to share his expertise in every other aspect of their lives.

Wanita knew that Layla and Charles had just returned from a nice romantic getaway in St. Maarten and wanted to hear how it was first-hand, so she decided to pay them a visit. Layla could not recommend St. Maarten enough, but Layla never had a bad thing to say about any place to which she traveled. As long as it was tropical she was happy. Charles recommended that Wanita and William stay on the French side of the island, because the American side was very touristy.

Wanita agreed with Layla, because she, too, loved the warmth, the ocean and the beautiful array of flowers that came with visiting a tropical paradise. She was trying to narrow her decision down to Venezuela, Curaçao, St. Maarten or Bermuda. Over the years, she

and William had visited several places. They used to make at least two
trips a year together. They had gone to Jamaica, St. Croix, St. Thomas,
St. Lucia, Costa Rica, the Cayman Islands, Argentina, the Dominican
Republic, Belize, Spain and even Hong Kong, all of which were nice
places, but she definitely wanted to stick with vacationing on an island.

The only other person she knew who traveled as much as she liked
was Sandy. Before she and Sandy got married, they used to get a group
of friends together and take summer vacations. It was still pretty early
in the morning, at least for a Saturday, but Wanita was so anxious to get
something booked that she decided to call Sandy anyway.

The phone rang a few times before someone picked up.

"Hello," Sandy answered, in a sleep-filled voice.

"Hey, Sandy, it's me, Wanita."

"Hey, girl, how are you? Is everything all right?" Sandy asked,
coming to.

Wanita envisioned Sandy in her girly nightgown and her matching
silk scarf wrapped around her perfectly curled hair. She didn't know
how Sandy did it. Sandy had to be the only person that she knew who
went to bed and woke up looking like her head never touched the pillow.

"Yeah, everything is great. I'm sorry if I'm waking you up."

"No, don't worry about it. I truly apologize for not calling you back
the other day. I just got so caught up and…"

"Sandy, are you still there?"

"Yeah, I'm here. Bedford is just tripping out here next to me. He
was sound asleep, and now he's trying to find out who's on the other
end. Girl, hold the line for a moment."

Wanita could hear the conversation between Sandy and Bedford.

"Why do you care who is on the other line? It's not for you," Sandy
said.

"I just want to know, because someone called here the other day
for you, and I forgot to give you the message. I just wanted to know just
in case it was that same person," Bedford responded.

"Then, who called for me?"

"I don't remember, that's why I wanted to know to see if the name
rang a bell."

"Bedford, go back to sleep, okay? I'm going to take this call downstairs so you can rest. You are a complete fool when you wake up before your time."

Wanita heard Bedford mumble something else to Sandy, but it seemed as though Sandy walked out of the room and closed the door behind her without bothering to respond.

"Yeah, you still there, girl?" Sandy asked.

"I'm here. What was that all about?"

"Girl, I wish you could tell me. Lately, he has been acting real crazy. Every cotton-picking time the phone rings, he rushes to answer it. He gets all paranoid and stuff, but for the life of me, I can't figure out why. Anyway, that's neither here nor there, so what in the world has you up this early? Wait, let me guess. You're pregnant?"

"Please, I wish. If I were, I'd probably fly up there personally to tell you. It's really nothing quite that pressing or urgent. William and I are planning our next vacation, and I've narrowed our search down to Venezuela, Curaçao, St. Maarten and Bermuda."

"Ooh, all of those are nice places. Girl, you love yourself some Spanish-speaking countries."

"Yeah, I know. I also know that you've visited Venezuela, Bermuda and Curaçao. Layla and Charles went to St. Maarten a few weeks ago, and they loved it, but I wanted to get your opinion on the other places before I made my final decision."

"How are Layla, Charles and the kids anyway?"

"As good as can be expected. You know how they always are, all touchy feely and stuff. You have to wonder if they ever stop; and, if they keep it up, they'll end up with at least two more."

"Listen, if it works for them, who are we to tell them how to run their marriage? Besides, I have enough of my own issues to deal with," Sandy said.

"I hear you loud and clear on that one. So, back to the vacation planning"

"Why don't you and William sit down and decide together?"

"William is more concerned about work and his upcoming gala for the Professional African American Men Association. His plate is filled with extracurricular activities, so he just leaves the vacation planning to yours truly. That's where you come in. I need your help."

"Okay, so what do you want me to tell you?"

"Which place did you like the most? I mean you've been every-where, girl, and I know that you'll give me the skinny on the places to go and not to go."

"All of those places are a complete haze to me now. I visited them so long ago."

"Oh, girl, come on! You had to have at least one favorite out of all of the ones that I mentioned. At least one, and then I can narrow my selection to two places, and I'll play a game of eenie-meenie-minie-moe!"

"Wanita, you are truly insane. If I had to do one of those places again, it would probably be Bermuda. No make that Venezuela."

"Okay, why Venezuela over Bermuda?"

"Just take my word for it."

"I will, after all you are travel queen."

"And don't you forget it," Sandy boasted.

"So how is work?" Wanita asked.

"Girl, it's funny that you should ask. The other day I had to call the district superintendent on my principal," Sandy said.

"What? What made you do that?"

"Wanita, she undermined me in front of one of the staff members. Shortly after, I had a talk with her, but that went absolutely nowhere. So, I decided to go over head."

"Your principal is tripping that hard? I wonder why."

"I guess she feels threatened by me, and I don't know why. I'm a neophyte."

"Sandy, please. That woman sees your potential and knows that it's only a matter of time before you take her position. How old is she, fifty-five, sixty? They are looking for youngblood with new ideas to develop the minds of these bad-ass kids."

"Wanita you are so silly, but truthful. Since I've stepped in the reading scores have improved significantly. I must say that I love my job and I'm damn good at it. Anyway, the meeting was to my advantage and Ms. Crabtree lost that battle."

"Is that her real name?" Wanita asked, laughing.

"No, but it's fitting."

"And you call me silly."

"Because you are. Bedford, stop! Why don't you go back to bed?"

"I see sleepyhead followed you to your hiding place."

"Yeah, he's just nosy and greedy. Why is it that they never bother you until you're busy or on the phone? I swear."

"That is so true. You can be sitting there butt-ass naked for hours on end, and as soon as the phone rings, and it's for you, they decide, okay, now I'll go over there and fondle her."

"For real. Anyway, let me go. I might as well feed this man since I'm downstairs in the kitchen. Bedford, behave yourself. Okay, now he's getting out of control. Girl, we'll catch up, but seriously, Venezuela would be your best bet. It's romantic and your fluency in Spanish will go over well there."

"Great! You've helped me narrow my selections down to St. Maarten and Venezuela. Thanks, Sandy."

"Anytime. *Adios, mi amiga.*"

"Adios."

After speaking to Sandy, Wanita headed out to the travel agency. She told an agent her choices and was given brochures for both. Wanita sat in the waiting area for more than an hour reviewing each pamphlet carefully. She wanted this to be the ultimate vacation. She wanted to have the red-carpet treatment all around and around-the-clock pampering. Wanita even went as far as to ask the travel agents if they had visited either location. To her surprise, all four of them had and three out of the four recommended that she go to Venezuela. The fourth woman didn't like the fact that the people in Venezuela weren't as fluent in English, but that wasn't an issue for Wanita. As a child, she grew up in Sunset Park in Brooklyn, which was a Spanish neighborhood, and when she got a little older, her parents moved to Clinton Hills. Upon entering high school, she took Spanish as a second language and took it again when she went to college.

The choice became obvious and Wanita arranged a fourteen-day vacation. They were scheduled to spend seven days at the Ritz Carlton in Venezuela and the other seven days on a smaller island off the coast. She booked them first class all around. They had an all-inclusive package and a luxury suite. When the woman told Wanita the cost, Wanita merely handed the lady her credit card and thanked her for the services. Wanita wasn't concerned about the money because that was no longer an issue in their household. William's six-figure salary and bonuses afforded them the ability to do things that they had only dreamed about when they first started dating.

A lot of things transpired during the course of Wanita and William's marriage. In the beginning, Wanita was the breadwinner, working at Beth Israel Medical Center in lower Manhattan. They lived in East New York, which was a less desirable section of Brooklyn, but that was all that they could afford. Wanita tried her best to get home as early as possible, because the sound of gunshots being fired was a common occurrence. William was in his last year of law school and worked part time as a teacher's aide in a public school. His salary barely covered the light, gas, cable and food expenses. It was a struggle, but they were happy. They didn't have much of a savings, and a vacation of any kind, even in driving distance, was almost out of the question. Although Wanita made decent money as a nurse, both she and William had accumulated credit-card debt as well as student loans.

When William graduated, he immediately got a job working for an assemblyman in Brooklyn. It wasn't William's dream profession, but it helped to pay the bills. Another great break came for them when the hospital she worked for offered Wanita an apartment in one of their buildings in the city. There was a long waiting list, but Wanita knew somebody who knew somebody else and they were able to speed up the process for her. In no time, they were living on Seventeenth Street and First Avenue, which was exactly one block away from Wanita's job. Things were starting to improve for them.

One evening, Wanita escorted William to a fund-raiser. William was busy making contacts and politicking for his assemblyman's party. Wanita wasn't really interested in the political mumbo-jumbo that was taking place around her, so she wandered around until she ended up meeting a former acquaintance now turned radio news reporter from high school. Wanita and her friend began talking and, before long, Wanita was networking and getting job information for William. Wanita's girl-friend told her that the company she worked for was new and growing rapidly. They were in need of an associate general counsel for regulatory affairs.

William wasn't satisfied with his present position and strongly dis-liked the bureaucracy. Except, at the time, he was simply happy to have a job, considering the fact that the market for lawyers was oversatu-rated. Wanita obtained the necessary information from her friend and passed it on to William. When Wanita first told William about the job, he refused to apply because he felt that he wasn't qualified. Wanita urged him to apply anyway and, after much persuasion, he finally turned in his résumé. It turned out that William's background truly didn't meet the criteria that Radio One was looking for, but since he was intelligent, motivated and highly referred by Wanita's friend, they made an exception.

Exactly four weeks later, Wanita and William were packing their belongings to relocate to the metropolis of Atlanta. William was respon-sible for overseeing and coordinating a wide range of regulatory and contractual legal services. The legal department was a two-man show, the vice president of legal affairs and William. The job was more than he could ever have dreamed, and allowed him the freedom to control his destiny with the company. He was developing and negotiating pro-vider contracts, standard financial agreements and real estate leases. He was also responsible for researching and reviewing applicable stat-utes and regulations affecting business to determine their potential im-pact to the company, as well as reviewing all marketing materials and other communications. To put it lightly, William's plate was full.

William became so entrenched in his job that everything else in his world became secondary. He pulled long hours all week and even some-times on the weekends. Wanita didn't notice the changes at the time, because she was busy working exhausting hours at the hospital. She also reconnected with her sorority by becoming active with the local chap-ter. This was where she and Sandy became familiar with each other. She hooked up with her old best friend from Brooklyn, Layla. Then, Layla introduced her to Maxine, and they became a foursome.

It wasn't until Wanita left her job that she realized how much William worked and how lonely she was. It was then that she decided to volunteer at the children's hospital, and even though she did, there was still a void. Wanita knew that she was married. She had the license and the ring to prove it, and, from time to time, she could even see that magical marriage island, but she couldn't quite swim to it.

On several occasions Wanita thought about returning to work, but each time she mentioned it to William, he suggested that she do something constructive at home. It wasn't as if money was an issue, so she never challenged his recommendation.

Now, here they were several years later with problems that Wanita never even fathomed. How was it possible for their relationship to become so volatile? They spent years building a friendship. Both she and William didn't want the focus of their union to be based on sex, which was where most couples went wrong. They had a very good sex life, but even more importantly, they became best friends. They got to know each other inside out, but was it ever possible to know everything about a person?

Wanita was so excited that she couldn't wait for William to come home and share the location and details of their next vacation with him. She filled her afternoon educating herself about Venezuela and was shocked to learn it had a population of 23,916,810 and it was more than twice the size of California. That was large in comparison to the other Spanish-speaking countries, minus Spain and Argentina. She and William were going to be staying in Caracas, which was the capital, but they would also spend one week on Margarita Island. Wanita made arrangements for William to take lessons in Spanish at the acclaimed Cela Spanish School located on Margarita Island. Since the island was thirty minutes from tourism and the mainland, they would have a chance to relax and reconnect.

This was a much-needed and deserved vacation for both she and William. Wanita had some things to sort out in her life. She realized that it was unfair for her to expect William to make her happy when her personal life was in disarray. Wanita had some firm decisions to make regarding returning to work as a nurse or the position that was recently offered to her as the basketball coach at the local high school. At present her plate was full. She was single handedly putting the PAAMA gala together. The director of events didn't have a clue about organizing an affair of this magnitude. It was the first time the gala was being held in Atlanta, so Wanita sympathized with them and basically took over the show. She was used to putting gatherings together since she did so many fund-raisers and parties for the children's hospital. The only thing that Wanita didn't do was find the venue. Aside from that, she hired the talent, caterers, created the invitations, put the program together, made follow-up calls, sent invitations to local government officials and media, and made several hotel and transportation arrangements for the expected out-of-town guests. Wanita was provided with a staff of ten people, but they didn't prove to be helpful, since most of them had daytime jobs.

Wanita couldn't wait for the gala to come and go and, as soon as everything was over, she and William were scheduled to go on a magnificent trip.

William pulled a long day at the office and didn't arrive home until late. Wanita was already upstairs in the bed fast asleep. Before joining his wife upstairs, William ate the food that Wanita left out on the counter for him.

When William entered the bedroom, he didn't bother to disturb Wanita. He undressed, took a quick shower and removed the brochures and papers that surrounded Wanita on the bed. The movement and noise awakened Wanita.

"Hey, sweetie," Wanita said, still half asleep.

"Hey. Welcome to the land of the living."

"What time is it?"

William buried the clock under the papers and brochures he placed on top of it.

"It's 10:23."

"Wow, it's pretty late. Are you just getting home?" Wanita asked.

"I got here about half an hour ago, but I ate and showered before coming to bed."

"I slept through all of that? Damn. So how was your day at work?"

"Busy. Nothing new there, but they're making some changes and furloughing people."

"Really, I hope none of this affects you."

"Don't worry, you'll still be able to live in the big house and drive the fancy car. My job is not in jeopardy. I'm not sure who it's really affecting, but I'm an asset and they know this."

"William, I know that you do a wonderful job, but everyone is expendable, no matter what the job."

"You must have me confused with you," William retaliated.

"What? That wasn't even called for. Why did you have to go there?"

"You brought that on yourself, talking all of that nonsense. How do you figure that they would fire me? Do you understand the amount of effort that I put into my job?"

"William, I'm more than aware of this, and all that I'm saying is that you shouldn't put all of your eggs in one basket."

"Wanita."

"What?" Wanita answered, slightly irritated.

"If I wanted your negative opinion, I would have asked. Now like I said, my J-O-B is not in jeopardy."

"Okay, fine," Wanita said, glad to move off that subject and on to something more positive. "Can you please pass me those pamphlets and things that you just placed on the floor?"

William reached over to retrieve the papers, then he held them before turning them over to Wanita.

"Whatever happened to the word *please*?"

"Damn, William. Please, now can you pass them to me?"

William shoved the papers at her, causing Wanita's attitude to turn sour.

"I just wanted to tell you about our upcoming vacation plans."

"Well, the floor is all yours, so show and tell me all about it."

"Okay, great!" Wanita said, feeling enthused again. "Here, look."

William took the glossy eight-page brochure that Wanita handed him. It displayed the hotel that they had reservations for in Caracas and all of the amenities that they could expect to receive once they arrived.

William's face didn't display any expression, and Wanita was curious to know what he was thinking and if he was as excited as she was.

"So, what do you think? Doesn't it look nice?"

"I guess it's okay."

"William, come on. It's beautiful, and you like tropical places."

"Yeah, but damn, don't you ever get tired of visiting these Spanish-speaking countries? How many of these places have we been to already? If you've seen one, you've seen them all."

"I just thought that you would like Venezuela. I asked for your opinion, and you didn't give me any ideas, so I came up with this."

"What other places did you consider?"

"St. Maarten, Curaçao and Bermuda."

"What was wrong with those places?"

"Nothing. I just figured that you'd like Venezuela, and you never complained about us visiting countries of Spanish origin before."

"I didn't realize that it was going to be an epidemic. I mean, what do you have planned for us for the next ten years—Puerto Rico, Bolivia, Chile, Columbia, Guatemala, Mexico, Panama, Paraguay, Peru, Uruguay?"

"William, don't be ridiculous. Why are you rattling off every Spanish country on the globe?"

"Because, more than likely, I'll be seeing all of those places. Please understand this, these places are nice, but I'd like to do something different. Any one of the aforementioned places you spoke of earlier would have been fine. Or maybe try this for an idea, how about someplace in Africa?"

"Okay, I'll keep that in mind for next time."

"Next time? Have we got our wires crossed again? Because I don't think that you understand. I'm not interested in visiting Venezuela."

"But the tickets are already purchased and the dates are already locked in."

"Now, why would you do that without consulting with me first?"

"William, I asked you for your help before I did all of this, and you told me to decide on my own."

"Yes, decide on a place, but that didn't mean you should book it right away. We should discuss it first."

"Since when? I've been doing this alone for years now and, all of a sudden, you want to set new rules. Why are you playing games with me? Why do you make things so difficult?"

"Why are you whining like a five-year-old? Grow the fuck up! All you have to do is go back to the travel agency and cancel the reservations, and I'll find the time to put something better together."

"That's what you should have done in the first place."

"Obviously!" William retorted.

"Let me ask you an important question?" Wanita sat straight up. She wanted William to take her seriously. This evening wasn't supposed to turn out this way. It was supposed to be filled with happiness and lovemaking. She was going to tell William about their awesome travel arrangements. He was going to be happy, and after they discussed the details and how much fun they were going to have he was going to notice her in her sexy negligee. She was going to give him the best head that he'd ever received, and he was going to return the favor to her by burying his head in her warm oven. She so longed to taste him and she forgot what it felt like to have a thick tongue lap her private area. It had been a while. Wanita lusted for William's tongue to circle her russet-colored nipples. She missed the warmth of his tongue and breath in her mouth. Unfortunately, none of those things were in the forecast.

"Go right ahead."

"Do you believe me to be capable of doing anything right?"

"Wanita, that is a ridiculous question. Speaking of which, how are things going with the PAAMA gala?"

"We're right on schedule, and things are going well. We're in the final stages and the only things left to do are add some final touches here and there."

"See, you always were a good organizer. Now, if I didn't have faith in you, I wouldn't have asked you to put one of the most important events together for PAAMA. After all, this is our biggest event of the year. Remember, you are my wife, and it's my rep at stake. Too much rests on this for me to not have faith in you."

Wanita's face immediately brightened after William's statement.

"That's true. Hey, has PAAMA decided who they're honoring this year?

"We have an idea. There are a couple of suggestions in the box, but we really want someone who has proven himself both in the organization, as well as within his community, and has a credible career. Someone who is seasoned and well accomplished."

"Then PAAMA should consider nominating you, because you are all of those things," Wanita said, snuggling up to William.

"You think so?"

"I know so," Wanita said seductively.

"Prove it," William dared.

"I will," Wanita said as she pressed her moist, warm, soft mouth against his, and William didn't object. Instead, he pulled her closer to his chest. Wanita inhaled his fresh-out-of-the-shower smell combined with his personal body cologne. Her body ached for his touch. Without hesitation, she palmed his manhood and, to her surprise, he was solid.

Wanita's wish was finally coming true. Within moments they were entangled and making sweet love.

21

"If Sybil Touches Me She Will Go to Jail!"

The blue overcast sky was only a sign of things to come. The weather was unpredictable. Hot one day and wintry the next. When Wanita spoke to Sandy a few days earlier she had reported that the weather in New York was in the mid-eighties. On that particular day, it was raining and brisk in Atlanta.

Wanita was in good spirits, enjoying her new ride on Interstate 285. She got off at the Camp Creek Parkway exit and drove the stretch toward her final destination. Wanita placed the gearshift in park and sat in the space of the short-term lot at Hartsfield International Airport in anticipation of her mother's arrival. *So much to do, and so little time,* Wanita thought. She really didn't have the energy to cater to her mother, but she couldn't very well tell her to go home, either. It was bad enough that William had turned her mother away once already. She'd had to plead with her mother in order to get in her good favor again. When her mother called informing Wanita that she was coming to town, Wanita simply accepted it. Under normal circumstances she would have chewed her mother out, because she never gave consideration as to what was on other people's agendas. Her mother had simply left her a message saying that she was tired of staying with her sister in hot, dry and boring Nevada. Her mother didn't know what it meant to stay anywhere longer than a week or two at a time. She didn't know what to do with herself now that she had retired. She was constantly roving from one city to the next. Her mother was a free spirit and very nomadic at heart. They were complete opposites. Wanita was more laid back and passive like her father, and her mother was high-strung and had a low tolerance for nonsense.

Wanita had never fully understood why her mother had decided to just up and divorce her father. Her parents, Sybil and Donald, were married for twenty-one years. When Wanita turned eighteen and went away to college, her mother said enough was enough and filed for a divorce. It was a shock to any and everyone who knew her mother and father. Her mother turned into a completely different person, claiming that she needed her independence and that Donald, her husband, no longer made her happy. When Wanita was about fifteen, her parents stopped sharing a bedroom. Her father slept in the guest room, and her mother stayed in their marital suite. They were very cordial to each other and still attended functions together and continued having their annual Fourth of July and Labor Day cookouts. They still shared laughter, split the bills, ran errands for each other, ate dinner as a family and made major decisions together. They obviously still cared for each other. Wanita couldn't understand why her mother would break up the family.

Wanita's parents had informed her of their split when Wanita returned home for the Christmas holidays during her first year of college. They sat her down and gave the spiel about it not being her fault and how they'd always love her and remain a family whether they were together or not. Wanita knew that this was all a bunch of crock and none of it made sense to her. Throughout the entire conversation, her father looked like he had rehearsed his lines over and over. His attempt at looking strong failed, because as soon as Wanita started crying, her father began shedding tears. Her mother was the only one holding it together. Wanita knew that the divorce had to have been her mother's decision, and her father had simply gone along with it to make her happy.

Wanita was in complete denial and hated both of her parents for giving up. She was bitter for years. She thought that marriage was something that was supposed to last forever.

Wanita returned to school, and her performance was miserable. She was placed on academic probation, almost lost her scholarship and was about to be removed from the basketball team. Wanita was smart enough to get it together. She became focused on school and her participation on the team. She also got herself a part-time job at the mall; so, when the holidays came around, she no longer went home. Wanita did her best to avoid seeing her parents. She was hoping that this part of her life was just a bad dream and, if she didn't go home right away, things would go back to normal.

Years later, when she finally decided to confront her mother about her choice to leave her father, her mother informed her that the things Wanita mentioned did not constitute a marriage. Her mother explained that she and Wanita's father were no longer compatible and broke the relationship down for Wanita, hoping to give her a complete and better understanding. Then she said, although she still loved Wanita's father she wasn't *in love* with him. The adage that would forever remain stuck in Wanita's memory was, "Convenience is no reason to stay in a marriage." Wanita couldn't understand why her parents couldn't work things out if they still loved each other. Convenience may not have been a reason to continue a marriage, but wedding vows were. When two people say "I do," that preordained a commitment for life, and Wanita didn't think that many people took that seriously anymore. A marriage commitment meant pledging or obligating oneself to another eternally. It wasn't like her father had ever disrespected her mother. He never cheated on her, and he didn't beat or treat her badly, so why couldn't they work things out? She was baffled to this day. The one thing Wanita did know was that the name Sybil befitted her mother very well because her behavior was truly schizophrenic.

Wanita didn't even bother to tell William that her mother was coming. He was just going to have to deal with it. After all, when his mother took ill, Wanita had welcomed her with open arms into their home. She didn't see why William was behaving the way that he was toward her mother, anyway. Yes, it was true that her mother could be a little bossy, but weren't all mothers?

Wanita looked at the clock and saw that she still had plenty of time before her mother arrived. She thought about getting out of the car and wandering around the airport to visit some of the stores, but she wasn't in a shopping mood. Instead, she opted to pop in her favorite Sade compact disc and relax until her mother's plane arrived.

The mellow tunes that Sade belted out made Wanita really sit and think about what her life had amounted to, and she began to realize just how unhappy she really was. She was an unemployed housewife with zero children, and her prospects of having any were even slimmer. She couldn't even have a puppy to keep her company. Her husband was difficult, stubborn, had a bad attitude, and she was starting to lose faith in him. Her best friend lived in New York, so she couldn't even cry on her shoulder like she really wanted, and she had two very judgmental friends with whom she refused to share her personal details. Before Wanita knew what was happening, she began to cry. She gripped the steering wheel and laid her head back on the rest hoping that this would deter the tears, but it didn't.

Not now, Wanita thought. The last thing she wanted was for her eyes to be red and puffy when her mother arrived. Of course, her mother would question her to death, and she would pry and pry until Wanita finally told her what the problem was. It was hard to answer such a question when Wanita didn't know exactly what the problem was herself. It was too hard to pinpoint. All married couples had their troubles, and this was merely a milestone that they would work through. William was still a decent husband. He took care of her and their household. She didn't have a need or want for anything. Money was at her disposal, and she had plenty of time to do whatever she desired. So what was the problem?

William worked too much, but was that a valid argument? He had to work hard since he was the only one supporting the family. After all, they lived in a big, beautiful five-bedroom home with a two-car garage, and an indoor swimming pool that sat on two acres in a gated community with a golf course they had to pay yearly dues for, whether they played or not.

William is inconsiderate.
William doesn't spend quality time with me anymore.
William is selfish.
William doesn't treat me like an equal partner in the relationship.
William doesn't seem to want children.

The list seemed to go on and on, and the more Wanita thought about each qualm, the sadder she became. She opened the glove compartment and pulled out some Kleenex. She wiped her eyes, blew her nose and searched her bag for her mascara. She stole a quick peek at herself in the mirror; she looked a mess.

How could Sade do this to her? Twenty minutes earlier she was in high spirits driving along in her new ride and then, out of nowhere, the dam had started to leak. She should have known better than to put in that particular CD in her player. Sade's music was for lovemaking and lovemaking only. If you were on the outs with your man, or if you had just parted ways, her songs could really play with your heart and mind.

Wanita and William were definitely on the outs, because it had been only two nights ago that she'd sat at the bottom of the steps dressed to the nines waiting for him to arrive from work and he had stood her up for a seven-thirty dinner reservation at the new upscale soul food restaurant in Buckhead, Black Pearl's. She had called him earlier to remind him to be home on time, and although he seemed preoccupied during their conversation, he said that he would be there. When he finally decided to come home one hour and twenty minutes late, he acted as if it were nothing. That was exactly what she meant by him being inconsiderate and his not valuing her time. Yet, when he wanted her to do something, it was to be done no matter what the circumstances. Wanita found herself jumping through hoops to keep up with William's requests, but, when it came to her needs, he was like a sleeping dog—not to be disturbed or bothered for fear of agitation. The conversation that evening was probably only a sign of more things to come.

Wanita had sat on the second-to-the-last step in the foyer as she waited for William, steeping with anger. She heard the car before she saw the headlights approaching and then pulling into the driveway. She knew the sound of that car all too well. The engine purred like a kitten because he paid more attention to the car than he did to her. She heard the driver's side door open and then gently close shut. Then, the passenger door behind the driver's seat opened and closed. William was bringing in his briefcase, which meant that he was probably going to do more work. Wanita continued to listen as William's wing tips hit the pavement in even strides until he reached the two steps that led to the threshold of their home.

The house keys jingled against the change in his pocket before he reached in to retrieve them. Slowly, the lock turned and the door was thrust open.

William entered the foyer, and his eyes were focused on the daily newspaper and getting the key out of the lock. When he achieved that he held up his head and was stunned at the sight of Wanita sitting on the steps.

"You scared the mess out of me. What are you doing sitting on the steps?" William asked. He looked at Wanita as if she were crazy.

"Well, hello to you, too, and how was your day?"

"Didn't I say hello?"

"Actually, no you didn't say hello, but to answer your question, I was waiting for you."

"Waiting for me? Why?" William asked.

"William, you can't be serious?"

"Wanita, how many times do I need to tell you? I'm not a mind reader. I have better things to do than to stand here and play guessing games with you, so are you going to tell me, or should I just walk away now?"

Wanita's dark-brown complexion burned black with fury. This had to be some kind of bad dream. Four years ago, this would never have happened. Three years ago, it might have occurred once in a blue moon. Two years ago, that blue moon became every full moon and, one year ago, it changed to just about every half moon.

"William, I called you earlier today to remind you about our dinner reservations at Black Pearl's. You rushed me off the phone, but you said okay, that you would be home before seven, and here we are going on nine o'clock."

"Well, like you said, I was busy. One thing came up and then the next, so what do you expect? Besides, I'm sure that I didn't commit to a time because I knew that this project was going to go well into the evening."

"I told you the time and you said okay, yes," Wanita said, pulling herself up by the handrail.

"Okay, now you're going senile on me. I don't remember this telephone discussion that you're referring to, and I damn sure didn't agree to do dinner or anything else, especially when I'm in the middle of contract negotiations."

"William, you are always in the middle of negotiations. That's your job! Anyway, I'm not going senile, crazy, insane or anything else that you and your creative imagination can come up with. I called and you spoke to me, so if anyone is going a little senile it's you."

"I don't have time for this crap right now. I have more pressing things going on."

"You know what, William, I'm sorry to burden you with our marriage. The fact that we barely see each other, make love or even communicate anymore isn't a pressing issue but your job is?"

"Why are you always putting words into my mouth? See, this is why we can't communicate, because there is a failure of comprehension."

"Oh, so now I'm stupid?"

"I didn't say it. You did! Now is that what you want to hear? Listen, I've had a long day. On top of that, the company wants all of its employees to be in one central location. Budgets are being cut and word is that it's too expensive for the company to fly me to Maryland every other week and still travel to different business sites between."

"So what exactly does that mean?"

"It means what you think it does, that we may have to move."

"Move?" Wanita said, walking over and standing directly in front of William. "Do I have a say in the matter?"

"Wanita, get real. This is bigger than both of us. How do you think this makes me feel?"

"I really don't know, seeing as how you're never here in the first place, but you're asking me to uproot myself and leave my friends, the children at the hospital and my latest opportunity at the high school."

"Get real! You're a volunteer at the children's hospital. It's not like you're holding down a real job, besides you can do all of those things in Maryland. You're good at making new friends, and you'll be closer to New York, so you can see Sandy again."

"You know, William, I don't even know why I bother anymore. You don't take anything that I do seriously, and, for your information, I was offered a job at Dunbar High School to be the girls basketball coach."

"You don't even play anymore."

"And, your point is?"

Wanita was waiting for the wounding remark. She hated to admit it, but Layla was right. Nothing she did or said was good enough anymore. All of her friends were right.

"My point is you don't play and what in the world qualifies you to become a coach? Your degree wasn't in physical education. It was in nursing, and now you want to veer off to the far right into something you know nothing about. I mean, Wanita, the hospital is one thing. This thing about becoming a coach, you aren't truly considering it, are you?"

"As a matter of fact, I was. I'm flattered that they would ask me and that someone, somewhere believes that I am good at something. It seems that nothing that I do in this household suits you. You don't believe in anything I do anymore."

"Wanita, I married a wife, not a nag, and I really don't want to come home to this shit each and every day. I'm sick and tired of fucking around with your silly ass. All you do is complain, 'You don't love me, You don't make love to me anymore, and you don't find me attractive anymore. You don't spend time with me anymore. You don't, you don't, you don't.' Damn, grow the fuck up!"

At that point, what was there to even say? Wanita should have expected to be disappointed. This wasn't the first time that he had broken an engagement between them, and it wouldn't be the last, but she still had hope. She had plenty of hope in her heart that things would go back to the way they once were. Wanita didn't think that she was asking for much, or were her expectations really and truly too much?

Wanita went upstairs to take off her clothes and carried a few items for William into the guest bedroom. Since he wanted to be alone in the relationship, then he should be made to sleep alone.

The last time they made love was two going on three weeks ago. The sex was very stiff and routine. The usual twenty- to thirty-minute foreplay was eliminated, and they went directly into action. William was more into self-satisfaction than he was on pleasing Wanita. She tried to change positions, but it was as if William were pinning her down. Wanita didn't even have the big orgasm. She barely had a tremor. William was steadily pumping away and the sweat from his brow dripped onto her face; and when he had completed his mission, he rolled over and went to sleep.

Afterwards Wanita got up and went into the bathroom to take a long soak in the tub where she cried her sorrows away. She seemed to be doing a lot of crying nowadays too. Wanita was beginning to have nightmares accompanied by anxiety attacks causing her to wake up in the middle of the night in a cold sweat. A year ago, she had zero strands of gray hair. This year, she had more gray than she could count, and in places she didn't believe possible.

Wanita didn't understand when their relationship had become so monotonous and conforming. This was exactly what she had wanted to avoid. She never dreamed that her marriage would one day mirror that of her parents' before their divorce. She'd always said that her marriage would remain spontaneous, loving, fun, harmonious and respectable, along with a host of other adjectives that were on the tip of her tongue. This was her life and things weren't supposed to happen this way. Her career had gone down the sewer, and now her marriage was in collapse. What was next?

Cleaning herself up and looking at her watch, Wanita realized that her mother's plane should have arrived five minutes ago. Her mother was probably already at baggage claim. Wanita grabbed her purse, popped out of the vehicle and armed the alarm. Car theft wasn't a big problem in Atlanta, but it paid to be cautious.

Sprinting across the parking lot, Wanita ran into the terminal. She didn't see her mother at the luggage carousel, so she walked over to the monitors to see the status of her mother's flight. To Wanita's dismay, the flight had arrived fifteen minutes before its scheduled time, which meant her mother must have been wandering around and pissed off at Wanita for being late. The last thing Wanita wanted was for her mother to be upset and have an attitude with her for not coming on time.

Wanita stole another quick glance to make sure that her mother wasn't inside before she walked back outside to find her. She walked outside into the core of a group of smokers, and the secondhand smoke almost gagged her to death. She waved the smoky air away from her face. *When will people learn how silly it is to smoke?* she thought. As Wanita walked through the chimney she heard someone call her name. She turned to see her mother smoking in the midst of the other secondhand killers.

"Ma, is that you?" Wanita asked.

"Of course it is, darling. Are you expecting someone else?" her mother asked as she put out her cigarette. She picked up her small carry-on bag and grabbed the handle to her pulley suitcase.

Wanita's mother was just as statuesque as her daughter, however, age made her appear more regal. She was tall and dark with smooth skin, very shapely for a woman in her late-fifties and she had her salt-and-pepper hair styled into a very sharp bob. She wore simple silver hoop earrings and a variety of silver bangles like a gypsy. She was heavy into collecting silver jewelry.

Wanita and her mother embraced, and the stench of tobacco assaulted Wanita's nose. It was then that she realized that only moments ago her mother had held a lit cigarette in her hand. Her mother had quit smoking when she and Wanita's father divorced. At the time, she'd said it was *that man* who had driven her to smoking, and when the relationship ended, she stopped. So Wanita was curious to know why she had picked up the habit again. Her parents had been divorced for almost fifteen years, so what was the new stress in her life that was causing her to revert to old bad habits?

"Ma, I know that you're not smoking again?"

"Oh, yes I am," her mother answered without chagrin. "And, might I add, enjoying it too!"

"Ma, you were doing so well. When did you start up again?"

"Oh, I don't know. It's not like I was looking at a calendar when I started. Now are we going to stand here and play trivia or can we go? I'm starving. You know they don't feed you on these flights anymore, and it wasn't a short flight, either. But I should have known better than to travel without eating first."

Wanita removed the small travel bag from her mother's shoulder and left her with the pulley. Wanita took note that her mother was actually using the designer luggage that Wanita purchased as a gift when her mother retired two years ago. At the time, her mother had made a big stink about Wanita spending so much money on luggage, but she obviously had the good sense to keep it. Her mother was frugal and that word was used kindly.

"We can go eat. What do you feel like?"

"Well, when in Rome do as the Romans do."

Wanita laughed. Her mother loved to use coined phrases.

"I take that to mean you want some good old southern cooking."

"That's right and with all of the fixin's!"

Twenty-five minutes later Wanita and her mother arrived at Black Pearl's. Since she was unable to dine there with her estranged husband two nights ago, Wanita figured she might as well take her mother.

It was the height of the lunch hour and Black Pearl's was jumping. Wanita and her mother had a thirty-minute wait, but the live jazz band kept them occupied while they sat at the bar and ordered drinks. They kicked back and enjoyed the ambience and the restaurant scene.

Black Pearl's seemed to be a restaurant for the Who's Who of Atlanta. They spotted a few celebrity basketball players and the singer India Arie.

Wanita's mother spotted the mayor leaving the restaurant with a group of colleagues. She started to get up to go over and meet him, but Wanita knew her mother all too well and stopped her.

"Wanita, why are you holding on to my wrist?"

"What were you about to go over there and do?"

"I was going to introduce myself to that fine man over there."

"Mmm-hmm, just as I thought. Ma, you need to leave that man alone. You are such a flirt."

"I'm a single, beautiful, intelligent black woman. And I don't recall needing your approval to handle my business. That man is a good catch."

"He's not available. He's married. Very married."

Wanita's mother turned back around to take a sip of her wine. She reached into her handbag to retrieve a cigarette.

"Ma, please don't," Wanita scolded.

"I don't need your permission to smoke, child. My goodness, are you going to pester me for my entire stay?"

"If you choose to smoke, yes. We don't allow smoking in our home, so don't get any ideas."

"Fine. I'll go outside. It won't kill me."

"Yeah, but your secondhand smoke can kill me."

The hostess came over to seat them before her mother could respond. The woman led them to an enclosed room that must have been the extension to the main dining room seeing as how the larger room was still filled with patrons. On the way in they spotted her friend, Layla and her husband getting up to leave, giggling and holding hands. Wanita went from smiling and chatting with her mother to solemn. Her mother immediately picked up on the change.

"Wanita, what's wrong?"

"Nothing. I don't feel quite as hungry anymore."

"Sweetie, we've been waiting for a little more than half an hour and we've both already selected our entrées, so what's really wrong? And don't say 'nothing,' because we may not live together anymore, but I know my daughter and that look smeared across your face is far from nothing."

"Ma, trust me, it's nothing."

Just then, Layla and her husband walked over to Wanita and her mother. They looked so happy. Wanita felt a tinge of jealousy lurking, and she wanted to shoot it down. She should have been pleased to see her friend and her friend's husband happy. Layla would be happy for her if things were the other way around. As a matter of fact, Layla was the one who had advised her to work on improving her marriage. Yet, there she was hating and, of all people to hate on, it was her friend.

"Hello, Wanita," Layla said, bumping purposely into Wanita. Her husband said hello to both Wanita and her mother before excusing himself to give the parking stub to the valet.

"Hey, girl," Wanita said, hugging Layla. She hoped that Layla didn't see through her fake grin.

"Hello, Mama Sybil. I'm surprised to see you down here. When did you arrive? When are you coming to spend some time with me, and what brings you to Hotlanta?"

Wanita's mother and Layla quickly embraced.

"Layla, you still haven't changed. Still asking fifty questions at a time, huh?" Wanita's mother said playfully.

"You know it, Mama Sybil. Listen, you guys are definitely going to enjoy the food. I don't know who their chefs are, but they better do whatever they can to keep these folks happy. You know how these restaurants start out with the bomb staff and win over patrons. Then, the restaurant management thinks they are the shit because business is good, and start to treat their staff like crap. People begin to quit, and the level and quality of food begin to taper off. If they want to maintain this kind of flow, they better work at keeping the back end happy. They have a four-page menu. Oh and Wanita, guess what?"

"What?"

"They have a section on the menu dedicated to vegetarians."

"Really, that's great." Wanita replied.

"Damn, don't get too excited," Layla said, noticing Wanita's aloofness for the first time. "Is everything okay with you?"

"She's fine. For whatever reason now she wants to play coy," Wanita's mother interjected. "Don't pay her any mind. Once she gets some food, she'll be back to normal."

"Layla, I'm fine. I'm just tired. I've had to deal with her mouth ever since she got off of that plane," Wanita said, looking at her mother in dismay.

Layla stared at both Wanita and her mother, and the look on her face indicated that she was going to steer clear of that one.

"Well, ladies, it was nice seeing both of you, but I have to run." Layla kissed both women and disappeared.

Layla was dead on when she said that the food at Black Pearl's was good. Wanita and her mother had to sit and let the food digest for a half an hour after they finished eating. Everything was a little on the pricey side, but the food was right. Wanita had a plate of steamed vegetables, which consisted of zucchini, carrots, broccoli and pumpkin, and she had pan-seared swordfish in butter and garlic sauce. Her mother said that she couldn't visit a soul food restaurant and eat the foods that Wanita selected, so she had collard greens, candied yams soufflé and fried catfish. She also had gumbo soup as an appetizer.

After the restaurant they visited Lenox Mall to try and walk the food off. Both women were only supposed to window shop, but, once they saw the sale at their favorite stores, their empty hands became filled with several bags.

When they arrived home the first thing that they did was unpack their bags and then they headed directly to bed for a quick nap. Talking, eating and shopping were exhausting affairs.

Wanita set the alarm, because she didn't want to oversleep. She had to get up to prepare dinner before William came home from work. She would do anything to avoid him and his mood swings while her mother was visiting. She didn't want her mother becoming involved in her personal affairs. She loved her mother, but she didn't want her living or running her life. As far as Wanita could see, her mother shied away from commitment and responsibility. Her longest relationship besides her marriage lasted for approximately two years.

Before going to the airport that morning, Wanita seasoned chicken for barbecue and she bought fresh corn and made mashed potatoes and string beans. Wanita was still full from her big lunch, so she had no intentions on eating. But she knew that her mother would eat as soon as she got up. Sybil had the metabolism of a lioness. She consumed enough food to feed a small congregation.

William arrived home just in time for dinner. Wanita was still in the kitchen snacking on celery and carrot sticks. She was flipping through the pages of *Shades* magazine when William walked into the kitchen.

They both met in the center of the room and embraced with a short, warm kiss. Wanita and William had been civil to each other since their disagreement two nights earlier. The lines of communication were improving. At the same time, this was also very common in their relationship. They went through constant highs and lows.

"I'm starving," William said as he walked over to the pot to see what smelled so enticing.

"As you can see, I prepared dinner."

"You know I love it when my woman cooks. That's what I'm talking about. Damn, woman, it looks like you cooked for an army. An entire tray of barbecue chicken, mashed potatoes and all these ears of corn. You must not plan to cook for the remainder of the week."

"That's not true."

"Then why all of the food?" William asked.

"Well, we have a house guest."

"A house who?"

"A guest, and don't try to act like you didn't hear me."

"I heard you, but you know how I feel about guests. Why didn't you just tell whoever it is to stay in a hotel? I really need my peace and quiet, and you know how you and your friends are when you get to-gether. Loud and obnoxious."

"First of all, William, it's my mother, so I'm not going to tell her to stay in anybody's hotel. Especially since we have all of this room. Rooms I might add that we don't seem to be filling with children any time soon, so we might as well have guests. Secondly, I detest your last statement. I do not get loud and obnoxious when I get with my friends. Third, you're hardly ever home, so what do you really care if we have com-pany or not?"

"Wanita, I don't know who you're talking to like that, but you'd better slow your roll and watch your fucking mouth. It doesn't matter whether I'm home three or four days out of the week, it's still my house, and I have a say as to who can and cannot stay here. Now, since you want to get technical, you *are* loud; look at how high and mighty you were just acting. Now I'm sick and tired of you and this talk about kids. Leave that shit alone. It will happen when the fuck it's supposed to happen."

"You know what, William? You are not the only one who is sick and tired."

"Oh, really, is that so?" William asked.

Wanita's mother nonchalantly entered the room while William and Wanita were at the height of their argument. She stood there and lis-tened on as they bantered back and forth.

"What is all of this loud talk about?" Wanita's mother asked.

Neither answered. Both William and Wanita looked at each other and then at Wanita's mother.

"Nothing for you to worry about, Mother. Why don't you just go back upstairs so William and I can continue our discussion?"

"I am not a child, and I don't like being told what to do," Sybil answered matter-of-factly.

"See, this is why I told her that she couldn't come here in the first place. Your mother doesn't know how to mind her own business."

"William, how dare you speak about my mother that way," Wanita said, both appalled and embarrassed that her mother had to hear and witness William's behavior.

"What exactly is going on here?" Wanita's mother asked again.

"You want to know what is going on so badly, I'll tell you," William answered, only inches away from Wanita's mother's face.

Wanita stood between them, because she knew that if William said the wrong thing to her mother that Sybil would haul off and slap the living shit out of him.

William backed up a few feet. "Where shall I begin?"

"William, why don't you stop being childish and wait so we can discuss this later?"

"Wait, oh fuck that. You started, so now we're going to finish. I told Wanita that I didn't want any guests in this house. I work hard, and I want my peace and quiet. The few days that I am here, I prefer to be left alone to rest. Now, I can't rest if you're here, can I?"

"Excuse me?" Sybil asked. "Now correct me if I'm wrong, but this is not only your home, but my daughter's as well, right?"

"This is my house, and I'm the king of this castle. I work, I pay the bills, I pay the mortgage. Therefore, I decide who can and can't stay here."

Tears began to well up in Wanita's eyes. She couldn't believe that William was actually standing there telling her mother all of this stuff. It was one thing for him to fill her head with all his bullshit, but it was surely another for him to impress the same nonsense upon her mother. How could he stand there and disrespect both she and her mother like that? This was totally inconceivable. This was definitely where Wanita decided that it was time to draw the line.

"William, you did not buy this house alone. We bought this house together. When your mother was sick and in need of someone to take care of her, who did it? Me!"

"Yes, you did and where is my mother now? Gone, so please don't do me any more fucking favors."

"William, now you're wrong. You need to apologize to my daughter and me," Sybil retorted.

"Apologize? Both of you are out of your damn minds. I'm not apologizing for jack. If I had put my mother in a facility that had able doctors and nurses, maybe she'd still be around."

Wanita's dark skin blazed beet red. She was beyond upset. The tears came to a cease and desist, because Wanita couldn't believe that William was blaming her for his mother's death. His mother would have died whether he had put her in a home with able doctors and nurses, as William so nicely put it, or not. His mother had terminal cancer and, unless by some miracle she went into remission, she was going to die.

"Are you blaming me for the death of your mother? Because let me tell you something, I did more for your mother in that one year than you probably did for her your entire life. You weren't even here half of the time to check on her prognosis, and you have the bravado to blame me? You damn bastard! I see what you're all about and now the truth comes to light. Now I understand what's been behind your sudden change in behavior."

"Wanita, whatever. Save the revelation for someone who cares. As far as I'm concerned, you and your mother can take your shit and get the hell out of my house."

"What? Get out? What exactly are you trying to say to me?" Wanita asked.

"Oh, enough of this shit, Wanita. Get out of the way, so I can knock the black off this nigga, because that's exactly what he's acting like," Sybil said.

Wanita had to restrain her mother, because she was two seconds away from doing something that Wanita wanted to do herself, but knew better.

"Let her go, let her go!" William said, leaning forward with his hands in his pockets. "If Sybil touches me, she'll go to jail! She'll go to jail tonight. I'll call the police on both of your asses and have you hauled out of here if you don't leave on your own."

William's threat riled Sybil up even more. Wanita was struggling to restrain her mother and took a few blows during her mother's wild fit. Sybil eventually calmed down when she realized that she was attacking the wrong person.

"I'm going upstairs to get my bags. I'm out of here. This is why I'm divorced now. I don't have the patience to deal with bullshit like this."

"You're alone now because you're a damn nag, just like your daughter."

"William, I'm ashamed of you. I'm hurt and ashamed, but don't worry, you won't have me to nag you anymore. I won't be around for you to get tired of anymore or bother you about children or expectations of having a healthy and happy marriage. The only thing that I can say is that I'm sorry that I came between you and your marriage to your job and yourself."

"Great, handle yours. I'll be fine. I'll be even better once you're completely out of here. Imagine that, us having a kid. You couldn't even take care of your patients, and you were registered and certified to do that. It would be the blind meeting the mentally challenged."

William's statement threw Wanita off for a moment, but more than anything it hurt her deep down to the core. Either he really hated her or he was being mean. The sad thing was she hadn't seen any of this and why it had taken her mother coming to visit for all of this to surface she would never understand. But if that was the way that William felt, then what more could she say? The last thing she ever wanted was for her marriage to fail, but it was apparent that her husband didn't respect, love or care for her.

"I'm sorry that you feel that way, and the only thing I have to say is that I wish that I would have known these things about you sooner, but like they say better late than never."

William looked at Wanita like she was an abomination. Wanita wanted to cry. She needed to cry, but she knew that crying wasn't going to solve anything. What she had to do was go upstairs and pack as much of her belongings as she could. Never in a thousand years would she have thought that things would end up this way.

Wanita decided to take the high road and leave on a good note.

"William, I just want you to know that I love you, and I'm sorry that things between us turned out this way."

With that said, she headed upstairs and, as soon as her back was turned to William, the river of sadness began to flow.

"Like I said, be gone!" William screamed.

22

Soulmate and Lover for Life

The doorbell rang. India didn't bother to flinch. Instead, she remained quiet. Lenora was working this afternoon and would answer the door on her behalf.

"I'm coming," Lenora answered to whomever was on the other side of the entrance.

India could hear Lenora scrambling about below her to get the door.

"Who is it?" Lenora asked.

India scampered quietly out of the bed to press the intercom to eavesdrop.

"It's me and my auntie Patience," Sierra answered.

India's heart began to race. She had figured that Patience would stop by even though she had specifically asked her to buy whatever Sierra needed.

India heard the thud of the bolts as they twisted and unlocked and the door squealed upon opening. Little feet scurried about and Sierra yelled, "Come up to my room, Veronica. You can pick out a toy to take with you too!"

"Did you all say hi to Miss Lenora?" Patience asked.

India could hear the pitter patter of feet come to a halt in the foyer.

"No," all three of the children answered. "Hi, Miss Lenora," the children said in unison, and then they all started running again.

"Don't run," Patience warned. "And don't take forever up there, either. Get what you came for and let's go."

"Hi, Miss Lenora, how are you doing?" Patience asked.

"Child, I'm doing well today. Once again, the good Lord has blessed me. Blessed me, and you?"

"I'm doing well. I guess I can say that I've been blessed today too. These kids have been driving me insane all morning. I thought that having twins was bad, but two girls against one boy? I'm sure you can relate," Patience said, chuckling.

"Oh yes, and I'm glad to say that those days are behind me. You know that I have four children."

"No, I didn't know that. How old are they?" Patience asked.

"My older boy Ken is thirty-seven, Celebrity is thirty-five, Nigel is thirty-four and Sepia is thirty-two."

"You were a busy woman. At this moment, I couldn't imagine having more than those two, and I know that Jonathan agrees. So you have a daughter named Celebrity? That's different."

"No different from you being named Patience, but her real name is Celia. When Celebrity was little, she was a beautiful little thing. She would sing and perform wherever we went—church, socials, parties. It didn't matter. She was not a shy child at all, and she would always tell us that when she got older she was going to become a celebrity. Celia said it so much that we all just started calling her just that, Celebrity."

"Wow, did she ever become a celebrity?"

"Well, she had minor successes here and there. She was a runway model for a while and got bored with that. Then she sang backup for a group and did really well there. Later on, she got her own recording contract, but then the label did something or other and the record never happened, but I have her demo and, I tell you, if she had continued to shop that thing, she would be big time now. Either way, I'm still proud of her. She set out to do big things, and Celebrity never let anything get in her way."

India never knew any of this about Lenora and was feeling a little down on herself for not becoming more familiar with her hired help. She could hear how proud Lenora sounded describing her children.

"So if you don't mind me asking, what's Celebrity doing now?"

"She lives in Los Angeles. She's the proud wife and mother of two. Celebrity ended up marrying her producer, and he is big-time out there.

They're very well off. I visit them during the holidays. My son Ken is an engineer, and he lives in Northern Virginia. Nigel is a banker; he's married with one child and lives near me; and Sepia is an architect in New York, but she travels a lot. She has no time for a serious relationship. In my day, we made time for relationships, now they seem to be an inconvenience for you young folk."

"That's funny, but true. I guess nowadays women are more liberated and have more choices. Women aren't as willing to put up with the crap that these men are out here dealing, thus refusing to settle."

"Ain't nobody saying that you have to settle. All I'm saying is that you all are screwing up the natural order of things. God made Adam and Eve. Not Adam, the animals and the world. Everyone is supposed to have a companion."

"Miss Lenora, I'm going to leave that one alone. Anyway, it sounds like you have a great family. Everybody seems to be doing very well. I can see why you're proud of your children."

"Oh yes. So what brings you here today?" Lenora asked.

India was glad that someone had finally brought up that interesting topic. She was curious to know as well. She continued to listen in on the conversation, but she was also trying to hear what the kids were doing down the hall. Nevertheless, even if they were misbehaving, she couldn't run down the corridor to stop them, or she would blow her cover.

"I called India this morning because we are taking a mini-vacation. Jonathan and I decided to go to Busch Gardens in Virginia this weekend. We're leaving tomorrow afternoon. I was able to run all of my errands, go to the mall, etc, etc. We got Sierra some play clothes. You know how my sister dresses her up every day like she's going to church or something. That was fine, but then Sierra started crying and throwing fits because she didn't want to go without her stuffed elephant. I offered to buy her a new one, but you know how children can be."

"Oh yeah, and as beautiful as that little girl is, she is headstrong like her father. When Grayson says he wants something, he doesn't stop until he gets it," Lenora added.

"Well, that's what brought me to this part of the valley. Is India home?"

"No. Didn't she go to work today?"

"No. I called her earlier and she was home. She said that she was going to run some errands, though, so I guess I missed her."

"Yeah, I haven't seen her since I got here, which was a little after ten. Her car wasn't parked in the driveway, and they rarely park inside of the garage."

"That's true. They have that double-car garage, and it's cleaner than I don't know what. They don't even use it for storage space. I don't know about those two neat freaks."

"Neat as all heck! They're a match made in heaven."

"If you say so," Patience said. "I wonder what is taking those kids so doggone long? Sierra, Veronica, Little John...come on now, we don't have all day. Get the toys that you came for and let's get going. Jonathan is in the car waiting for us."

"Oh, well tell him that I said hello. I haven't seen him in a while now. I guess the restaurant is keeping you two pretty busy."

"Yes, it is. It's more than we ever imagined, but we're thankful. We're ever so thankful, because when we started out we didn't think that we would have made it through the year, and now we're booked for private parties and reservations for the next couple of months."

"Congratulations, I know how fickle starting a new business can be. You're either very successful or you fizzle and burn quickly."

"Miss Lenora, you should come out and visit *Pájo Soul*. We would love to have you and a guest. Where do you live?"

"Oh, I live not too far from here. Maybe ten minutes or so," Lenora answered.

"I'm scared of you," Patience joked.

"Why?"

"It's expensive living out here," Patience responded.

"Well, I own my home free and clear from the bank. When my husband died, he left me a nice little policy, and the first thing I did was pay the mortgage off. See, all of my life I was a housewife. When my husband passed, I needed something to do, so I started doing house-work here and there to keep me busy. With the exception of Celebrity, my children were already pretty established. She would come back and forth, depending on what she was up to, and I knew eventually she would leave the nest permanently, so that's why I'm here now.

It's not for the money, but I simply need to keep busy."

The kids came running down the steps.

"Didn't I tell you all no running, especially while coming down the steps?"

The quick shuffle of feet slowed down to a jog.

Once Veronica, Little John and Sierra got to the foot of the steps, they picked up the pace once again and hauled out of the front door pushing and squealing, and said good-bye to Lenora.

"Well, we have to pick up on this conversation another day. I really enjoyed talking to you, and I hope that you'll take me up on my invitation and come to Baltimore to *Pájo Soul*. It would be such an honor to have you as our guest."

"I'll see what I can do. Perhaps one of these upcoming weekends, but I'll call you before I come out."

"That sounds great! Oh, and when India gets home, tell her that I stopped by for Sierra's favorite stuffed animal. I'm sure that she'll get a laugh out of it."

"I sure will. Take care and drive safely," Lenora said as she shut the door behind Patience.

India took in the entire conversation. That was a close call.

Earlier, when she sat in the kitchen drinking her tea, she had had the feeling that Patience would make a surprise visit. She figured that something would go awry with her sister's plan, and she would find some reason or another to stop by, so India decided to park her car inside the garage. She should have known to pack Sierra's elephant before taking her to Baltimore for the weekend. This morning, right after India drank her tea, she had grabbed her keys and run outside to move the car before Lenora arrived. Then, she took a goody bag of snacks and bottled water, a few office supplies, her fax machine and laptop into her room to avoid having to venture outside of her quarters.

From the very beginning, she instructed Lenora that whenever her room door was closed that she wasn't to enter. However, if her room door was open, then she could come in and clean as she saw fit. India was happy that she had established that rule from early on.

The good thing was that Lenora didn't even suspect that she was home. All morning, India had as remained quiet as a mouse. When the phone rang, she didn't answer it, but looked at the caller I.D., and then returned the call on her cell phone from inside her bathroom. She was getting antsy being in her room, but there was no other option.

India decided to take a short nap because she had worked harder that day than she did all week. She was able to speak to Veronica Webb's publicist and secure her for the upcoming fall issue, and she got in touch with the singing sensation Mary J. Blige for an interview. She edited the stories that Nashelle faxed over from her folder and even came up with some new ideas to change the image of the fashion and beauty section of the magazine. After doing all of that, she deserved to rest. The only thing that concerned India was Nashelle telling her that Nala, her boss wasn't happy about India's absence. Other than that India was on a roll. Nala's concern should be whether India was doing good work or if it suffered because of her days off. However, neither was the case. Nala knew that India was the best in the industry, and other magazines would be more than happy to snap her up.

When India woke up, it was nearly seven o'clock. The smell of food almost made her drift downstairs, but she wanted to make sure that Lenora was already gone for the evening. India located her cell phone and dialed her home number. She was beside the phone when it rang and, even though she knew whom it was on the other line, the sound startled her. After four rings, the machine came on, so she knew the coast was clear.

Grayson's letter was still on the pillow beside hers just the way he'd left it. India figured it was time for her to read it. She had to read it before he came home. She located her letter opener, which was in her nightstand, and unopened the note. The letter was written in calligraphy. Grayson always did have beautiful handwriting.

Dear India,
    You look so beautiful and at peace when you are resting. Sometimes I wonder how I ended up with a princess named India. Both you and Sierra have blessed my life in so many ways.

I am thankful to our Creator for placing you in my world.

I hope that you will be able to forgive me for my irrational behavior last night. I'm so sorry for all of the pain and anguish that you've suffered. It's just that I get overprotective about my position at the firm. The last thing I need is my peers looking upon me as being feeble minded or to be a laughingstock. Unfortunately your message put me in that predicament. I cannot afford to jeopardize all that I've worked for. It is important that you know that I love you. The way I fight to maintain our family and uphold our image in our community and at my workplace is the same way I will always fight for and love you. I will always be there for you and Sierra. You are my life, and I will sacrifice all that I have to make sure that we will always be a family.

India you are my life, my love, my source, my energy, my universe, and you make me whole. I love you and hope that you will find it in your heart to forgive me.

Your soul mate and lover for life!

Gray

Grayson's words were poetic and moved India to tears. She knew that he hadn't meant to hurt her. He'd even said it in the letter. He was only defending their name and his reputation. It took India a couple of minutes to regroup and regain her strength to get up.

India maneuvered herself into the bathroom to clean herself up. She didn't want to be smelly when Grayson got home. She knew that he'd had a long and arduous afternoon because, before going to sleep, she was able to catch a snippet of his trial. This was one of Grayson's biggest cases yet. India was proud as she watched him in action live on television. Grayson waltzed across the courtroom as if he owned the place. He was a natural, and he knew it. He had a calm, cool and collected exterior and, even when the prosecution began playing dirty, his demeanor remained the same.

India eagerly watched the telecast. It appeared that the prosecution was trying to bring prejudicial evidence against X-Tasy into the case. Grayson argued that the information was prejudicial, irrelevant and non-material. The issue at hand was that female rapper X-Tasy sang lyrics that the prosecution felt would implicate her in the assault and murder.

X-Tasy was quiet the entire time as Grayson pleaded her case. X-Tasy denied that she was ever involved with the woman sexually or otherwise, and she said she was not responsible for her miscarriage nor was she present when this so-called lover was assaulted.

India waited patiently as the court officer prepped the recorder to play the lyrics to X-Tasy's song. The jury was comprised of two middle-aged white women, an Asian man who looked to be in his early thirties, three black men ranging from the age of twenty to forty, three black women and three Latino women. The courtroom was silent and within moments the song began.

> *Whoever said pimpin' ain't easy was wrong*
> *I got niggas on the corner wearin' thongs*
> *My bitches work hard to please me*
> *I make sure that they're well rewarded*
> *Pockets so phat I can more than afford it*
> *Step out of line I'll be forced to abort it*
> *X-Tasy don't throw no fits*
> *Pistol-whip your ass, punch your belly with my fist*
> *You're telling me lies and loose lips sink ships*
> *I can wreck shop and bust up your shit*
> *X-Tasy has the best little whorehouse this side of town*
> *You only playa hating 'cause you wanna be down*
> *X-Tasy don't have time for no black-mailer*
> *Exert your efforts elsewhere ya fuckin' failure*
> *When I come down the streets, you'll have to watch ya backs*
> *Cross me, you'll be looking at the bottom of my Timberland*
> *tracks*

India watched Grayson's expression, and it remained unreadable the entire time. X-Tasy looked as if she had seen a ghost, and it was obvious that Grayson was trying to console and reassure her, but worry washed all over her face. Things were no longer looking that great for Grayson, so India immediately turned off the television.

India knew this case could either make or break Grayson at the law firm. This was as big as Johnny Cochran representing P. Diddy aka Puff Daddy. If Grayson won the case, he would make senior partner, and India wanted that for Grayson even more than he wanted it for himself. They would have it made and would be set for life.

Candles burned and soft music played to set the mood. India busied herself putting out the good silverware and china for dinner. She wanted this evening to be special to celebrate Grayson's first official week at trial. There was a good chance that he would be in a foul mood since things hadn't gone his way in court. So, the candlelight and music were distractions and an effort to thwart a repeat incident of the night before.

The front door opened, and Grayson entered—his hands filled with flowers, gifts and his briefcase. India saw him struggling and immediately ran to his aid. She removed his briefcase and the beautiful arrangement of flowers from him, and he gave her a peck on the lips. India smiled because this meant that he wasn't in a bad mood. When they got into the living room, India placed his briefcase on the sofa table and then headed into the kitchen to find a vase for the flowers.

"How was your day?" Grayson asked.

"It wasn't bad. I got a lot of work done today."

"Really, like what?" Grayson asked as he removed his blazer and loosened his tie.

"I didn't go in today, well, because you know," India said. She went from looking directly at Grayson to focusing on the floor. "Anyway, I got in touch with Veronica Webb's publicist and that went well. I also spoke with Mary J. Blige, the singer, and she graciously agreed to be in one of our upcoming issues; and I edited a ton of stories today."

"That's great. Where is our little angel?"

"Oh, she's still with Patience and Jonathan. They were going to Busch Gardens for the weekend and asked if she could come along, and I said it was fine. I hope that was alright with you. I wasn't sure if you had anything planned," India said cautiously.

"Oh, that's fine. We could use a nice long weekend together, don't you think?" Grayson asked as he perused the stack of mail that was beside his briefcase on the table.

"Most definitely."

"Besides, I want to pamper you this weekend. You deserve it. So, how are you feeling otherwise?" Grayson asked as he moved closer to India to take a look at her face and the rest of her body.

"I'm a little sore, but nothing that won't heal or get better over the weekend."

"Well, that's good to know. Did you read my note?" Grayson asked.

"Yes, I did, and it was beautiful. I forgive you. Really, I do."

"India, baby, that means a lot to me, and I'm going to use this entire weekend to make things up to you. I can go out and get a couple of movies if you're not up to going out. We can decide on that later, but, first, here's a little something that I got for you." Grayson handed India two beautifully wrapped gifts.

India got excited and gushed as she took the boxes from Grayson. She knew from the moment that Grayson walked in that the boxes were for her. It never failed. After every altercation, Grayson's way of making up was to purchase an expensive gift for her. Most times, she would put a little buzz in his ear letting him know what her latest fancy was, but this time she hadn't. Either way, she trusted his taste. He had style and plenty of class.

India shook the box to see if she could guess what was inside and Grayson beamed at her.

"Woman, you are not going to be able to guess, so open it."

"Okay, okay. Hold your horses."

India neatly removed the wrapping paper. It wasn't as if she had plans to keep the paper, but it was habit. When she opened the box, she was surprised to find a mango-gold-colored evening dress. It was a Vera Wang no less. Grayson always did have spectacular taste. India held the dress up to her, and it looked gorgeous against her skin.

"Grayson, this is beautiful, but where will I wear this?"

"You will be escorting me, the newly nominated man of the year for the Professional African American Men Association."

India shrieked with enthusiasm.

"Oh my goodness! I can't wait. Where is the ceremony taking place this year and what is the date? I'm so excited. I have to save the date for my sweetheart."

"This year it takes place in Atlanta, and it's June 16, so we have plenty of time."

"You are the man. The man of the year, that is," India commented.

"That's right. Your baby just received word today that not only is my chapter being nominated for three awards like I set out for, but that they also want to honor me. Can you believe that? They want to honor yours truly!" Grayson stood in front of India and took a bow.

"You are so silly. How did you get that way?"

"I learned from the best!"

"I wonder who that is," India said, laughing.

"You, of course. Now, open up the other box."

India opened up the smaller box, which had to be some kind of jewelry, and, to her delight, it was. There was a choker that had more diamond baubles on it than even Grayson could afford, matching earrings and bracelet.

"Grayson, what is this?"

"Isn't it beautiful?" Grayson asked as he took the necklace out of the box and began putting it around India's neck.

"It is, but how can we afford this? I mean, this has to be about, about, about...damn I can't even guess."

"Then don't. Just enjoy it!"

India put the pear-shaped diamond earrings into her ears and the matching bracelet on her wrist. She quickly walked over to the mirror to see how the ensemble looked on her. She stood there speechless as she admired the set.

"Grayson, this is beautiful. I can't even thank you enough. I thought only the rich and famous were able to wear stuff like this or the cheap and tacky wannabes. I'm still curious to know how you were able to afford this."

"Do you really have to know?"

India didn't want to upset him, but she really wanted to know. The earrings alone were probably worth between ten and fifteen thousand dollars. The clarity of the diamonds was unbelievable, and she knew that Grayson would never get faux anything.

"Well, you know that I'm representing X-Tasy. After the trial to-day, we were discussing the next steps. She didn't have time to do it formally because she needed to pick something up at the jewelers. I told her that I would accompany her so that we could talk along the way. We walked into the jewelry store, and people were treating me like I was some kind of superstar. I didn't know if it was because I was with X-Tasy, because of course, everybody knows her. If they didn't know her before, they know her now because of the trial. I commented to Mr. Bovïr, one of the owners of the shop, that the jewelry was beautiful."

"You spoke to the owner of Bovïr and Crïchton? Oh my goodness, go on. I'm sorry for interrupting." India was in awe of the people that her husband was becoming acquainted with. She knew that Bovïr and Crïchton hand made jewelry for the celebrities who walked the red carpet for the Oscars and the Grammy award shows.

Bovïr and Crïchton was also one of *Shades'* biggest advertising accounts and, on occasion, they would allow stars who were being showcased on the cover to borrow their lower-end jewelry.

"I sure did. We talked for a while, and then he brought me over to a showcase of fine jewelry. I told him about my upcoming function and my nomination for man of the year. He asked me if I was there to shop, and I told him about my representing X-Tasy. He recognized me from television, and then we had a good old time."

"Okay, but that still doesn't explain how I ended up with this fortune on my ears, my neck or wrist."

"I'm not done. He asked me if I had a wife. Of course, I told him yes, and he went to the back. He said that he had personally made this set for one of the stars, but she decided that she didn't want it, and that it was just sitting. He asked me to make an offer and, after looking at it, I said there was no way that I could afford to pay what it was truly worth."

"Right," India said, trying to get him to spit it out.

"So, I told him to just tell me what he wanted for it, and we would work from there. I worked him down and when I mean down, I mean way down. Now the thing is, it is a lot of money, so don't ask me the price. But after this case, when I make partner, my bonus alone will cover that and then some. I have stock options that are presently going through the roof, so please don't worry about it. Just know that I love you and this is a gift from me to you."

"I still can't believe this is mine," India boasted.

"Believe it, baby, and from here on out, it's nothing but the best for my special lady. And on the evening of the gala, you are going to be the envy of all women because, not only will you the best-looking woman out there, but you will be dressed to kill and armed with jewelry and a husband that are both lethal."

"I know that's right!" India said, hugging and then kissing Grayson on the mouth.

23

"You Better Stop Abusing My Sister"

atience, Jonathan and the kids arrived at India's house late Sunday evening. India did her best to hide all of the bruises. They had at least healed to the point where she could easily concoct a convincing lie.

Grayson was out with his boys working on a project for the Professional African American Men Association's upcoming gala. He was so excited that they were honoring him, and India was pleased to see him so happy. He told India that he planned on flying his foster mother down for the occasion, and he was going to extend an invitation to both Patience and Jonathan. India was just happy for him. His trial seemed to be going well. To date, the prosecution hadn't tried to bring any additional evidence to the table, but that wasn't to say that they didn't have something else hidden in the back alley.

India fed everybody and, when they were done, the kids went into the family room to play, and Jonathan went to watch a sporting event in the den after Patience mentioned that she wanted to talk to India.

"So, how was Busch Gardens?"

"Fun! The kids ran Jonathan and me ragged, but they had a ball. We stayed at the Hilton Garden Inn Hotel. It wasn't too far from Busch Gardens. We had two adjoining rooms. The kids stayed in one room, and we stayed in the other, but we left the doors open between the two."

"That sounds like a lot of fun. So I take it that you and Jonathan never...you know?"

"Please, when those kids were fast asleep, we closed the door for about an hour and we handled our business," Patience said, smiling.

"You go, girl!" India said, holding up her hand to give her sister a high-five.

"So what else is there to do in Williamsburg?" India asked.

"There's a shopping outlet, a PGA tour stop, Kingsmill, Golden Horseshoe, Ford's Colony, Williamsburg National and some other junk."

"What?"

"Exactly, that's why we stuck with Busch Gardens. The kids went on the rides, saw shows and some animal attractions. That part was kind of corny, but the kids learned some things about birds and animal preservation, so it was cool. What did you do this weekend?" Patience asked, taking a keen look at India.

"A little of this, a little of that," India replied. "Grayson is being honored with the PAAMA Award this year, so we celebrated and stuff."

"I know exactly what the stuff was; with no Sierra to disturb y'all, you probably got too much stuff."

Both women laughed long and hard.

"I am not mad at you! So, what happened to your arm?" Patience asked.

India had figured that this question was coming sooner or later, and she'd had all weekend to come up with something credible and creative.

"Girl, when was the last time I rode a bike?" India asked, biting into a health bar.

"You act like I remember. Probably when you were in junior high or something because when you got to high school you were too fly to be seen riding anybody's bike. That is, unless it was a motorcycle."

"You know that. Anyway, Grayson wanted to do something different this weekend, so we went out and rented bicycles and went to the park. Girl, they say you never forget how to ride, but this chick busted her ass several times. I'm telling you, Grayson got such a good laugh out of seeing me fall so many times. Then, you know that I was too cute to wear a helmet or arm and kneepads. Now look at the results," India said, extending her arm for Patience to examine.

"You are out of your mind. At your age, you should really know better. Some of those marks are not going to go away, either."

"Well, I've been using cocoa butter and vitamin E, so hopefully they'll go away. My skin is too beautiful to have scars. Patience, I really can't thank you enough for looking after Sierra for me this weekend. I was able to get a lot of stuff done, and Grayson and I spent a lot of quality time together. We really needed that."

"No problem. Now, I want to tell you something, but you have to promise me that you won't get upset."

"Why would I get upset?"

"Just promise me that you won't have an attack or try to attack me," Patience said, reaching across the table to hold her sister's hands.

"Oh boy, what did you do now?" India asked, looking into her sister's face, but Patience simply gave her hands a light squeeze. "Alright, I promise that I won't have an attack or hurt you."

"Okay," Patience said as she let go of India's hands. "We saw Daddy this weekend."

"You what?" India stood and placed her hands on her hips. "I thought that you said you went to Virginia. Did you fly my child all the way to Florida to see that loser?"

"India, you promised you wouldn't have an attack."

"I don't have time for bullshit promises. Now where did you see that man at?"

"He met us down in Williamsburg, Virginia. I told you that I had been speaking to him, and he really is trying to change. He has a little job down in Florida. You know, just something to keep him occupied. Daddy really looked good."

"I don't give a damn how he looked."

"When are you going to forgive him? Life is too short. Haven't you learned anything from the September 11?"

"Yes, life is too short, and you know whose life was too short? Huh? Huh? Our mother's, or did you forget that he was the culprit behind her leaving us so quickly? Listen, what you do is your business. If you want to be a good Samaritan and forgive him, then you do that, but I don't want anything to do with him. That's my choice and it's final."

"India, all of that anger, and for what? Where's it going to get you? And, just because you don't want to have anything to do with him doesn't mean that you should keep Sierra from him. He wants to be involved in his grandchildren's lives. Don't you think that he has lost and suffered enough? I mean, he lost a son, a wife and one of his daughters. We're all the family he has left. India, please believe me when I say that I understand where you're coming from, but you should really put the past to rest."

"Are you finished?" India asked, taking a seat.

"Yes, I'm done."

"Fine, now I don't appreciate you taking my daughter behind my back to see that man."

"If I'd told you, you wouldn't have allowed me to take Sierra, and he wanted to see all of his grandkids."

"I didn't interrupt you, so please don't interject on me."

Patience had a look on her face that read, "Well excuse the hell out of me."

"Like I was saying, I don't like that you took Sierra to see him without telling me, but you're right. It's unfair of me not to allow Sierra to see him. It's bad enough that Grayson doesn't have any immediate family to speak of. I still maintain the feelings that I have for our father. I despise him. I will never, ever consider him to be a father again. He lost my respect years ago after what he did to our family."

Patience and India sat in silence. They could hear the children romping in the adjoining room. Once again, Veronica and Sierra were beating up on Little John and he was screaming, "Stop hitting me!" Neither Patience nor India bothered to tell them to behave. Instead, India got up from the table and went to the sink to place the dirty pots, glasses and plates into the dishwasher.

A few moments later, Patience got up to join her.

"You need some help?" Patience asked.

"No, I just wanted to come over here and think to myself for a moment."

"Do you mind if I join you?"

"You're already over here," India said as she gave her sister a stern look. "Patience, I'm really mad at you."

"I'm sorry to hear that, and I really didn't want to go behind your back and do that, but it was important to me that Sierra saw her grandfather. You know that this was the first time that he's seen Sierra in person? I didn't realize that."

"Yeah, I know, but I sent him pictures when Sierra was born."

"Yeah, that was four, going on five, years ago now. That man cried and cried when he hugged those kids. I thought that he was going to scare them away, but he didn't. They rallied around him, and he really enjoyed their company."

India thought about her father and how loving he was to her and Patience when they were kids. She remembered how he used to carry her on his shoulders through the park while Patience and their brother, Cleveland, rollerskated. After a long and exhausting day at the park, he would take them to their favorite fast-food restaurant. He would tell them imaginary stories and sometimes reflect on things that he had done when he was child. India remembered those days all too well. Their father was very cultured, and the family often took trips to the museum and went to plays that came to town. That was the one thing that she could thank her father for, her love for the arts. When she attended college her major was journalism, but she minored in art history. In hindsight, she knew her father wasn't all that bad. Nevertheless, it was hard to forgive him for all of the damage he had inflicted on the family.

"We had a really long talk. He wants to have you back in his life. Daddy is really sorry for everything. Don't you think that if he could go back and do things differently, he would?"

"Why do you have to have such a big heart?" India asked.

"Why do you have to be so damn evil?"

The water from the sink was on, and India put her hand under the faucet and flicked a few droplets at Patience.

Patience wiped her face and gathered some water in her palms and splashed it all over India. They went back and forth until both of their shirts were soaked.

"You know what? You and Daddy are more alike than you'd ever care to admit," Patience said.

"Whatever."

"No, seriously. You're both very stubborn and evil as all hell. I mean, you both can be nice when you want to be, but don't get either one of you upset. Oh, and you both hold grudges longer than necessary."

"Hardy, har, har! You are so funny."

Grayson came home shortly after India and Patience finished putting the dishes into the dishwasher. He came into the kitchen and gave India a nice peck on the lips and hugged Patience. Patience obliged, but it was apparent from her body language that she didn't want to be bothered with him. Grayson was too preoccupied to notice anything.

"What are you ladies in here gossiping about now?" Grayson asked, looking at India.

"Nothing that concerns you," India replied.

"Oh, well in that case, what's for dinner?" Grayson lifted the lids off the two pots on the stove. He practically submerged his head into the first pot. When he resurfaced, he clapped his hands and rubbed them together. "See, now that's what I'm talking about. After a long laborious day, a man likes to come home to his favorite meal. Steak with roasted potatoes, asparagus tips, and I know that my lady has made some salad to go along with this dinner."

India laughed bashfully.

"You know that I did," she answered.

Patience looked at the two of them and looked up at the ceiling in disgust. "Oh, please give me a break," she said.

Grayson walked over to Patience and gave her a kiss on the forehead.

"I love you too, Patience." Grayson walked over to the cabinet to get a plate. After fixing it, he returned to the table where India and Patience were and sat beside Patience.

"So, how was the trip, and did our little angel behave herself?"

"The trip was nice, and the children had a lot of fun. You know Sierra is always on her best behavior. She's a little India in disguise. Grown for her four years and bossy as all heck, but she gets that from her mother."

India spiked Patience a derisive look and sucked her teeth.

"Hey, hey, watch what you say about the women in my life," Grayson joked.

"I was just telling India that we saw our father in Busch Gardens."

"Really?" Grayson put his fork down.

"Yeah, it's no big deal. We arranged this trip a little while back. It just worked out that Sierra came along with us. Jonathan and I wanted to take her, anyway. I didn't know how to approach India because I knew she would probably say no way."

"You're probably right," Grayson replied. "So, was Sierra surprised to see her grandfather?"

"Yeah, I guess. You know, she's too small to really understand what's going on. All the same, she enjoyed his company, and we all had a good time."

Grayson returned to eating his food.

"Where's Jonathan?" Grayson asked.

"In the den watching television. As you can imagine, he is dog tired."

"Oh, yeah! Three kids this weekend? I definitely don't envy the brother, but I want to do something similar real soon with the kids. After this case, I want to take two vacations. One with the entire family to someplace like Orlando. Then, I want to take a nice, quiet one with my beautiful wife. That trip is long overdue, and she deserves it for putting up with my difficult behind." Grayson smiled and nudged India with his elbow.

"Well you can take the kids. That will give me and Jonathan some time alone for a change."

"We'll let you know when we plan on going. This trial is going to be the death of me."

"Why, what's going on?" India queried.

"Yeah, I've been keeping up with it on television. That judge is really a stickler," Patience added.

"All I can say is that I'm glad it's her and not that craggily old Judge Pinch. I probably wouldn't have made it this far if she were behind the bench."

"So what's going on?" Patience asked.

"You know that I'm not at liberty to disclose information or discuss the details of the case with you and don't say that you won't tell anyone else. You both know that's a lie. India works for one of the largest black magazines in the country, and, Patience, you have a ton of friends who will question you to death if they know that I'm your brother-in-law. Ah-ah-ah, don't lie," Grayson said, cutting Patience off before she could interject.

Patience and India looked at each other and rolled their eyes at Grayson.

"I don't care, you can both stay mad at me, but I bet India won't stay mad after I tell her that I've asked X-Tasy to do an exclusive interview with *Shades!*"

India immediately perked up.

"Get the hell out of here! Are you serious?" India asked, wrapping her arms around Grayson's neck.

"Yes, I did, and she said yes," Grayson boasted.

"Oh shit! The editor-in-chief is going to love me. Oh my goodness. I knew there was a reason that I love you."

"I hope that there's more reason than that for you to love me."

"I hope so, too," Patience added.

"Hey, Patience, speaking of good news, did India tell you that I'm being honored by the Professional African American Men Association next month?"

"Yes, India mentioned it. Congratulations, I'm happy for you."

"Yeah, it means a lot to me. This is huge. Well, I want to invite you and Jonathan to the big bash. It would really mean a lot to me if you all could make it."

"I'll see what we have going on then," Patience answered.

"Well, let me and India know."

"Definitely, so when and where is it being held?" Patience asked.

"It's taking place in Atlanta."

"Oh, that should be nice. You know what?" Patience's brain was ticking quicker than a time bomb.

"What?" Grayson and India asked in unison.

"You should invite our cousin Sandy and her husband Bedford. It would be a real nice reunion. Plus, her good friend Wanita lives down there."

"Oh yeah," India said, seeing exactly where her sister was going.

"We should invite them. Didn't Bedford inquire about joining PAAMA the night he saw you at their party?"

"He sure did. Okay, I'll have an invitation sent out to them."

"Great! As long as we don't have a huge party taking place that week, we'll definitely be there. You can count us in," Patience said enthusiastically.

Jonathan entered the kitchen with a beer can in his hand.

"Hey, what's up, man?" Grayson said, getting up to give Jonathan a pound.

"Nothing much, man. I'm just ready to go home and sleep."

"Man, I hear you. I just want to thank you for taking care of Sierra for us this weekend. We appreciate it and plan to return the favor soon."

"That sounds good," Jonathan said, putting the can in the receptacle. "Patience, you ready? I'm about through for the night. You may have to drive us back to Baltimore."

"That's fine," Patience replied.

"I'll go get the kids ready to go," India said, heading into the family room.

"I'm going to drain the dragon before we leave. This was my second can of beer," Jonathan said.

Patience and Grayson were left alone in the kitchen together. Grayson got up to place his plate into the sink and, when he noticed it was empty, he opened up the dishwasher and placed it with the other plates. Patience cleared her throat.

"Would you like something to drink before you leave?" Grayson asked, walking to the fridge.

"No, I'm fine. So, India tells me that you two went bike-riding this weekend."

Grayson didn't answer her immediately. Instead, he kept staring into the fridge like something new was going to appear.

"Ah, is that what she said. Yeah, we went biking."

Patience knew that he was lying by the way he hesitated. She figured that her sister had lied to her. She had known India long enough to know that she would never go bike riding. She'd hired a personal trainer to avoid having to go to the gym. India was into posh and pampering, not outdoor exercise. That was as far-fetched as India going rock climbing. India was too concerned about chipping a nail or the high altitude making her hair frizzy.

"So, where did you two go?"

"Oh, we went here and there. You know, around the way."

"Hmm, India said that you all rode around the lake."

"Yeah, that's what I meant by here and there."

"Grayson, you are such a damn liar. India didn't tell me jack about going to the lake. She told me that you two went bike riding around the park. But let me tell you one thing. You better stop abusing my sister. I don't know why she puts up with your crap or even sticks around when she could do better, but if you continue I'll have you fucked up!"

"Patience, I don't know what you're talking about," Grayson answered.

"Like I said, you see how messed up my sister looks right now. She's telling me that she fell off some damn bike like I'm supposed to believe that shit. You'll look even worse and that's if you survive."

"Patience, are you threatening me?" Grayson asked, getting serious.

"You're an attorney. You're a very smart man, so you take it anyway you want. But just remember, the next time I see a mark on my sister, you better watch your back."

The kids came running out of the family room with their jackets on and Jonathan returned from the bathroom.

Both India and Jonathan sensed that something wasn't quite right.

"What's going on in here?" India asked with a concerned look on her face.

"Oh, nothing," Patience answered. "I was just telling Grayson about something that might transpire in the future if certain events continued to occur. Isn't that right, Grayson?" Patience said.

"Yeah, something like that," Grayson replied and exited the room.

24
"So What's the Bad News?"

onday was Bedford's least favorite day of the week. After having a nice leisurely weekend he loathed having to come into the office, even if he did work for himself. Bedford rationalized that it was always better to walk into your own office and make your own money than it was punching in the clock like a flunky for someone else.

Bedford had to pry himself out of the bed that morning. He'd spent a good thirty to forty minutes burying his tongue in Sandy's hot spot. That always helped him to get his work week off to a good start.

On his way into the office, Bedford made a pit stop at his favorite bagel and coffee shop. He purchased a cranberry nut muffin and a cup of café au lait. He also picked up a glazed doughnut and regular coffee for his third favorite girl, Shirley.

Bedford stepped out of the elevator and checked himself in the large mirror that was in the corridor on the opposite side. He thought, as he adjusted his tie, *Damn, I look good!* He didn't stare too long because another door opened, and a few people exited the elevator.

As he strolled down the hallway he stole a quick look into one of the newly renovated office spaces. Two weeks earlier workmen were putting up the Sheetrock and painting the walls. One week earlier, they were laying the carpet, hanging paintings and installing the furniture. This week, Bedford had new neighbors. Ironically, the sign on the door read PROFESSIONAL AFRICAN AMERICAN MEN ASSOCIATION OF NEW YORK, CORPORATE HEADQUARTERS. It was an organization that he'd considered joining and, now that their offices were only a few doors down the hall, he would definitely take the initiative. Now he had no excuse.

Bedford glanced at his watch to see if he had time to stop in and introduce himself to his new neighbors. The watch read five minutes after nine, but he didn't have anything pressing or waiting for him at the office. It was going to be a typical, uneventful and boring Monday morning. Just as Bedford was about to open the door to enter, a twenty-something woman with big bright eyes, long lashes and a beautiful smile walked out. Bedford held the door open for her, and they both gazed at each other a moment longer than necessary. Bedford bowed his head to acknowledge and greet his new neighbor, and she responded by doing the same. She walked by him, and the soft sensual smell of her perfume lingered beneath his nose. He continued to hold the door open and his eyes followed her as she ambled down the hall in a skirt that reminded him of a tube top.

"Sir, may I help you?" a voice from inside of the office beckoned.

Bedford cleared his throat and focused his attention on the little beauty behind the desk. She flashed him a look of interest, but the look immediately changed once she saw the wedding band on his finger.

"Yes, you may," Bedford replied. "I work down the hall, and I just wanted to introduce myself and welcome you to the building."

"Well, thank you sir, and your name is?"

"Pardon me. My name is Bedford Jackson. I'm the owner of Jackson and Jackson Financial Consultants, Inc." Bedford shook hands with the woman behind the desk.

"Oh, I saw your company listed on the directory out by the elevator. It's nice to meet you, Mr. Jackson. My name is Cinnamon S. Wells. I'm the receptionist-slash- office-assistant-slash anything else that they assign to me."

"Nice to meet you, Ms. Cinnamon S. Wells."

"Same here. So, you said Jackson and Jackson. Are you in business with a family member, like your brother, cousin, *wife*?" Cinnamon placed extra emphasis on the word *wife*. Bedford immediately picked up on her little charade.

"It's actually my ex-wife, but we still maintain an amicable relationship."

"Oh," Cinnamon said with renewed interest.

Since you asked me a question, let me ask you one. What does the "S" stand for?"

"It stands for anything you want it to stand for."

Wow, Bedford thought. This was going to be easier than he thought. Miss Cinnamon S. Wells was rolling out the red ass for him. He knew that, once again, he was probably asking for trouble, especially getting involved with a woman this young who worked down the hall. He would have to feel her out and up first before making that vital move. The last thing he wanted was a fatal-attraction scenario. He'd had too many close calls as it was, and Patience just wouldn't go away. She was still leaving messages and now his daily task was to check their answering service every hour on the hour because he never knew if and when she was going to call.

"Let's see…Cinnamon tastes good, but it tastes even sweeter with Sugar."

Cinnamon laughed at Bedford's joke.

"Okay," Cinnamon said as she regained her composure. "Mr. Jackson, you are both funny and good looking. What does a girl have to do to get on you—I mean on your calendar for lunch? That was a little slip of the tongue."

Cinnamon licked her lips after making her statement.

"You can slip your tongue anywhere you want," Bedford said, playing along. He knew that if he played his cards right, he could have this tasty little treat one day this week, but he was also interested in the delicious young lady who had crossed his path earlier. He wanted to ask Cinnamon who she was without being obvious.

Cinnamon's face piqued with interest.

"By the way, if we're going to be friends, you don't need to call me Mr. Jackson. Bedford is fine."

"Yes, Bedford is," Cinnamon countered.

Bedford continued to hover over the reception desk, making small talk and laughing with Cinnamon, when Beautiful Smile with the tube top for a skirt returned. She stopped at the desk to make idle chat with Cinnamon, and then assigned her several tasks before walking away. Beautiful Smile glanced over her shoulder to steal one last look at Bedford before entering her office and closing the door.

Bedford wanted her. She wasn't going to be an easy conquest. He knew that he could have her if he really pursued her, but she wasn't going to make it as easy for him as Cinnamon.

"I can't stand her," Cinnamon said, rolling her eyes and clucking her tongue as soon as her coworker went into the office.

Great, Bedford thought. They weren't friends, so he could have his cake and pie and eat them too.

"Well, you know we don't have control over the people we work with, but we can definitely make it easier on ourselves if we remain respectful and cordial," Bedford said.

"Yeah, you're right. It's just that she thinks that she's all that. The only reason she got this job is because her uncle is the cofounder of the New York branch, but she ain't hardly qualified. I could do what she does," Cinnamon said, huffing.

"Just hang in there and prove yourself and maybe you'll get that job or even one better."

"True."

"Anyway, I'd better get to work," Bedford said, reaching into his inside jacket pocket to fetch his business card holder. He found it and pulled out a card for Cinnamon. "Here's my card. Give me a call sometime this week."

"You know I will."

"I expect nothing less," Bedford said before he departed.

Two minutes later, Bedford walked into his domain. He greeted everyone as he breezed through. He was looking good and feeling great. He took a deep breath as he approached his office. Things were going to be quite interesting over the next few weeks.

Shirley was on a call when he walked up to her and placed the bag with the coffee and the doughnut on her desk. Although she was on the phone, she held up a finger telling him to wait before walking off. Bedford stood and waited until Shirley completed her call. He couldn't help but listen to her talk to one of his clients, and he loved her professionalism. She could win anyone over.

"Well, good morning, Mr. Jackson," Shirley sang in her southern drawl. "Thank you for picking up my coffee and doughnut. You know I appreciate it."

"Anything for my Shirley. So, what's going on? Did you need me for something?"

"Oh yes, two things. I need to leave the office a little early on Thursday. I have to go down to motor vehicles to turn in my old tags."

"That's fine. Just remind me on Thursday morning. What else is going on?"

"Mrs. Jackson is in your office."

"What? Why?" Bedford asked.

"She said that it was urgent, and she needed to speak to you immediately. She's been sitting in there waiting for you since nine A.M. I told her that you had a meeting and would probably be in late, but she didn't budge."

"Damn it. What does Felice want now? It damn well better be important," Bedford said, storming past Shirley's desk.

"I'm sorry," Shirley said sympathetically. "I tried to derail her, but she was adamant about seeing you. She said something about you not returning her calls."

"Don't worry about it. It's not your fault, and I'll get to the bottom of whatever it is."

Bedford opened the door to his office and Felice was sitting at his desk reviewing the files that were lying there. She didn't acknowledge Bedford until he slammed the door shut.

"Well, good morning to you too," Felice said.

"Good morning, Felice. What can I do for you on this bright Monday morning?"

Felice removed herself from the plush leather seat and sat on the opposite side of the desk while Bedford hung his jacket up in the closet.

"Why haven't you returned my calls?"

"I've been busy," Bedford said as he restacked his folders in the order that he had originally left them.

"You are so freaking anal," Felice said and laughed.

"It's not about being anal. I have a particular order in which I want to review these materials, and I arranged them this way for a reason.

Anyway, one thing has nothing to do with the other. You came by because you obviously need or want something. So, what is it now?"

Felice was looking good as usual. She was nicely dressed. Her hair was longer than the last time Bedford had seen her, and she had gained a little weight, but, from what he could see, in all of the right places. As much as he liked sexing Felice, he knew that she was a bad habit, especially since they were business partners. Felice had a short fuse and was unpredictable. She was a typical Gemini woman.

"Do you want the good news or the bad news first?" Felice asked.

"I'll let you decide which one you want to give me first."

"Okay, fine. Be that way. Here goes…" Felice said, pausing for an extended amount of time as Bedford looked on. "I'm pregnant."

"That's great! Your boy Aaron must be happy. So what's the bad news?"

"You're the father."

25

"Bitch Set Me Up..."

edford removed himself from his comfortable leather chair and placed himself directly in front of Felice. This had to be a nightmare. He and Felice had been married for several years, and not once during the course of their matrimony had she ever managed to get pregnant. So why and how could this be happening to him now? Felice had to be lying. The last time they'd gotten their freak on was well over a month ago. He definitely knew that it was a while back. They got together once or twice after Sandy's trip to North Carolina when she had gone to visit her mother. Felice had to be mistaken. That would mean that she was at least…Bedford didn't want to think about it. He was not the only person Felice was sleeping with. She had a man, and his name was Aaron.

Bedford was feeling like the former mayor of Washington, D.C., Marion Barry: "Bitch set me up . . .I shouldn't have allowed her to suck my dick . . . damn bitch."

Bedford pulled himself together because he didn't want to offend Felice by saying the wrong thing, but based on the current situation, anything that came out of his mouth was bound to be foul.

"Let me get this straight, you're pregnant."

"Yes, okay, so you were listening. You had this bewildered look in your eyes, and then everything went blank, so I thought that I lost you there for a moment," Felice joked.

"I'm glad that you find humor in this situation. Now, why in the world do you think that I'm the father of this…this baby you're supposed to be carrying?"

"B.J., are you trying to call me a liar?"

"Woman, I'm not calling you anything, but I would like to know why you believe me to be the father."

Bedford leaned back against his desk and folded his arms. The stern look on his face was more out of anxiety and fear than anger. Yes, he did want to start a family, but with his current, not his ex-wife.

"Because you are, that's why."

"Felice, that's not good enough and you know it. Now, please explain yourself. I mean, I know I'm not the only person you're sleeping with. Are you selecting me because you feel that I'll take responsibility for this?"

"B.J., don't flatter yourself! The fact of the matter is that Aaron is not the father and, aside from him, you are the only person that I've slept with in the last few months—or weeks, for that matter. I know that Aaron is not the father because he was overseas playing basketball at the time that this baby was conceived. Not that it's any of your business, but I was with Aaron one month prior and two months after."

"Not that it's any of my business. You have the gumption to sit here and tell me this shit. Oh Felice, come on. What do you expect me to do or say? Do you want me to own up to this? Because I won't until the test results tell me otherwise."

"B.J., don't you think that this is hard on me too? Do you really think that I would intentionally put myself into this kind of a predicament?"

"Felice, I don't know what you would or wouldn't do anymore. I've stopped guessing when it comes to you."

Felice didn't say a word. She held her head down in her hands and began to cry. Bedford went back to his side of the desk and unsympathetically began working on the files that sat before him. Bedford tried to remain calm. After all, he was still at work and if any of what Felice said was true, he didn't want this to spread. Shirley was stationed right out in front of his office and he knew that she had keen hearing. To an extent, he knew that Shirley was aware of his occasional indiscretions, but she never flaunted them. Shirley never got involved in his personal affairs, but this case was a little different. She wouldn't want to get involved especially since she really worked for Bedford. Shirley would be placed in an awkward position as his secretary having to answer the phone and lie to Sandy about his whereabouts, or even to Felice when he didn't want to see her. It would definitely put her in a compromising position.

Bedford felt uncomfortable treating Felice so coldly, but he didn't know what else to do. If he were to become sympathetic, she would probably assume everything was okay and move forward with having this baby, of which he truly wanted no parts. He didn't understand how something like this could happen to him. Why hadn't Felice told him that she wasn't using any contraception? He was also pissed off at himself for failing to use protection. Bedford knew Felice was clean, so he took having sex with her for granted. They had been doing it for so long without getting caught that he had thrown caution to the wind. What he didn't take into consideration was that she could still end up pregnant.

Bedford wanted to punish himself for being so stupid. This couldn't be happening at a more inopportune time. He was already working overtime trying to avoid having Sandy find out about his little fling at their anniversary party. Aside from that, things were going on the right track between them. Sandy was beginning to trust him again and if this ever got back to her, things would definitely be over. How in the world could he talk himself out of this one?

He had used his nephew's death as part of the reason that he lapsed the first time around. To an extent it was true, but it didn't excuse his sleeping with Keyanna. Why did he allow himself to get mixed up in things like that? Why did he use his dick as a guide instead of his brain? Less than an hour ago he was flirting with Ms. Cinnamon S. Wells. He had to use mind control to calm himself down because she was coming at him like a bulldozer to a building. Cinnamon was an interesting character, and Bedford was already conjuring up scenarios in which he planned to devour her. He could see that she was a hot little tart. She was nicely dressed in a lavender business suit, but she'd had her jacket off, and her camisole showed off her twenty-something perky, *I-want-you-to-suck-me-now* breasts. Bedford just knew that with her pretty brown complexion, her nipples had to be the color of caramel, and he'd never had Cinnamon and caramel at the same time. Just thinking about it was making his dick hard, and now was not the time or the place. Then, he tried to figure out how he could get both Cinnamon and Beautiful Smile together at the same time. Bedford had to stop thinking about sex. That's exactly what had gotten him into this jam with Felice, and he really had no intention of owning up to the pregnancy until it was confirmed. Conversely, he knew that Felice wouldn't lie to him about something this big or important.

Bedford put the papers down and focused on Felice. He never did like to see her cry. It used to hurt him when they were married and, in some strange way, it still bothered him to see her upset or sad.

"Felice, talk to me. What do you want to do?"

Bedford handed her a few pieces of Kleenex from the box on his desk. Felice took them to clean her face and blow her nose. She was trying to stop the tears from flowing and get her breathing under control.

"I don't know," Felice said, choked up.

Bedford was still feeling uncomfortable and was trying hard to find the right words to help soothe her.

"Is it too late to…you know?"

Felice quickly held up her head and gave Bedford a look that made him wish that he'd never asked.

"I can't believe you. Are you suggesting that I have an abortion?"

"I-I don't know what you want to do. Were you planning on having the baby? Is that what you want to do?"

"B.J., I really don't know what I want to do. I haven't told my fiancée, Aaron, yet, and, quite frankly, I don't think that I can."

"You didn't tell me that you guys were engaged," Bedford said, sounding a little envious and noticing the boulder swallowing her finger for the first time.

"You don't return people's phone calls. I called you more than a month ago to share the good news with you and…well, whatever. I don't have time to chase you down. We work in the same damn office, and I have to make an appointment to see my business partner!"

"Felice, I'm sorry. I've been dealing with some problems of my own, and it seems that my stack of things just keeps piling up. Besides, I thought that you had gone to Europe to see Aaron, and I didn't know when you were returning."

"Well, I've been back for a while now and, like I said, we work in the same office. You can walk over to my office just the same way I mosey on over here."

"You're right. You'll get no argument from me there."

"As for what I want to do…if this were Aaron's baby, I wouldn't even have a second thought about keeping it. It's not like we're not in a position to provide for a child. The only problem there is that he's overseas, but he'll be retiring in another year or so. The truth is that I would love to have this baby and, at the same time, I know that I can't. Then, there's my conscience that I have to deal with. How do I go about murdering this baby? I mean, at this stage, it is a baby."

"How long have you known about it?" Bedford queried.

"I've known about it for a month now. I was still getting my period, so I had no reason to suspect that I was pregnant. Then, I started to notice little things changing about me, and I couldn't hold certain things down. I went to the doctor, and he ran some tests and, low and behold, I found out that I was fine, but that I'm expecting."

Damn, Bedford thought. That was a new one. He thought that being pregnant interrupted the menstrual cycle instantly. Apparently, he was wrong.

"Then, why didn't you do something before this?"

"Because I wasn't sure what I wanted to do. B.J., this is a big decision. I'm not getting any younger, and this is the first time in my thirty-something years that I have ever gotten pregnant. If I abort it, will I ever be able to conceive again?"

"Maybe, maybe not, but don't you think that you're botching up any future that you may have with Aaron? Seriously, what do you think this guy is going to say when you tell him that you are carrying another man's baby?"

"I honestly don't know."

"Felice, he's a man. You've just crushed his ego. He's going to feel real fucked up and, no matter how much he loves you, he's going to walk away from this. He may have understood if you just had an affair, but to leave the trail of evidence? Hell, I couldn't even deal with that."

"If he got some woman in Europe pregnant, I'd be understanding."

"You're only saying that now because it's happening to you and, honestly speaking, by nature, women are more forgiving. Let me be blunt with you. Aaron may know that you are over here getting your groove on, but there has never been any proof to substantiate that. Besides that, no man wants to know that someone else is tapping his piece of ass. We may know the truth deep down, but once it comes to light we no longer want the soiled goods. We toss them to the side and move on to the next woman. That's a man by nature. We can do it, but our women cannot."

"That's real foul and chauvinistic."

"Felice, that may be so, but it's the damn truth."

"What would you do if I decided to keep it?"

Bedford hoped this was a trick question.

"Do you want me to blow smoke up your ass, or do you want me to tell you the truth?"

"I'm in search of the truth right now."

"I'd be upset. It's not on my agenda to have a child outside of my marriage. My wife and I are trying to start a family, and this could put a hitch in things. I mean, if it were five years ago when you were my wife, fine. However, this is the here and now, and your pregnancy could destroy everything that I have with my wife."

"You weren't thinking about that when we were straddling your desk," Felice retaliated.

"Neither were you." Bedford paused. "I'm not looking for a match with you, Felice. What I want is for us to resolve this matter immediately. Firm decisions have to be made, and we can't afford to delay things any further."

"I agree," Felice said, throwing the damp tissue into the receptacle and pulling herself together.

"Do you need me to go with you to the doctor?"

"First, let me talk to my physician. Then I'll let you know my final decision, but I think I already know what I have to do," Felice said, sounding remorseful.

"Felice, I want you to know that whatever the decision, I'll be here for you, but it won't be in the way that you'll need me."

"B.J., I know…I know. Well, I'll have to act fast and deal with my conscience later."

"I'm real sorry, Felice." Bedford left his desk to give Felice a hug of support.

"I'm even sorrier," Felice said, welcoming Bedford's embrace.

26

The Dead Have Come to Life

anita felt like crap. She was back in New York with her mother in her old childhood bedroom. She loathed staying with Sybil. She hadn't left the room since she'd arrived three days earlier. Wanita would give anything to go back home to her husband, but William wasn't taking or returning her calls. According to his assistant, he was on a business trip and Wanita wasn't in a position to either deny or confirm this information.

Depression was starting to set in. She had been crying from the moment she'd left her house. On the first night, she and her mother booked a room and stayed in a hotel. The following day, Wanita went back to the house to retrieve a few more items because she had no idea how long she was going to be gone. She didn't know if this was definite or indefinite. She really hoped that it was the latter.

Sybil wasn't making the transition any easier. Throughout the entire plane ride to New York, all she did was complain about men and their faults—men ain't shit, men this and men that. Sybil was set on telling Wanita things that she didn't want to hear. It was the longest two-hour flight that Wanita had ever had to endure. It was plumb painful. Then, her mother told her that she was better off without William, and, if Wanita didn't know any better, she would have thought that her mother was a lesbian. Sybil didn't have one good thing to say about the male species, and she was trying to recruit Wanita to feel the same way.

Wanita refused to leave the confines of her pink bedroom with the white canopy bed. Her room was just the way she'd left it more than fifteen years ago. Her jewelry chest was still on the shelf along with her favorite books, *Assata* and several Toni Morrison novels. Wanita felt out of place. This was no longer her home. Wanita's place and heart were in Atlanta

Eight years of marriage down the tubes. No, Wanita was not willing to give up that easily. She needed to use this time apart to pull herself together. How could William be so cruel? She didn't understand why he would be so quick to just throw everything out of the window. This marriage was not over. They needed to talk things out rationally because there was nothing that they couldn't work out. William was a good husband, when he was acting like one, and she knew that that person still existed somewhere. Wanita knew that she might have to dig deep to find that person, and she was prepared to roll up her sleeves and put in the extra muscle to get the job done.

More than anything, Wanita was embarrassed and hurt. She didn't know why William would choose to show out in front of her mother. She was aware of the fact that he was never very fond of Sybil, but to behave the way that he did was simply outrageous. He'd acted as if he were possessed. The words that he flung at both her and her mother still resonated in her head.

"This is my house, and I'm the king of this castle. I work, I pay the bills, I pay the mortgage. Therefore, I decide who can and can't stay here...If Sybil touches me, she'll go to jail!"

If William's mother were still alive, Wanita would never dream of ever being disrespectful to her. Wanita was taught to respect her elders, and she knew that William was brought up in a similar manner.

Over the past few days, Wanita had been praying on the situation. She asked the good Lord to guide and give her the strength to make the right decision. In her heart, she knew that in order for things to work between her and William he was going to have to change. Wanita knew that she wasn't without fault, but her issues were minor in comparison. Otherwise, she would be going home to the same exact thing.

One of the most important things that Wanita wanted and needed to do was sit down with William and get to the bottom of his blaming her for his mother's death. He had to know deep down that she had done everything she could to make his mother comfortable while she was alive. Wanita had treated her as if she were her own birth mother because she would have expected if William were in a similar situation that he would have done the same.

Wanita decided she would get up and bathe. She had been neglecting her personal hygiene and only left the room two to three times a day to use the bathroom or grab a quick bite to eat. She really didn't even have an appetite. The only thing that she had consumed in the past three days was ginger ale, tea, water, two slices of toast, an egg and, the night before, her mother had made her to eat a salad. She knew that her mother meant well, but she was getting on her last nerve. Every night, she forced herself into the room with Wanita and tried to get her to talk, but Wanita wouldn't budge. She was just grateful that her mother left the house to run errands every day. That was the only reason that Wanita had been able to put up with her this long.

Wanita had never truly felt like a failure until now. For many years, she had been down on herself for having made that fatal error with Mr. Bowen, her patient, but she hadn't felt like a loser or a failure before, but today she did. Wanita didn't know how she could possibly face her family and friends. Layla and Maxine were too judgmental. She'd already heard enough *I told you so*s to last her a lifetime. She knew Sandy wouldn't judge her, but she didn't want to be a burden with her problems. Sandy had told her that she was working on some things in her marriage, but she hadn't gone into detail, and Wanita didn't force her to divulge any information. Wanita figured that it couldn't possibly be that bad, because from what she could tell, Bedford loved Sandy very much. They were probably just having problems trying to conceive. Many women were ashamed to discuss that openly, even if they considered a person their best friend. Wanita needed to talk to someone, and she needed to leave the house for some fresh air.

The phone stared at Wanita. She wanted so badly to call her girl, Sandy. She needed to talk. She wanted someone to help her through this, and the only person she felt content talking to about it was Sandy.

After ten minutes of staring, she decided to finally pick up the phone. Slowly she dialed Sandy's office number. It was eleven o'clock, and she hoped that Sandy was in her office. The phone rang three times before someone answered.

"Hello," Wanita said. "May I please speak with Mrs. Sandy Jackson?"

"Please hold the line," an abrupt voice instructed.

"Hello, this is Mrs. Jackson. How may I help you?"

Wanita was relieved to hear Sandy's voice. Everything that had been bottled up came spilling out over the phone. Without realizing it, Wanita began to bawl.

"Hello…hello? Is somebody there?" Sandy asked.

"Sandy, it-it's me. Wanita." Wanita began to sob uncontrollably.

"Wanita, is everything alright? What's wrong?" Sandy asked, concerned.

Wanita didn't mean to worry Sandy with her problems. All she wanted to do was talk, but she could barely get the words out.

"William and I…" Wanita hiccupped. "William and I, we…we broke up."

"Wanita, oh my sweet Jesus. Sweetie, where are you? Are you going to be okay?"

"I'm up here in New York. I-I'm at my mother's house. I've been here since Monday."

"Wanita, baby, I'm so sorry. Do you feel up to having visitors? I can swing by your mom's house after work if you want."

"Yes, I'd like it if you stopped…by." Wanita was trying to get her breathing under control.

"I'll come by right after work. Your mother lives in Brooklyn, right?" Sandy asked.

"Yes."

"What part of Brooklyn, and what's her address?"

"She lives in Clinton Hills. It's the big house on the corner of Lafayette and Vanderbilt. You can't miss it."

"Oh yeah, I remember now. I'll see you later on this evening."

"Okay…and Sandy…"

"Yes, sweetie?"

"Thank you for coming by."

"No problem. You'd do the same for me."

Wanita tried to get herself cleaned up before Sandy came. She unpacked her suitcase and put all of her clothes in the drawers and closets. She had at least three weeks' worth of clothes, and she was hoping that was all she would need. The Professional African American Men Association's gala was taking place in the next three weeks; by then she prayed that everything would be resolved.

Sandy arrived at 5:15. She was looking as radiant as ever, and Wanita wished that she could say the same about herself. Wanita's long hair was pulled back into a ponytail, and she had on a pair of old sweats that she'd found in her dresser drawer and an old T-shirt from college. She looked and felt like a bum.

After hanging up from Sandy earlier, she'd cried for another hour until she fell asleep. Not having William in her life was worse than losing her job. She could always get another position, but there was only one William.

When Wanita opened the door, the first thing Sandy did was give her a big hug. They hugged for a good two minutes before letting go. Wanita used all of her strength to keep herself from crying. She knew that the tears would start to flow once she started telling Sandy her story.

Sandy's hands were full. She had her laptop, handbag and another bag, which looked like it contained food. If Wanita wasn't mistaken, it smelled like Jamaican, and Sandy knew how much she loved West Indian food.

"How's my baby girl doing?" Sandy asked, stepping back to get a good look at her friend.

"I'm holding up. I won't lie, though; it's been a rough couple of days."

"Wanita, I can only imagine. You know, they should have given us an instructional manual about marriage because I don't think half of us would do it if we knew how difficult it really was."

"Isn't that the truth," Wanita replied. She walked Sandy down the hall and into the kitchen because the food in Sandy's bag was making her hungry. She was glad to see her friend and happy to have some kind of feeling again. Wanita's body, soul, spirit and heart had been quite numb.

"I got your favorite dish. Escoveitch fish, rice and peas and a salad. I remembered the last time that you were up here you took me to that restaurant, 3D's Place on Washington Avenue, so I made a pit stop on my way here."

"Girl, you know that I love you. I'm so glad that I decided to call you."

"I'm glad too!"

Wanita went to the cupboard to retrieve two plates and glasses. She wasn't sure if she should jump right in and tell Sandy what had happened, or if she should wait until they were done eating.

"So, how's Bedford doing?" Wanita asked, trying to make small talk.

"Bedford is doing well."

"Good." Wanita could feel the awkwardness seeping into their space. "So, where should I begin?" Wanita asked.

"Wherever you feel comfortable. I'm just here to listen, unless you ask me to do otherwise."

Wanita took a deep breath and sat in the chair opposite Sandy. She felt like she was going on the main stage to perform.

"You know that things have been rocky in my marriage over the past couple of months. Really, the last couple of years, but they didn't really escalate until earlier this year."

"I know."

"Well, remember when I told you that William told my mother not to come down to Atlanta?"

Sandy compassionately nodded.

"Well, you know Sybil. She wouldn't take no for an answer, and she eventually just came. Now, Sandy, that's my mother, so I'm not going to turn her away. I can't have any man do that to my mother, either. I really should have addressed that when he first told her that *I* said she couldn't stay with us. That's a bunch of bullshit, but I didn't. Looking back, there were a number of things that I should have addressed."

"You know that hindsight is always 20/20."

"Yeah, that's true. Anyway, the night that she came, he practically cussed her out. Then he turned on me, and, get this...he blamed me for his mother's death."

Sandy had an astonished look on her face, and her mouth formed the perfect "O."

"Get the hell out of here! Why in the world? What is this world coming to? I swear this mess is in the air that we breathe. It's making folks go crazy," Sandy added.

"You can just imagine my surprise too. Anyway, to make a long story short, he threatened to call the cops on my mother and me. We all got into it, and he told us both to leave, and here I am."

"Damn, girl," Sandy said, getting up to give Wanita another hug. "Everything is going to be alright. Just trust in our wonderful Creator. He never gives us more than we can bear."

"I know...I know. I've been praying for guidance."

"Wanita, we're not all without problems," Sandy confided. "A few months back, Bedford and I were also on the brink of...I don't even want to say it, but we were on the road to separation, divorce. I don't know, but we have worked through our problems. Now, I have to say that our marriage is as good as new."

"Really? I hope that I can look back and say the same in a couple of months. I can't wait for all of this to be over."

"If you have faith and an ounce of patience, it will be over soon."

"Sandy, I'm just still shocked. It has and it hasn't hit me. You know what I mean?"

"Yeah, I do. I never confided what transpired between Bedford and me. When everything was happening, it looked and felt like a complete haze. I could barely put one foot in front of the other. I almost lost the faith, but thanks to my mother and Robby, I stuck it out."

"Any regrets?"

"None. Bedford made one mistake. He slept with this woman and, well, it's over now. We've gone through counseling, and he's been on his best behavior ever since."

"Bedford, cheat? He doesn't even look like the type. Sandy, he's so into you. I swear I wouldn't have guessed that in a million years."

"I know. It happened, and we worked through it."

"Well, I'm happy for you. William has this gala in three weeks, and I plan to be there, because I was working on the event. I basically put it all together, so I'll be going back down."

"Are you talking about that Professional Men's thing?"

"Yeah, it's the Professional African American Men Association. Their gala is in June."

"Yeah, my cousin India sent me and Bedford an invitation. Maybe we'll go with you."

"I'd be glad to have you. What makes me really sad is that I had that great Venezuelan vacation planned for the last week in June, and we won't be going on that trip."

"Well, you never can tell. William may come around by then."

"Oh, I didn't tell you. He hated the idea of going to Venezuela. He claimed that he was tired of visiting Spanish-peaking countries."

"What? Didn't you ask him where he wanted to go, and he told you to just go ahead and pick a place?"

"Umm-hmm, but that didn't matter. We had a big argument over that too. I'm telling you, it's been rough lately. He told me to cancel the trip, but I got so busy that I didn't even remember to do it."

"Like I said, you two may end up taking that trip, so don't count him out yet."

"Girl, I'm not. I'm keeping my fingers, toes and anything else that I can crossed. I really want my man back."

"I hear you. Then, you fight for what you want and believe in. Wanita, my only word of advice is that you seek counseling. It can do wonders to jumpstart your marriage in the right direction. Without it, I honestly don't know what would have become of Bedford and me."

"I will heed your advice. The only problem is convincing William to do the same."

"Like you said, just continue to pray on it."

Sandy and Wanita vibed for two hours. They made dinner plans for the following evening. Sandy had a two-thirty doctor's appointment in the city, and they would meet afterward.

Wanita was still shocked at Sandy's revelation about Bedford. She was confident that William had never cheated on her. That was the one thing that she never ever worried about. William wasn't the type, but, then again, what was the type? Wanita didn't give it a second thought, because she didn't need to conjure up any additional troubles. The ones that she had were more than enough.

Sybil came home while Wanita was still downstairs. This was the first time that she had come out of her room while her mother was home. Sybil heard the noise in the kitchen and came to see what the commotion was. "Oh, my goodness! The dead has come to life," she joked.

Wanita wasn't really in the mood for her mother's bad humor.

"Good evening, Mother," Wanita said and started to leave the kitchen.

"Wanita, don't leave the kitchen on my account. You're welcome to stay as long as you like. You can make yourself at home."

"Thanks, but I'm tired. I'm going to head upstairs to take a nap."

"Wanita, I didn't do anything to you. If anything, I've helped you to see the light and to see that man for what he really is. I wish that you would stop shutting me out like this."

"You're right. You didn't do anything, but I don't need you to keep reminding me of my situation. Now, Ma, when I'm ready to discuss my affairs you'll be the first to know."

Wanita left the kitchen and returned to her room. She really was tired, but she had to make one last call before going to sleep. She dialed her home phone number. Once again the machine came on.

The automated voice came on, "Freeman residence, please leave a message after the tone...*beeeeep.*"

"Hello, William, it's me again. I just wanted to talk to you. I'm in New York with my mother and I really miss you. William, I don't know where things went wrong between us, but I want you back in my life. What we have deserves a second chance. Marriage is sacred and we are supposed to stay in this through thick and thin, sickness and health and until death do us part. Let's talk. My cell phone is still on, so you can call me on that or 917-555-1990. William, I love you, and I know that you still love me, so please let's work this out."

Beeeeep. "The machine is full."

27

"It's My Cousin, Patience"

andy had a busy day ahead of her. She got up at 6:00 A.M. and
decided to take a thirty-minute jog around Fort Green Park. Since
her schedule was full, she wanted to get her day off to a good start.
She had a morning meeting with the fellow vice principals within her
district, and after that she had a cabinet meeting.

Sandy was more than aware of the problems that existed between
Wanita and William, but she didn't think that it was to the point that they
would part ways. Sandy had had her share of ups and downs in her
own relationship, so she truly sympathized with Wanita and wanted to
support her as much as possible.

When Sandy returned from her jog, she stopped in the kitchen to
brew some coffee. She went upstairs to jump in the shower, and she
heard the water running. Sandy was just about to go in and join Bedford,
but the phone rang. Just as she picked up the phone, Bedford turned the
water off.

"I got it," Sandy yelled. "Good morning."

"Hello, Sandy?"

"Yes, this is Sandy. Who's speaking?"

"Sandy, girl, it's about time that I got you. It's your cousin, Patience."

"Oh my goodness, girl, I was thinking about you the other day.
We've been playing phone tag for so long."

"I know. That's why I said let me call Sandy early in the

morning, because every time I call I get Bedford or your voice mail."

"Yeah, we're working hard."

Bedford strode out of the bathroom with the towel wrapped around his waist. Drops of water cascaded down the center of his chest. He dried his face with the hand towel before walking over to Sandy to give her a kiss. He was about to ask Sandy a question, but she pointed to the phone and he stopped.

"Who is calling us at this hour?" Bedford asked.

"Girl, hold on," Sandy said before muting the mouthpiece with her hand. "It's my cousin, Patience."

"Oh," Bedford said, looking alarmed. "What does she have to say this early in the morning?"

"Bedford, I don't know. She's been trying to reach me for some time now, so I'll find out soon enough."

"Okay, but try to make it quick. I have to use the phone. I forgot about a call that I have to make."

"Then go downstairs and use the phone in your office, or did you forget that you have one?" Sandy returned to Patience. "Patience, I apologize for taking so long. My husband is over hear trying to talk my ear off."

"Really? Well, tell Bedford that I said hi." Patience laughed deep and throaty. "I'll make this quick. I wanted to see if you received the invitation that India sent you?"

"As a matter of fact, I did. I was just talking about that yesterday with my girl, Wanita. You remember her? She was at my wonderful anniversary party."

"Yeah, I remember her. Speaking of your party, it was even more wonderful than you'd ever imagine."

"Tell me about it. My husband knows how to do it right," Sandy said.

"Apparently, that's not all that he knows how to do," Patience said.

Sandy was busy trying to pull her sweaty shirt over her head and missed Patience's comment. She took the remainder of her clothes off and put them in the hamper in the bathroom. When she reentered the bedroom she noticed that Bedford kept applying the skin lotion to the same area while staring into space.

"Are you all right?" Sandy whispered to Bedford.

"I'm fine, but shouldn't you be getting ready? I thought that you said you had a meeting this morning?"

Sandy looked at her wristwatch to confirm the time.

"Oh, I have at least an hour to get ready. Oh, by the way, Patience told me to tell you hi."

Bedford didn't answer. He just continued rubbing the lotion onto his thigh.

"Sandy, are you there?" Patience asked.

"Yeah, I'm here. I was just tending to my husband for a second."

"Well, I won't take up too much of your time. I wanted to make sure that you both are coming to the Professional African American Men Association's annual gala."

"I haven't discussed it with Bedford yet, but I don't see why not. After all, my cousin-in-law is being honored, and I've been seeing Mr. Big-Time on television. India must be so excited."

"You can say that," Patience replied dryly. "Well, I really want you to come. I have something really important that I want to discuss with you."

"Oh, okay. Is everything alright? You sound so serious."

"Yeah, everything is fine. I won't lie, though, it is an important matter. I'd just really prefer to see and speak to you in person. We can sit back and have a few drinks and just talk."

"That sounds like a plan. Wanita will be there too. She's the one who worked on the gala like a dog. "

"Then it should be really nice. Listen, I have to get these kids out of here for school. I just wanted to make sure that you are coming. Please don't bail on me, or I'll have to come up there and hunt you down."

"I don't want to make any false promises, but I definitely want to come. I just need to check our schedules first."

"Okay, that's fine. If you're unable to come, just let me know. All you have to do is book your flight. The hotel is already taken care of."

"Wow, that sounds like a huge incentive. I may not be able to pass that one up."

"I hope not, but if you do, I still want to see you. Call me and let me know your schedule. Perhaps we can bring the family up to New York," Patience said.

"You can definitely do that. We have the room, and school will be out soon, so that won't be a problem."

"Great, then either way, we'll see you."

"Definitely, so we'll chat later. I have to start getting ready for work."

"Okay. You have a good day."

"Same to you," Sandy said and placed the receiver into its cradle.

"What was that all about?" Bedford asked as Sandy headed into the bathroom.

"Oh, nothing urgent, Patience just wanted to know if we were coming to the Professional African American Men Association's annual gala."

"Is that it?" Bedford asked, sounding almost relieved.

"Yeah, what else did you think?" Sandy asked curiously.

"No, it's just that…oh nothing. I figured that it was something more pressing than that. Anyway, when is the gala?"

"The invitation is over there on the dresser, but if I'm not mistaken, it's the second weekend in June. That's only two weeks away."

"Oh, I may not be able to go," Bedford countered.

"Why not?" Sandy asked. "It's a great networking opportunity for you. Besides, I thought that you were interested in joining the organization."

"Yeah, I am, but I have a lot of work to do. I'll make it up to you by taking you someplace nice the weekend after."

"That sounds real good. Well, I guess Wanita will be my date, but I'd much prefer to have you," Sandy said, laughing.

"If you stay, you can have' as much of me as you want," Bedford replied.

"Oh, is that so? I just may have to reconsider going, then," Sandy said, stopping to kiss him on the lips before heading to the shower.

By the time Sandy returned to her school, she was exhausted. Sitting in a roomful of people who couldn't agree on anything was draining. This was the reason the schools were failing. They had poor direction, and everyone wanted to be a captain instead of a skipper.

Sandy was the new kid on the block, so for the most part, she just took notes. Every now and again, she would add her two cents, but the group was going to do what they wanted, anyway.

All of the teachers were already seated in the makeshift conference room when Sandy arrived. The students were attending a two-hour assembly. Sandy had no intentions of making this meeting any longer than necessary. She barely had time to scarf down her lunch on the way back, and she really didn't have that much to report. Her earlier meeting had proven to be a complete bust, and she didn't want to waste any more of her staff's time than necessary. Sandy updated her cabinet on the overall results for the city's standardized tests. She informed them of where the Daniel Hale Williams School stood in comparison, and what the expectations would be for the following year. She opened the floor for questions and concerns. Then she answered them to the best of her knowledge, and within one hour, the meeting was over.

When Sandy got to her office, she saw that it was almost one o'clock. She had to finish completing her paperwork and hurry up to leave soon, or else she'd be late for her 2:30 doctor's appointment in lower Manhattan. The train ride would only be about fifteen minutes long, if she caught the express. However, the express didn't start running until about four o'clock.

Dr. Espinosa's office was practically empty when Sandy arrived. It was 2:15 so she had another fifteen to spare. She had called Wanita before she left work, and they decided to meet right after her doctor's appointment in Manhattan. Sandy figured that it wouldn't take more than an hour total, since all she came for were results. They agreed to decide which restaurant that they wanted to eat at later. There were so many to choose from, especially around the Thirty-fourth street area.

Sandy approached the nurse's station to inform the nurse of her arrival. The woman looked up her file and then handed her a form to complete. Sandy didn't know why she always had to fill out forms when she came to this office. She was seriously thinking about switching doctors because this was ridiculous. They never had the correct information on file, and this was not her first visit. Maybe this was their formality, or a way to keep patients occupied while they waited. Either way, Sandy thought it was a pain in the neck.

"Dr. Espinosa will see you soon," the nurse exclaimed after Sandy returned the clipboard.

"Okay, thank you."

Sandy grabbed a copy of the latest issue of *Shades* magazine and returned to her seat. She immediately flipped to the beauty and fashion section to see what tips her cousin India had for her. There was an interesting article on how to treat skin blemishes and another on painless hair removal in the bikini region. Sandy became so immersed in the magazine that she didn't realize that almost thirty minutes had passed. Aside from her, there was only one other patient in the waiting room, who was still waiting. Sandy's cell phone rang, and the nurse looked up at her, so she took the call out in the hallway.

"Hello," Sandy said in a whisper.

"Sandy, it's Wanita. I'm here in the city. Are you almost done?"

"Girl, no. I broke my neck to get here and they are moving slower than molasses. Where are you?"

"I'm on Thirty-fourth and Seventh. Do you want me to come over to the doctor's office?"

"Yeah, you might as well swing over this way, because I don't know how much longer this will be. It might be a little walk from where you are, though. I'm on Thirty-third and Park."

"That's okay. I'll hop in a cab."

"Good, so I'll see you in about ten minutes. More than likely, I'll still be sitting here in the waiting area. Just come to the fourth floor, gynecology."

"Okay, I'll see you."

Sandy walked back into the waiting area, and she was glad to see that the other patient was absent. She hoped that she was being seen by the doctor and not in the rest room.

Ten minutes later, the woman who was waiting when Sandy arrived walked out of one of the rear offices. She greeted Sandy and left.

"Mrs. Jackson," the nurse called.

"Yes," Sandy replied.

"Dr. Espinosa will see you now."

"Great!"

The nurse opened up the door and led Sandy down a separate passageway from the one that Sandy had entered. She passed several examining rooms. The nurse knocked twice on a door and then entered.

Dr. Espinosa was not at all what Sandy expected. For starters, Dr. Espinosa was a female, and Sandy preferred male doctors. That really wasn't important since she wasn't coming in to be examined.

Dr. Espinosa stood and shook Sandy's hand. Then she pointed her toward the chair to take a seat. Sandy also sat down, and the nurse turned over Sandy's chart, closed the door and left.

"Mrs. Jackson, how are you doing today?"

"Not too bad," Sandy answered.

Dr. Espinosa reviewed Sandy's chart before responding.

"Good, good. Well, I don't really see why they called you in here today. Everything appears to be fine."

"I don't know, either. Your office called me and said something about results, and I know that they don't disclose information over the phone, so I came in."

"Let me check something out," Dr. Espinosa said.

Sandy waited while the doctor called the nurse at the front desk to see if she knew what was going on. After hanging up, she excused herself and walked out of the office. Two minutes later, she returned.

"Mrs. Jackson, I'm sorry to have kept you waiting. It seems that there was a little mix-up. I'm embarrassed to say that we had another Mrs. Jackson on file and we confused the information. Apparently, you two had the same phone number on file, and we called you by mistake. That's why we had you fill out a new patient information form."

Sandy thought about it for a moment and laughed.

"Oh, do you mean Felice Jackson?"

"Yes, do you know her?" Dr. Espinosa asked, surprised.

"Yeah, we did have the same phone number. I'm married to her ex-husband. That's why the number is the same. That is so ironic. I didn't realize that we shared the same gynecologist. Well, it's really a small world."

"It sure is. As a matter of fact, the other Mrs. Jackson came in earlier. We thought that somehow we messed up in the computer by entering the same number twice. Again, Mrs. Jackson, we truly apologize, and we didn't mean to make you wait so long."

"Oh, don't worry about it. I'm just happy to know that there is nothing wrong with me. I was getting a little concerned, considering the last time I came here was a few months back."

"No, nothing for you to concern yourself over. You are fine."

"Thanks," Sandy said as she stood to shake the doctor's hand before leaving.

When Sandy returned to the waiting area, she saw Wanita sitting patiently and reading the same magazine that she had left in the chair. Wanita didn't see her until Sandy stood directly in front of her.

"Is the story you're reading that interesting?" Sandy asked.

"Not really."

"It sure looked like it was. I could have been anyone sneaking up on you like this."

"Anyone like whom? Girl, we're in a doctor's office."

"Yeah, crazy people come to the doctor's office too. "

"No crazier than you," Wanita replied.

"So, did you decide on which restaurant you wanted to go to?"

"Yeah, there's a nice little spot that I passed back over there near Thirty-second and Broadway. That is, if you're in the mood for Chinese?"

"Chinese sounds good to me. Since we're going over there, I can pop in and surprise Bedford. He works across the street from Madison Square Garden."

"Oh, really?"

"Yeah. I can tell him about the mix-up at the doctor's office."

"What mix-up?"

"You won't believe this. Out of all of the gynecologist's offices in New York City, can you believe that Felice and I share the same physician?"

"Get out of here."

"Apparently, they called me by mistake, but it was Felice that they really wanted. I know if I tell Bedford, he'll get a huge kick out of it."

"Damn, y'all shared the same man, now the same doctor? What's next?"

"Don't even go there!" Sandy laughed. "It's a nice enough day. We can walk over there instead of hopping in a cab," she suggested.

"That's fine."

By the time they arrived at Jackson and Jackson, it was four-thirty. Sandy greeted the staff members and introduced Wanita to the few account executives that she knew. When they got to Shirley's desk to see if Bedford was there, she was gone. Someone passing by told Sandy that Shirley had to leave early for the day, but she was more than sure that Bedford was still in his office.

Sandy started to buzz him from Shirley's phone, but decided against it. She proceeded to knock on his door, and both she and Wanita entered.

28

Cinnamon Sugar

edford was beginning to see the light at the end of the tunnel. He was no longer concerned about Patience. It looked like he had been worried for nothing. When he got out of the shower and saw Sandy talking on the phone and she informed him that it was Patience, he saw his marriage flash before him. It was like an out-of-body experience. He saw the relationship begin and then come to an abrupt end, but that was no longer an issue. If Patience had something up her sleeve, she would have told Sandy over the phone this morning—or would have been even more persistent in calling. As far as he was concerned his worries were over.

Bedford exited the train and strolled down the street with a smile on his face. He felt like he'd gotten over, and he should have known man-to-man that Jonathan wouldn't drop the dime on him. Men were cool like that. There were lines that men didn't cross with each other, and certain things were often left unspoken. You might know that your boy was a dog, but as long as he's not dogging your sister or some relative, it was more like, to hell with it! Let that brother handle his business, and let you mind your own.

There was definitely an extra pep in Bedford's step as he entered the bagel and coffee shop. He ordered his usual as well as Shirley's. He was aware that he had a huge smile plastered across his face, but he could care less. Things were starting to look up, and as soon as Felice confirmed that she was going to take care of that little matter he would be straight. The only place to go was up. His sister, Isis, had even agreed to meet him for lunch the next day. Apparently Isis and Sandy had had a nice, long talk, and his wonderful wife told his sister that they had gone to counseling and their relationship was back on solid ground. Sandy would never know just how much he appreciated her doing that for him. He hadn't put her up to talking to his sister, but she felt comfortable around Isis, so who was he to argue?

Bedford entered his office building and tipped his head to the door-man. He walked toward an elevator and, just as he was about to step in, the doors closed. One second later, they reopened, and there before him stood Beautiful Smile. She had a set of teeth that looked better than Lena Horne's. Beautiful Smile grinned at him as she released the Door Open button and pushed the button for their floor.

"Thank you!" Bedford exclaimed.

"You are very welcome. I saw you enter the building, and I was going to wait for you, but the elevator arrived."

"Well, it's the thought that counts, right? Hi, my name is Bedford Jackson." Bedford reached to shake her hand.

"Hi, and I'm Belinda Black. So you work on our floor?"

"Yes, and actually you work on my floor. I was there before you," Bedford laughed coyly. "Jackson and Jackson is my company."

"Oh, very nice," Belinda said, stepping out of the elevator, and Bedford followed.

They walked down the hall and made small talk until they got to Belinda's office. Bedford politely opened the door for Belinda and Cin-namon must have thought that he was coming in to see her because she beamed at Bedford. The smile quickly vanished once she saw Belinda walk through the door.

"Hi, Cinnamon," Bedford said, waving, and Cinnamon greeted him. "Belinda, it was nice speaking to you, and I hope that we have the opportunity to do it again."

"I'm sure we will," Belinda replied and walked to her office.

Bedford watched her walk until she disappeared behind her double door office.

"Bye, Bedford," Cinnamon said.

"Bye, Cinnamon Sugar."

"Good morning, Bedford," Shirley said as he handed her the bag with her doughnut and coffee.

"Top of the morning to you, Shirley," Bedford sang.

"Someone is in a very good mood. What's got you feeling so good this morning?" Shirley asked. "Maybe I don't want to know the answer to that," she added.

"It's not what you think. Can't a man just be happy?"

"Yes, it's very possible, but something led to this newfound happiness. I'll leave you alone. Oh, by the way, remember I told you that I have to leave early today to go to motor vehicles."

"Yes, Shirley. What time are you getting out of here?"

"Around three, three-thirty. It should be empty by the time I get there. At least that's what I hope and, if it is, I'll get a new photo I.D. card."

"Okay, if you want to get out of here earlier today that's fine too. I don't have a lot going on today," Bedford said and walked into his office.

The first thing Bedford did was follow up with his list of clients to see if there was anything new going on, and to offer help in any areas that he could be of assistance. Bedford was big with customer service and believed that was the key to retaining business. He firmly felt that, aside from the good work that his company performed, many of his clients had remained because of the satisfactory service and attention.

By noon, Bedford had already attended to the majority of client folders that were on his desk from the evening before. He hadn't heard from Felice, and she told him that she would get back to him, and it was already Thursday. He hoped that she was smart enough to realize that having their baby would be a mistake. He decided to buzz her.

"Good afternoon, Felice Jackson's office."

"Hey, it's Bedford. Is Felice in?"

"Yes, Mr. Jackson. Hold on a second."

"This is Felice."

"Felice, it's me, Bedford. Are you busy?"

"I was about to step out to grab a bite to eat."

"Where are you going?" Bedford asked.

"Nowhere in particular. Why?"

"If you're going alone, I can come with you and we can talk."

"That's fine. I'll meet you by the elevator in five minutes."

Bedford arrived at the elevator area before Felice did. He read the newspaper that sat on the table while he waited. The voices of women heading his way stole his attention, and when he looked up, he saw Felice and Cinnamon walking and talking. Bedford greeted both women, but focused his attention on Felice to avoid Cinnamon making any lewd remarks. He hoped that she knew better, but one could never tell.

Felice and Bedford ended up walking thirteen blocks to one of their favorite restaurants, Caribbean Spice. They were seated immediately by the window and it was a nice day to people watch.

"So, I went to the doctor's earlier this morning," Felice said sadly.

"Yeah, so what happened?"

"I had an ultrasound, and I found out how many months I am."

"How far along are you?" Bedford asked.

"Too far. Let's just put it this way, at this stage, I'm killing a person."

Bedford and Felice sat in silence. Beres Hammond filled the room, but neither was able to focus on the music. Bedford knew that Felice was hurting, and it bothered him that he wouldn't see his seed grow, but it just wasn't plausible for them to have a child together. He just wanted this to be done and over with.

"What did you decide?"

"I'm going to go through with it."

Bedford's heart raced. Why would Felice do this to him? Didn't she know that this was the biggest mistake that she could ever make?

"I want you to be there for me."

"Are you sure that this is what you want to do?" Bedford asked, alarm filtering his voice.

"Yeah, this is the best thing for us. You were right when you said that I'd be messing up my chances of marriage to Aaron. I love him, and there is no way that I could lie to him and say that this is his baby.

I really don't want to do this because I'm putting my life at risk, but this baby was just not meant to be."

"Oh," Bedford said, relieved.

"B.J., you don't have to sound so damn happy."

"Felice, I'm sorry. Really I am, and I know that this is hard on you, and I wish things were different. You are my friend, and I still have love for you. You know that. You also know that I'm trying to stay married this time around, so please understand where I'm coming from."

"It's hard, but I'll try."

Bedford pulled her hands across the table and held on to them until the food arrived.

Felice and Bedford had only intended to take a one-hour lunch, but they ended up talking and were too full to budge, so, they took a cab back to the office. Shirley was still in the office when Bedford returned, and she handed him a stack of messages from returned calls that he had made earlier.

Bedford turned on his work switch and began returning calls again. He hated the game of phone tag. He knew it could be days before he was able to get a hold of someone. Bedford dialed so many numbers that he was beginning to feel like a telemarketer. He decided to take a short break when Shirley knocked on the door to tell him that she was leaving for the day.

Bedford was just about to step out to go purchase himself a cup of coffee when his phone rang, and he remembered that Shirley was gone.

"Bedford Jackson."

"You answer your own phone?" a female voice asked.

"Not usually, but my secretary is gone for the day."

"Then, it must be my lucky day to get you in person."

Bedford was trying to see if he could identify the voice.

"I guess so."

"I have a twenty-minute break, and I wanted to come down the hall to see your office."

Just then Bedford realized that it was Cinnamon.

"Well, you're more than welcome to come on down. The main receptionist will point you to my office. Like I said, my secretary is gone for the day, so just knock on my door when you arrive."

"Okay, I'll be right down."

Bedford decided to time Cinnamon to see how long it would take her to get to his office. To his surprise, she arrived in less than two minutes, which meant that she'd hauled ass to get there.

Cinnamon didn't bother to knock, she just let herself in and closed the door behind her.

"That was quick," Bedford joked.

"I told you that I only have twenty minutes. I don't like going over that time because I don't want people talking about me taking extended breaks."

"Well, you sound like you're very dedicated to your job."

"It's a job. They hire me to work, and that's what I'm going to do, even if I don't really like it."

"What's your ideal job?" Bedford asked.

"I really didn't come down here to talk about work," Cinnamon said, stepping out of her skirt and pulling her blouse over her head, revealing her thong panties and matching bra.

Bedford was both surprised and speechless as he marveled over Cinnamon's very ripe and appetizing body. He'd expected them to hook up, but he hadn't thought that it would happen this quickly.

Bedford thought, it really was a good thing that Shirley was gone for the day.

Cinnamon walked around to his side of the desk and began to unbutton his shirt and pants. He didn't lift a limb. He watched as she nimbly removed his penis through the opening in his briefs. She didn't suck it immediately. Instead, she appeared to be examining him while she proffered him a hand massage. Bedford reclined in his chair and placed his hands behind his head for further comfort. He was a happy man. He got even happier when he felt a warm set of lips glide from the base of his shaft to the tip. Bedford thought to himself as he enjoyed the warmth of Cinnamon's soft, full, warm lips, one down one to go. His next conquest would be Beautiful Smile.

Damn, Bedford thought. *Where have you been all of my life?*

Cinnamon was just as skillful as Felice, if not better. His hands quickly left the comfort of his head to remove Cinnamon's sheer black bra. He unhooked the thin strap and pulled the bra off her arms and her breasts lightly dangled.

Bedford was really excited. If Cinnamon continued sucking him this way he wouldn't be able to give her any just desserts. He leaned forward and palmed her bare ass. She looked up at him, and he opened his top drawer and went into a hidden compartment to retrieve a condom. When he was done placing it on, he directed her to sit on him, and Cinnamon quickly obliged.

"Did you like the way I sucked your yam sacks?" Cinnamon asked, as she bounced up and down.

"You know that I did," Bedford answered.

Bedford was so ensconced with Cinnamon that he didn't hear the knock on the door, but he did see the look of surprise and horror on his wife's face as she and her friend entered his office.

29

Click!

anita had the phone pressed against her ear and listened as
William chastised her. The phone conversation started out hostile and that wasn't the direction which she had intended to go. However, it seemed inevitable, and the longer he talked, the more she came to realize that maybe there was no hope of rekindling their marriage.

The tunnel was looking darker and darker as Wanita pressed forward. The love in her heart wouldn't allow her to surrender that easily. Eight years of marriage. There was no way that she could just bow out on twelve years of being together. Sure they'd had their moments, but that had come along with the territory. How could William give up so easily on twelve years? He was raised with both of his parents, and the only thing that had separated them was death. His father died in a car accident and his mother died after a long illness. Wanita and William both believed in the importance of family and keeping a unit together. At least, that's what she'd thought. It seemed like William was having a memory lapse about what he believed and didn't believe. It appeared that his ideals had changed over the years.

Wanita heard people talk about the seven-year itch, but what did the eighth year bring? A monsoon? Wanita had prayed more this week than she probably had in her entire life. She knew that it was unfair to go to the Lord only when she wanted or needed something, but she promised that if things were to change, she would continue praying. It wasn't like she didn't believe in God or have faith. She did believe, and she had faith, but she wasn't a holy roller or regular church attendee. The churches were already filled with enough hypocrites, at least all of the churches that she had attended—people more concerned about their clothes than the scriptures and pastors getting their mack on.

William was finally winding down his sermon, and Wanita snapped out of her daze.

"Are you coming back down for the Professional Men's gala?" William asked.

"Do you need me to?"

"I don't need you to, but you started something, and you should finish."

"I was only doing it for you. Now, if you don't need me, then no. I see no real reason that the rest of the staff can't do whatever is left to be done."

"They aren't as organized as you. Things are starting to get a little haywire."

"I'm sorry to hear that, but unless you personally need me, the answer is still no," Wanita voiced firmly.

Wanita waited for William's answer. Although there was silence on the line, she could hear him sighing. She knew that he was thinking of a way around saying the words that she wanted to hear, *I need you.* Wanita was patient. Being in New York these past two weeks had given her time to think. Instead of mourning over William last week she'd spent the time consoling Sandy. She and Sandy were supposed to have a nice dinner and talk about her problems. Along the way, Sandy had decided to pay Bedford a surprise visit. It was definitely a surprise, and they caught Bedford with his pants down, literally! Wanita thought that Sandy was going to kill both Bedford and his little trollop. Sandy went crazy. When they opened the door and saw what was happening, and it actually registered in Sandy's head, she charged at him with an unbelievable amount of strength. She beat on Bedford as if he were a mugger trying to steal her purse. Then the girl tried to get away, but Sandy had something for her too. Sandy made such a commotion that both Sandy and Wanita had to be escorted out of the building by security.

Sandy was a bigger person than Wanita, because she actually took the time out to pack Bedford's belongings. She even took the time to fold them neatly to enable her to get as much of his stuff in the bags as possible. She left the suitcases on the doorstep, so anyone passing could have taken them. Then, she changed the locks before he got home.

Sandy was a complete basket case for the remainder of the week, so Wanita had decided to stay with her to make sure that she didn't do anything extreme to herself or Bedford. Seeing something like that could push anyone over the edge, even levelheaded Sandy.

It never crossed Wanita's mind that William would ever cheat on her, but maybe that was the reason he was so quick to get her out of the picture.

"If you don't come back down and tie up these loose ends, it will look bad on you," William countered.

"Bad on me? You must be losing it. I don't belong to that organization. I'm not even officially on the event planning committee. I was only doing all of you a favor, but what happens from here on out is their problem. If anyone looks bad, it will be you. What are you going to tell people, that your wife left you? Or that you put me out?"

"That's no one's business."

"It will be when you can't deliver me to complete the job. The event is in two weeks. You don't have much time left. When I don't show up as your date for the event, what excuse are you going to use then? Or, do you already have a replacement for me?"

"Where is all of that coming from? And what are you trying to accuse me of?"

"I don't know. You tell me. You were in such a haste to get rid of me."

"Wanita, now you're playing games."

"William, I'm only playing the game that you started."

"Listen, I don't have time for this. If you come down, then you come down. If not, things will work themselves out."

Wanita felt a surge of courage overcoming her. She wanted to push William to the limit.

"I hope so for your sake. Anyway, there's no reason to continue this conversation, because it doesn't seem to be going anywhere," Wanita retorted.

"I don't understand what you're trying to say."

"Maybe you'll understand this, have a nice life." *Click!*

Wanita knew that she was taking a big chance hanging up on William. His ego was too big for his own good, and she was getting tired of being the one to kiss up to him, so she placed the ball in his court. If he called her back, then she knew that she had broken him.

On her way down to the kitchen, Wanita heard the phone ring. She wasn't near the phone, so her mother picked up. William was on Sybil's shit list, so he'd be lucky if she decided to turn the phone over to Wanita. She listened intently as Sybil gave William a few choice words and slammed the phone down in his ear. Wanita laughed and continued her path to the kitchen for a snack. A few moments later, she heard her cell phone ring. Wanita knew that the phone was in her handbag, but couldn't locate it. Although the bag had to be near, she could hear the chime of the phone loud and clear. By the time Wanita located the bag, the phone stopped. She checked the LCD screen, and it displayed one missed call. When she checked, it was indeed her former Atlanta home phone number. A few seconds later, the phone beeped, indicating there was a new message waiting.

After getting some cookies, she headed back into her room. She picked up the phone and was just about to dial William when she heard a knock on the door.

"Come in."

Sybil entered the room looking classy, as usual. She had to be the only person who could wear a warmup suit and still look like she was dressed up. She sat on the edge of Wanita's bed. Sybil had a way of saying the wrong thing at the wrong time, so she looked like she was trying to choose her words carefully.

"How are you doing today?"

"Not too bad. Things could be better."

"I hope you aren't still trying to chase after that man."

"Mother, please don't involve yourself in my marriage."

Sybil looked sympathetically at her daughter and shook her head in pity.

"Anyway, how's Sandy doing? I haven't seen her in a few days."

"Sandy is hanging in there. She needs some time alone, and she promised me that she wouldn't do anything crazy."

"What's she going to do? Now that marriage is really caput!"

"It looks that way, but that's none of my business. I have my own problems to deal with."

"Isn't that the truth?"

"Don't start. Who called earlier?" Wanita asked, even though she already knew.

"Than man of yours, if you can call him that. I don't understand why you would continue to waste your time. You are a smart and beautiful young woman. There are other fish in the sea."

"Is that why you're alone now?"

"Excuse me? I'll have you know that my being alone is by choice. If I wanted a man, trust me I could get one just like that." Sybil snapped her fingers.

"If you say so, Mother."

"You act like you are an old lady. Don't be afraid to get out there and start over. It's okay to get your feet wet again."

"I'm not afraid of starting over, or so-called getting my feet wet, but I'm not interested in either. I have a husband, and I believe that we can work things out."

On that cue, Sybil stood and pressed her clothes out with her hands. "All I can say is that I hope that you eventually come to your senses," Sybil advised.

"Any decision I make has to be mine, and I hope that you respect that."

"I'm starting to understand that I don't have any other choice."

When Sybil left the room, Wanita called her voice mail to re-trieve her message. It was William telling her to come back for the gala in his insincere way. Then he had the nerve to say that she was acting like a child by not answering the phone. She didn't even bother to return his call. If he wanted her to come back, it had to be for more than a stupid gala. And upon that return, she had some conditions that she wanted to establish. As much as she wanted him back, Wanita was keeping her wits about her, because she couldn't allow herself to be *dos veces la tonta*. She was too smart to be *the same fool twice*.

30
"What the Hell is This?"

ndia and Grayson as well as Patience, Jonathan, Sandy and Wanita arrived in Atlanta a day before the PAAMA awards. They all stayed at the Grand Hyatt hotel where the gala was taking place. The hotel was booked to capacity and only had smoking rooms available. When India made the reservations, she had specifically requested a non-smoking room. India was mad as hell. She reamed the woman at the front desk and then threw a verbal acid attack at the general manager who was extremely apologetic and ended up giving them a deluxe suite. India immediately changed from Mrs. Hyde to a princess.

The hotel was located in the heart of Buckhead, Atlanta's most prestigious and fashionable area, which pleased India. She had access to the city's finest shopping, dining and entertainment and took complete advantage of it all.

While India, Patience, Sandy and Wanita shopped, Jonathan decided to visit the restaurants in the area for ideas and Grayson attended to PAAMA business. He had a break from the trial because the jury was deliberating. The alleged charges brought against X-Tasy were first-degree murder on the baby, plus assault and battery and obstruction of justice by tampering with prospective witnesses. There was a good chance that she would get off on all charges because the prosecution hadn't provided sufficient evidence. The only thing that they had, to date, that really concerned Grayson was X-Tasy's song, and that wasn't good enough. X-Tasy's lyricist testified on her behalf and stated that X-Tasy only cowrote the song.

India was happy to be surrounded by family and friends. She didn't remember the last time that she'd had this much fun. They didn't have to worry about the kids because Lenora had volunteered to stay at the house and take care of them. Patience even convinced her to invite their father for this grand occasion and, after much persuasion, she finally broke down and sent him an invitation. She had no intentions of calling him. Patience informed her that he had received the invitation and was looking forward to coming. He didn't have to come far since he was already in Florida. His drive from Tampa would only take him about six hours. India wasn't really looking forward to the reunion, but it really was time that she confronted him. It didn't make sense to continue harboring those negative feelings.

India pretended to be sad when Sandy told her about the breakup with Bedford. India and Patience knew that it was inevitable because of what Jonathan had witnessed. Patience decided that it didn't even make sense to tell Sandy at this point. It would probably only upset her more. Then Wanita shared her marital problems with the group. Apparently, everyone was having difficulties, but India didn't dare discuss her business with anyone. Not only was it none of their business, but it wasn't anything that she couldn't handle or control.

After India completed her shopping extravaganza, she had to hail a cab for the three-block trip. The Grand Hyatt was in walking distance from Phipps Plaza, but she had too many bags to return on foot. When she arrived at the hotel she had to enlist the concierge to bring her bags to the room. India couldn't remember the last time she had shopped like that. Sandy ran a close second, while Patience had just picked up a few items for the kids; and Jonathan and Wanita's purchases consisted of only bath and body products. India had no idea how any of her items were going to fit into her luggage carrier. Another bag would have to be purchased.

India had found two beautiful evening gowns in Neiman Marcus. She was torn between the two dresses. If she had her choice, she would've worn both of them to the gala. One was peach with gold sequins, and she loved the way she looked in peach. The other dress was a soft green. It wasn't a color that she was very fond of, but she'd fallen in love with the style and design of the dress. There was still one day to decide on what she would wear, and she wanted to surprise Grayson. She knew that he would be flabbergasted at the sight of her in either outfit.

Grayson came back to the hotel just in time to take his favorite girl out to dinner. He was in a good mood, and India loved to see him that way. If only things were like this all of the time. Originally, India had told Patience, Sandy and Wanita that she would go out with them for dinner earlier, but plans have a way of changing. India hadn't expected Grayson to come back to the hotel until later on that night. She called Patience to inform her that Grayson had returned early, and that they were going out to dinner for an early celebration.

They took a cab to Black Pearl's, which Wanita highly recommended. When they entered the restaurant, the hostess immediately recognized Grayson. She asked him a chain of questions and even requested his autograph. Grayson was flattered and signed the napkin that the hostess put before him. India just stood by basking in her husband's glory. If this was a sign of things to come, India couldn't wait. There was a forty-five-minute wait, but Grayson's reputation preceded him, and they were seated within five minutes of arrival. They were taken to a separate area, which they learned was the VIP room. There were several patrons there, some of whom they recognized as professional athletes, and others who were probably local politicians with whom they weren't familiar.

The waitress came by with a bottle of Kristal, compliments of the house. India lightly tapped Grayson on the hand out of excitement.

"My Grayson is a celebrity," India fawned.

"If you only knew the half," Grayson boasted.

"The half of what?"

"This trial has people catering to my every beck and call. Everywhere I go, people are calling me Mr. McCall. The only people who call me by my last name are court officials and such. Now, it's Mr. McCall, what can I get you? Mr. McCall, how can I help you? 'Mr. McCall, Mr. McCall.' Now, don't get me wrong, I don't mind the attention, but I can't even cross the street at home anymore without being recognized."

"Mmm…I knew that this case was going to bring you fame, but

damn. Well, this just means that when you win this case, Lever and Bard will definitely make you senior partner."

"That's already in the works. Do you know how hard I worked for this? And India, I couldn't have done any of this without your support. Speaking of support, *Shades* is interviewing X-Tasy on Monday. The features editor called me to ask a few questions for quotes, but I can't remember her name for the life of me. I already instructed X-Tasy as to what she could and should not reveal."

"Features editor? Odetta Karim, is our features editor. She is really good. Well, you know what that means right?"

"No. Should I?" Grayson questioned.

"It means that X-Tasy will be featured in our August issue. I heard them talking about using it to replace the J-Lo story, but I didn't know in what capacity until now.

"Well all right!" Grayson slapped both hands on the table for emphasis, disturbing the centerpiece and the cutlery. "And you know that we are going to win this case, so that's even more reason for celebration."

Grayson popped the top of the Kristal, and poured them both a glass.

"Baby, this is for your unconditional love and support and for putting up with my mood swings. For knowing that my love for you is deeper than the core of the earth."

India was moved beyond words and lifted her glass after Grayson completed his toast. Their glasses joined and clinked together.

"Grayson, you have made me the happiest woman on this earth, and you also mean the world to me. I love you!"

June 16

Everyone was busy. Wanita ran around like a madwoman in an asylum, and Grayson was going crazy trying to locate his acceptance speech. India, Patience and Sandy chose to go to the sauna and take it easy. They decided to be onlookers and stay away from both parties. India didn't understand why Wanita felt so compelled to help out especially since she wasn't being compensated by the organization. From what India gathered, William had pulled a guilt trip on Wanita. India didn't say anything, but she saw how William was wielding his power to manipulate Wanita, and it was sad.

The evening couldn't come soon enough. India was almost done getting dressed and, after much thought, she decided to wear the green dress to the gala. She was in the bathroom applying the final touches to her makeup when Grayson returned. He walked into the room, agitation tincturing his face. During his absence, India had tried to locate his speech. She went through every piece of luggage that they carried, and even checked the closets, drawers and any other place that he could have misplaced it. Unfortunately, she turned up empty. India even went through the trouble of trying to prepare him a new one. She didn't exactly remember what the first one read verbatim, but she did the best to her recollection.

"India," Grayson huffed.

India quickly stepped out of the bathroom to see what Grayson needed. She knew that he was in a bad mood, but the bass in his voice indicated the actual degree.

"Yes?" India answered.

"Did you have the hotel steam my tuxedo?" Grayson asked. He pulled the tuxedo out of the bag to examine it closely.

"No, I wasn't aware that it needed to be steamed. It should be fine."

What do you mean you weren't aware? Use your common sense. The tux has been in transit, and even though it's in the garment bag, it still gets wrinkled."

"Don't worry," India said, walking over to the phone. "I'll call up now and have them take care of it right away."

"Do you see the time? We should be getting ready to walk out of the door. I can't believe this crap. What the hell have you been doing all day besides shopping?" Grayson looked at India with sheer disgust in his eyes.

India saw that all-too-familiar look. He was beyond the stage of vexation. She knew that he wouldn't do anything crazy this evening, especially since he was going to be accepting an award. They were both supposed to sit at the table on stage among other prestigious couples. Several government politicians were scheduled to attend and two celebrity guests.

"I was trying to find your speech."

"And?" Grayson questioned.

"I didn't have any luck, but I tried to put something together for you." India ran to retrieve the sheet of paper from the living room and handed it over to Grayson.

Grayson quickly glanced over the information.

"What the hell is this? You expect me to get up in front of all of these people and recite this? My speech has to be somewhere here. It was in a bright orange folder. I purposely put it in that folder so it would stick out like a sore thumb."

"You mean the orange folder that was sitting on the sofa table at home?" India asked.

"Yes, it was on the table. I asked you to grab it when the cab came to pick us up."

India would have remembered that. Grayson didn't instruct or ask her to bring that folder. Furthermore, something as important as his speech should have been packed way in advance.

"By the way, what is that you're wearing?"

"Oh, do you like it?" India asked, swinging around so Grayson could get a full view of the dress. She was happy that he had taken notice.

"What the hell happened to the dress that I bought you?"

"Oh, I left it home," India answered nervously.

"Left it home...left it home. The same way you left my fucking speech at home?"

"I didn't intentionally leave your speech at home," India said, taking the blame. "I didn't bring the dress because it didn't fit right."

"What, you didn't like the dress? You seemed to like it the night that I brought it home for you. You damn sure didn't forget to bring the jewelry that you're wearing." Grayson tugged at the choker around India's neck.

"Grayson, you're going to break the necklace."

"Do you think that I give a damn about some stupid-ass necklace?

Huh? What the hell do you think?"

"I'm sorry," India exclaimed. She was starting to get afraid. Grayson was winding himself up, and his temper was flaring.

"Sorry for what? For leaving my speech at home, or for not appreciating the things that I get for you? Tell me."

"Grayson, I liked the dress very much. It's just that it made me look frumpy."

"Frumpy? I'll give you something that will make you look frumpy alright." Without a second thought, Grayson pushed India, and she fell to the ground. He kept coming at her, and she didn't have time to get up. Instead, she used the palm of her hands to back up. Then she found herself up against the wall with no place to go.

"Grayson, please stop. We have to get ready to go. I can call Lenora at home and she can fax your speech over to the hotel. It will be downstairs by the time we get there."

Grayson didn't hear a word that came out of India's mouth. The Mr. Hyde transformation was already in full effect. Grayson picked India up by the strap of her dress, causing it to tear. India struggled to pull herself from his grasp. She couldn't allow this to happen again. She ran toward the living room, and Grayson came after her. He leaped forward and pounced on her. She was trapped under his hold as he hit her. India managed to block the majority of the blows, but she was taking a beating. She kneed him in the groin and when he doubled over in pain, she got up and ran toward the door. Grayson recovered quickly, caught her and flung her up against the wall. India's head struck the large hand-crafted framed mirror that hung on the wall. The force of her head hitting the mirror caused it to crack and crash to the floor. Broken glass and specs of blood dotted the off-white Berber carpet.

India's head was pounding, and she felt woozy. Grayson watched as India's body slumped and fell to the ground. Through blurred vision, India could see that Grayson wasn't quite done. She felt the broken glass beneath her bloodied hands, and when he came at her, she grabbed a huge shard and speared it into him.

Epilogue

andy walked to the mailbox to get the mail. There were two packages and a huge envelope with a New York return address. She immediately turned her attention to the envelope because she recognized the logo in the upper-left-hand corner. It was from her divorce attorney's office. She hastily opened the letter while walking to the porch to rejoin her mother.

A smile swept across Sandy's face as she read the divorce decree. It was finally over. The final order of business that needed to be taken care of was the sale of the brownstone in New York. She had gained the house as part of the divorce settlement. Sandy didn't really care about it, but she knew how much it meant to Bedford. So, to be spiteful, she requested to have it, and it was granted. She decided that Bedford had hurt enough people, and that the house needed to be exorcised from him and his deceit. When she returned to New York, she was scheduled to see a real estate agent. She wanted to sell the brownstone and then purchase a nice two-bedroom condo in the Park Slope section of Brooklyn or the upper east side of Manhattan. If she moved to the upper east side she would be closer to work.

Sandy was spending one month of her summer vacation in North Carolina with her mother and brother, and the other month with her cousins and friend—India, Patience and Wanita—in Maryland.

After all the dust settled between India and Grayson, Wanita and Sandy took a nice two-week vacation together in Venezuela. When they returned Wanita spent another three months in New York with Sandy.

Wanita prayed on her relationship with William every day but, she had told Sandy that she wasn't going to run after him anymore. If William didn't see that he was missing out on a good thing, it was his loss. Wanita didn't have to pray long, because during her short stay with Sandy, William pursued her long and hard. He was almost unrelenting in his quest to get her to return home. Radio One did eventually move William to Maryland. William drove up every weekend for two months until Wanita decided to return to her marriage. He stayed in corporate housing for a while and begged Wanita to come back and help him find them a home. He wanted a home for them to start a family in. Wanita agreed, on the condition that they seek counseling, and that she return to work, full-time.

Sandy was just happy that she didn't have to travel all over the place to see the people who mattered to her most. Instead of making three and four trips, she really only had to make two—one to North Carolina and the other to Maryland, and, if she felt like it, she could drive to Atlanta to see Layla and Maxine.

Sandy took a seat next to her mother while looking over the final divorce papers. She couldn't believe that just one year ago she was married to a no-good man named Bedford Jackson. How could he have deceived her for so long? He was a complete dog, and she didn't even know it. Here she was thinking that he had only slipped up once, when he had several other women waiting in the wings, one of whom she found out was pregnant. As far as she knew, Bedford and Felice had probably had the baby, but that wasn't her concern. She should have known, and the signs were all there, but she ignored them. When she met Keyanna in the restaurant and was told that Bedford said she was crazy and suicidal, she should have paid attention. He'd even told Keyanna that they had children. Sandy should have taken those things to heart. Instead, she laughed it off as nothing. Women were quick to believe anything that sounded good, just as long as they ended up with the prize, which in reality was no prize at all.

Bedford was a liar and a cheat and would do the same thing that he did to her to the next woman that he settled with. Cheating was his nature. It was what he did best. He was a good charmer and a good liar. He would get his just desserts. Sandy reasoned that he could now have his cake, but he could no longer eat hers.

Sandy thought about a speech that the Reverend Farrakhan once made. One line stood out in particular. He said, "There is no such thing as a no-good woman. She was made no good by a no-good man."

Patience sat in the car and honked the horn for India, Sierra and her father to come outside. It was Memorial Day weekend, and India insisted on going to visit Grayson's gravesite. Patience couldn't believe that Grayson had died almost a year ago. Her mind flashed back to the headlines after Grayson's death. They read *Defense Attorney Slain in Domestic Situation,* which was ironic. The jury returned that following Monday and found X-Tasy not guilty. Grayson's name remained in the headlines for well over three months, and the media harassed India the entire time.

Patience was reluctant to go to the cemetery with her sister, but she knew how much it meant to India and didn't want to disappoint her. She begged Jonathan to accompany them, but he declined, because he felt the same way Patience did about Grayson and the entire situation. However, *Pájo Soul* was so busy for the holiday weekend that it was necessary that one of them was there to manage the restaurant.

On the evening of the gala, Patience, Jonathan, Sandy, Wanita and their father sat at the table reserved for the guests of honor. Patience noticed that the two seats reserved on stage for India and Grayson were empty. As the night progressed, and the actual ceremony started, Patience began to worry. She went to the hotel house phone and called India and Grayson's room, but didn't get an answer. She summoned Jonathan to accompany her to their room. They knocked and knocked and still there was no answer. Patience called housekeeping and insisted that the door be opened. At first, they were hesitant, because there was a "do not disturb" tag on the door. Jonathan threatened to knock the door down himself if they continued to refuse. When they entered the room, they found India unconscious and Grayson surrounded by a pool of blood. He was bleeding heavily from the chest and his breathing was shallow. They rushed both of them to the hospital. A lot of time passed between the incident and when Patience found them, and Grayson had already lost a lot of blood. The glass had pierced his heart and when he got to the hospital he was pronounced dead on arrival.

India was in a coma for two days. When she finally came to, the first person she asked for was Grayson. Patience didn't want to tell India the truth.

When India returned to Maryland, she took an indefinite leave of absence from work and locked herself in the house for weeks. She refused to do anything, so Patience took Sierra for the summer. Then their father came to Maryland to spend time with India and, after a few weeks of his staying in a hotel near her house, she allowed him to stay with her.

Patience was about to get out of the car when the house door opened. India came out holding both Sierra's and her father's hands. She was dressed in all black, even though the weather was well into the eighties. Their father opened the doors. Sierra jumped into the back, and India joined Patience in the front. He closed India's door and returned to the back to sit with Sierra. Patience waited for everyone to buckle up. She closed all of the windows and turned on the air conditioner.

"Is everyone ready?" Patience asked.

"As ready as I'll ever be," India replied. "Ready to start a new beginning."

From the Author

Writing *Shattered Vessels* was a challenge, particularly because of the subject matter. It is sad to know that women endure such pain every day. *Shattered Vessels* is not the first novel to cover this topic, and I'm sure that it won't be the last. Abuse is nothing new in our society. Yet, we still allow it to exist. If I can help one woman to see that the volatile/hostile situation that exists in her present relationship is unhealthy, and she is able to say, "I love myself, and I deserve better," then my job is done.

Many people will question and disagree with the occurrences that take place in *Shattered Vessels*. Some may feel it is over the top, and others may say that situations such as this are too minor to warrant these kinds of consequences or extremities. However, I have spoken to women who were beaten for lesser reasons than those stated in this novel. The question at hand is when is it okay for a man to raise his hand to his girlfriend or spouse? The answer is *never*. Is it ever acceptable to belittle, disrespect, cheat or neglect your girlfriend or spouse? The answer is *no*. Is there *ever* a reason to remain in an abusive relationship? Again, the answer is *no*.

Women, realize your power. Woman is Mother Earth. We bear and give life to the flowers in bloom today and tomorrow.

Love yourself enough to put *you* first!

—Nancey Flowers

Cited Statistics on Domestic Violence

It is estimated that every nine seconds, a woman is battered.

The Department of Justice, 1991

Ninety-five percent of the victims of domestic violence are women.

"Report to the Nation on Crime and Justice"
Bureau of Justice Statistics, 1983

Research suggests that wife-beating results in more injuries that require medical treatment than rape, auto accidents and muggings combined.

"Violence Among Intimates", E. Stark and A. Filtcraft, 1987

In the United States, a woman is more likely to be assaulted, injured, raped, or killed by a male partner than any other assailant.

"Resource Availability for Women at Risk"
A. Browne and K.R. Williams

Violence will occur at least once in two-thirds of all marriages.

The Abusive Partner, M. Stark, 1982

During a six-month time period following an incident of domestic violence, approximately 32% of the women are victimized again.

National Crime Survey, 1983

Twenty-five percent of the women in the U.S. (12 million) will be abused by their current or former partners at some point during their lifetime. Three to four million women are physically abused each year.

"Partner Abuse in Illinois: Knowing the
Facts and Breaking the Cycle," IDPH, Report
to the General Assembly, 1996

The average battered woman is attacked three times each year.

Intimate Violence, R. Gelles and M. Straus, 1988

The National Women's Study results indicate that 3.7% of women who have ever been married have suffered at the hands of a husband or ex-husband. These results mean that over 3.5 million American women are survivors of wife battering.

"The National Women's Study", D. Kilpatrick, et. al.,
National Crime Victims Research and Treatment Center,
Charleston, SC, 1992

At least forty-two percent of women who are murdered, are killed by their partners.

"Domestic Violence: A National Curriculum
for Family Preservation Practitioners,"
S. Schecter and A. Ganley, San Francisco
Family Violence Prevention Fund, 1995

Four women each day and more than 1,000 women each year are killed by their partners.

"Partner Abuse in Illinois: Knowing
the Facts and Breaking the Cycle"
IDPH, Report to the General Assembly
1996

Approximately 3.3 million children witness abuse between their parents each year, based on estimates of partner abuse.

Domestic Violence: A National Curriculum
for Family Preservation Practitioners,
S. Schechter and A. Ganley, San Francisco
Family Violence Prevention Fund, 1995

Each year, more than one million women seek medical assistance for injuries caused by battering

"Medical Therapy as Repression"
E. Stark and A. Filtcraft, 1982

Battered Women are four to five times more likely than non-battered women to require psychiatric treatment.

"Violence Against Women: A Global Problem"
C. Everett Koop

Families in which domestic violence occurs use doctors eight times more often, visit emergency rooms six times more often, and use six times more prescription drugs than the general population.

"Domestic Violence: A Community Crisis
Waiting for an Effective Response"
Seattle Domestic Violence Intervention Project, 1989

Twenty to thirty percent of women in the emergency room are there due to abuse.

"California Hospital Emergency Departments'
Response to Domestic Violence Survey Report"
D. Lee, P. Letellier, E. McLoughlin, and P. Salber
San Francisco, Family Violence Prevention Fund, 1993

Every year, domestic violence results in almost 100,000 days of hospitalizations, almost 30,000 emergency department visits, and almost 40,000 visits to a physician.

"Five Issues in American Health," Chicago
American Medical Association, 1991

In a study of 691 white, African-American and Hispanic women, sponsored by the Centers for Disease Control, one in six reported physical abuse during their present pregnancy. One in four reported physical abuse in the last calendar year.

"Assessing for Abuse During Pregnancy:
Severity and Frequency of Injuries and
Associated Entry in to Prenatal Care,"
J. McFarlane, et. al.
Journal of American Medical Association, 267 (23)
pp. 3176-3178

Being abused or neglected as a child increases the likelihood of arrest as a juvenile by fifty-three percent as an adult by thirty-eighty percent, and for violent crime by 38%.

"The Cycle of Violence," C.S. Widom
National Institute of Justice
Washington, DC, 1992

Approximately 3.3 million children witness abuse between their parents each year, based on estimates of partner abuse.

"Domestic Violence: A National Curriculum
for Family Preservation Practitioners,"
S. Schechter and A. Ganley, San Francisco
Family Violence Prevention Fund, 1995

Women are more likely to be victims of homicide when they are estranged from their husbands than when they live with them. The risk of homicide is higher in the first 2 months after separation.

"Spousal Homicide Risk and Estrangement"
M. Wilson and M. Daly
Violence and Victims, 8:3-16, 1993

Four women each day and more than 1,000 women each year, are killed by their partners.

Partner Abuse in Illinois: Knowing
the Facts and Breaking the Cycle
IDPH, Report to the General Assembly
1996

At least forty-two percent of women who are murdered, are killed by their partners.

"Domestic Violence: A National Curriculum
for Family Preservation Practitioners,"
S. Schecter and A. Ganley, San Francisco
Family Violence Prevention Fund, 1995

A Fools Paradise

Brought to you by the author of *Shattered Vessels*.
In stores now!

Prologue

My father, Trevor, called me Star, so I grew up believing that I had the ability to attain anything the world had to offer. As a result I grew up with very high aspirations and determined to reach for the sky—or die trying.

I have three passions: My boyfriend, Donovan, is the first one. We've been friends from infancy. The second is school. I love learning new things. The last thing is my desire to travel to America. Jamaica, my birthplace, and the country where I reside, is in an economic decline and the opportunities are becoming few and far between. Whenever I watch American programs on television I see how differently the people live, and I want to one day experience that lifestyle. I've dreamed about this ever since I can remember. Seeing black people like Benson assisting the governor at his mansion and like the Jeffersons who were moving on up, I, too, wanted a piece of the pie. I could just imagine being in America where the streets would glitter like gold with unlimited opportunities. The only catch was that I wouldn't be able to have all three of my passions. I would have to give up one or two, but which would it be?

The sexual attraction that Donovan and I have for each other was sinful. I can't recall a time when I was able to visit him in closed quarters and we were able to accomplish anything other than good, hot sex. When Donovan caressed my breasts and kissed the nape of my neck, I could feel the wetness oozing out of me. Just imagine popping the top from a bottle of champagne and the flow of liquid that rushes from the bottle. That's exactly what Donovan did to me.

Then there's school. Presently, I'm an honor student studying premed at the University of the West Indies. The challenge of working hard and learning something new gives me a rush. In the end my reward is a well-deserved A. Generally, good grades especially, A's lead to acknowledgement from my parents and professors for my exemplary efforts. There is nothing more gratifying or fulfilling.

I would love the chance to travel and go away for a while, but such a situation has never presented itself to me. If it had I know I, Anne-Marie Saunders, would jump at the chance.

As it turned out, one of my passions would eventually be my downfall. The other would do me the most harm, and the third would be my salvation.

NN'N
Soulmates